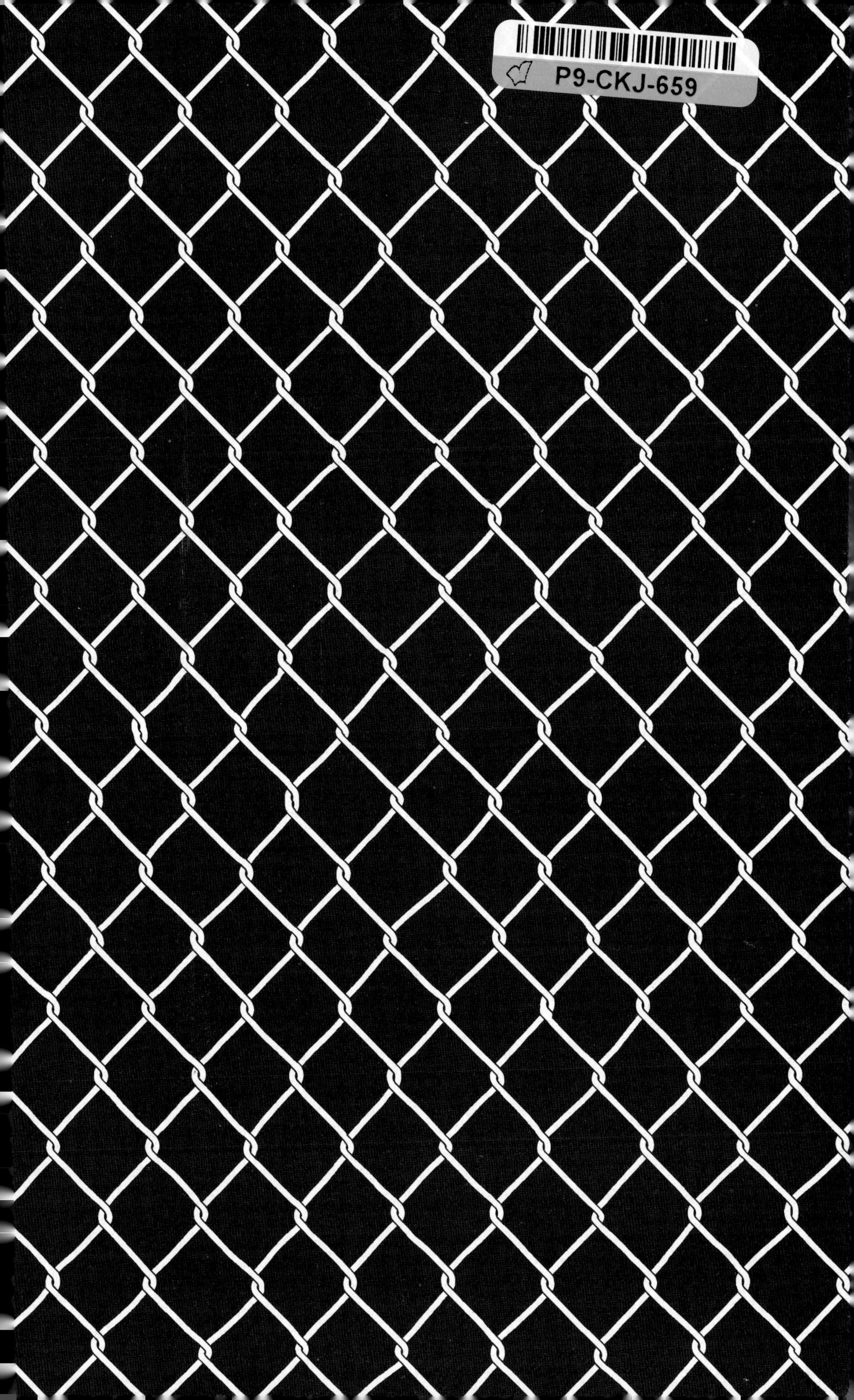

Writer
Julio Anta

Artist
Anna Wieszczyk

Colorist
Bryan Valenza

Letterer
Hassan Otsmane-Elhaou

Cover
Lisa Sterle

Logo Design
Dylan Todd

Publication Design
Ryan Brewer

Copy Editor
Melissa Gifford

Library Consultant
Chloe Ramos

Educator Guide Provided by
Re-Imagining Migration

Abeer Shinnawi
Amber Cook
Jodi Grosser
Robin Hawley-Brillante

Re-Imagining Migration

HOME, VOL. 1. First printing. November 2021. Published by Image Comics, Inc. Office of publication: PO BOX 14457, Portland, OR 97293. ISBN: 978-1-5343-1997-4.

image

HOME

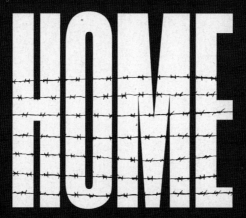

Introduction
by Frederick Luis Aldama

We are in the middle of a cultural neo-Renaissance, with extraordinary Latinx comics creatives like Miami-raised Cuban-Colombian Julio Anta at its gravitational center. In his short-form (*Between Two Worlds, Unbow Your Head, and The Price of Freedom*) and long-form comics (Home), Julio seeks to infuse complexity and nuance into otherwise untold or occluded Latinx histories, identities, and experiences. As a boat of Haitian refugees reaches US shores in the short-form comic *Balseros*, Julio asks readers to take an ethnoracial pause and soak up the systemic racism that has long informed geopolitical migration policies that deem some émigrés desirable and others not. One way or another, Julio uses comics to make visible the systems of oppression experienced by Black and Brown people, from the horrors of forced migration to everyday racial surveillance and profiling and misogynistic violence.

That Latinx comics are a significant power in this neo-Renaissance is not surprising. Given that we live in an epoch where the visual dominates, the visual-verbal storytelling power of Latinx comics has more than proven its mettle. They wrest us from Twittersphere echo chambers and perfunctory left-right swipes. Latinx comics invite us to breathe in the complexities of Latinx identities and experiences.

Many of today's Latinx creatives choose the visual-verbal devices of comics to shape stories of our *hermanas y hermanos* across the Americas—those who've been violently displaced from homelands and forced to make dangerous and deadly journeys in the hopes of finding safer havens. I think readily of Augusto Mora's deeply haunting *Illegal Cargo*, which follows Salvadoran papa José in his ultimately failed search to find his daughter, Helena; she disappeared during her journey north. José encounters the murderous menace of Mexican migra officers, gangs, and traffickers. Pablo Leon's visually arresting webcomic, *The Journey*, follows the journey of 11-year-old Linda, whose attempt to gain lawful asylum in the US leads to a horrific experience in an ICE detention center.

Latinx creatives like Julio, Augusto, and Pablo are not alone in their attentive and nuanced storytelling focus. As more and more of the planet's population are displaced, many other comics creatives are using the power of sequential storytelling to shape stories of trauma and loss. Comics creatives such as Thi Bui (*The Best We Could Do*), Mohamed Arejdal and Cedric Liano *(Amazigh*), J.P. Stassen (*Deogratias: A Tale of Rwanda*), Nnedi Okorafor (*LaGuardia*), and Eoin Colfer, Andrew Donkin, and Giovanni Rigano (*Illegal*) to name a few.

Julio is an eyes-wide-open realist storyteller. He's also a superheroic optimist. With *Home*, we see how Julio (with artist Anna Wieszczyk) at once opens eyes to the barbarity of forced migration *and* creates moments of triumph and hope. Julio's protagonist, the chavalito Juan, is violently separated from his mamá, Mercedes, and locked up in an ICE detention center. However, it's here that Juan comes into his mutie superpowers to ultimately vanquish marauding *migra* villains who declare him a "serious threat" to the security of the US. Like some of his Latinx comic book predecessors—Bobby da Costa as Sunspot and Bonita Juarez as Firebird—Juan can create, wield, and hurl balls of fire.

Other Latinx comics creatives deployed the superhero storytelling form to strip down, then reconstruct and amplify, the experience of Latinxs like Juan who fall prey to the panoptic eye of restrictive sociopolitical systems powered by xenophobia. I'm reminded of the titular hero of Héctor Rodriguez's *El Peso Hero*, who defends women and children from predatory narcos and *migra*. With *Jalisco*, Kayden Phoenix throws readers into the deep end of the murderous violence against women that has plagued US/Mexico borderland life and the life of Latina superhero Alicia Cuevas (aka Jalisco), who fights for justice along with her newfound league of Latina warriors.

We need our Latinx superheroes like Juan, El Peso Hero, and Jalisco. Indeed, these and other Latinx superheroes demonstrate that a comic book like Julio's *Home* is more than escapist, wish-fulfilment fantasy. It doesn't shy away from showing the violence, trauma, and systems of exploitation and oppression that target Latinx peoples across the Americas. It also wakes us to truth-to-power actions as a way to heal, transform, and build community. Finally, comics like *Home* forcefully remind us that Latinx youth, in all their *superheroic* struggles of survivance, can and do offer us a radical openness to combat the real and mind-forged manacles daily thrust upon us.

Frederick Luis Aldama, aka Professor Latinx, is an Eisner Award-winning author and the Jacob & Frances Sanger Mossiker Chair in the Humanities at UT Austin.

Chapter One

GUATEMALA CITY

FROM THE DESK OF THE ATTORNEY GENERAL OF THE UNITED STATES: "TODAY, AS ORDERED BY THE PRESIDENT, WE HAVE OFFICIALLY PUT IN PLACE A ZERO TOLERANCE POLICY FOR ILLEGAL ENTRIES ON OUR SOUTHWEST BORDER.

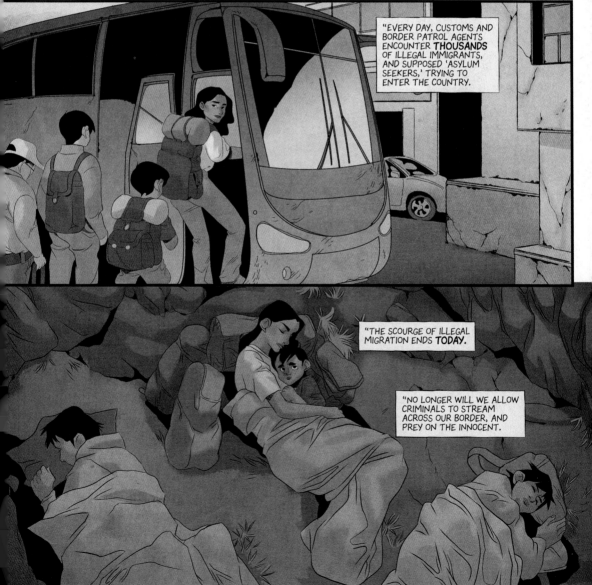

"EVERY DAY, CUSTOMS AND BORDER PATROL AGENTS ENCOUNTER **THOUSANDS** OF ILLEGAL IMMIGRANTS, AND SUPPOSED 'ASYLUM SEEKERS,' TRYING TO ENTER THE COUNTRY.

"THE SCOURGE OF ILLEGAL MIGRATION ENDS **TODAY.**

"NO LONGER WILL WE ALLOW CRIMINALS TO STREAM ACROSS OUR BORDER, AND PREY ON THE INNOCENT.

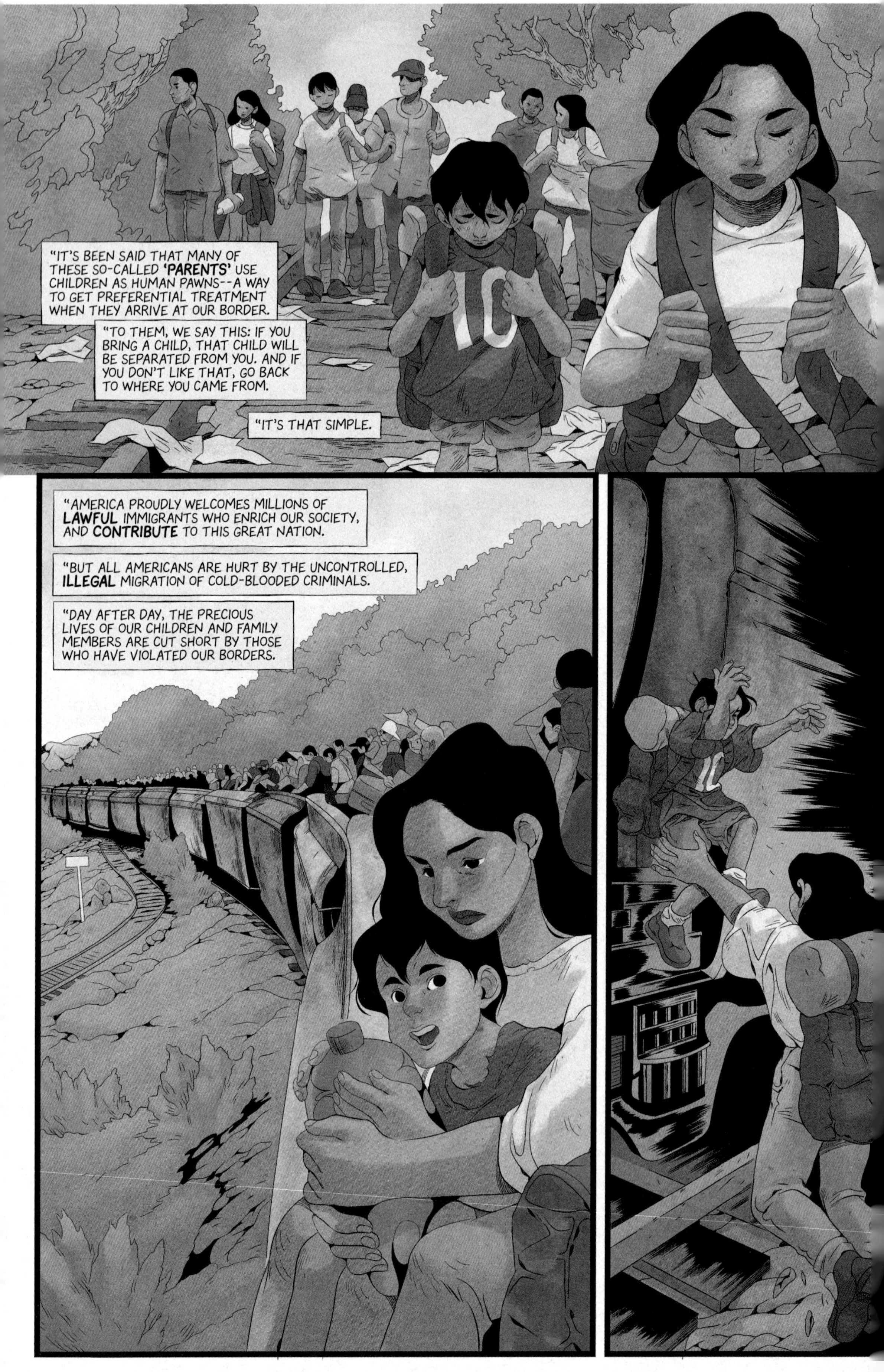
"IT'S BEEN SAID THAT MANY OF THESE SO-CALLED 'PARENTS' USE CHILDREN AS HUMAN PAWNS--A WAY TO GET PREFERENTIAL TREATMENT WHEN THEY ARRIVE AT OUR BORDER.
"TO THEM, WE SAY THIS: IF YOU BRING A CHILD, THAT CHILD WILL BE SEPARATED FROM YOU. AND IF YOU DON'T LIKE THAT, GO BACK TO WHERE YOU CAME FROM.
"IT'S THAT SIMPLE.
"AMERICA PROUDLY WELCOMES MILLIONS OF LAWFUL IMMIGRANTS WHO ENRICH OUR SOCIETY, AND CONTRIBUTE TO THIS GREAT NATION.
"BUT ALL AMERICANS ARE HURT BY THE UNCONTROLLED, ILLEGAL MIGRATION OF COLD-BLOODED CRIMINALS.
"DAY AFTER DAY, THE PRECIOUS LIVES OF OUR CHILDREN AND FAMILY MEMBERS ARE CUT SHORT BY THOSE WHO HAVE VIOLATED OUR BORDERS.

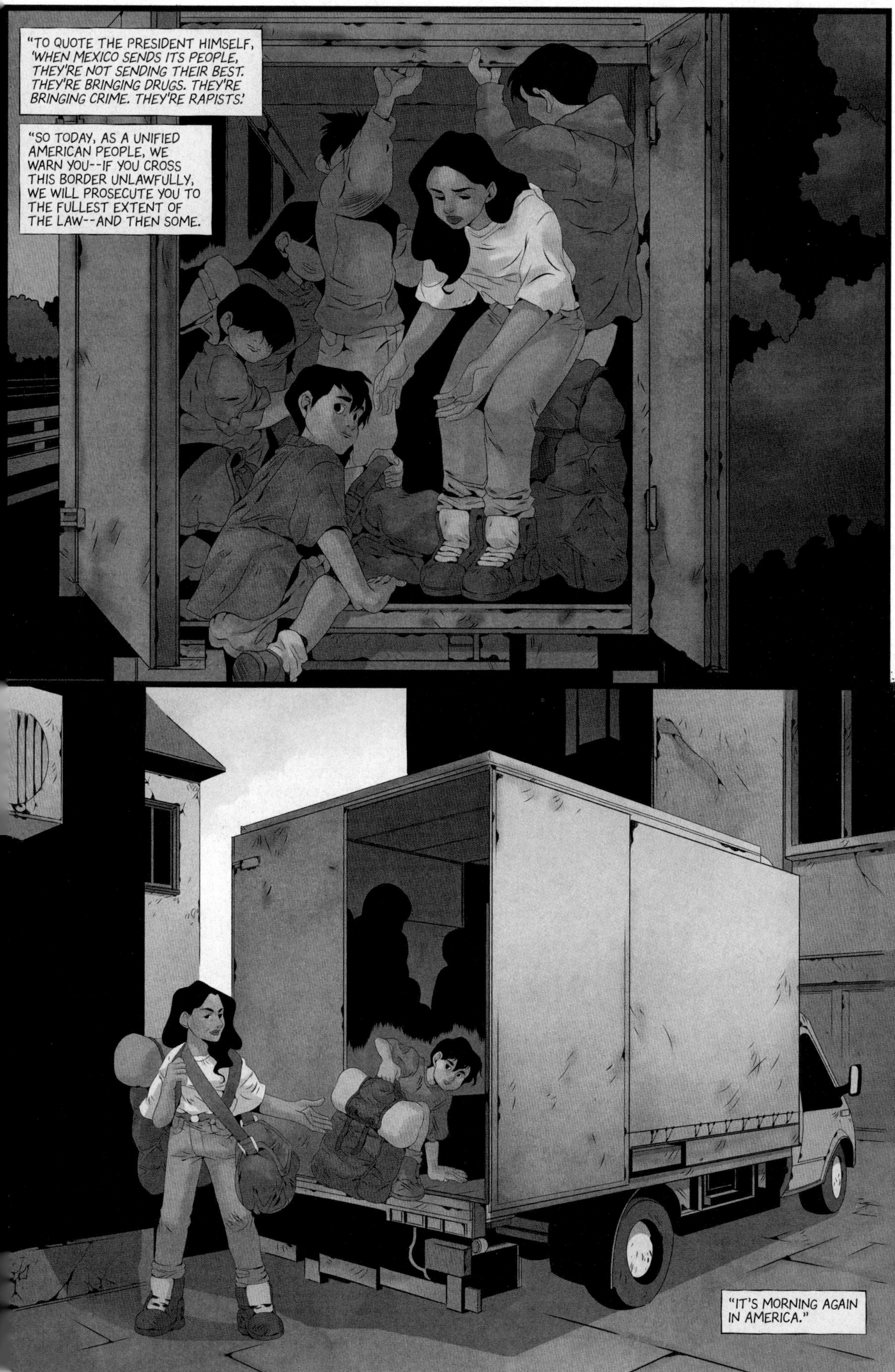
"TO QUOTE THE PRESIDENT HIMSELF, 'WHEN MEXICO SENDS ITS PEOPLE, THEY'RE NOT SENDING THEIR BEST. THEY'RE BRINGING DRUGS. THEY'RE BRINGING CRIME. THEY'RE RAPISTS.'
"SO TODAY, AS A UNIFIED AMERICAN PEOPLE, WE WARN YOU--IF YOU CROSS THIS BORDER UNLAWFULLY, WE WILL PROSECUTE YOU TO THE FULLEST EXTENT OF THE LAW--AND THEN SOME.
"IT'S MORNING AGAIN IN AMERICA."

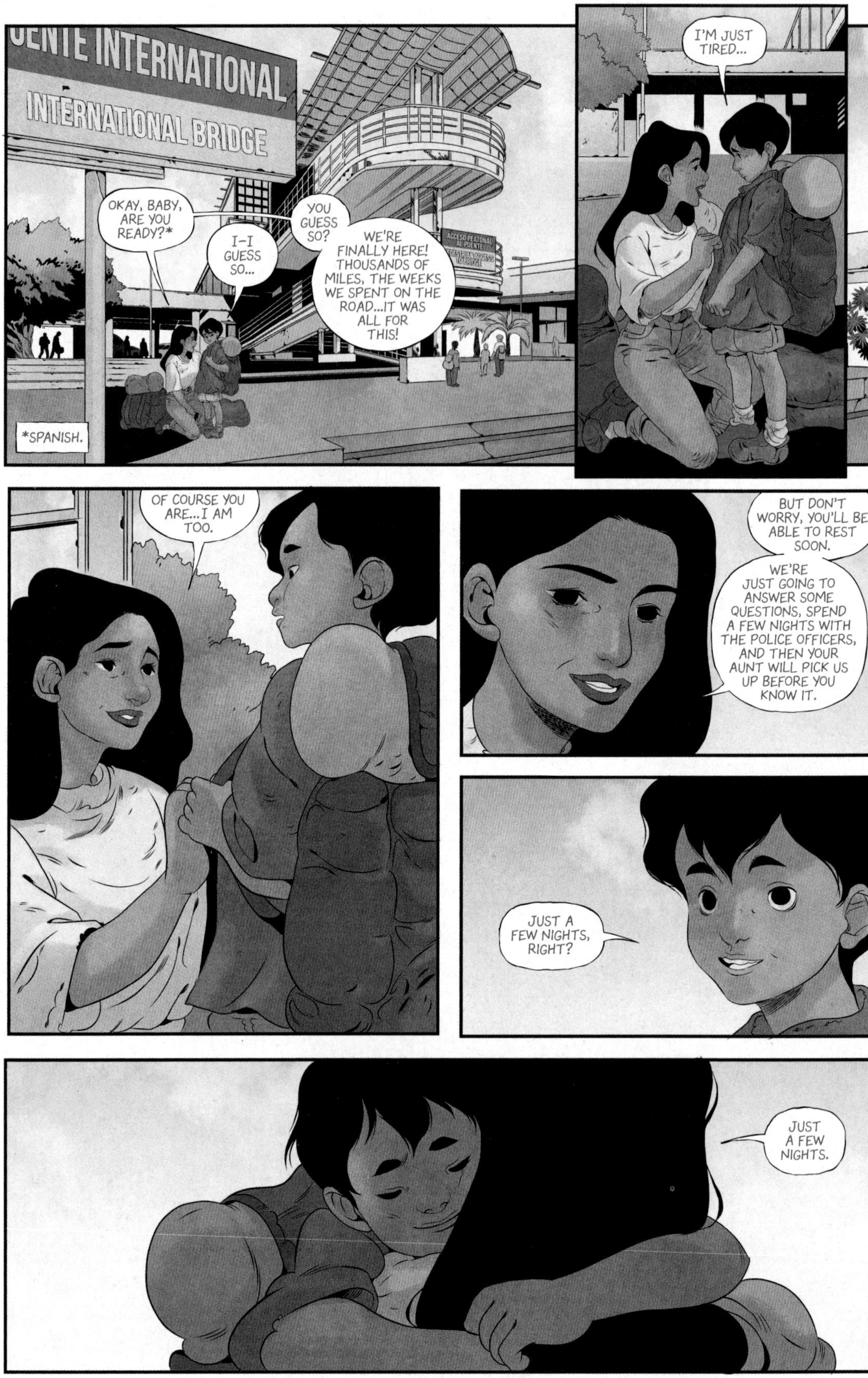
UENTE INTERNATIONAL
INTERNATIONAL BRIDGE
OKAY, BABY, ARE YOU READY?*
YOU GUESS SO?
I-I GUESS SO...
WE'RE FINALLY HERE! THOUSANDS OF MILES, THE WEEKS WE SPENT ON THE ROAD...IT WAS ALL FOR THIS!
ACCESO PEATONAL AL PUENTE
PEDESTRIAN ACCESS TO BRIDGE
*SPANISH.
I'M JUST TIRED...
OF COURSE YOU ARE...I AM TOO.
BUT DON'T WORRY, YOU'LL BE ABLE TO REST SOON.
WE'RE JUST GOING TO ANSWER SOME QUESTIONS, SPEND A FEW NIGHTS WITH THE POLICE OFFICERS, AND THEN YOUR AUNT WILL PICK US UP BEFORE YOU KNOW IT.
JUST A FEW NIGHTS, RIGHT?
JUST A FEW NIGHTS.

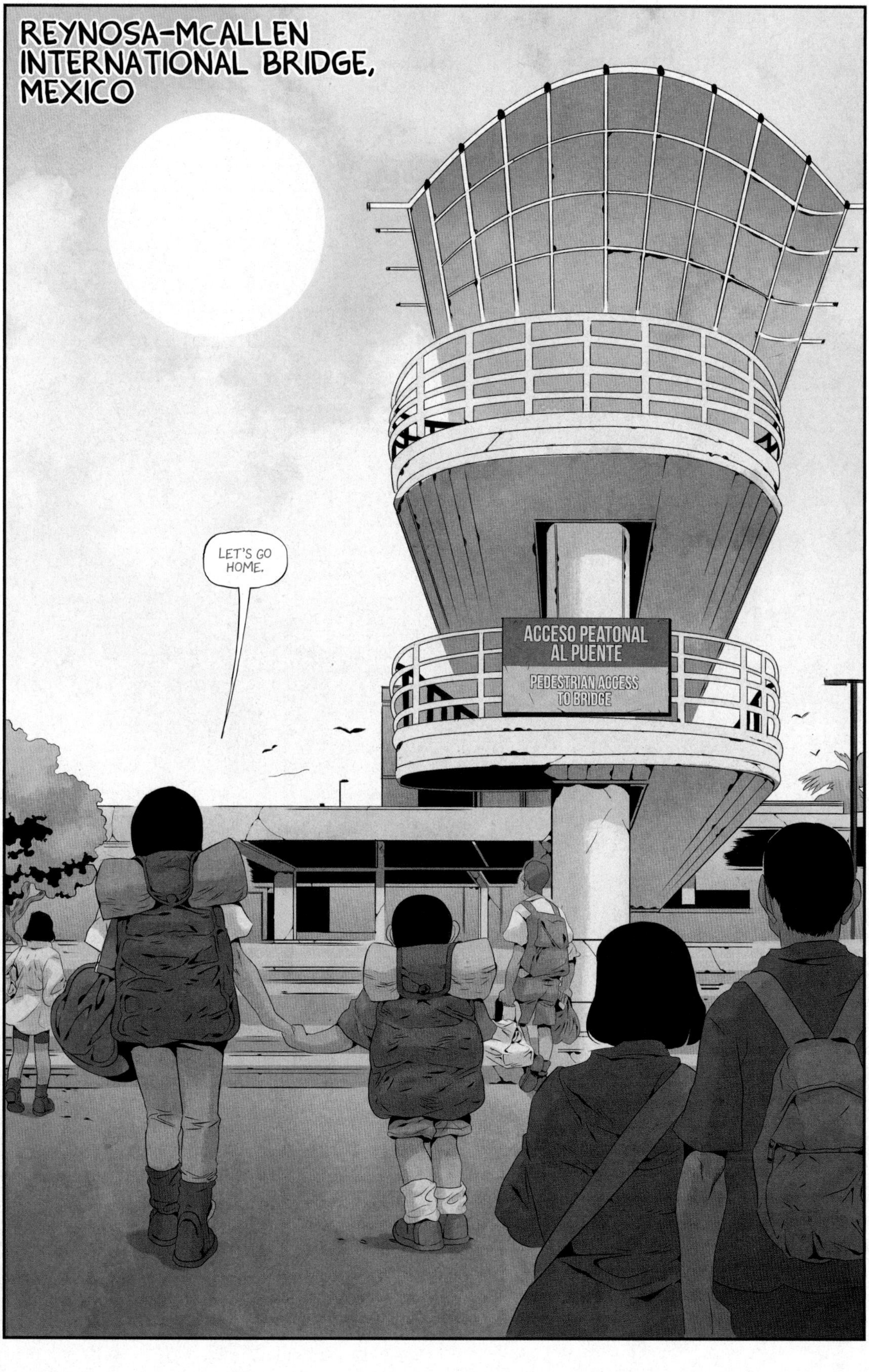
REYNOSA-McALLEN INTERNATIONAL BRIDGE, MEXICO
LET'S GO HOME.
ACCESO PEATONAL AL PUENTE
PEDESTRIAN ACCESS TO BRIDGE

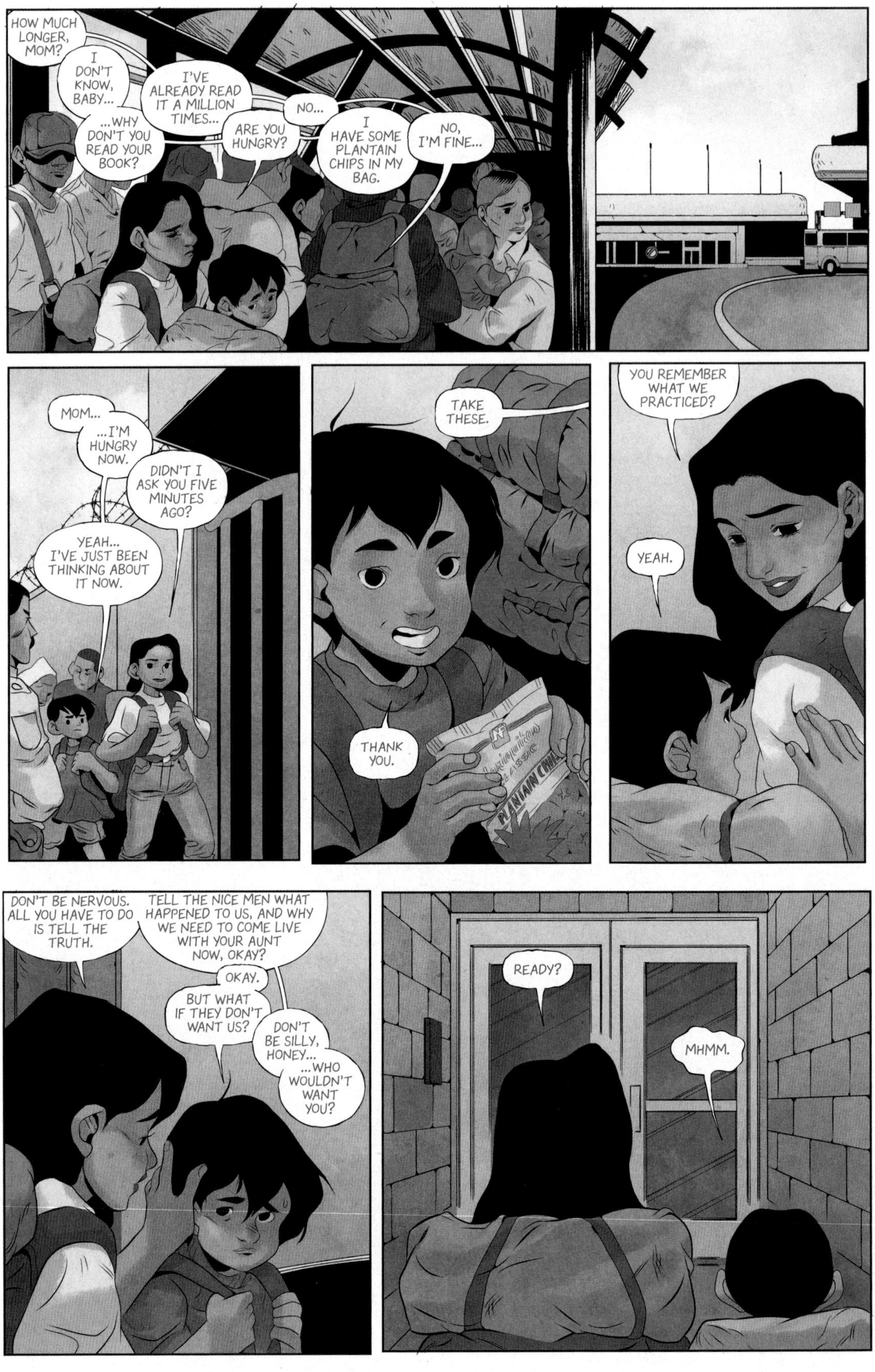
HOW MUCH LONGER, MOM?
I DON'T KNOW, BABY...
...WHY DON'T YOU READ YOUR BOOK?
I'VE ALREADY READ IT A MILLION TIMES...
NO...
ARE YOU HUNGRY?
I HAVE SOME PLANTAIN CHIPS IN MY BAG.
NO, I'M FINE...
MOM...
...I'M HUNGRY NOW.
DIDN'T I ASK YOU FIVE MINUTES AGO?
YEAH... I'VE JUST BEEN THINKING ABOUT IT NOW.
TAKE THESE.
THANK YOU.
PLANTAIN CHIPS
YOU REMEMBER WHAT WE PRACTICED?
YEAH.
DON'T BE NERVOUS. ALL YOU HAVE TO DO IS TELL THE TRUTH.
TELL THE NICE MEN WHAT HAPPENED TO US, AND WHY WE NEED TO COME LIVE WITH YOUR AUNT NOW, OKAY?
OKAY.
BUT WHAT IF THEY DON'T WANT US?
DON'T BE SILLY, HONEY... ...WHO WOULDN'T WANT YOU?
READY?
MHMM.

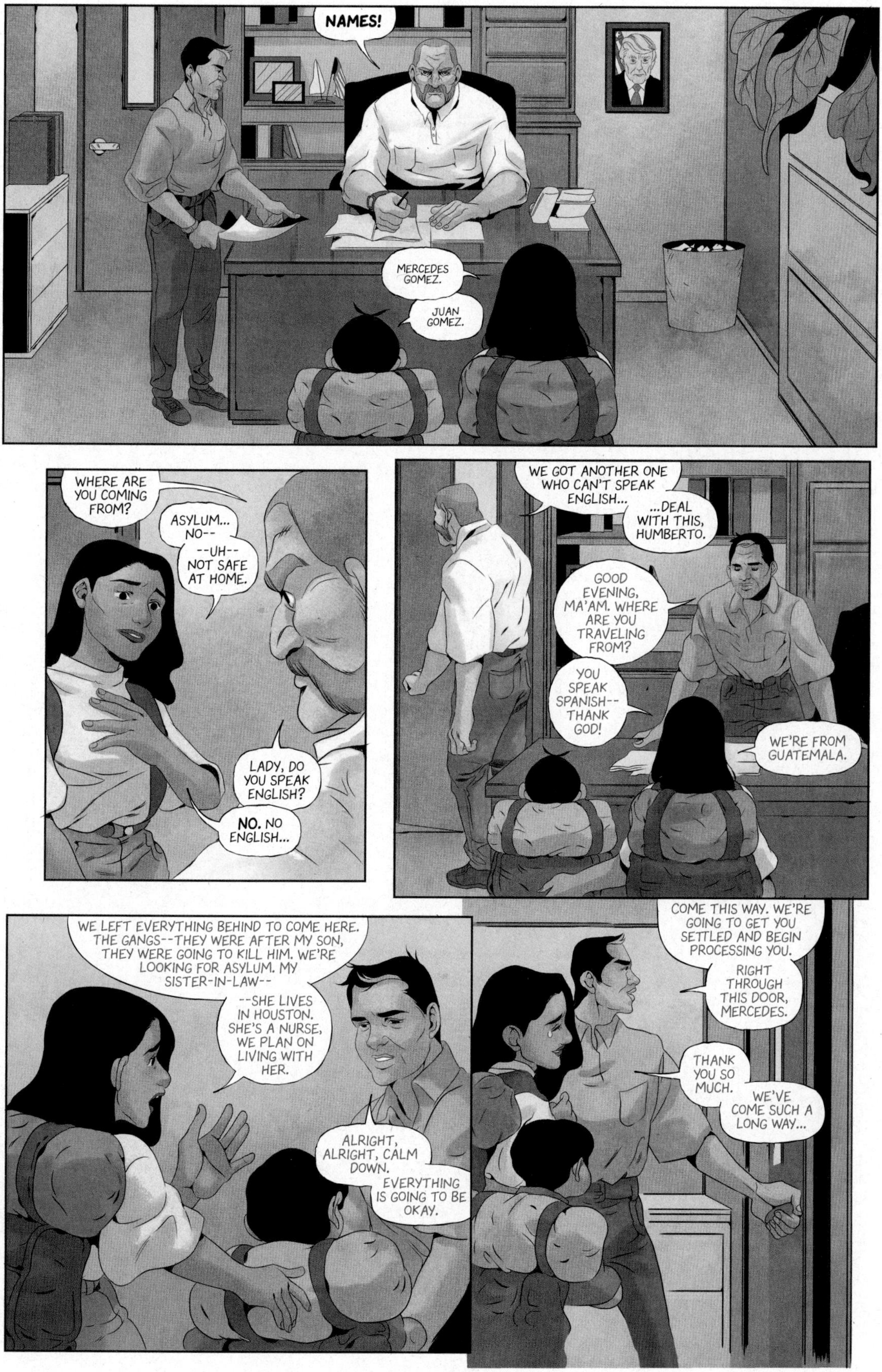
NAMES!
MERCEDES GOMEZ.
JUAN GOMEZ.
WHERE ARE YOU COMING FROM?
ASYLUM... NO--
--UH-- NOT SAFE AT HOME.
LADY, DO YOU SPEAK ENGLISH?
NO. NO ENGLISH...
WE GOT ANOTHER ONE WHO CAN'T SPEAK ENGLISH...
...DEAL WITH THIS, HUMBERTO.
GOOD EVENING, MA'AM. WHERE ARE YOU TRAVELING FROM?
YOU SPEAK SPANISH-- THANK GOD!
WE'RE FROM GUATEMALA.
WE LEFT EVERYTHING BEHIND TO COME HERE. THE GANGS--THEY WERE AFTER MY SON, THEY WERE GOING TO KILL HIM. WE'RE LOOKING FOR ASYLUM. MY SISTER-IN-LAW--
--SHE LIVES IN HOUSTON. SHE'S A NURSE, WE PLAN ON LIVING WITH HER.
ALRIGHT, ALRIGHT, CALM DOWN.
EVERYTHING IS GOING TO BE OKAY.
COME THIS WAY. WE'RE GOING TO GET YOU SETTLED AND BEGIN PROCESSING YOU.
RIGHT THROUGH THIS DOOR, MERCEDES.
THANK YOU SO MUCH.
WE'VE COME SUCH A LONG WAY...

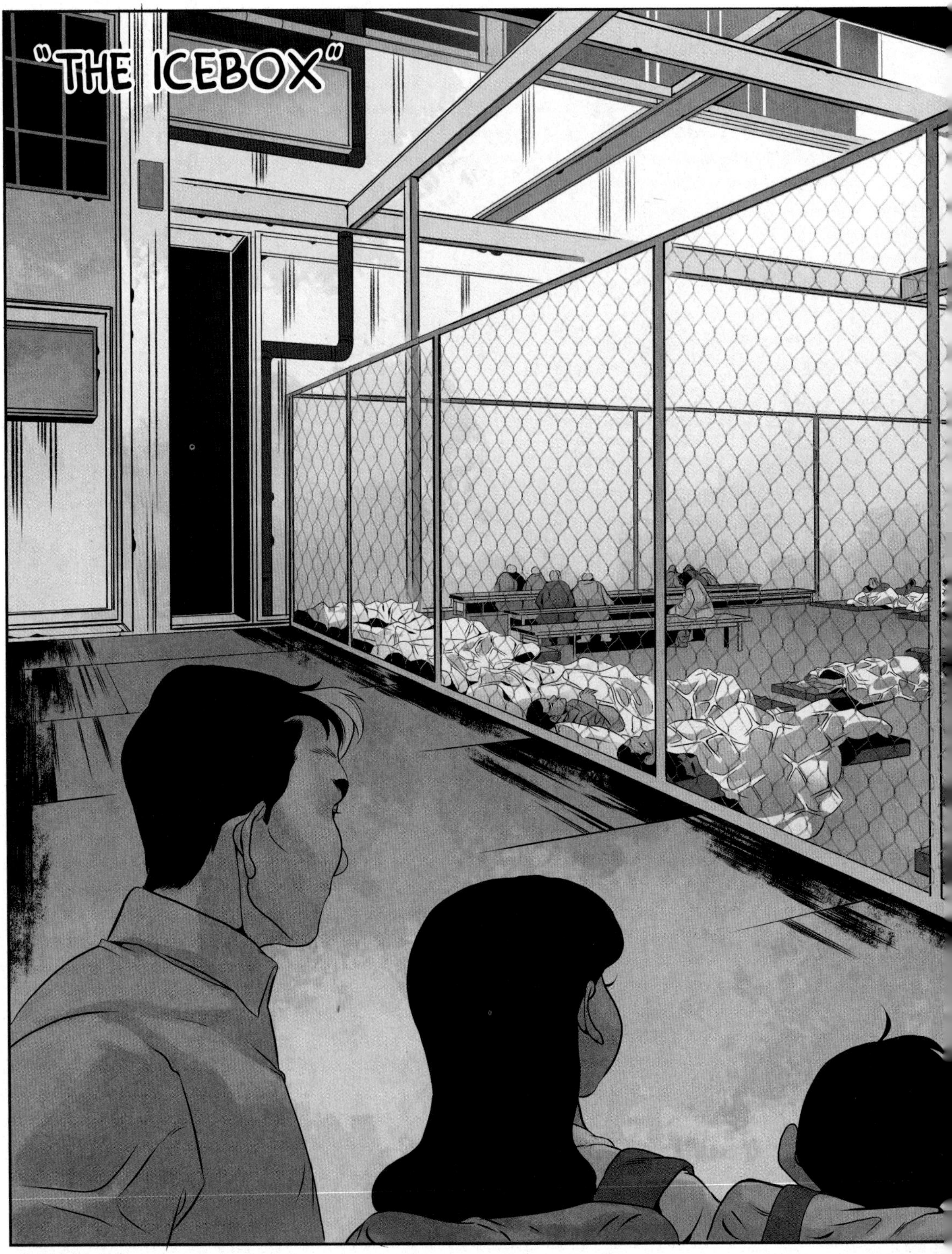
"THE ICEBOX"

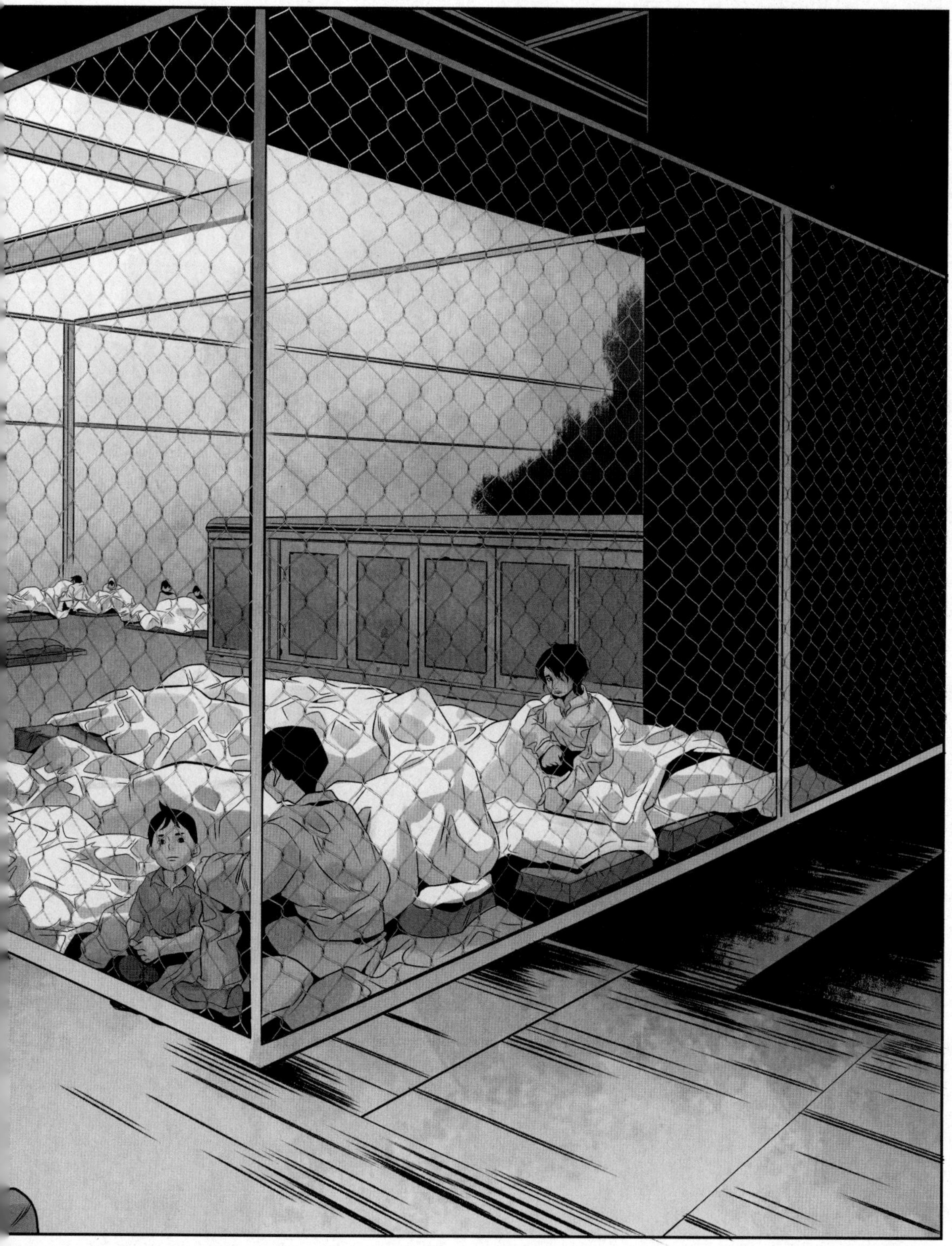

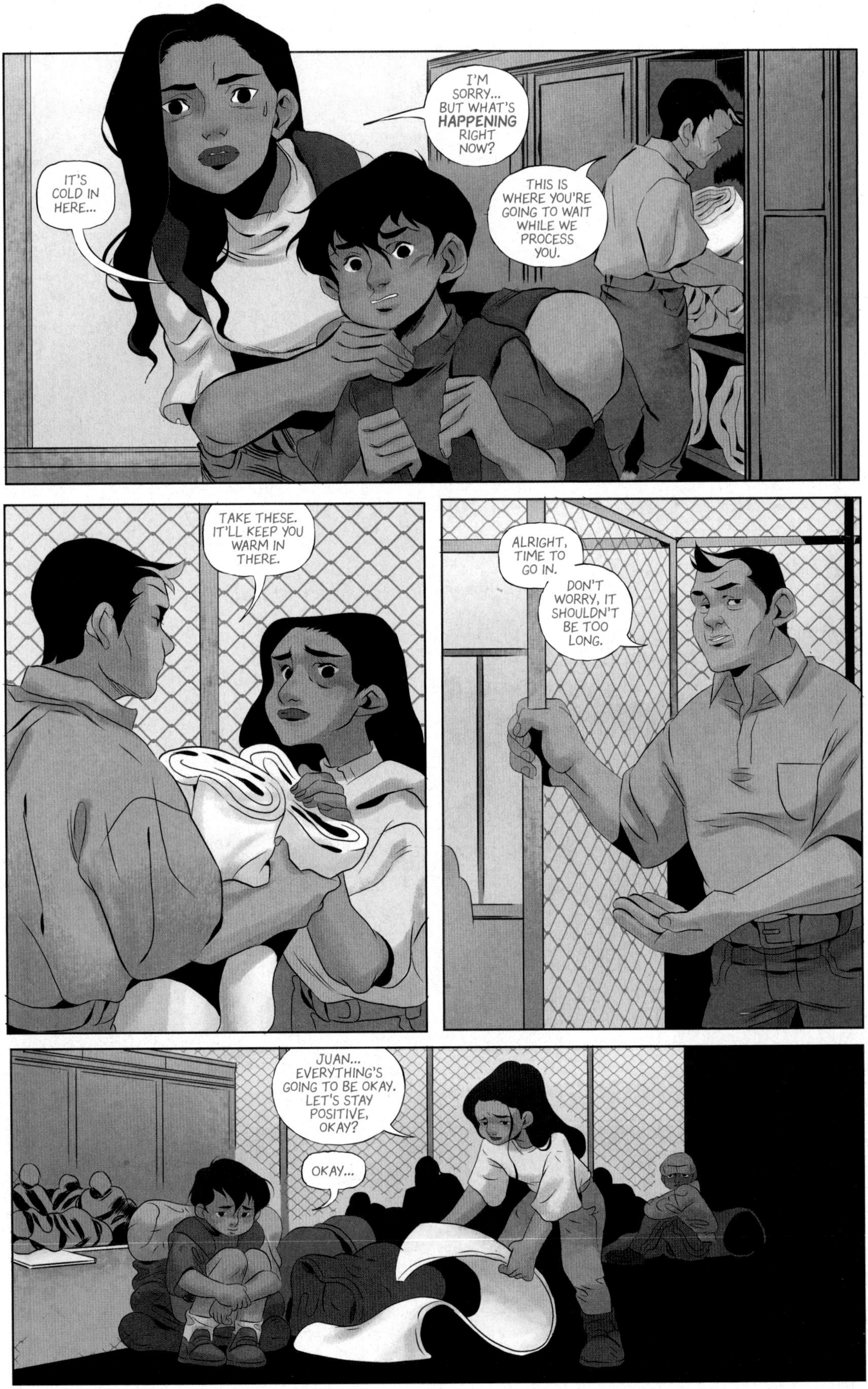
I'M SORRY... BUT WHAT'S HAPPENING RIGHT NOW?
IT'S COLD IN HERE...
THIS IS WHERE YOU'RE GOING TO WAIT WHILE WE PROCESS YOU.
TAKE THESE. IT'LL KEEP YOU WARM IN THERE.
ALRIGHT, TIME TO GO IN.
DON'T WORRY, IT SHOULDN'T BE TOO LONG.
JUAN... EVERYTHING'S GOING TO BE OKAY. LET'S STAY POSITIVE, OKAY?
OKAY...

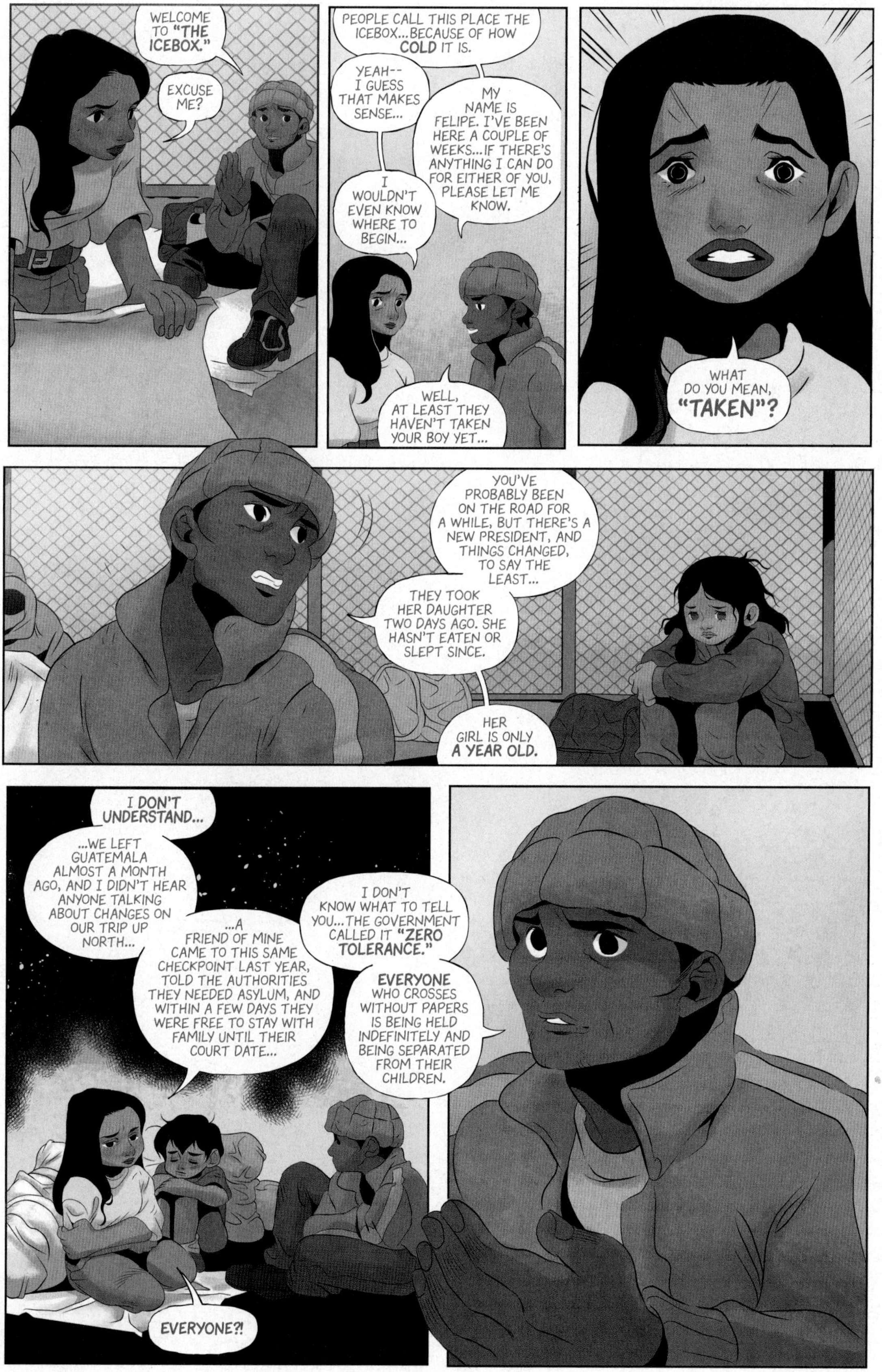
WELCOME TO "THE ICEBOX."
EXCUSE ME?
PEOPLE CALL THIS PLACE THE ICEBOX...BECAUSE OF HOW COLD IT IS.
YEAH-- I GUESS THAT MAKES SENSE...
MY NAME IS FELIPE. I'VE BEEN HERE A COUPLE OF WEEKS...IF THERE'S ANYTHING I CAN DO FOR EITHER OF YOU, PLEASE LET ME KNOW.
I WOULDN'T EVEN KNOW WHERE TO BEGIN...
WELL, AT LEAST THEY HAVEN'T TAKEN YOUR BOY YET...
WHAT DO YOU MEAN, "TAKEN"?
YOU'VE PROBABLY BEEN ON THE ROAD FOR A WHILE, BUT THERE'S A NEW PRESIDENT, AND THINGS CHANGED, TO SAY THE LEAST...
THEY TOOK HER DAUGHTER TWO DAYS AGO. SHE HASN'T EATEN OR SLEPT SINCE.
HER GIRL IS ONLY A YEAR OLD.
I DON'T UNDERSTAND...
...WE LEFT GUATEMALA ALMOST A MONTH AGO, AND I DIDN'T HEAR ANYONE TALKING ABOUT CHANGES ON OUR TRIP UP NORTH...
...A FRIEND OF MINE CAME TO THIS SAME CHECKPOINT LAST YEAR, TOLD THE AUTHORITIES THEY NEEDED ASYLUM, AND WITHIN A FEW DAYS THEY WERE FREE TO STAY WITH FAMILY UNTIL THEIR COURT DATE...
I DON'T KNOW WHAT TO TELL YOU...THE GOVERNMENT CALLED IT "ZERO TOLERANCE."
EVERYONE WHO CROSSES WITHOUT PAPERS IS BEING HELD INDEFINITELY AND BEING SEPARATED FROM THEIR CHILDREN.
EVERYONE?!

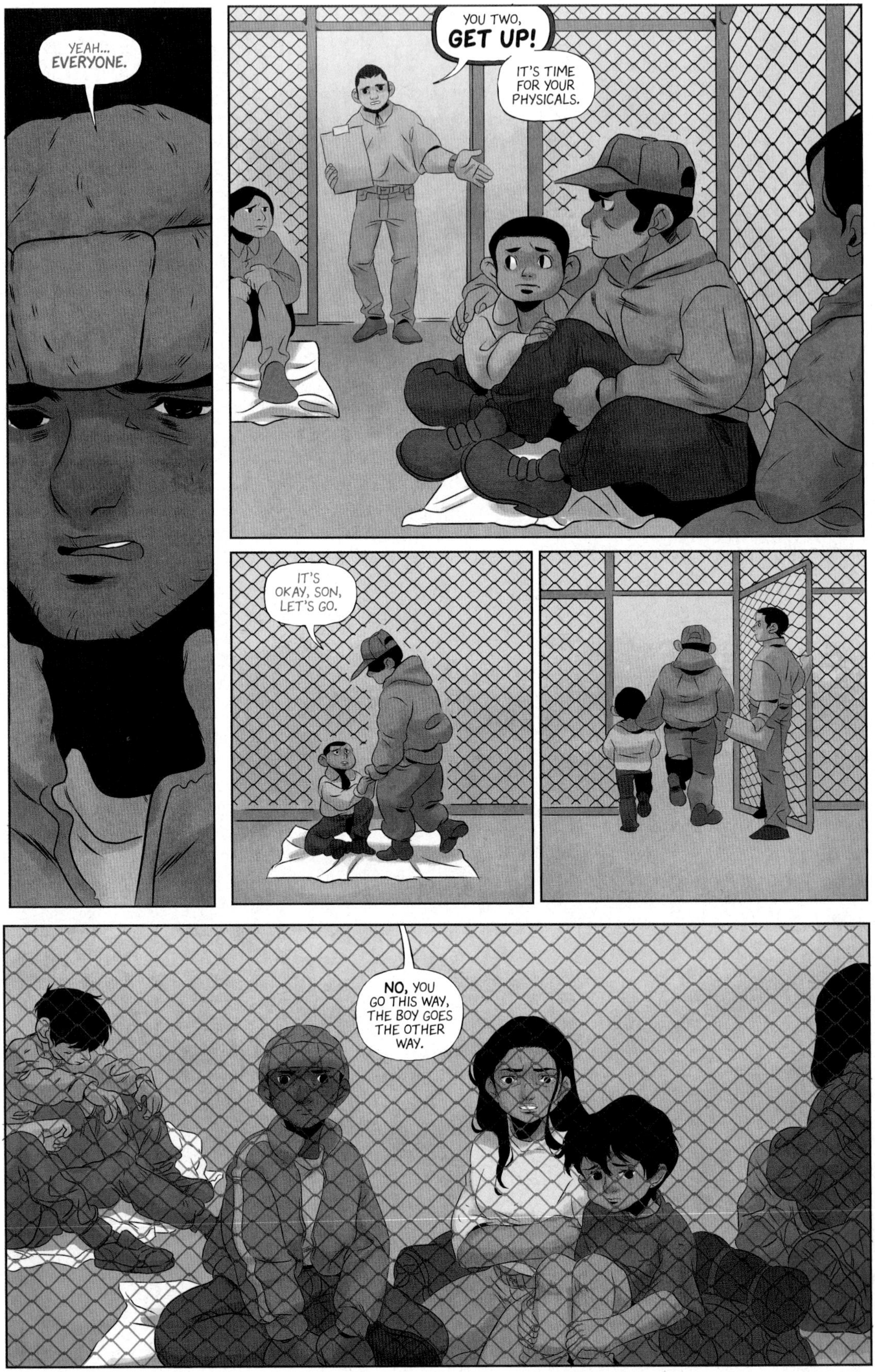
YEAH... **EVERYONE.**
YOU TWO, **GET UP!**
IT'S TIME FOR YOUR PHYSICALS.
IT'S OKAY, SON, LET'S GO.
NO, YOU GO THIS WAY, THE BOY GOES THE OTHER WAY.

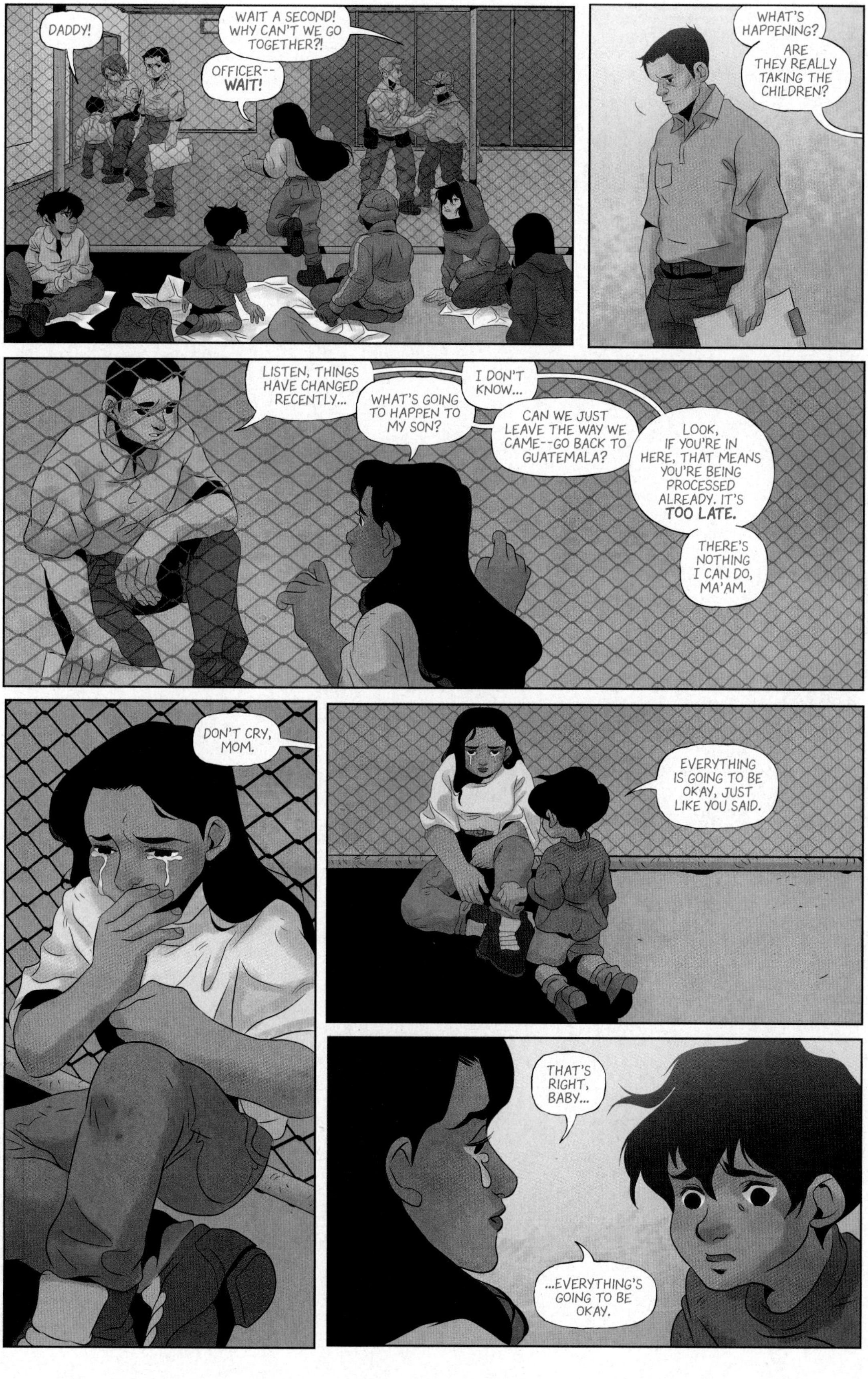
DADDY!
WAIT A SECOND! WHY CAN'T WE GO TOGETHER?!
OFFICER-- **WAIT!**
WHAT'S HAPPENING?
ARE THEY REALLY TAKING THE CHILDREN?
LISTEN, THINGS HAVE CHANGED RECENTLY...
WHAT'S GOING TO HAPPEN TO MY SON?
I DON'T KNOW...
CAN WE JUST LEAVE THE WAY WE CAME--GO BACK TO GUATEMALA?
LOOK, IF YOU'RE IN HERE, THAT MEANS YOU'RE BEING PROCESSED ALREADY. IT'S **TOO LATE.**
THERE'S NOTHING I CAN DO, MA'AM.
DON'T CRY, MOM.
EVERYTHING IS GOING TO BE OKAY, JUST LIKE YOU SAID.
THAT'S RIGHT, BABY...
...EVERYTHING'S GOING TO BE OKAY.

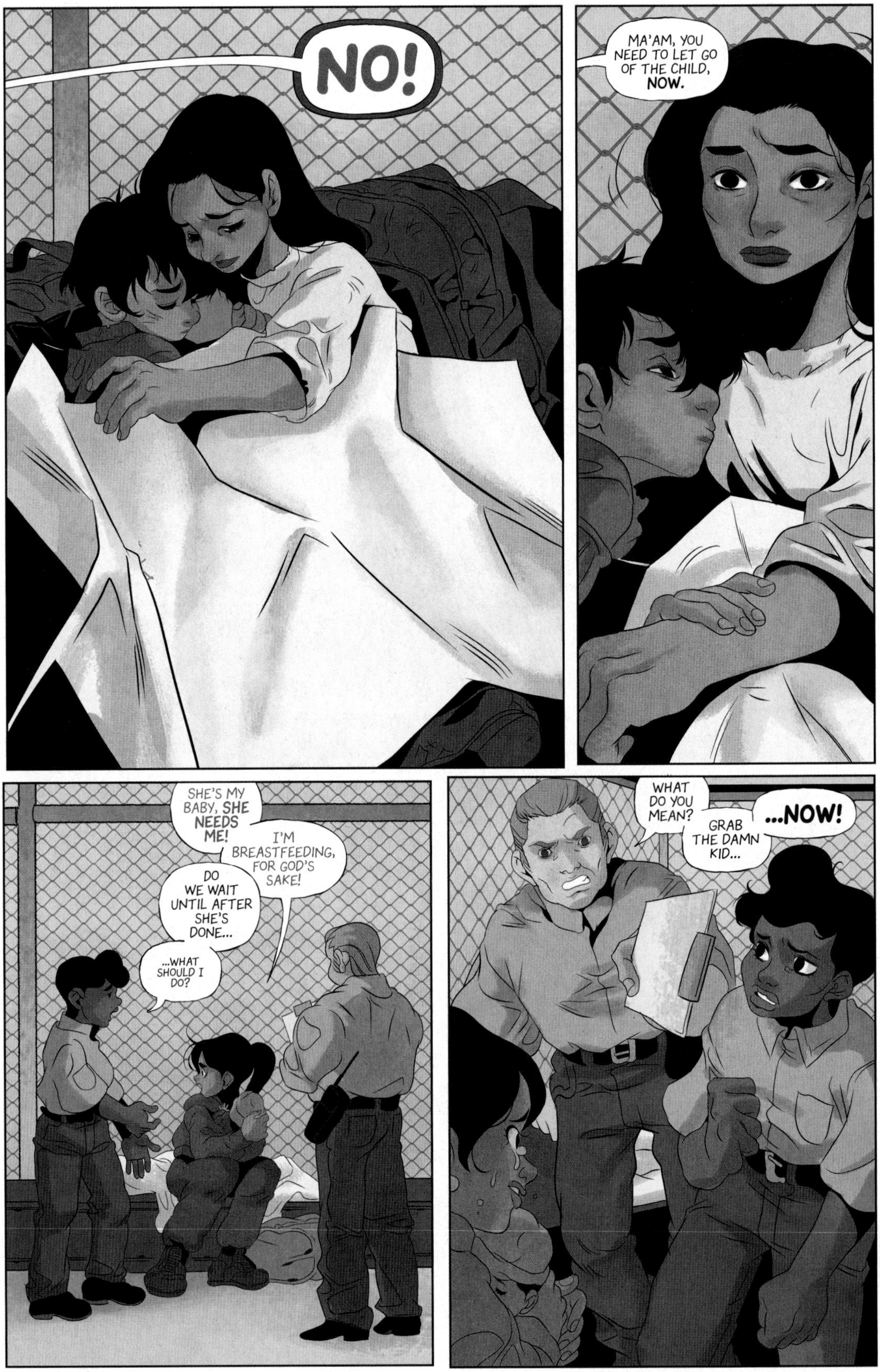
NO!
MA'AM, YOU NEED TO LET GO OF THE CHILD, NOW.
SHE'S MY BABY, SHE NEEDS ME!
I'M BREASTFEEDING, FOR GOD'S SAKE!
DO WE WAIT UNTIL AFTER SHE'S DONE...
...WHAT SHOULD I DO?
WHAT DO YOU MEAN?
GRAB THE DAMN KID...
...NOW!

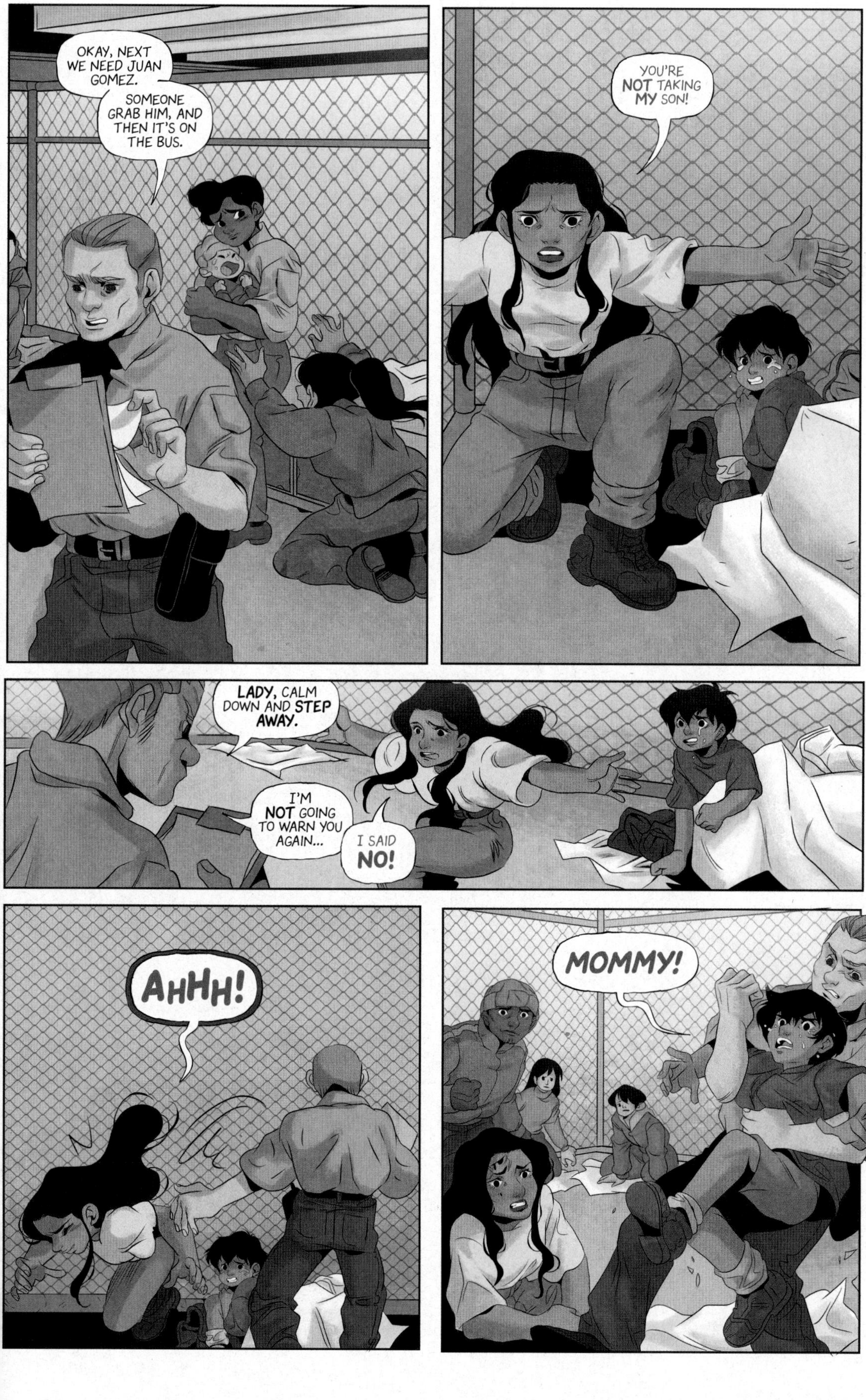
OKAY, NEXT WE NEED JUAN GOMEZ.
SOMEONE GRAB HIM, AND THEN IT'S ON THE BUS.
YOU'RE NOT TAKING MY SON!
LADY, CALM DOWN AND STEP AWAY.
I'M NOT GOING TO WARN YOU AGAIN...
I SAID NO!
AHHH!
MOMMY!

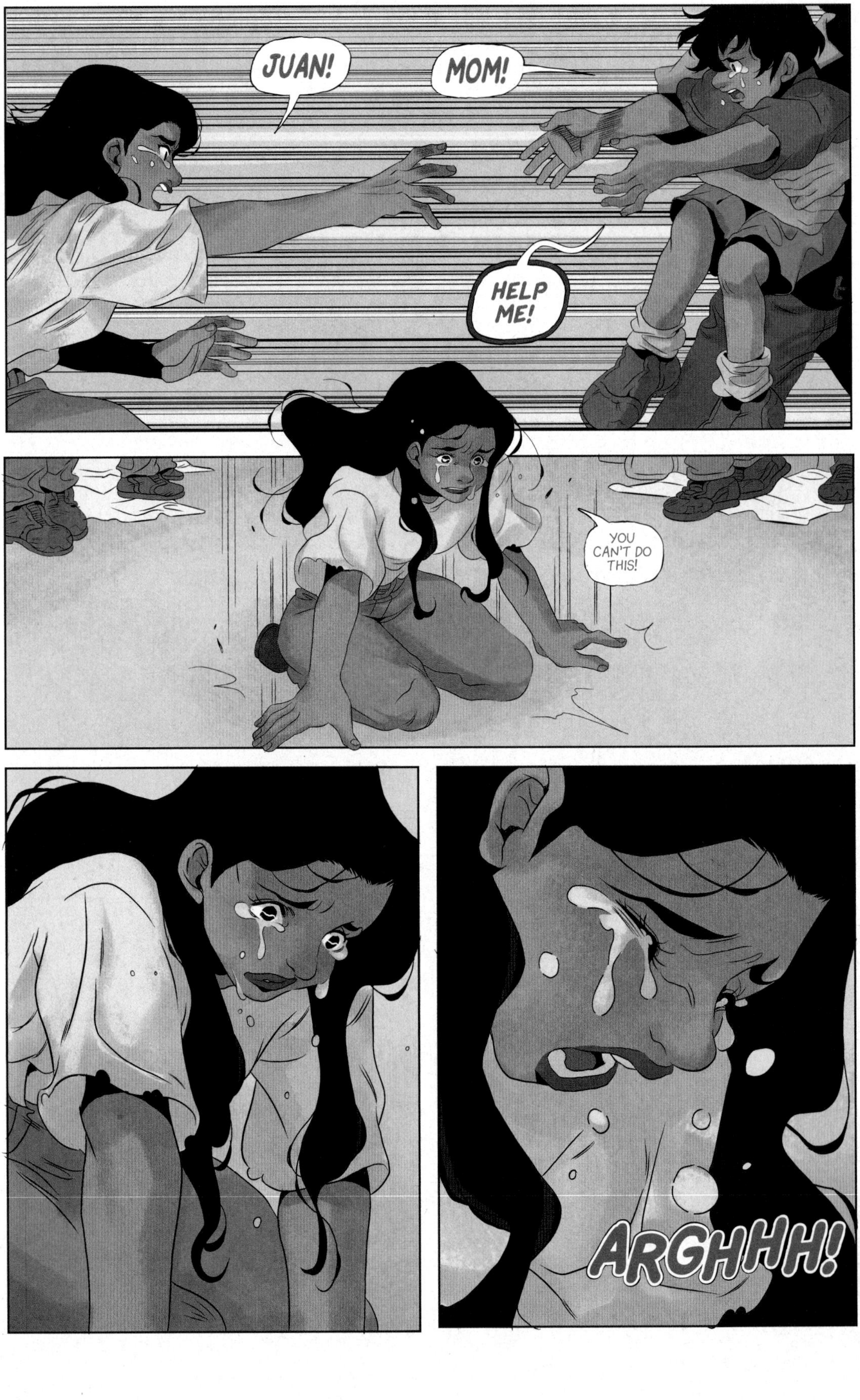
JUAN!
MOM!
HELP ME!
YOU CAN'T DO THIS!
ARGHHH!

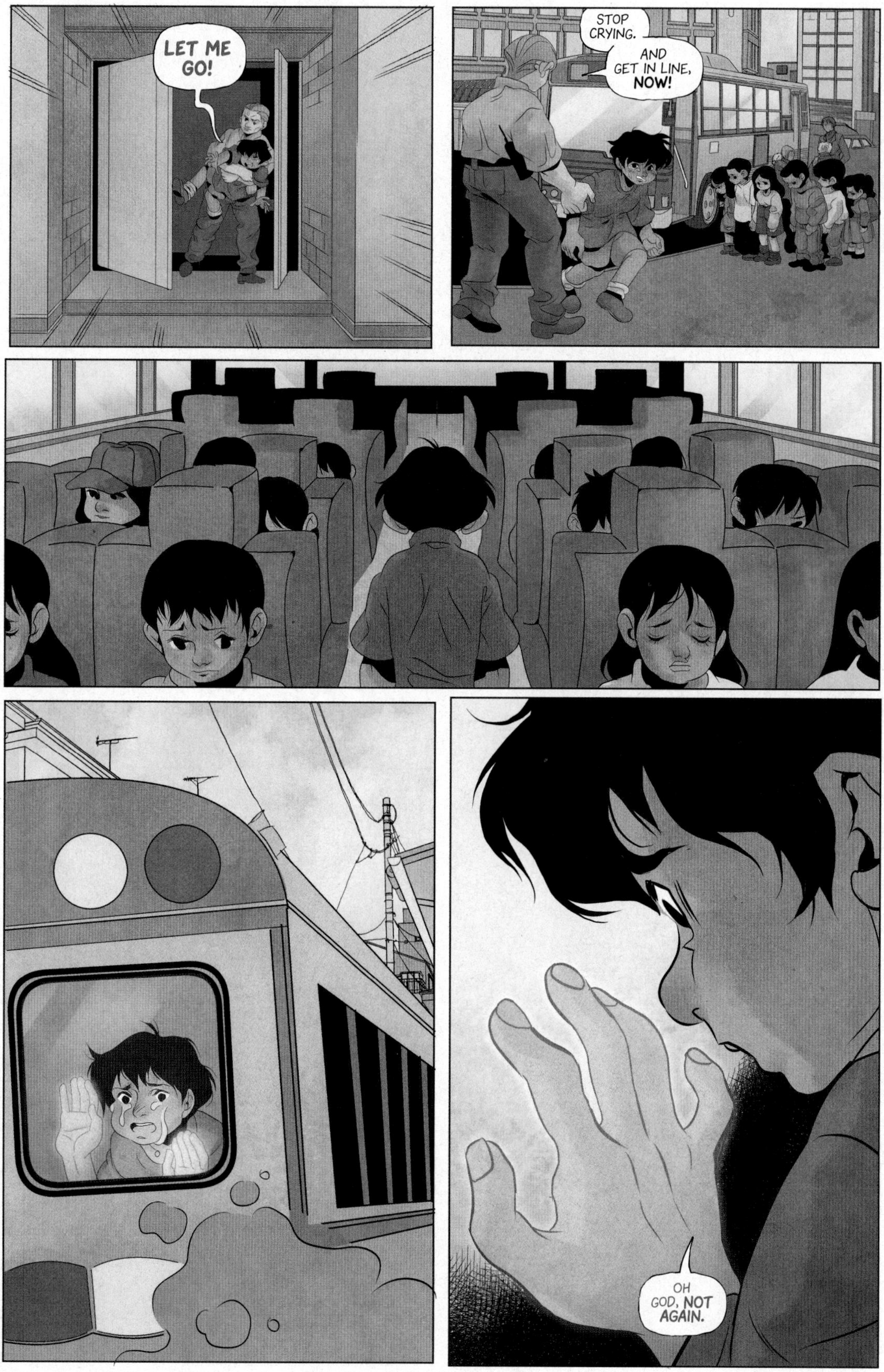
LET ME GO!
STOP CRYING.
AND GET IN LINE, NOW!
OH GOD, NOT AGAIN.

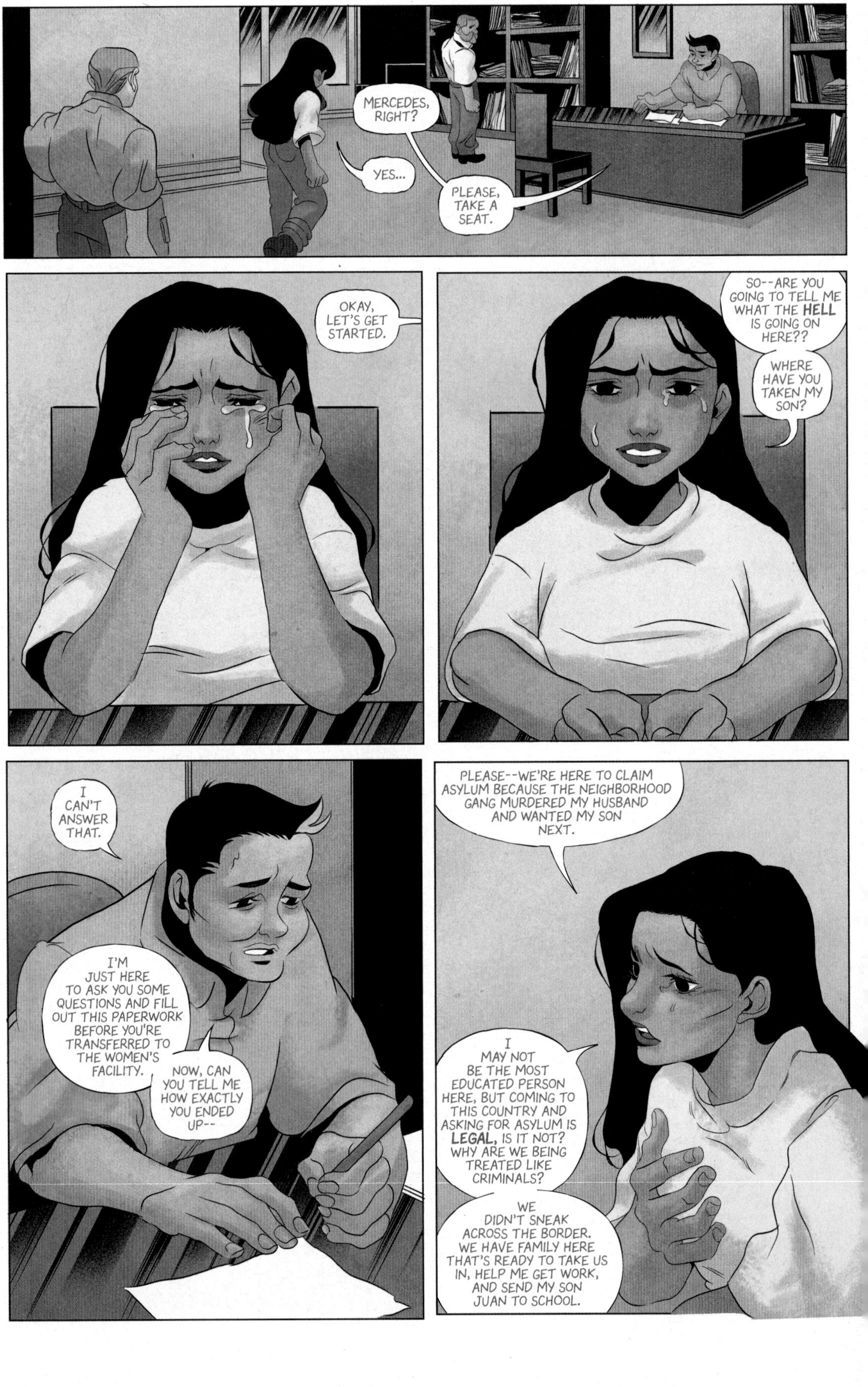
MERCEDES, RIGHT?
YES...
PLEASE, TAKE A SEAT.
OKAY, LET'S GET STARTED.
SO--ARE YOU GOING TO TELL ME WHAT THE **HELL** IS GOING ON HERE??
WHERE HAVE YOU TAKEN MY SON?
I CAN'T ANSWER THAT.
I'M JUST HERE TO ASK YOU SOME QUESTIONS AND FILL OUT THIS PAPERWORK BEFORE YOU'RE TRANSFERRED TO THE WOMEN'S FACILITY.
NOW, CAN YOU TELL ME HOW EXACTLY YOU ENDED UP--
PLEASE--WE'RE HERE TO CLAIM ASYLUM BECAUSE THE NEIGHBORHOOD GANG MURDERED MY HUSBAND AND WANTED MY SON NEXT.
I MAY NOT BE THE MOST EDUCATED PERSON HERE, BUT COMING TO THIS COUNTRY AND ASKING FOR ASYLUM IS **LEGAL**, IS IT NOT? WHY ARE WE BEING TREATED LIKE CRIMINALS?
WE DIDN'T SNEAK ACROSS THE BORDER. WE HAVE FAMILY HERE THAT'S READY TO TAKE US IN, HELP ME GET WORK, AND SEND MY SON JUAN TO SCHOOL.

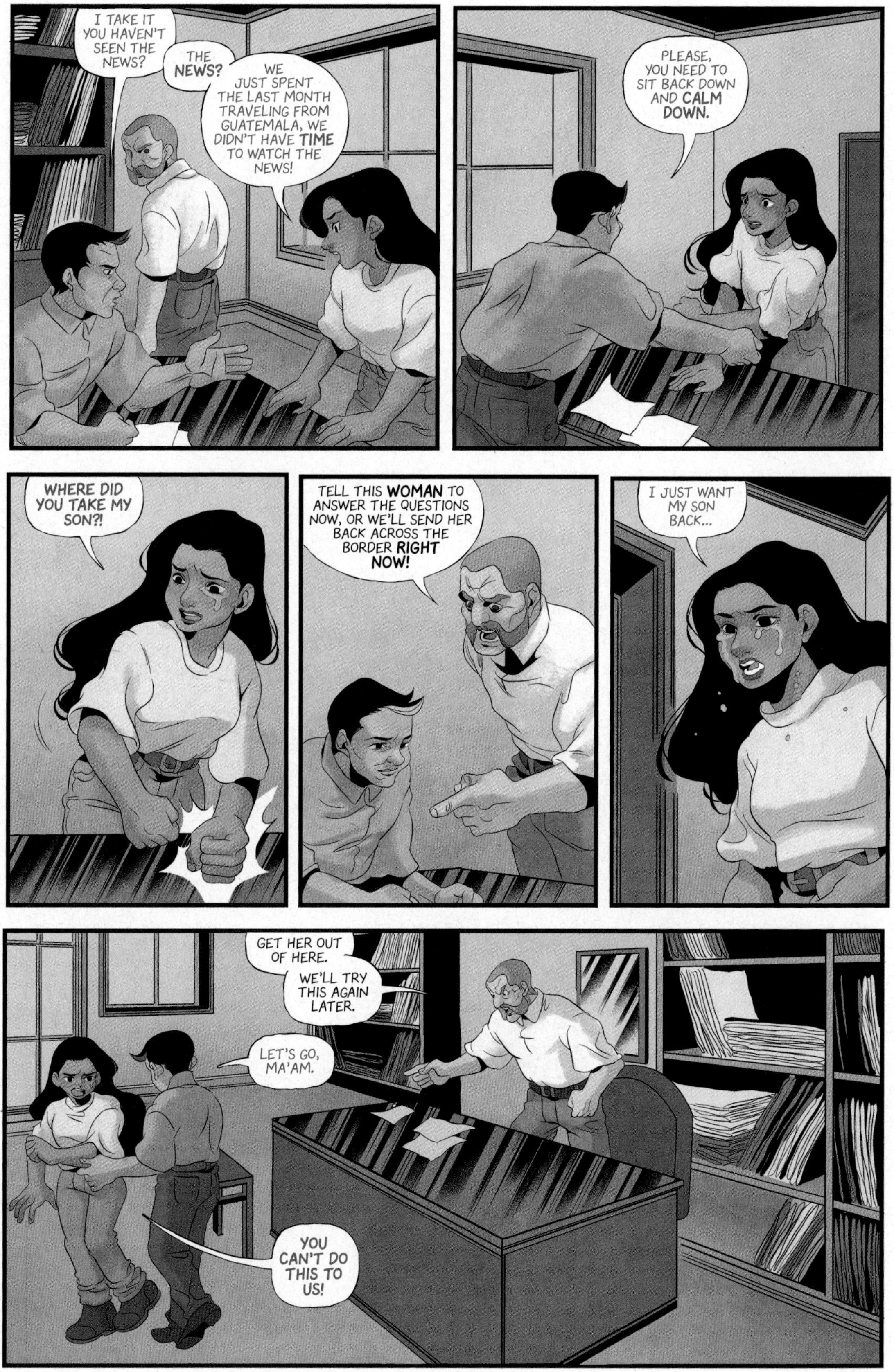
I TAKE IT YOU HAVEN'T SEEN THE NEWS?
THE NEWS?
WE JUST SPENT THE LAST MONTH TRAVELING FROM GUATEMALA, WE DIDN'T HAVE TIME TO WATCH THE NEWS!
PLEASE, YOU NEED TO SIT BACK DOWN AND CALM DOWN.
WHERE DID YOU TAKE MY SON?!
TELL THIS WOMAN TO ANSWER THE QUESTIONS NOW, OR WE'LL SEND HER BACK ACROSS THE BORDER RIGHT NOW!
I JUST WANT MY SON BACK...
GET HER OUT OF HERE.
WE'LL TRY THIS AGAIN LATER.
LET'S GO, MA'AM.
YOU CAN'T DO THIS TO US!

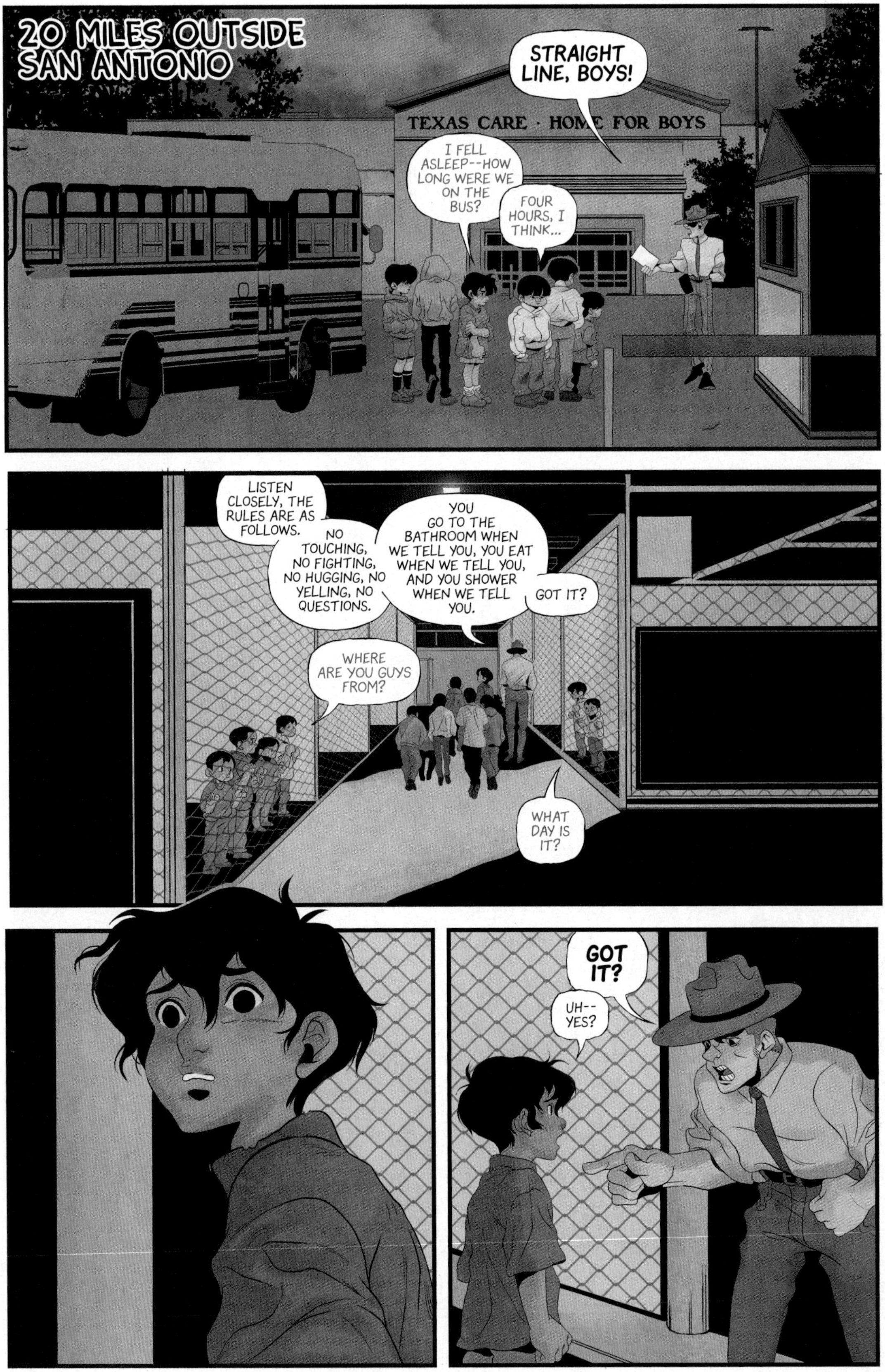
20 MILES OUTSIDE SAN ANTONIO
STRAIGHT LINE, BOYS!
TEXAS CARE · HOME FOR BOYS
I FELL ASLEEP--HOW LONG WERE WE ON THE BUS?
FOUR HOURS, I THINK...
LISTEN CLOSELY, THE RULES ARE AS FOLLOWS.
NO TOUCHING, NO FIGHTING, NO HUGGING, NO YELLING, NO QUESTIONS.
YOU GO TO THE BATHROOM WHEN WE TELL YOU, YOU EAT WHEN WE TELL YOU, AND YOU SHOWER WHEN WE TELL YOU.
GOT IT?
WHERE ARE YOU GUYS FROM?
WHAT DAY IS IT?
GOT IT?
UH--YES?

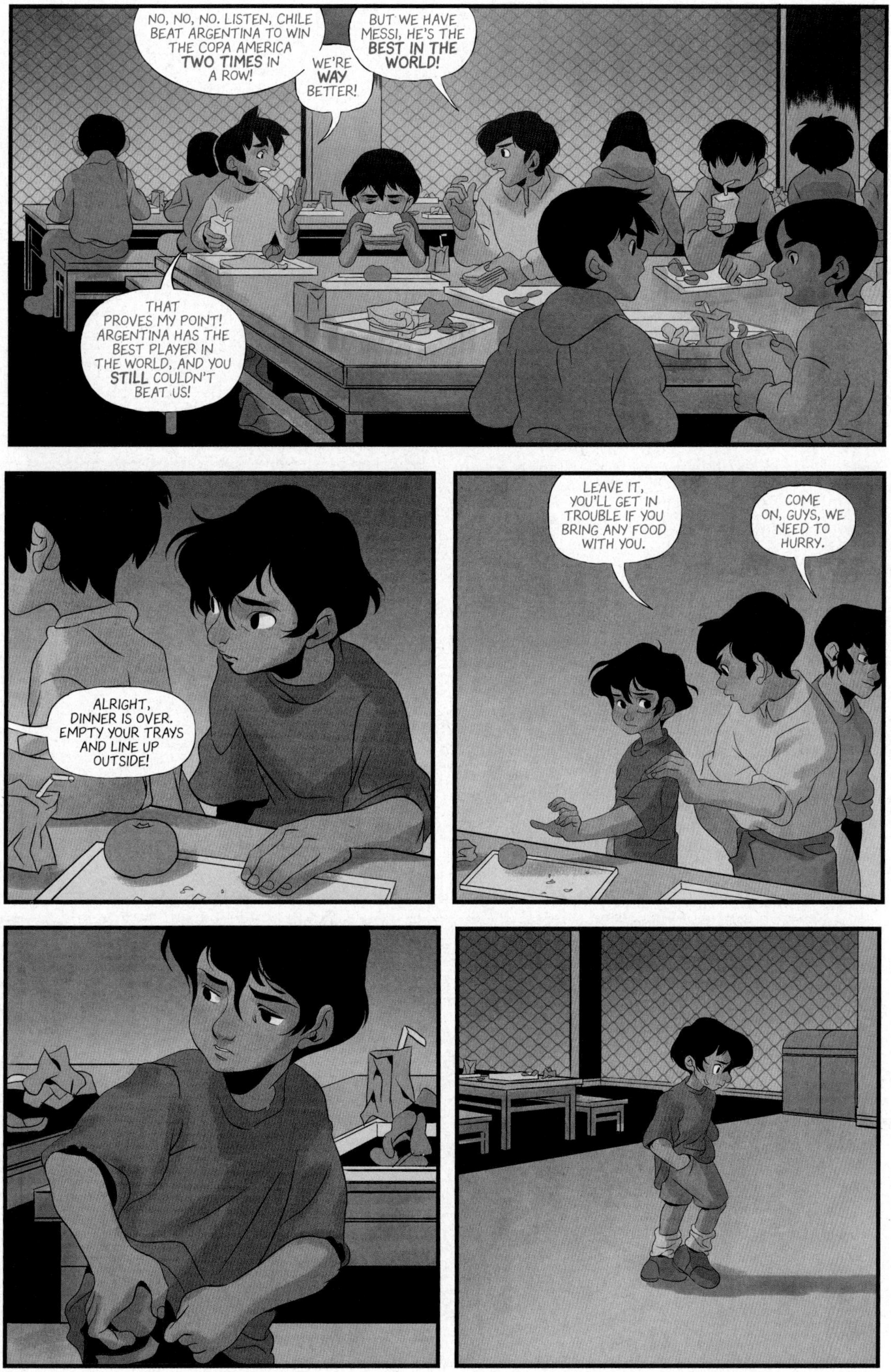
NO, NO, NO. LISTEN, CHILE BEAT ARGENTINA TO WIN THE COPA AMERICA TWO TIMES IN A ROW!
WE'RE WAY BETTER!
BUT WE HAVE MESSI, HE'S THE BEST IN THE WORLD!
THAT PROVES MY POINT! ARGENTINA HAS THE BEST PLAYER IN THE WORLD, AND YOU STILL COULDN'T BEAT US!
ALRIGHT, DINNER IS OVER. EMPTY YOUR TRAYS AND LINE UP OUTSIDE!
LEAVE IT, YOU'LL GET IN TROUBLE IF YOU BRING ANY FOOD WITH YOU.
COME ON, GUYS, WE NEED TO HURRY.

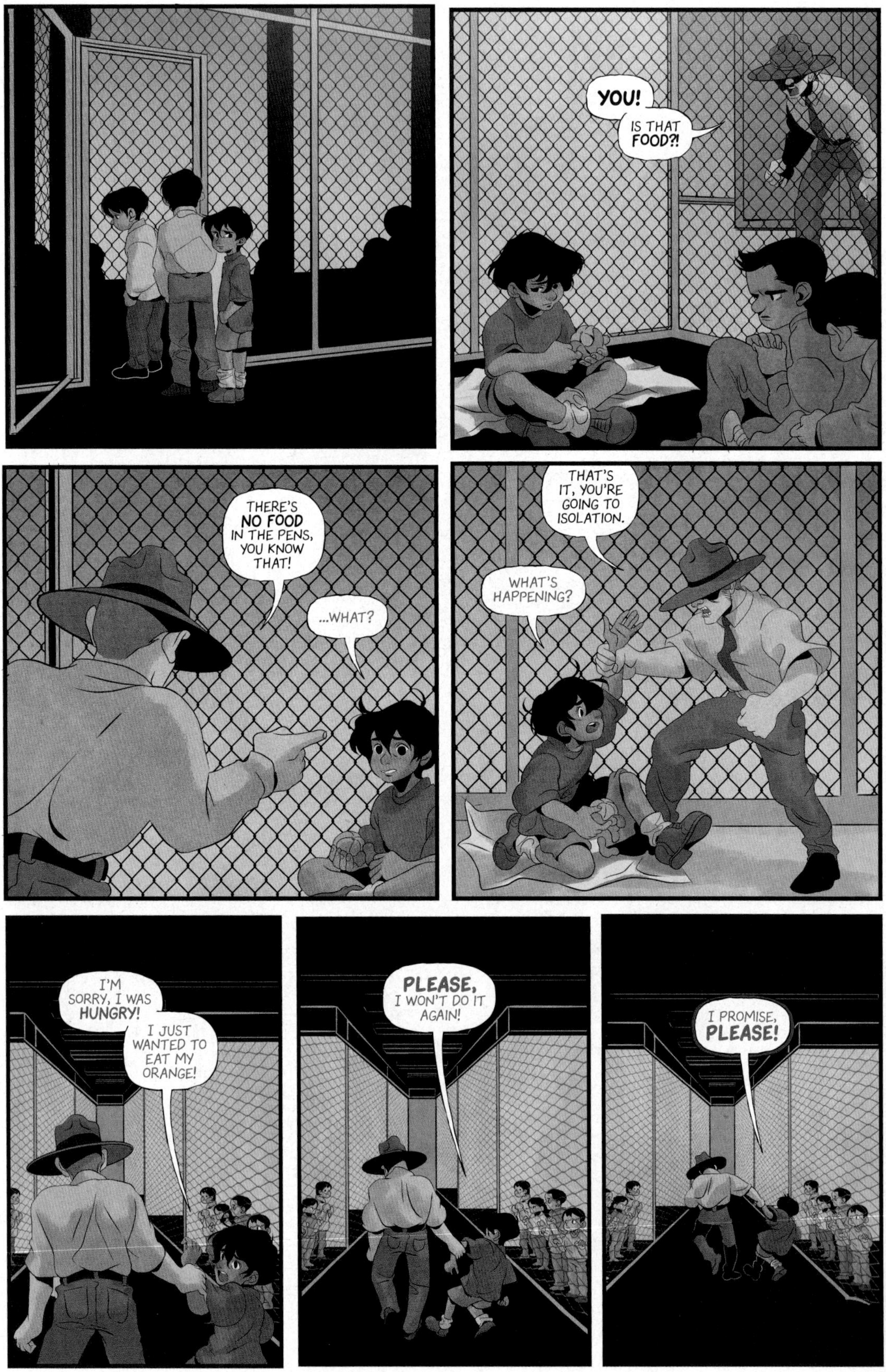
YOU!
IS THAT FOOD?!
THERE'S NO FOOD IN THE PENS, YOU KNOW THAT!
...WHAT?
THAT'S IT, YOU'RE GOING TO ISOLATION.
WHAT'S HAPPENING?
I'M SORRY, I WAS HUNGRY!
I JUST WANTED TO EAT MY ORANGE!
PLEASE, I WON'T DO IT AGAIN!
I PROMISE, PLEASE!

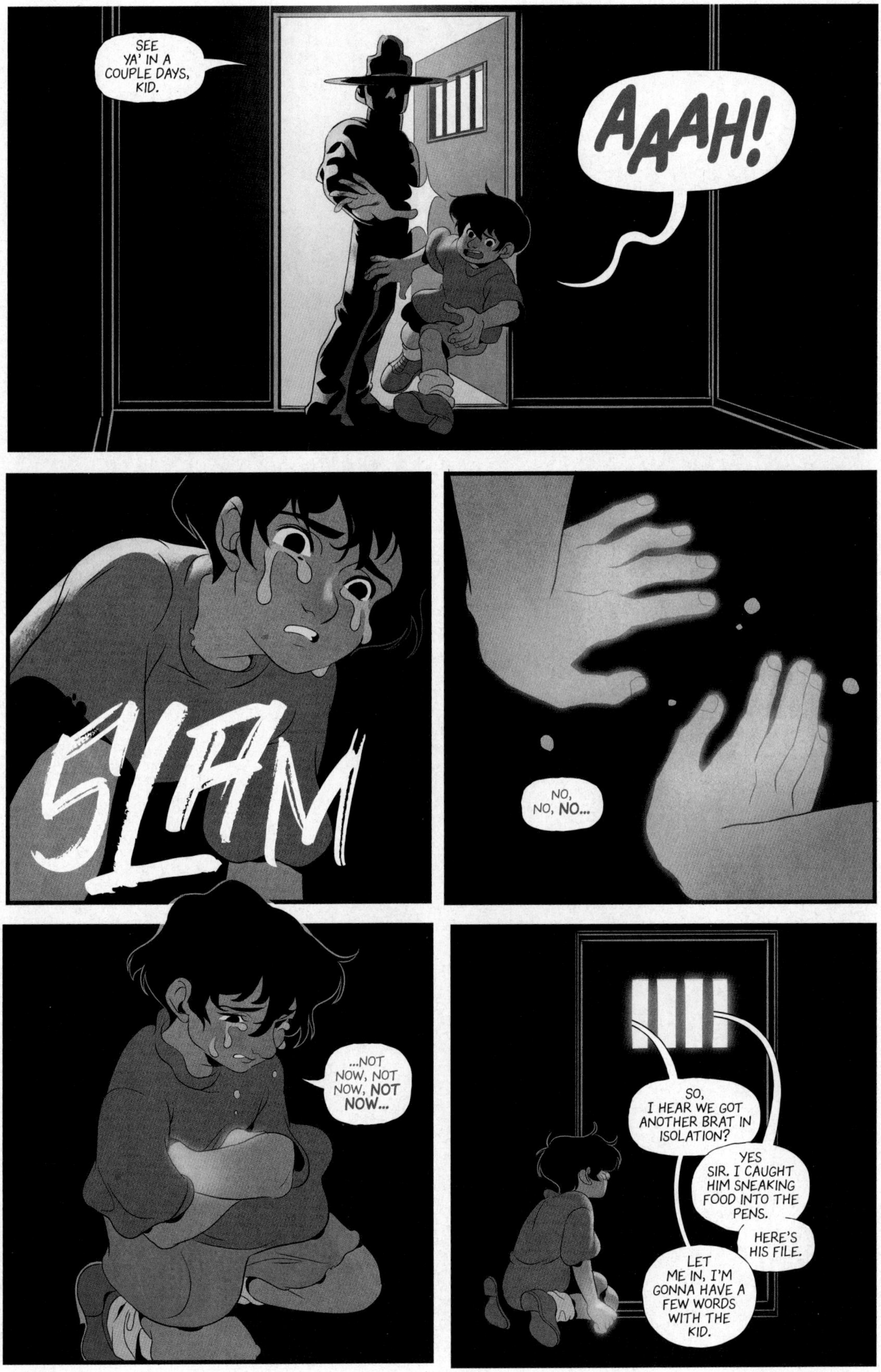
SEE YA' IN A COUPLE DAYS, KID.
AAAH!
SLAM
NO, NO, NO...
...NOT NOW, NOT NOW, NOT NOW...
SO, I HEAR WE GOT ANOTHER BRAT IN ISOLATION?
YES SIR. I CAUGHT HIM SNEAKING FOOD INTO THE PENS.
HERE'S HIS FILE.
LET ME IN, I'M GONNA HAVE A FEW WORDS WITH THE KID.

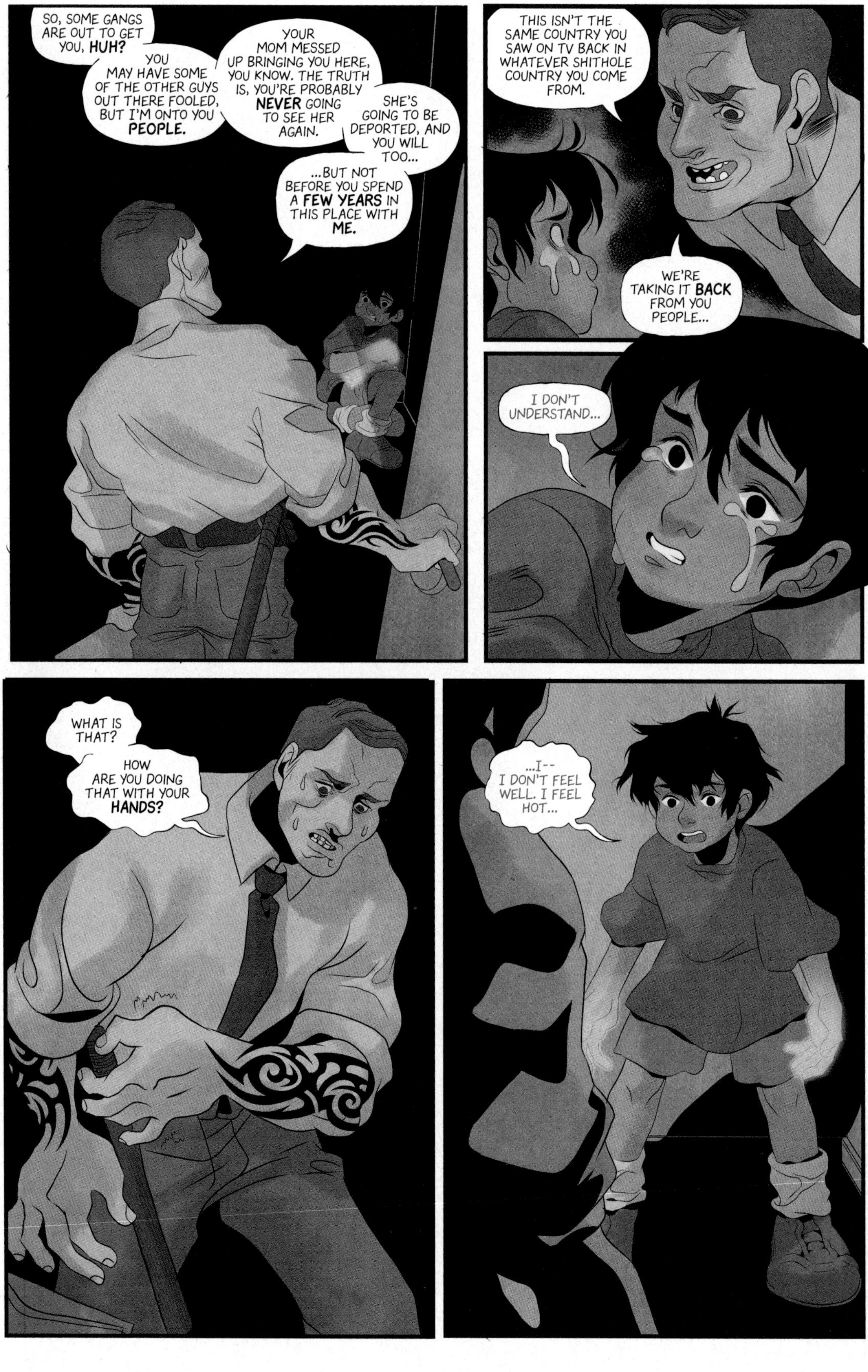
SO, SOME GANGS ARE OUT TO GET YOU, HUH?
YOU MAY HAVE SOME OF THE OTHER GUYS OUT THERE FOOLED, BUT I'M ONTO YOU PEOPLE.
YOUR MOM MESSED UP BRINGING YOU HERE, YOU KNOW. THE TRUTH IS, YOU'RE PROBABLY NEVER GOING TO SEE HER AGAIN.
SHE'S GOING TO BE DEPORTED, AND YOU WILL TOO...
...BUT NOT BEFORE YOU SPEND A FEW YEARS IN THIS PLACE WITH ME.
THIS ISN'T THE SAME COUNTRY YOU SAW ON TV BACK IN WHATEVER SHITHOLE COUNTRY YOU COME FROM.
WE'RE TAKING IT BACK FROM YOU PEOPLE...
I DON'T UNDERSTAND...
WHAT IS THAT?
HOW ARE YOU DOING THAT WITH YOUR HANDS?
...I-- I DON'T FEEL WELL. I FEEL HOT...

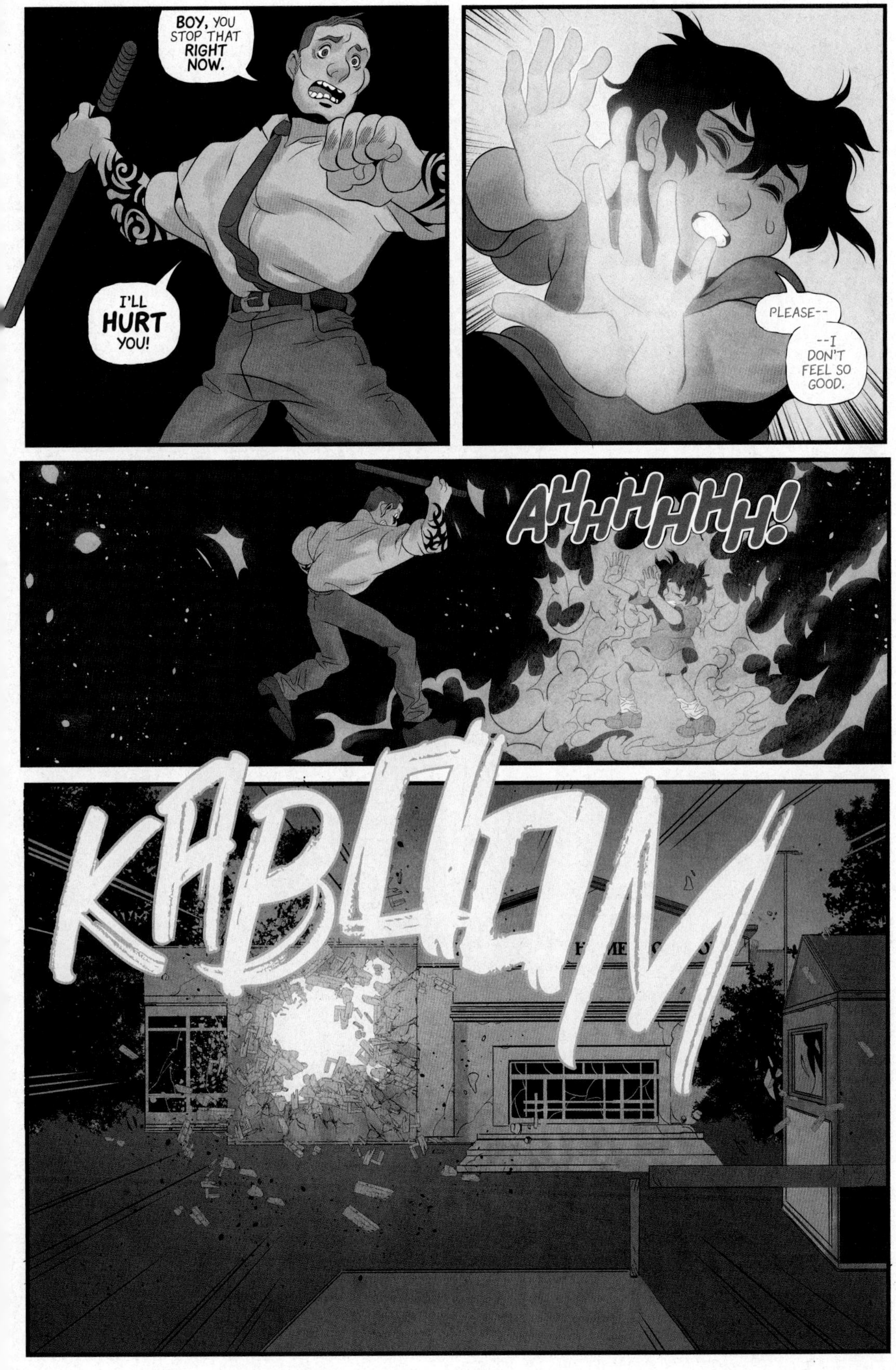
BOY, YOU STOP THAT RIGHT NOW.
I'LL HURT YOU!
PLEASE--
--I DON'T FEEL SO GOOD.
AHHHHHHH!
KABOOM

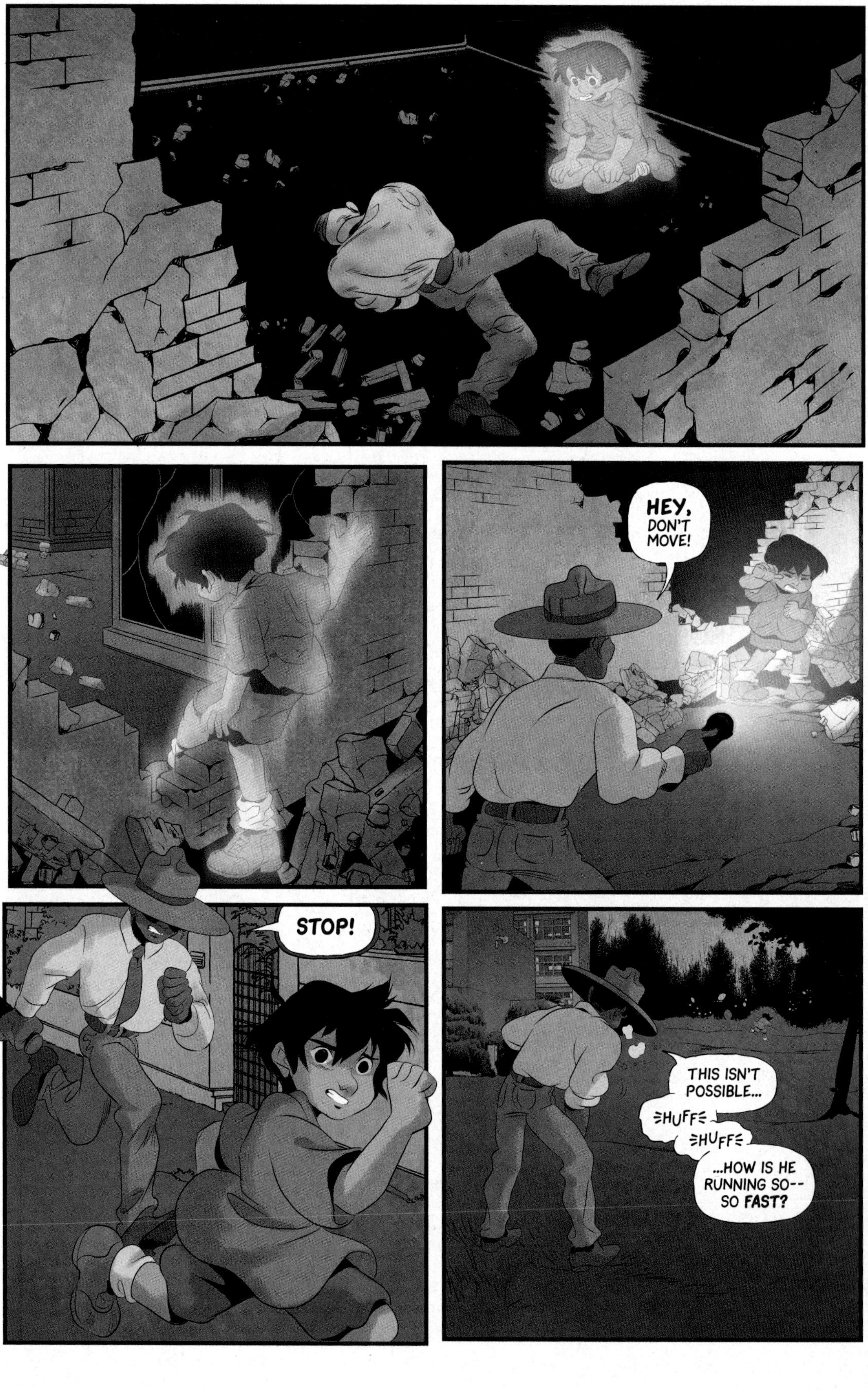
HEY, DON'T MOVE!
STOP!
THIS ISN'T POSSIBLE...
HUFF
HUFF
...HOW IS HE RUNNING SO-- SO FAST?

Chapter Two

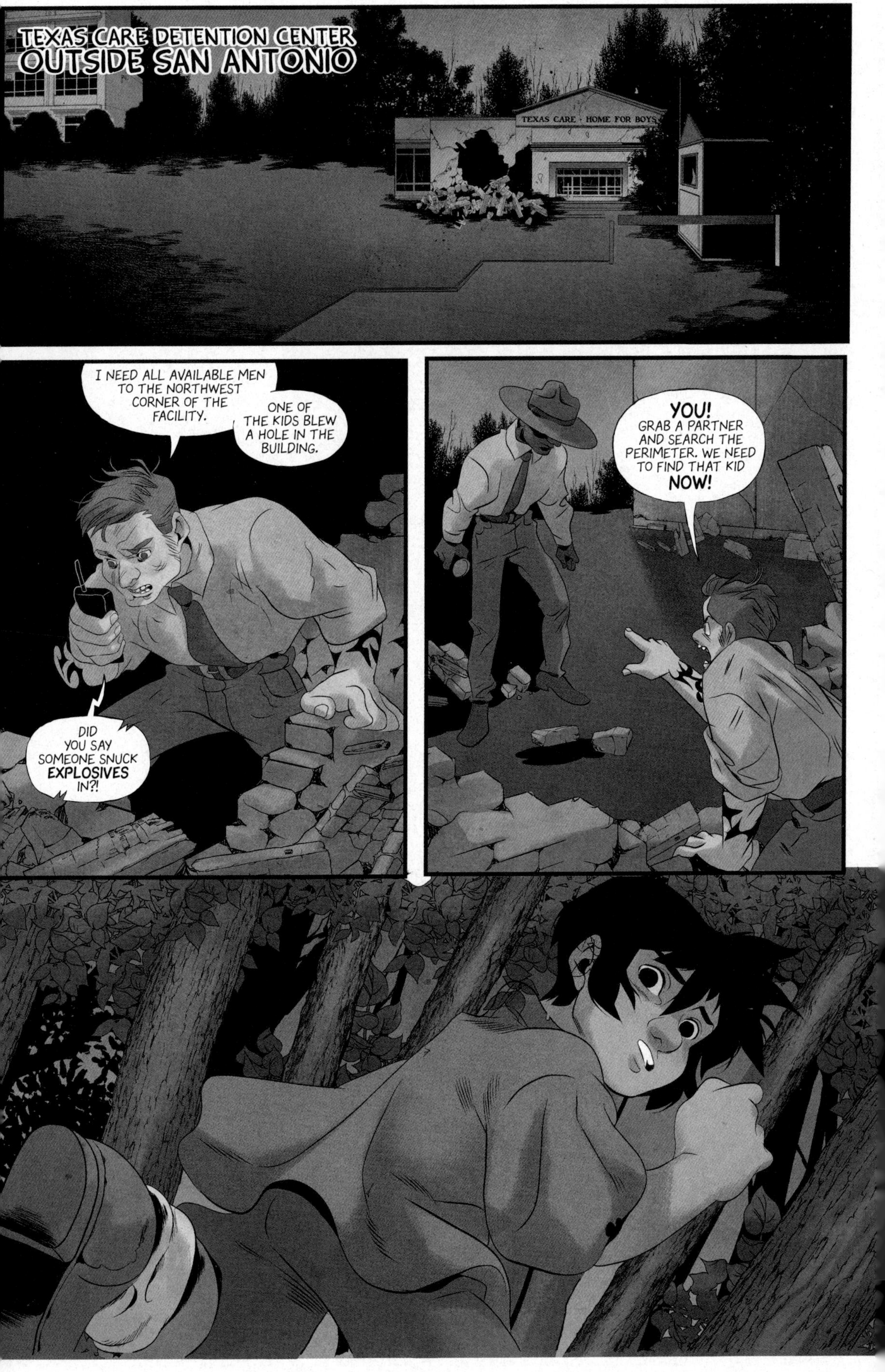
TEXAS CARE DETENTION CENTER
OUTSIDE SAN ANTONIO
TEXAS CARE · HOME FOR BOYS
I NEED ALL AVAILABLE MEN TO THE NORTHWEST CORNER OF THE FACILITY.
ONE OF THE KIDS BLEW A HOLE IN THE BUILDING.
DID YOU SAY SOMEONE SNUCK EXPLOSIVES IN?!
YOU! GRAB A PARTNER AND SEARCH THE PERIMETER. WE NEED TO FIND THAT KID NOW!

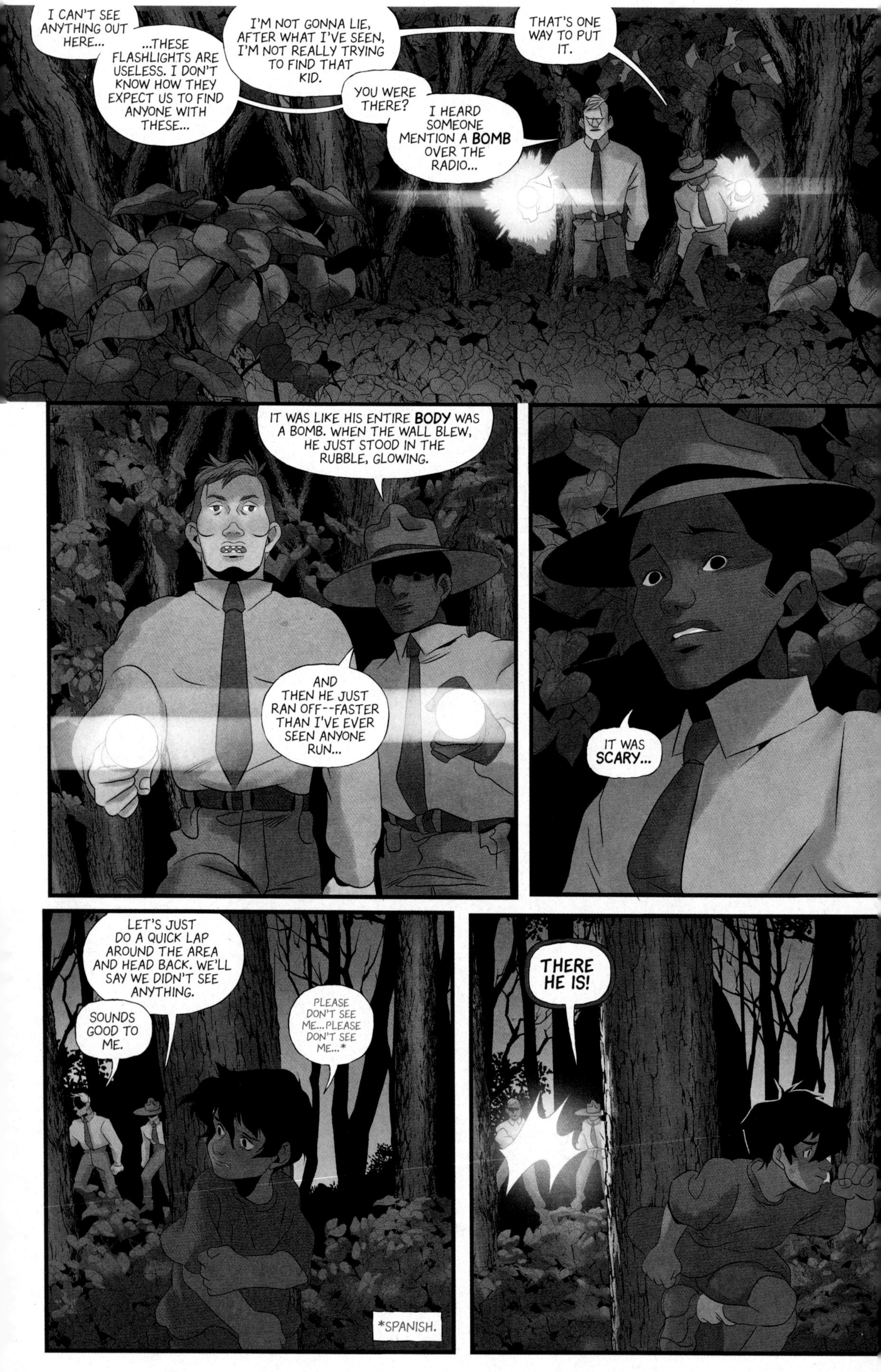

I CAN'T SEE ANYTHING OUT HERE...
...THESE FLASHLIGHTS ARE USELESS. I DON'T KNOW HOW THEY EXPECT US TO FIND ANYONE WITH THESE...
I'M NOT GONNA LIE, AFTER WHAT I'VE SEEN, I'M NOT REALLY TRYING TO FIND THAT KID.
YOU WERE THERE?
I HEARD SOMEONE MENTION A **BOMB** OVER THE RADIO...
THAT'S ONE WAY TO PUT IT.
IT WAS LIKE HIS ENTIRE **BODY** WAS A BOMB. WHEN THE WALL BLEW, HE JUST STOOD IN THE RUBBLE, GLOWING.
AND THEN HE JUST RAN OFF--FASTER THAN I'VE EVER SEEN ANYONE RUN...
IT WAS **SCARY...**
LET'S JUST DO A QUICK LAP AROUND THE AREA AND HEAD BACK. WE'LL SAY WE DIDN'T SEE ANYTHING.
SOUNDS GOOD TO ME.
PLEASE DON'T SEE ME...PLEASE DON'T SEE ME...*
*SPANISH.
THERE HE IS!

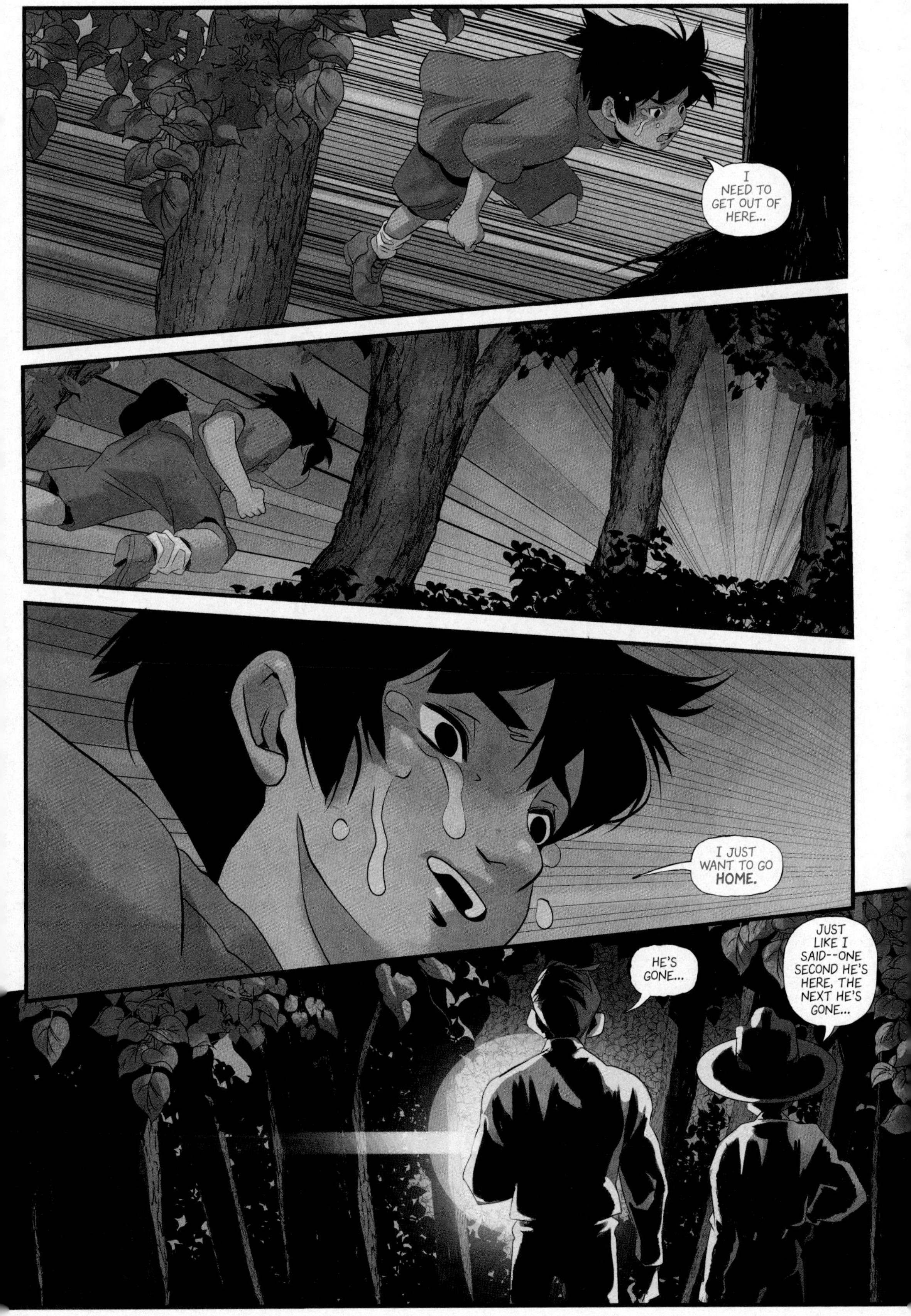
I NEED TO GET OUT OF HERE...
I JUST WANT TO GO HOME.
HE'S GONE...
JUST LIKE I SAID--ONE SECOND HE'S HERE, THE NEXT HE'S GONE...

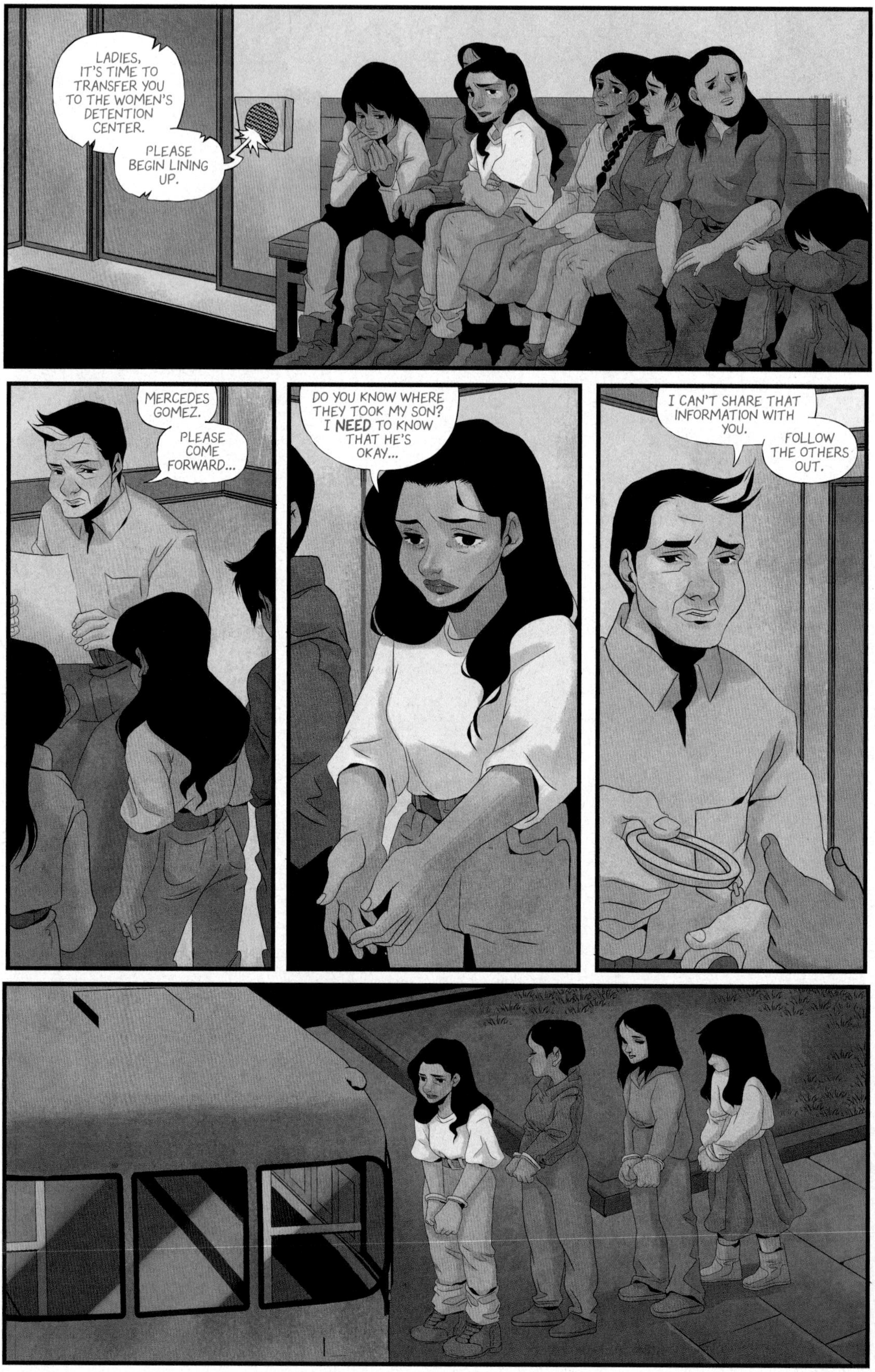
LADIES, IT'S TIME TO TRANSFER YOU TO THE WOMEN'S DETENTION CENTER.
PLEASE BEGIN LINING UP.
MERCEDES GOMEZ.
PLEASE COME FORWARD...
DO YOU KNOW WHERE THEY TOOK MY SON? I **NEED** TO KNOW THAT HE'S OKAY...
I CAN'T SHARE THAT INFORMATION WITH YOU.
FOLLOW THE OTHERS OUT.

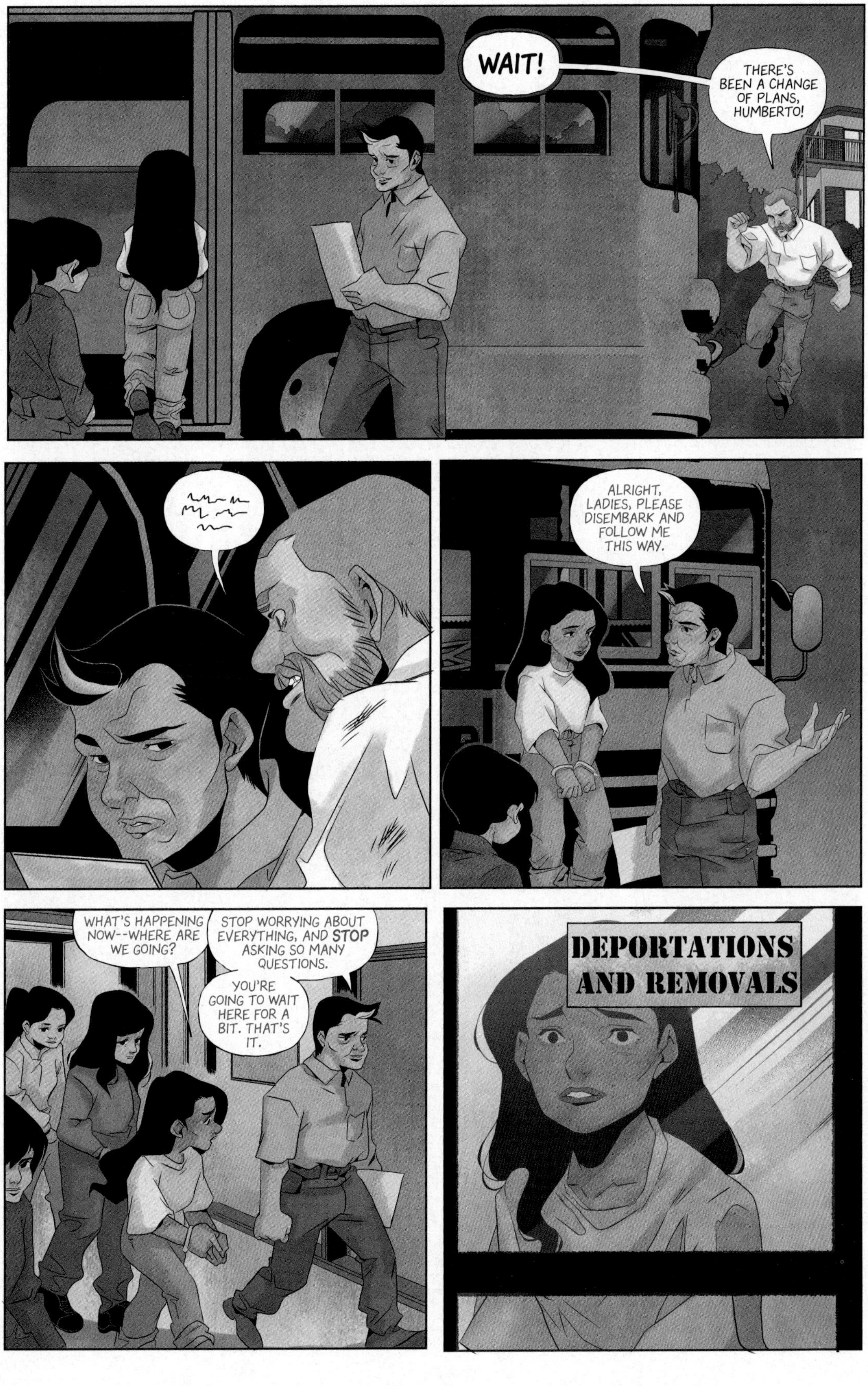
WAIT!
THERE'S BEEN A CHANGE OF PLANS, HUMBERTO!
ALRIGHT, LADIES, PLEASE DISEMBARK AND FOLLOW ME THIS WAY.
WHAT'S HAPPENING NOW--WHERE ARE WE GOING?
STOP WORRYING ABOUT EVERYTHING, AND **STOP** ASKING SO MANY QUESTIONS.
YOU'RE GOING TO WAIT HERE FOR A BIT. THAT'S IT.
DEPORTATIONS AND REMOVALS

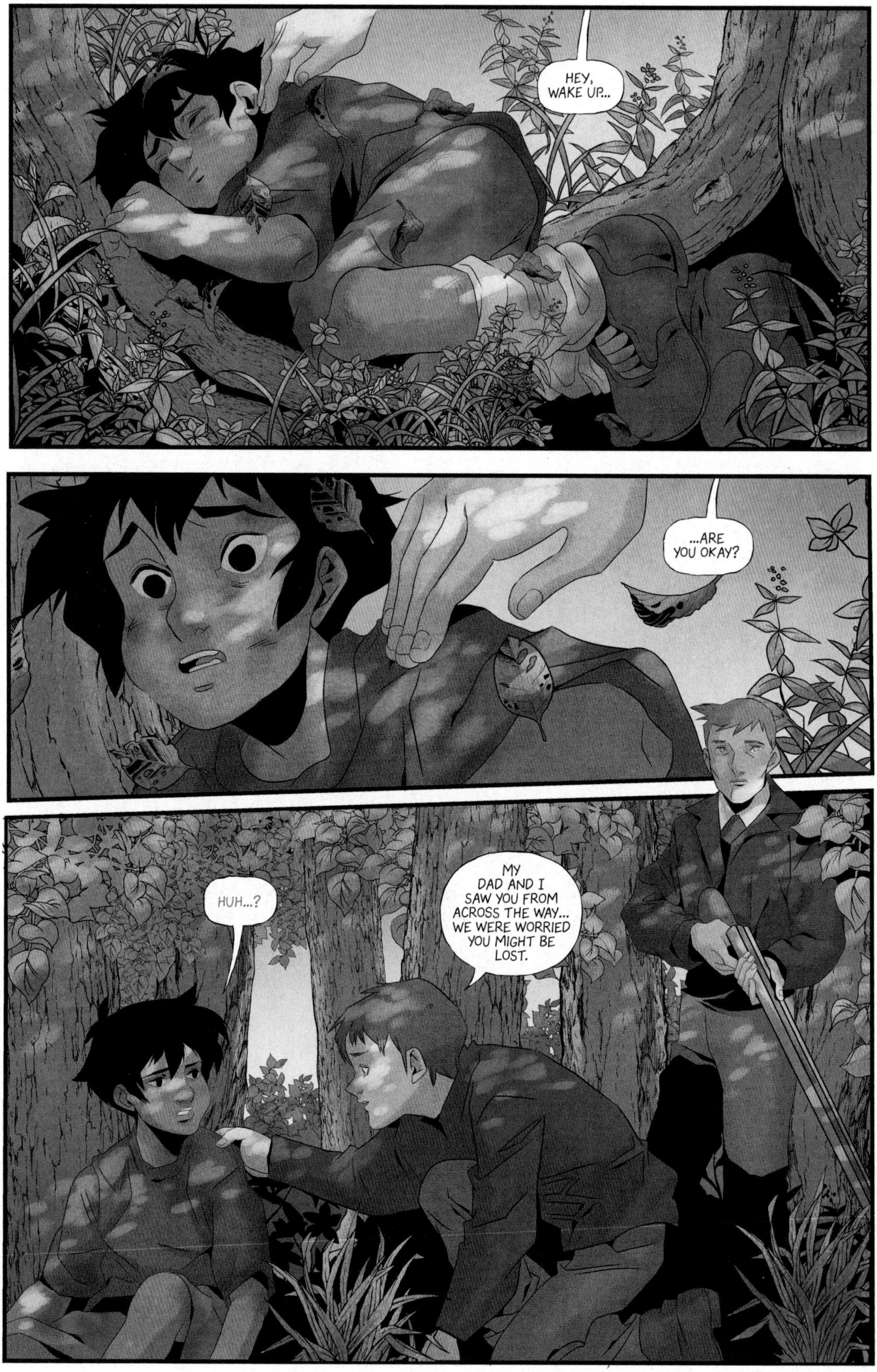
HEY, WAKE UP...
...ARE YOU OKAY?
HUH...?
MY DAD AND I SAW YOU FROM ACROSS THE WAY... WE WERE WORRIED YOU MIGHT BE LOST.

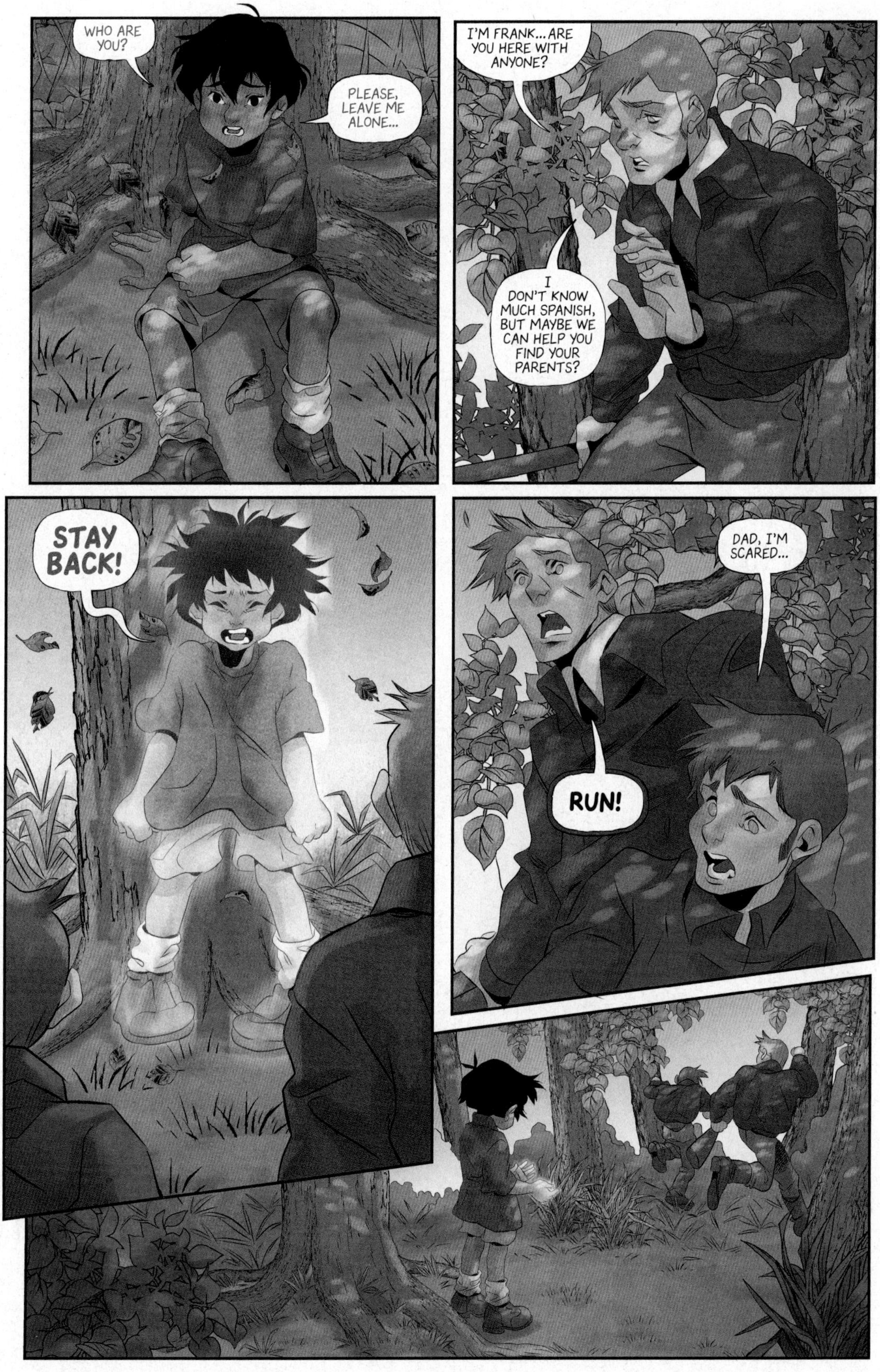
WHO ARE YOU?
PLEASE, LEAVE ME ALONE...
I'M FRANK... ARE YOU HERE WITH ANYONE?
I DON'T KNOW MUCH SPANISH, BUT MAYBE WE CAN HELP YOU FIND YOUR PARENTS?
STAY BACK!
DAD, I'M SCARED...
RUN!

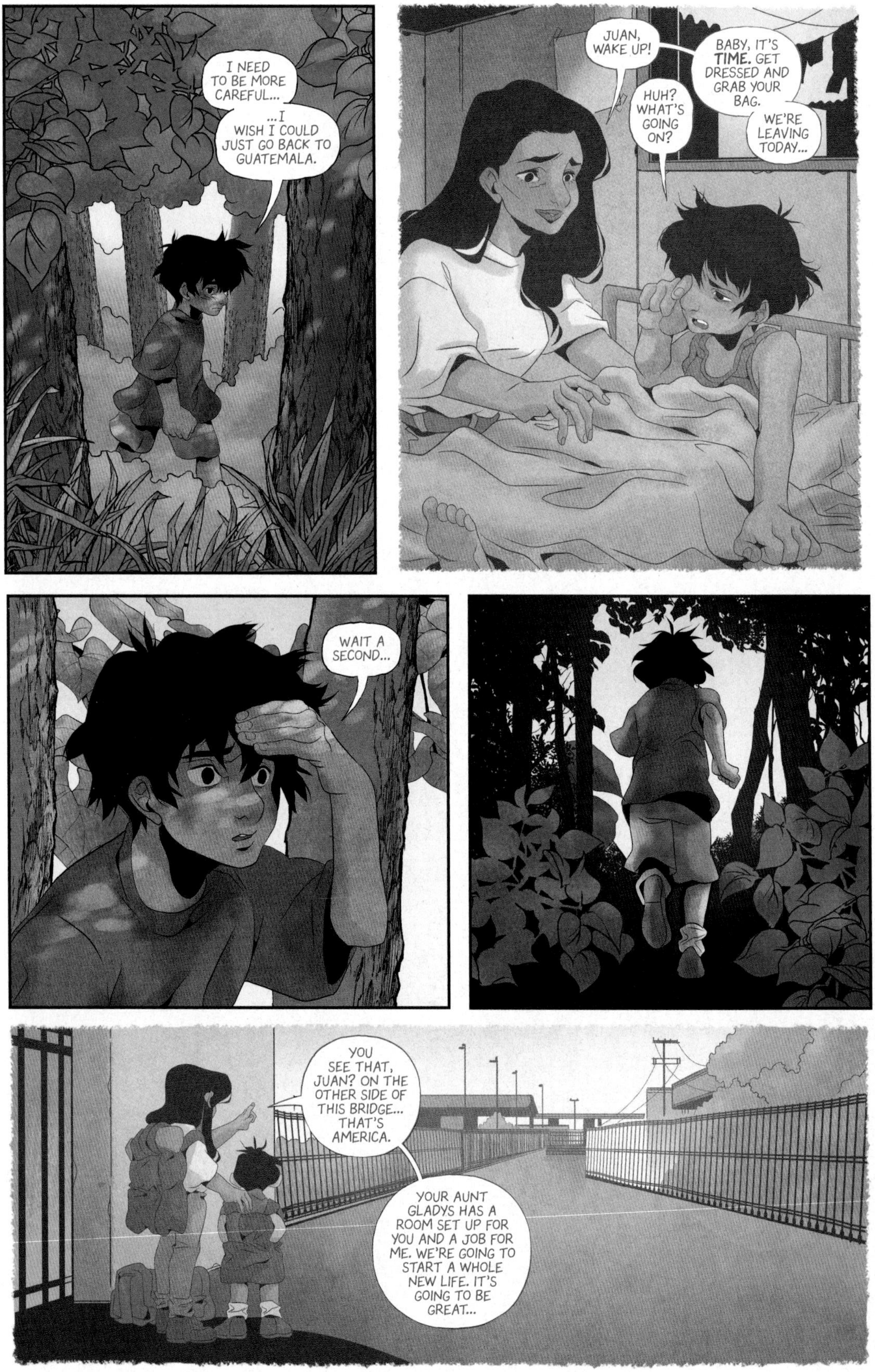
I NEED TO BE MORE CAREFUL...
...I WISH I COULD JUST GO BACK TO GUATEMALA.
JUAN, WAKE UP!
BABY, IT'S **TIME.** GET DRESSED AND GRAB YOUR BAG.
HUH? WHAT'S GOING ON?
WE'RE LEAVING TODAY...
WAIT A SECOND...
YOU SEE THAT, JUAN? ON THE OTHER SIDE OF THIS BRIDGE... THAT'S AMERICA.
YOUR AUNT GLADYS HAS A ROOM SET UP FOR YOU AND A JOB FOR ME. WE'RE GOING TO START A WHOLE NEW LIFE. IT'S GOING TO BE GREAT...

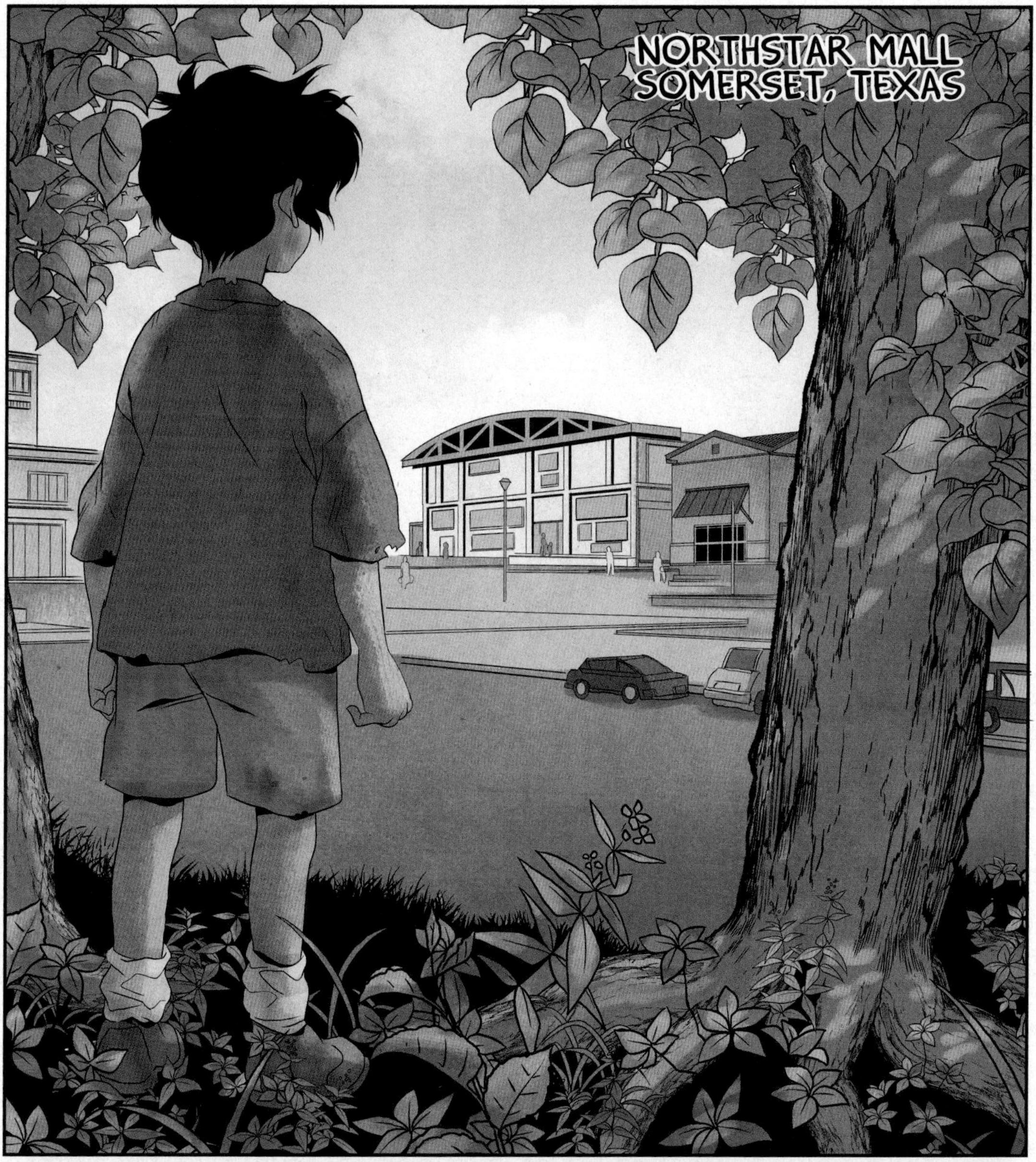
NORTHSTAR MALL
SOMERSET, TEXAS
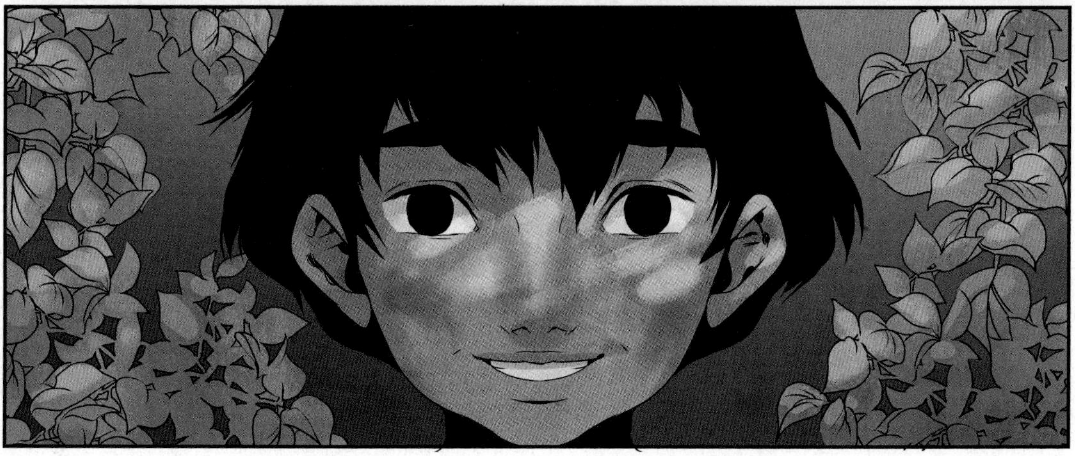

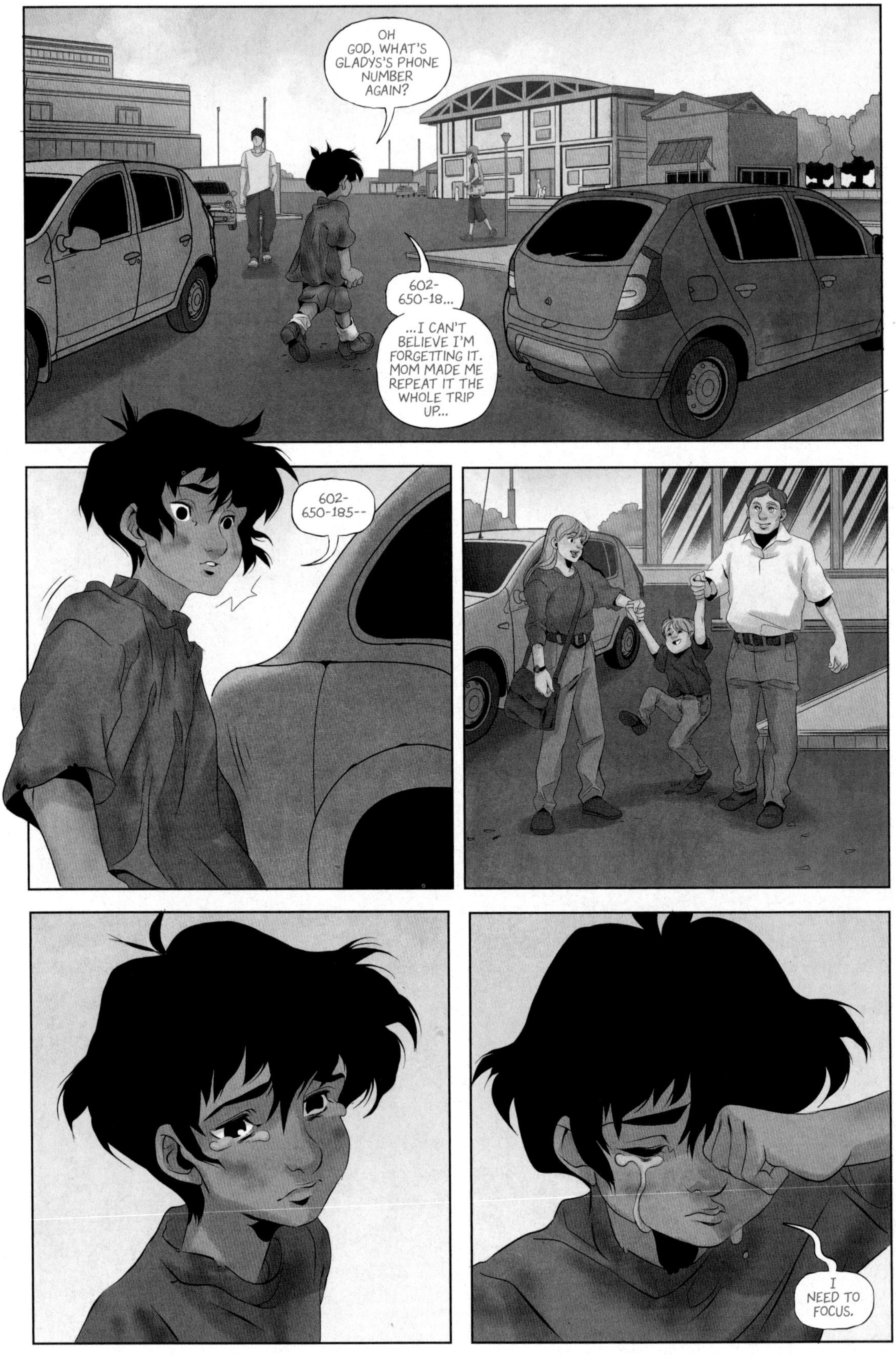

OH GOD, WHAT'S GLADYS'S PHONE NUMBER AGAIN?
602-650-18...
...I CAN'T BELIEVE I'M FORGETTING IT. MOM MADE ME REPEAT IT THE WHOLE TRIP UP...
602-650-185--
I NEED TO FOCUS.

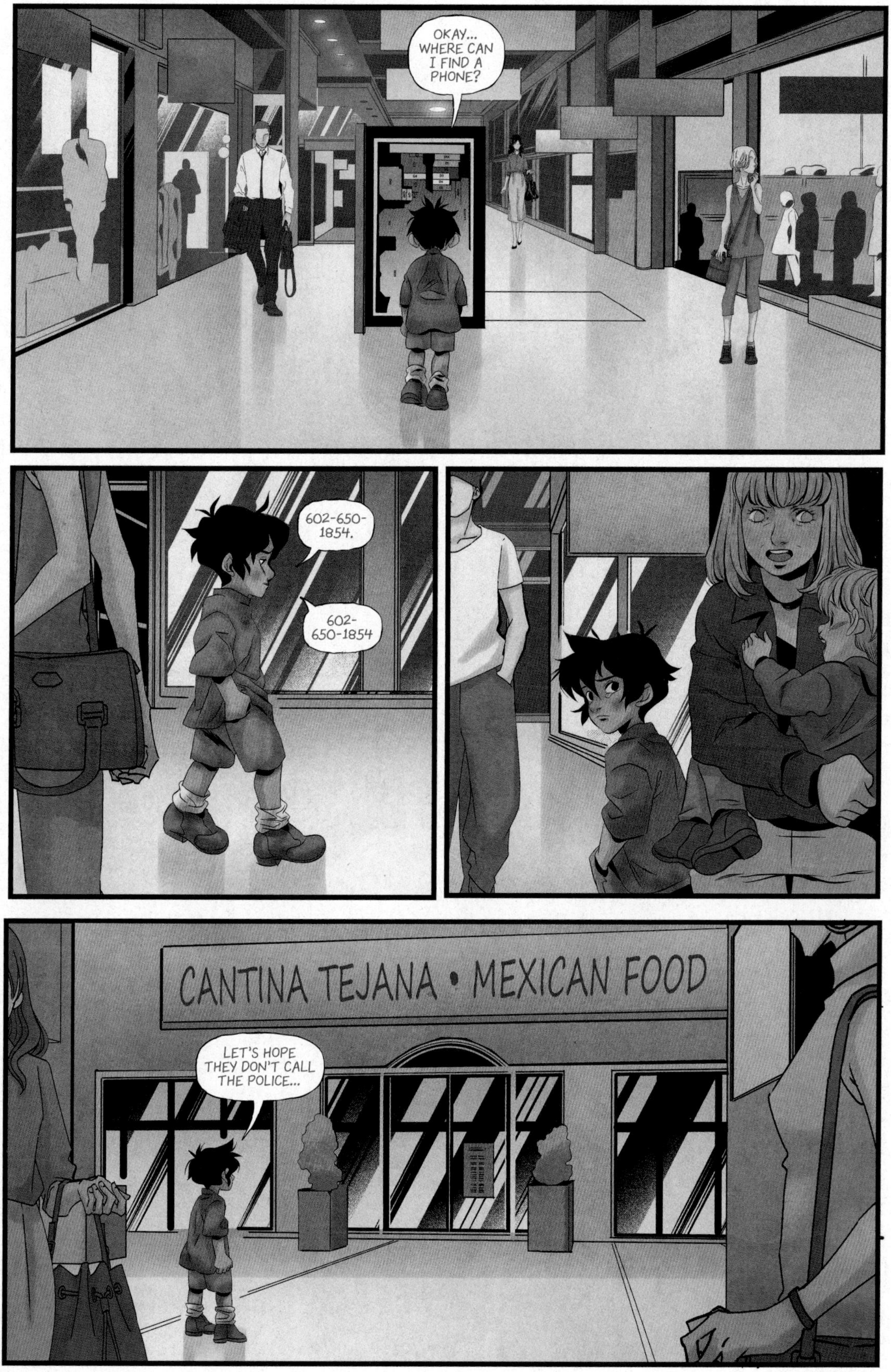
OKAY... WHERE CAN I FIND A PHONE?
602-650-1854.
602-650-1854
CANTINA TEJANA • MEXICAN FOOD
LET'S HOPE THEY DON'T CALL THE POLICE...

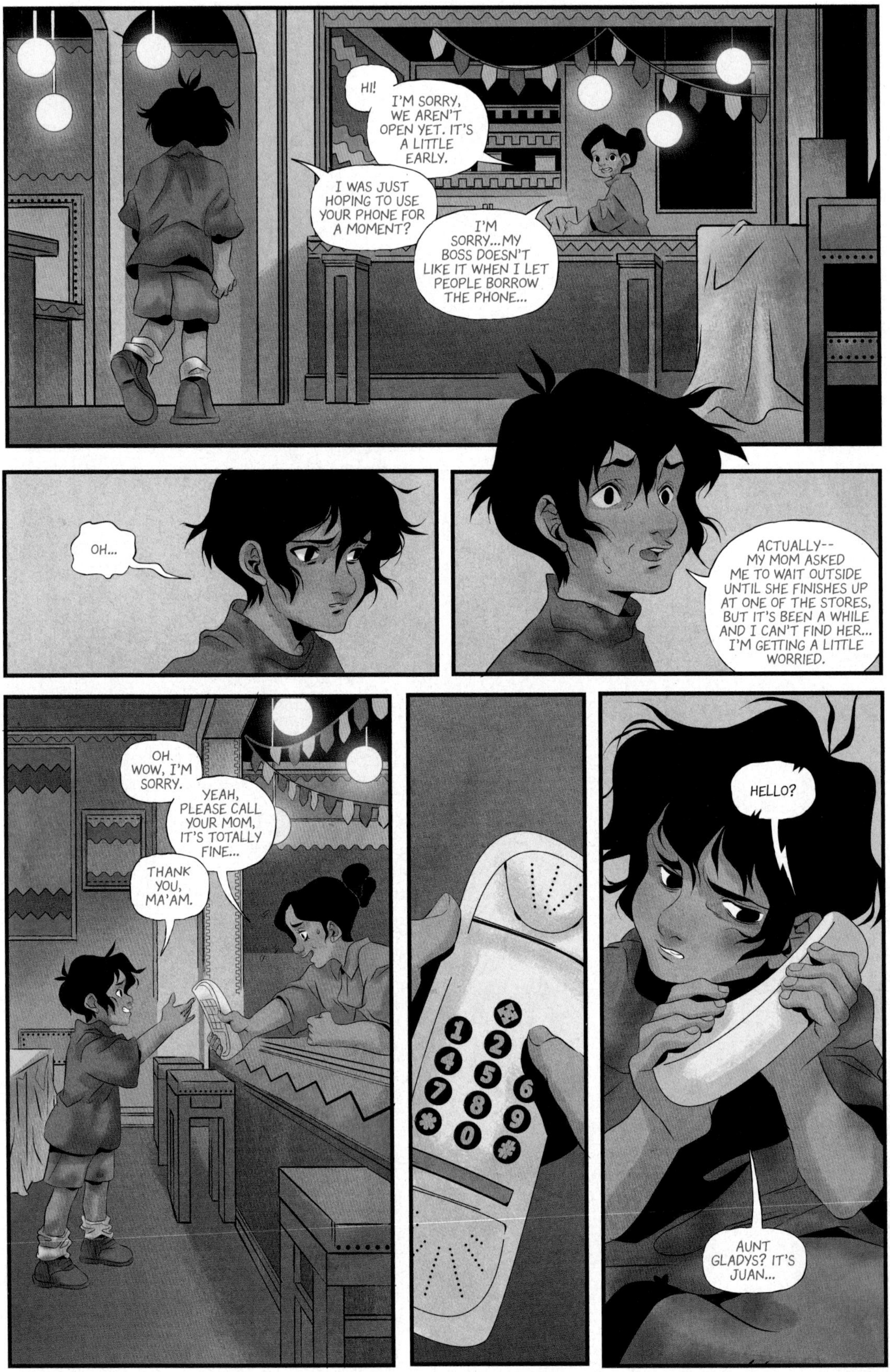
HI!
I'M SORRY, WE AREN'T OPEN YET. IT'S A LITTLE EARLY.
I WAS JUST HOPING TO USE YOUR PHONE FOR A MOMENT?
I'M SORRY...MY BOSS DOESN'T LIKE IT WHEN I LET PEOPLE BORROW THE PHONE...
OH...
ACTUALLY-- MY MOM ASKED ME TO WAIT OUTSIDE UNTIL SHE FINISHES UP AT ONE OF THE STORES, BUT IT'S BEEN A WHILE AND I CAN'T FIND HER... I'M GETTING A LITTLE WORRIED.
OH WOW, I'M SORRY.
YEAH, PLEASE CALL YOUR MOM, IT'S TOTALLY FINE...
THANK YOU, MA'AM.
HELLO?
AUNT GLADYS? IT'S JUAN...

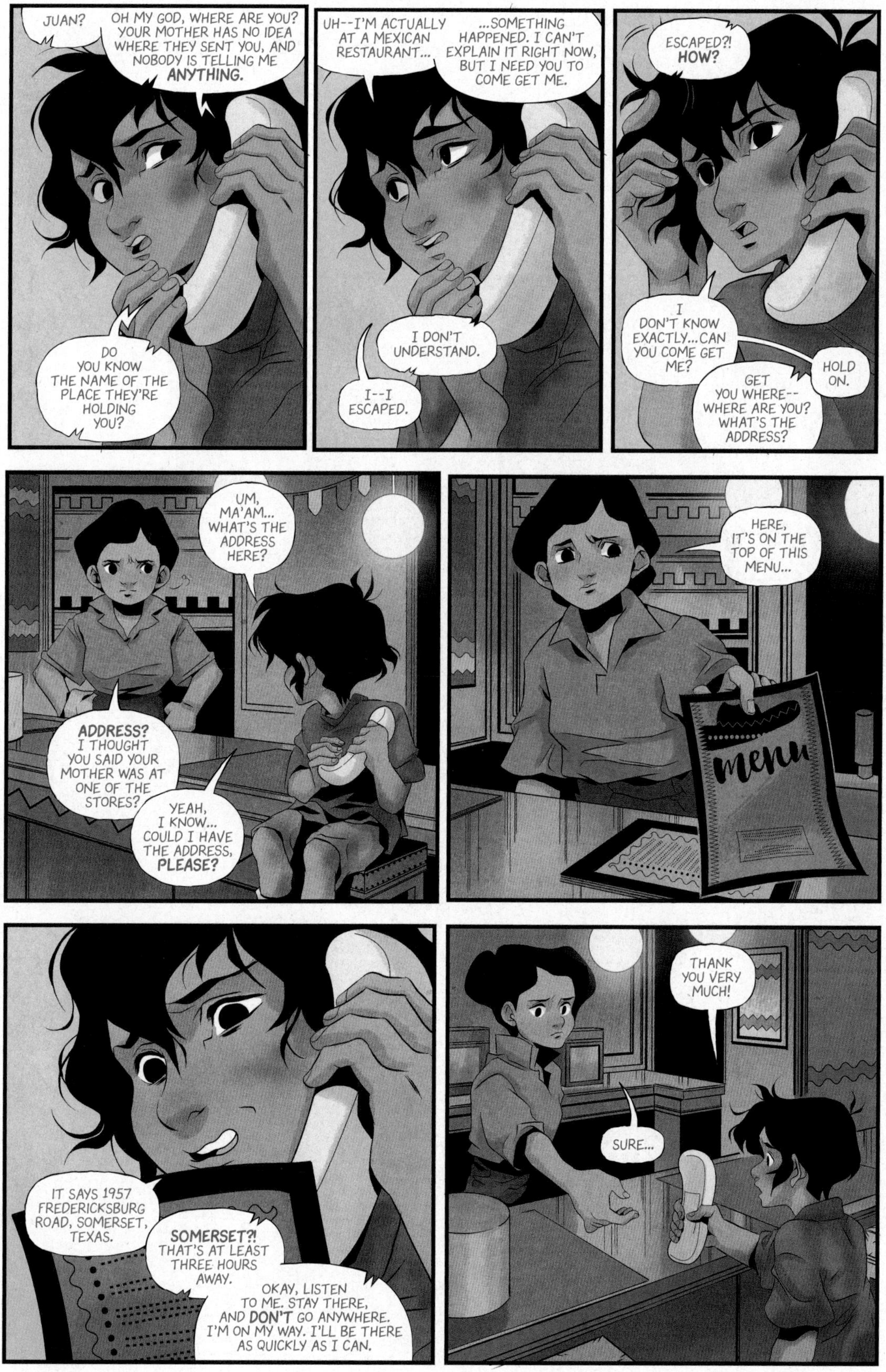
JUAN?
OH MY GOD, WHERE ARE YOU? YOUR MOTHER HAS NO IDEA WHERE THEY SENT YOU, AND NOBODY IS TELLING ME **ANYTHING.**
DO YOU KNOW THE NAME OF THE PLACE THEY'RE HOLDING YOU?
UH--I'M ACTUALLY AT A MEXICAN RESTAURANT...
...SOMETHING HAPPENED. I CAN'T EXPLAIN IT RIGHT NOW, BUT I NEED YOU TO COME GET ME.
I DON'T UNDERSTAND.
I--I ESCAPED.
ESCAPED?! **HOW?**
I DON'T KNOW EXACTLY...CAN YOU COME GET ME?
GET YOU WHERE--WHERE ARE YOU? WHAT'S THE ADDRESS?
HOLD ON.
UM, MA'AM... WHAT'S THE ADDRESS HERE?
ADDRESS? I THOUGHT YOU SAID YOUR MOTHER WAS AT ONE OF THE STORES?
YEAH, I KNOW... COULD I HAVE THE ADDRESS, **PLEASE?**
HERE, IT'S ON THE TOP OF THIS MENU...
menu
IT SAYS 1957 FREDERICKSBURG ROAD, SOMERSET, TEXAS.
SOMERSET?! THAT'S AT LEAST THREE HOURS AWAY.
OKAY, LISTEN TO ME. STAY THERE, AND **DON'T** GO ANYWHERE. I'M ON MY WAY. I'LL BE THERE AS QUICKLY AS I CAN.
THANK YOU VERY MUCH!
SURE...

YOU REALLY THINK THAT'S WHAT WE SHOULD DO?

I REALLY DON'T THINK I COULD LEAVE THIS PLACE...

THE GANGS ARE NOT GOING TO LEAVE JUAN ALONE...YOU NEED TO LEAVE GUATEMALA. YOU SAW WHAT THEY DID TO MY SON-- YOUR SWEET HUSBAND.

LISTEN TO ME. IT ISN'T GOING TO BE EASY, BUT THE THING MY SON LOVED THE MOST ABOUT YOU WAS YOUR STRENGTH. YOU CAN DO THIS.

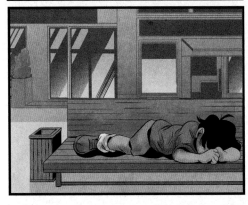

I'VE ALREADY SPOKEN TO GLADYS. SHE SAYS YOU CAN LIVE WITH HER FOR AS LONG AS YOU NEED. SHE SAID SHE'LL EVEN GET YOU A JOB AT THE HOSPITAL.

I KNOW IT'S WHAT HE WOULD WANT FOR YOU BOTH IN THIS SITUATION.

I'LL HAVE A ROUTE, SOME MONEY, AND BUS TICKETS FOR YOU BY NEXT WEEK. YOU CAN'T WAIT ANY LONGER THAN THAT.

BUT I DON'T WANT TO LEAVE YOU, OR THE REST OF THE FAMILY.

LEAVING HERE WAS NEVER THE PLAN FOR US.

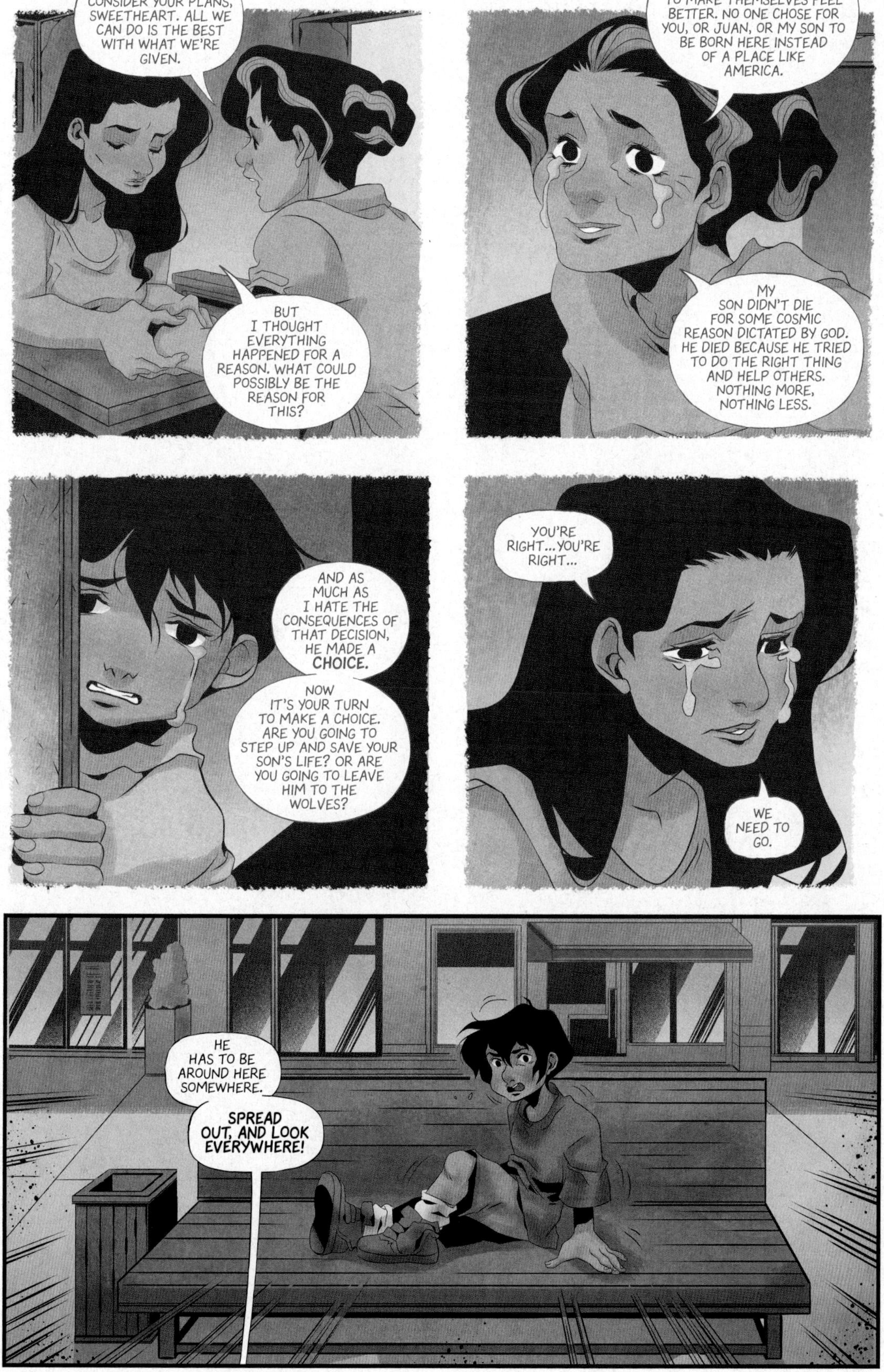
LIFE DOESN'T CONSIDER YOUR PLANS, SWEETHEART. ALL WE CAN DO IS THE BEST WITH WHAT WE'RE GIVEN.
BUT I THOUGHT EVERYTHING HAPPENED FOR A REASON. WHAT COULD POSSIBLY BE THE REASON FOR THIS?
THERE IS NO REASON--THAT'S JUST SOMETHING PEOPLE SAY TO MAKE THEMSELVES FEEL BETTER. NO ONE CHOSE FOR YOU, OR JUAN, OR MY SON TO BE BORN HERE INSTEAD OF A PLACE LIKE AMERICA.
MY SON DIDN'T DIE FOR SOME COSMIC REASON DICTATED BY GOD. HE DIED BECAUSE HE TRIED TO DO THE RIGHT THING AND HELP OTHERS. NOTHING MORE, NOTHING LESS.
AND AS MUCH AS I HATE THE CONSEQUENCES OF THAT DECISION, HE MADE A **CHOICE.**
NOW IT'S YOUR TURN TO MAKE A CHOICE. ARE YOU GOING TO STEP UP AND SAVE YOUR SON'S LIFE? OR ARE YOU GOING TO LEAVE HIM TO THE WOLVES?
YOU'RE RIGHT... YOU'RE RIGHT...
WE NEED TO GO.
HE HAS TO BE AROUND HERE SOMEWHERE.
SPREAD OUT, AND LOOK EVERYWHERE!

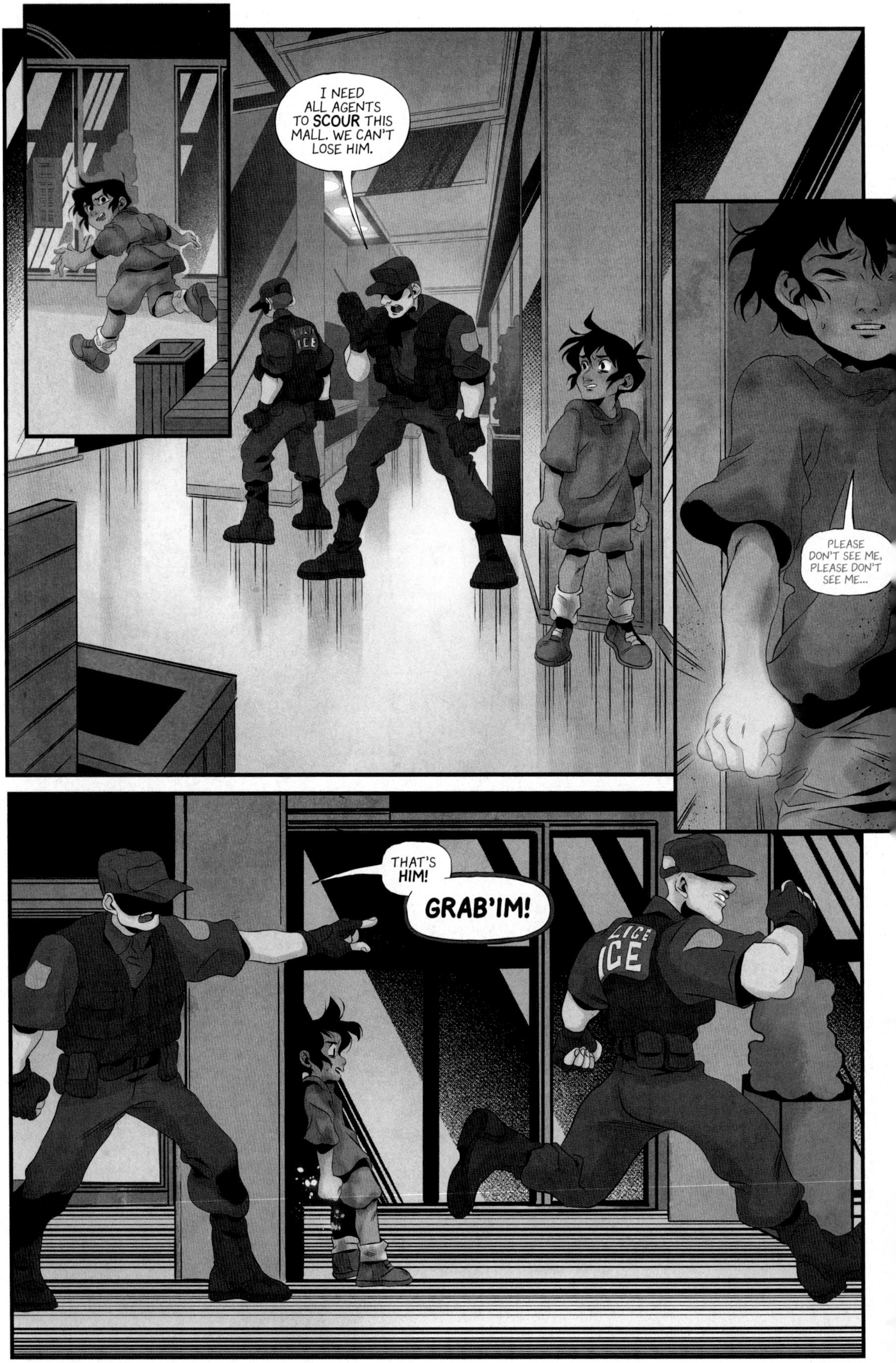
I NEED ALL AGENTS TO **SCOUR** THIS MALL. WE CAN'T LOSE HIM.
PLEASE DON'T SEE ME, PLEASE DON'T SEE ME...
THAT'S HIM!
GRAB'IM!

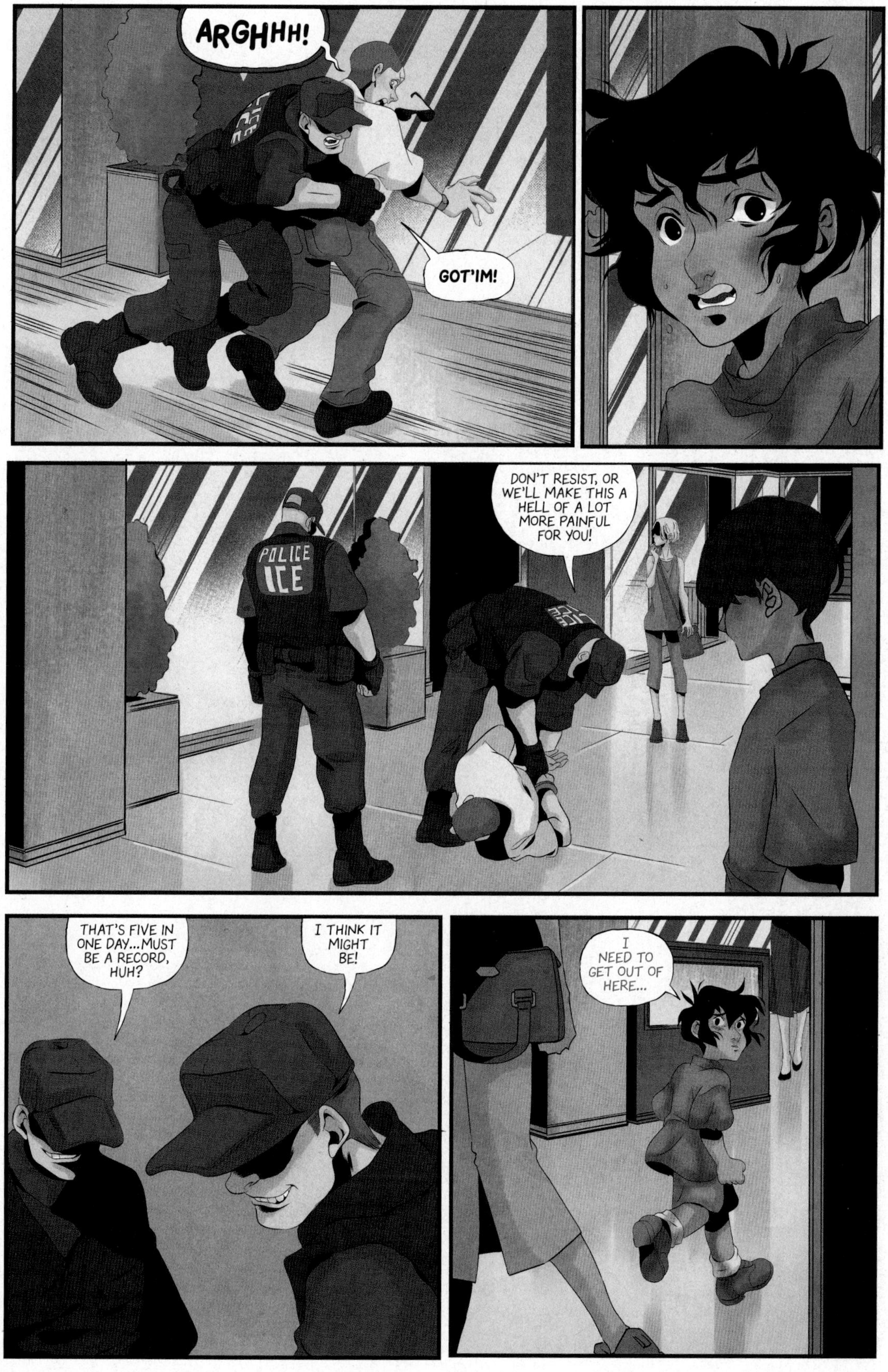
ARGHHH!
GOT'IM!
DON'T RESIST, OR WE'LL MAKE THIS A HELL OF A LOT MORE PAINFUL FOR YOU!
POLICE ICE
THAT'S FIVE IN ONE DAY...MUST BE A RECORD, HUH?
I THINK IT MIGHT BE!
I NEED TO GET OUT OF HERE...

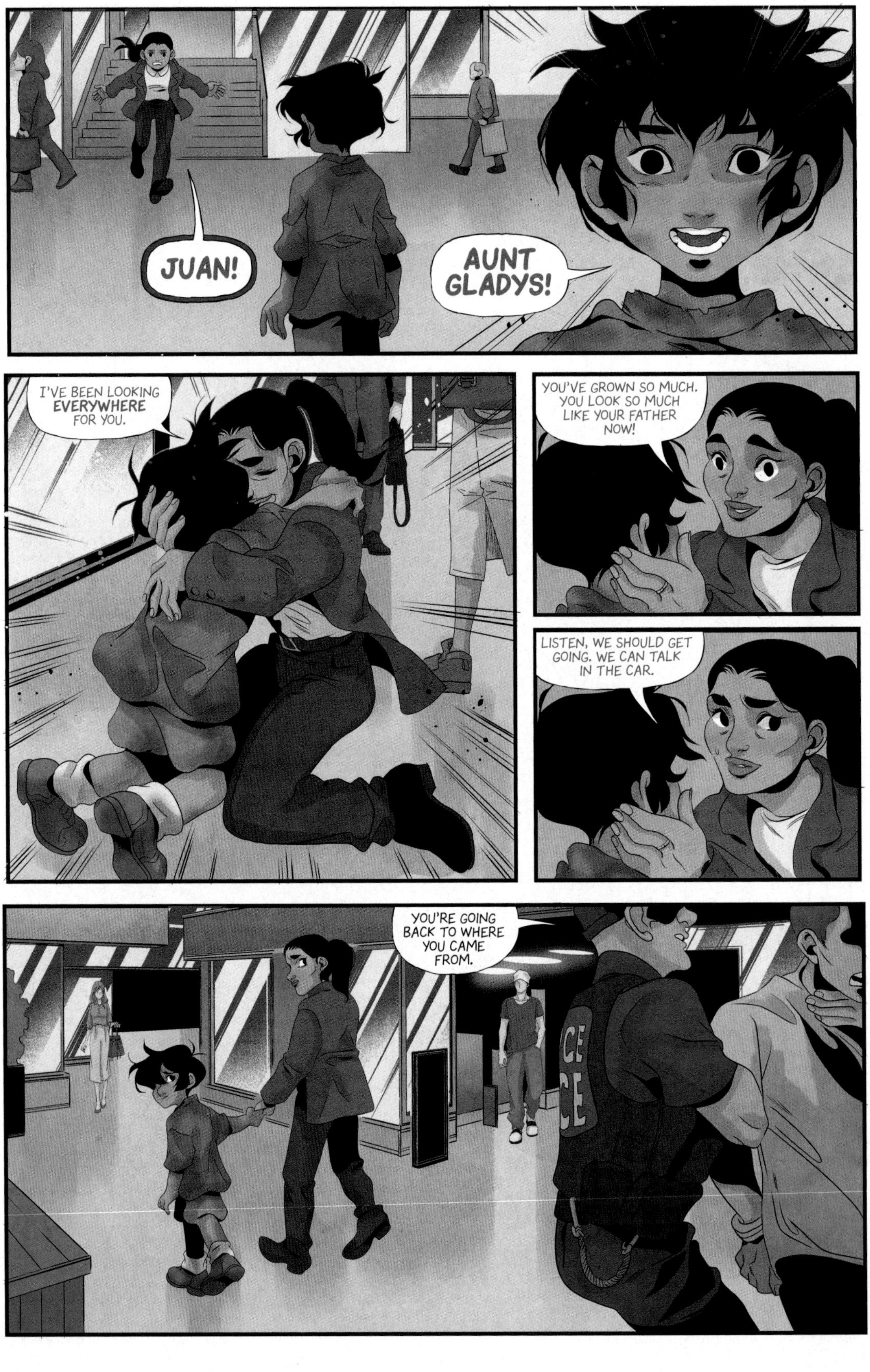
JUAN!
AUNT GLADYS!
I'VE BEEN LOOKING EVERYWHERE FOR YOU.
YOU'VE GROWN SO MUCH. YOU LOOK SO MUCH LIKE YOUR FATHER NOW!
LISTEN, WE SHOULD GET GOING. WE CAN TALK IN THE CAR.
YOU'RE GOING BACK TO WHERE YOU CAME FROM.
CE
CE

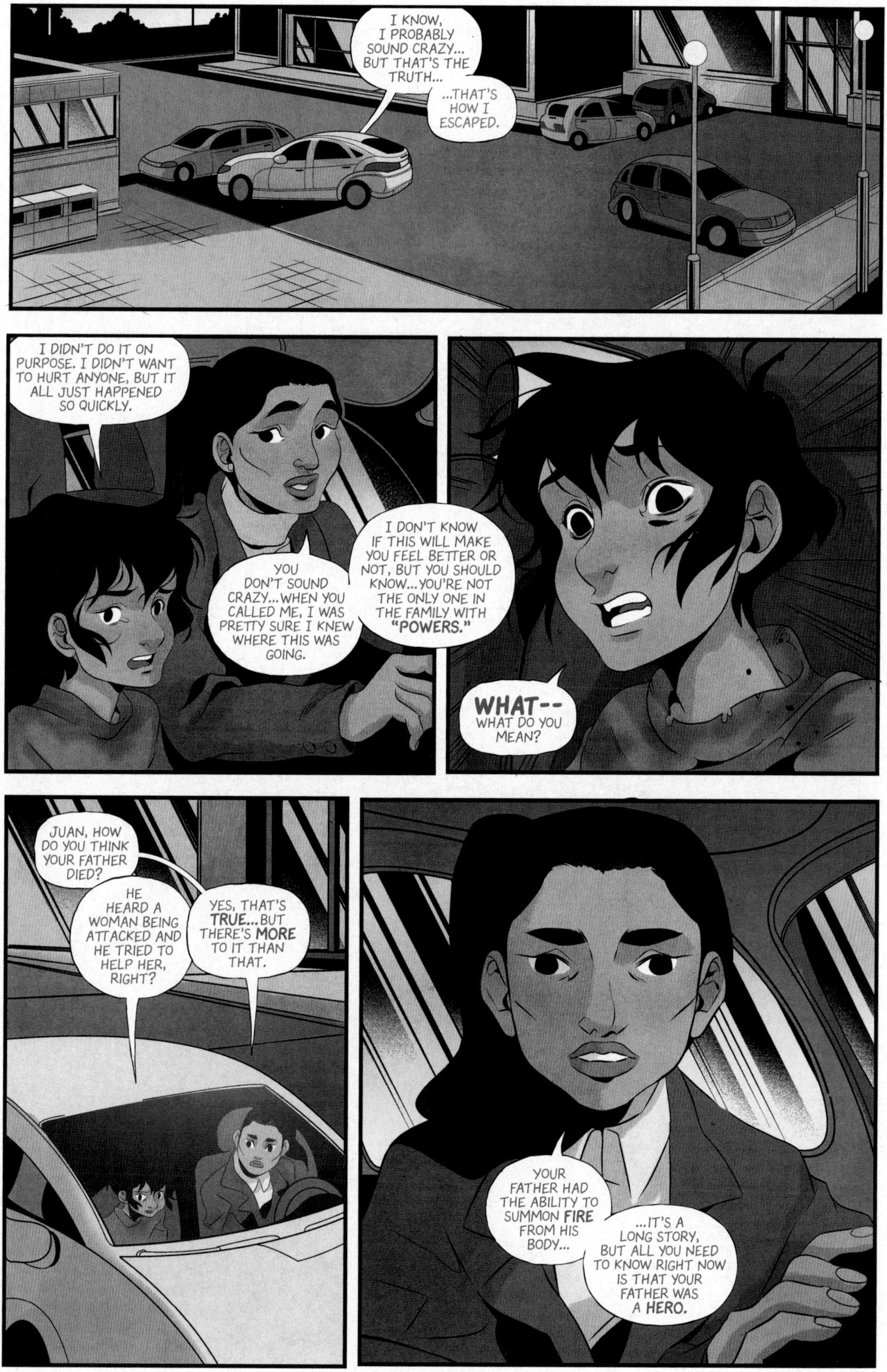
I KNOW, I PROBABLY SOUND CRAZY... BUT THAT'S THE TRUTH...
...THAT'S HOW I ESCAPED.
I DIDN'T DO IT ON PURPOSE. I DIDN'T WANT TO HURT ANYONE, BUT IT ALL JUST HAPPENED SO QUICKLY.
YOU DON'T SOUND CRAZY...WHEN YOU CALLED ME, I WAS PRETTY SURE I KNEW WHERE THIS WAS GOING.
I DON'T KNOW IF THIS WILL MAKE YOU FEEL BETTER OR NOT, BUT YOU SHOULD KNOW...YOU'RE NOT THE ONLY ONE IN THE FAMILY WITH "POWERS."
WHAT-- WHAT DO YOU MEAN?
JUAN, HOW DO YOU THINK YOUR FATHER DIED?
HE HEARD A WOMAN BEING ATTACKED AND HE TRIED TO HELP HER, RIGHT?
YES, THAT'S TRUE...BUT THERE'S MORE TO IT THAN THAT.
YOUR FATHER HAD THE ABILITY TO SUMMON FIRE FROM HIS BODY...
...IT'S A LONG STORY, BUT ALL YOU NEED TO KNOW RIGHT NOW IS THAT YOUR FATHER WAS A HERO.

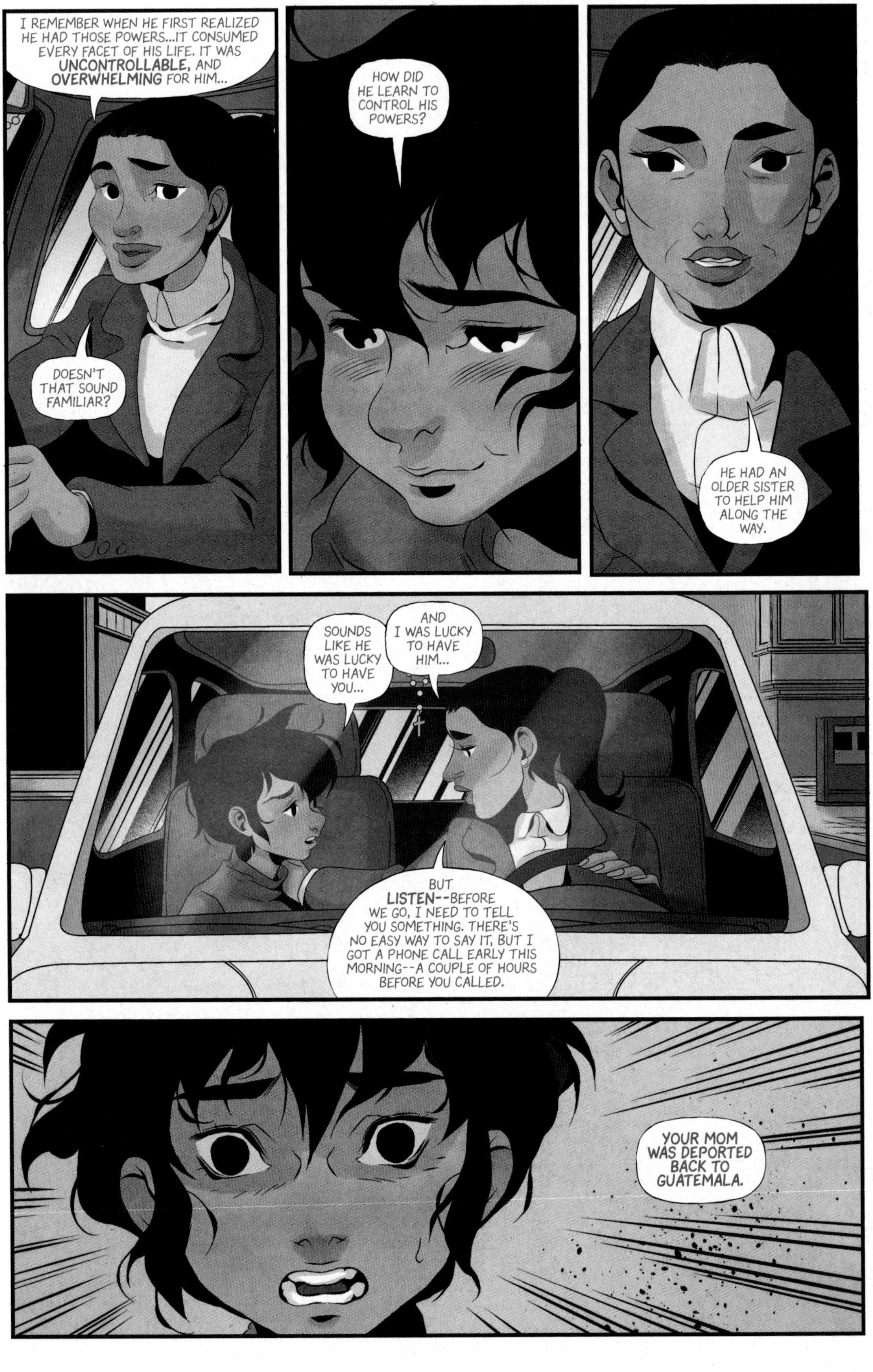
I REMEMBER WHEN HE FIRST REALIZED HE HAD THOSE POWERS...IT CONSUMED EVERY FACET OF HIS LIFE. IT WAS **UNCONTROLLABLE,** AND **OVERWHELMING** FOR HIM...
DOESN'T THAT SOUND FAMILIAR?
HOW DID HE LEARN TO CONTROL HIS POWERS?
HE HAD AN OLDER SISTER TO HELP HIM ALONG THE WAY.
SOUNDS LIKE HE WAS LUCKY TO HAVE YOU...
AND I WAS LUCKY TO HAVE HIM...
BUT **LISTEN--**BEFORE WE GO, I NEED TO TELL YOU SOMETHING. THERE'S NO EASY WAY TO SAY IT, BUT I GOT A PHONE CALL EARLY THIS MORNING--A COUPLE OF HOURS BEFORE YOU CALLED.
YOUR MOM WAS DEPORTED BACK TO GUATEMALA.

Chapter Three

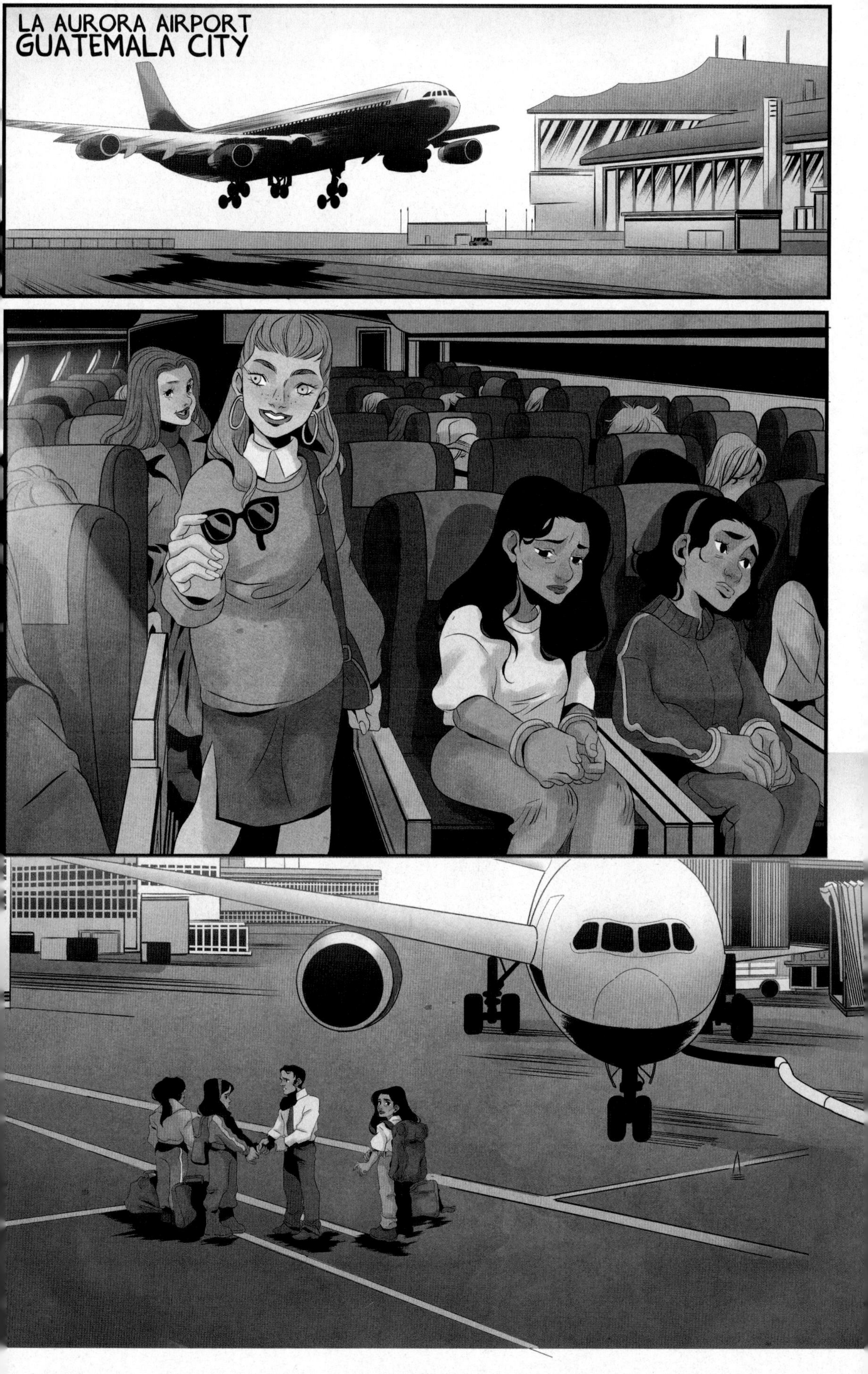
LA AURORA AIRPORT
GUATEMALA CITY

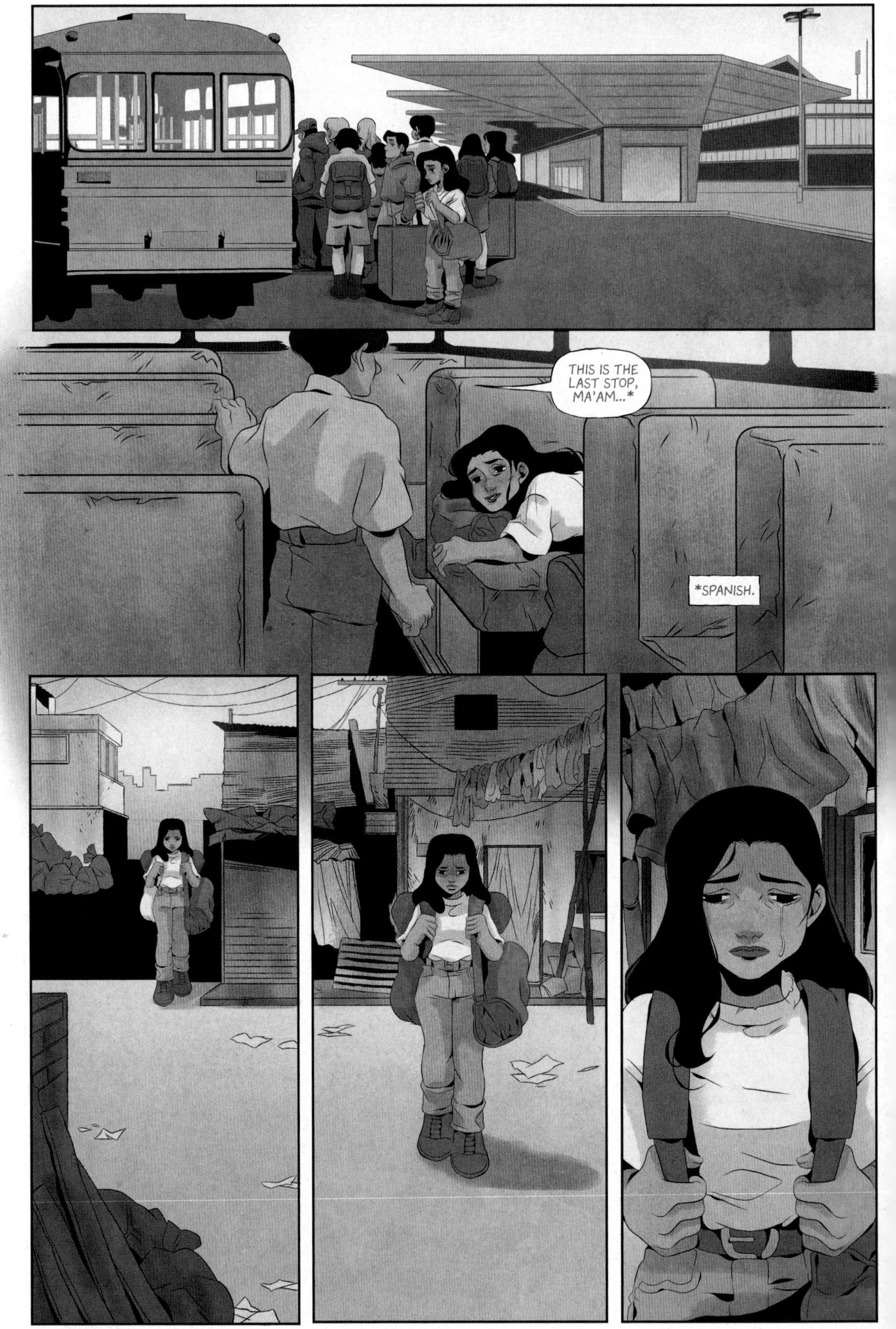
THIS IS THE LAST STOP, MA'AM...*
*SPANISH.

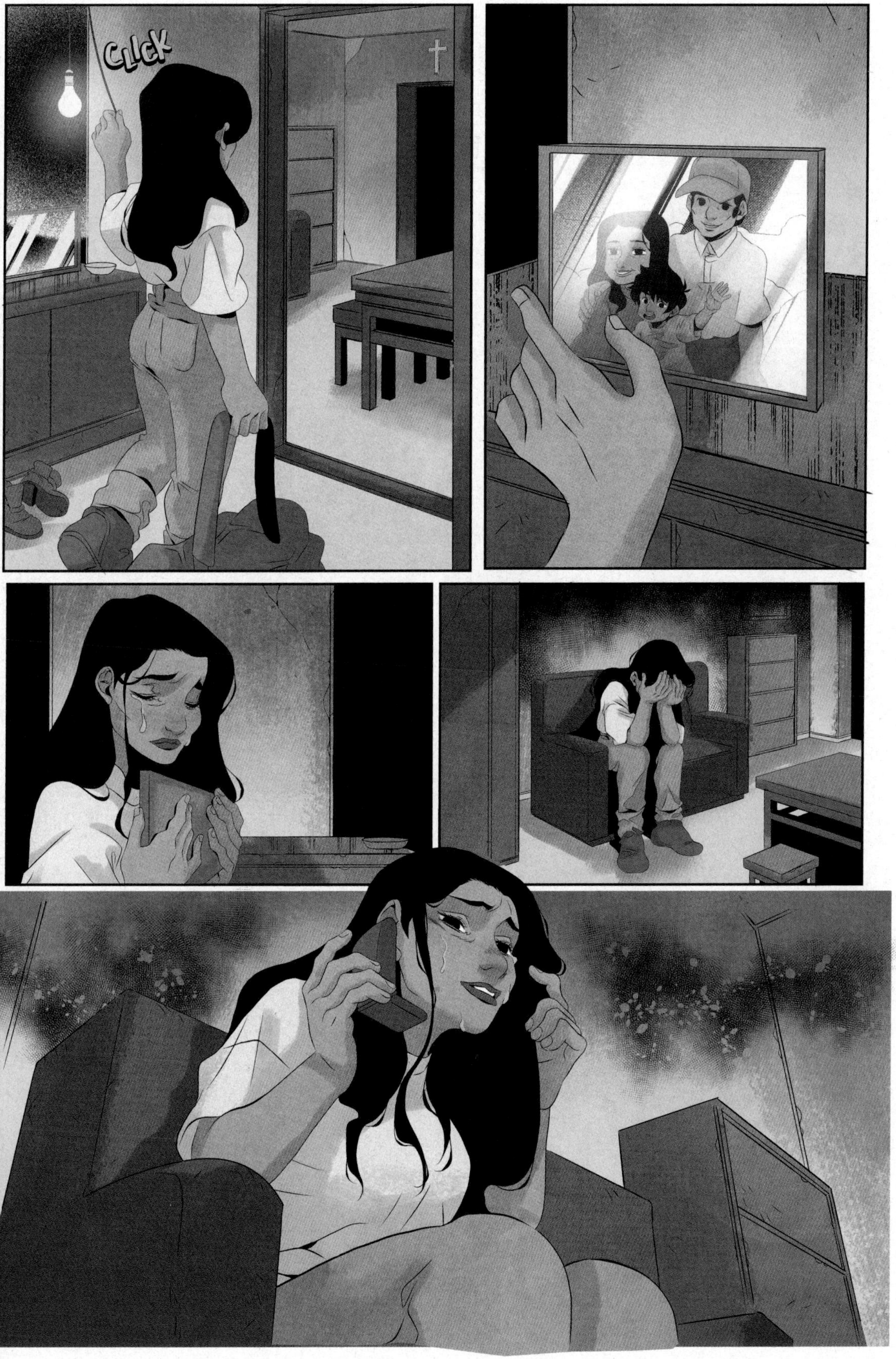
CLICK

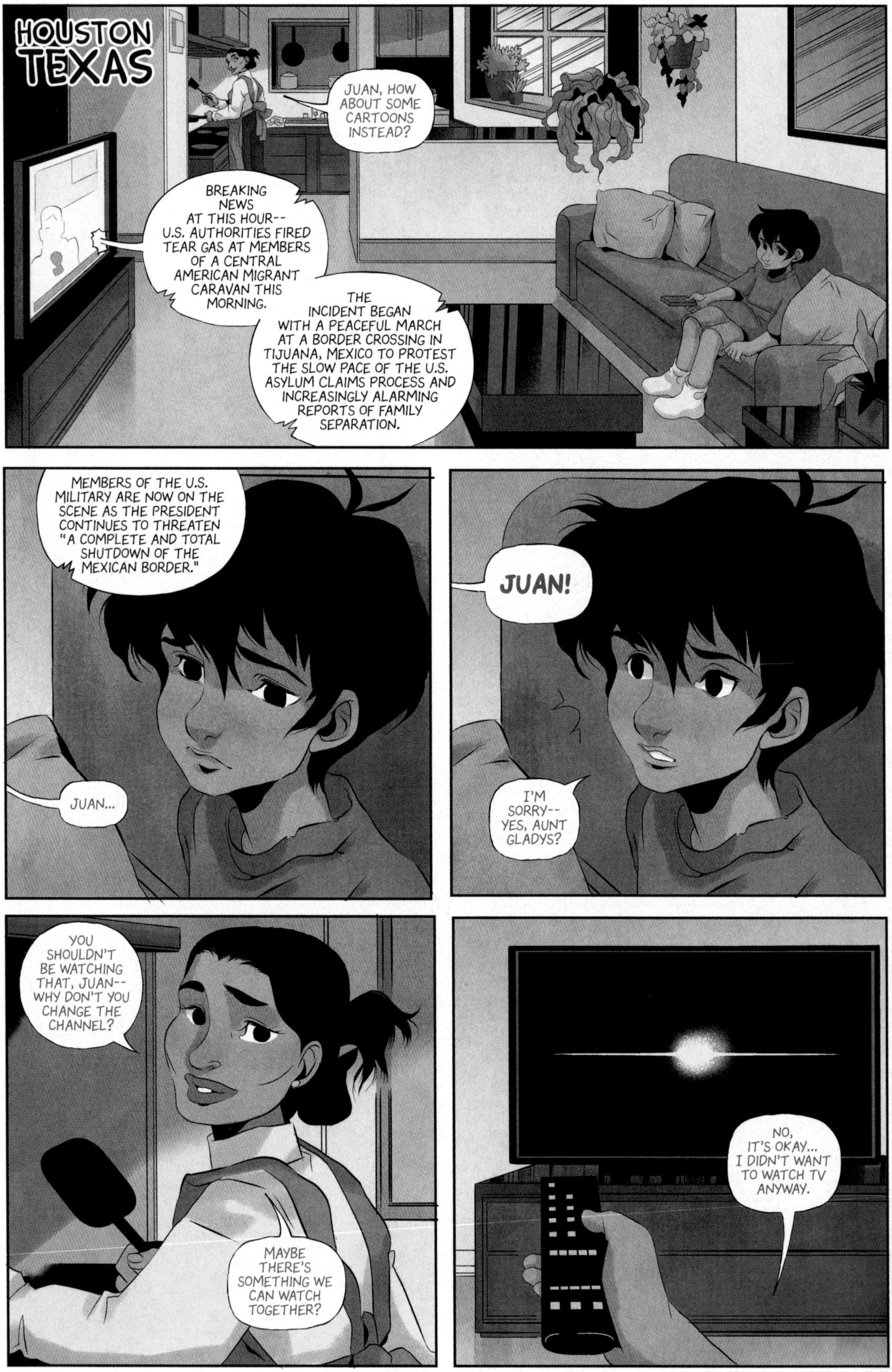
HOUSTON TEXAS
JUAN, HOW ABOUT SOME CARTOONS INSTEAD?
BREAKING NEWS AT THIS HOUR-- U.S. AUTHORITIES FIRED TEAR GAS AT MEMBERS OF A CENTRAL AMERICAN MIGRANT CARAVAN THIS MORNING.
THE INCIDENT BEGAN WITH A PEACEFUL MARCH AT A BORDER CROSSING IN TIJUANA, MEXICO TO PROTEST THE SLOW PACE OF THE U.S. ASYLUM CLAIMS PROCESS AND INCREASINGLY ALARMING REPORTS OF FAMILY SEPARATION.
MEMBERS OF THE U.S. MILITARY ARE NOW ON THE SCENE AS THE PRESIDENT CONTINUES TO THREATEN "A COMPLETE AND TOTAL SHUTDOWN OF THE MEXICAN BORDER."
JUAN...
JUAN!
I'M SORRY-- YES, AUNT GLADYS?
YOU SHOULDN'T BE WATCHING THAT, JUAN-- WHY DON'T YOU CHANGE THE CHANNEL?
MAYBE THERE'S SOMETHING WE CAN WATCH TOGETHER?
NO, IT'S OKAY... I DIDN'T WANT TO WATCH TV ANYWAY.

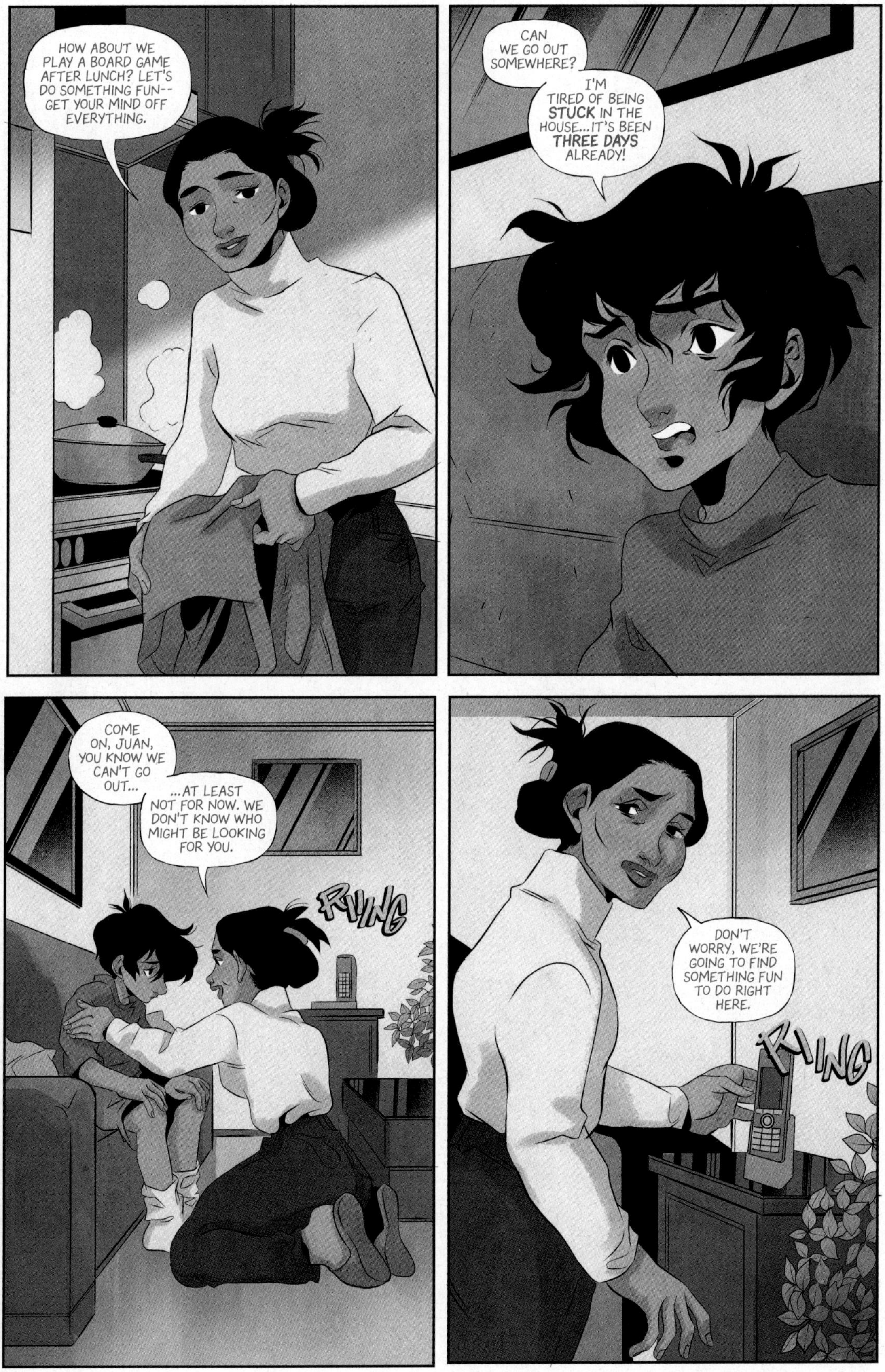
HOW ABOUT WE PLAY A BOARD GAME AFTER LUNCH? LET'S DO SOMETHING FUN-- GET YOUR MIND OFF EVERYTHING.
CAN WE GO OUT SOMEWHERE?
I'M TIRED OF BEING **STUCK** IN THE HOUSE... IT'S BEEN **THREE DAYS** ALREADY!
COME ON, JUAN, YOU KNOW WE CAN'T GO OUT...
...AT LEAST NOT FOR NOW. WE DON'T KNOW WHO MIGHT BE LOOKING FOR YOU.
RING
DON'T WORRY, WE'RE GOING TO FIND SOMETHING FUN TO DO RIGHT HERE.
RING

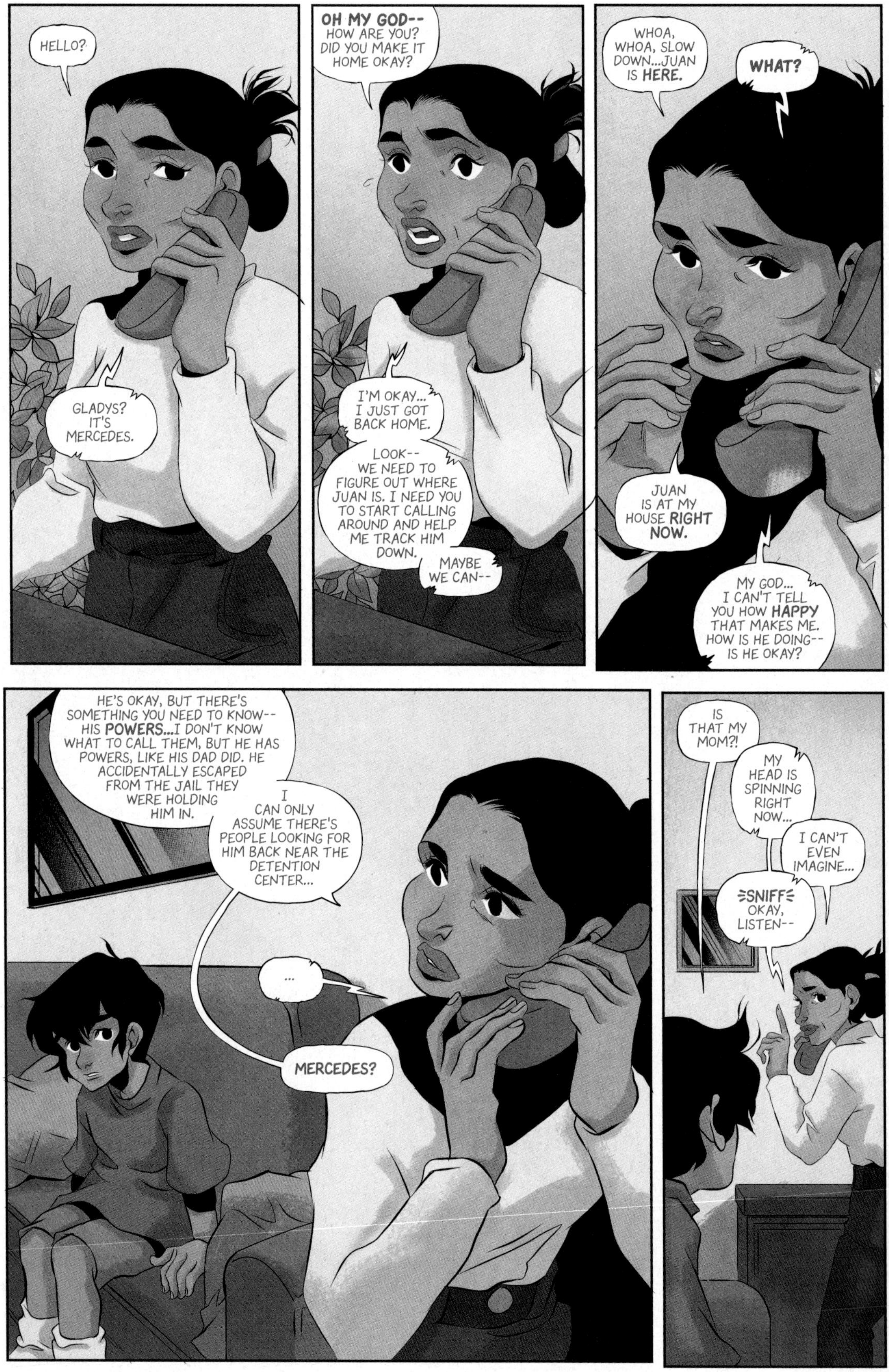
HELLO?
GLADYS? IT'S MERCEDES.
OH MY GOD-- HOW ARE YOU? DID YOU MAKE IT HOME OKAY?
I'M OKAY... I JUST GOT BACK HOME.
LOOK-- WE NEED TO FIGURE OUT WHERE JUAN IS. I NEED YOU TO START CALLING AROUND AND HELP ME TRACK HIM DOWN.
MAYBE WE CAN--
WHOA, WHOA, SLOW DOWN...JUAN IS HERE.
WHAT?
JUAN IS AT MY HOUSE RIGHT NOW.
MY GOD... I CAN'T TELL YOU HOW HAPPY THAT MAKES ME. HOW IS HE DOING-- IS HE OKAY?
HE'S OKAY, BUT THERE'S SOMETHING YOU NEED TO KNOW-- HIS POWERS...I DON'T KNOW WHAT TO CALL THEM, BUT HE HAS POWERS, LIKE HIS DAD DID. HE ACCIDENTALLY ESCAPED FROM THE JAIL THEY WERE HOLDING HIM IN.
I CAN ONLY ASSUME THERE'S PEOPLE LOOKING FOR HIM BACK NEAR THE DETENTION CENTER...
...
MERCEDES?
IS THAT MY MOM?!
MY HEAD IS SPINNING RIGHT NOW...
I CAN'T EVEN IMAGINE...
SNIFF OKAY, LISTEN--

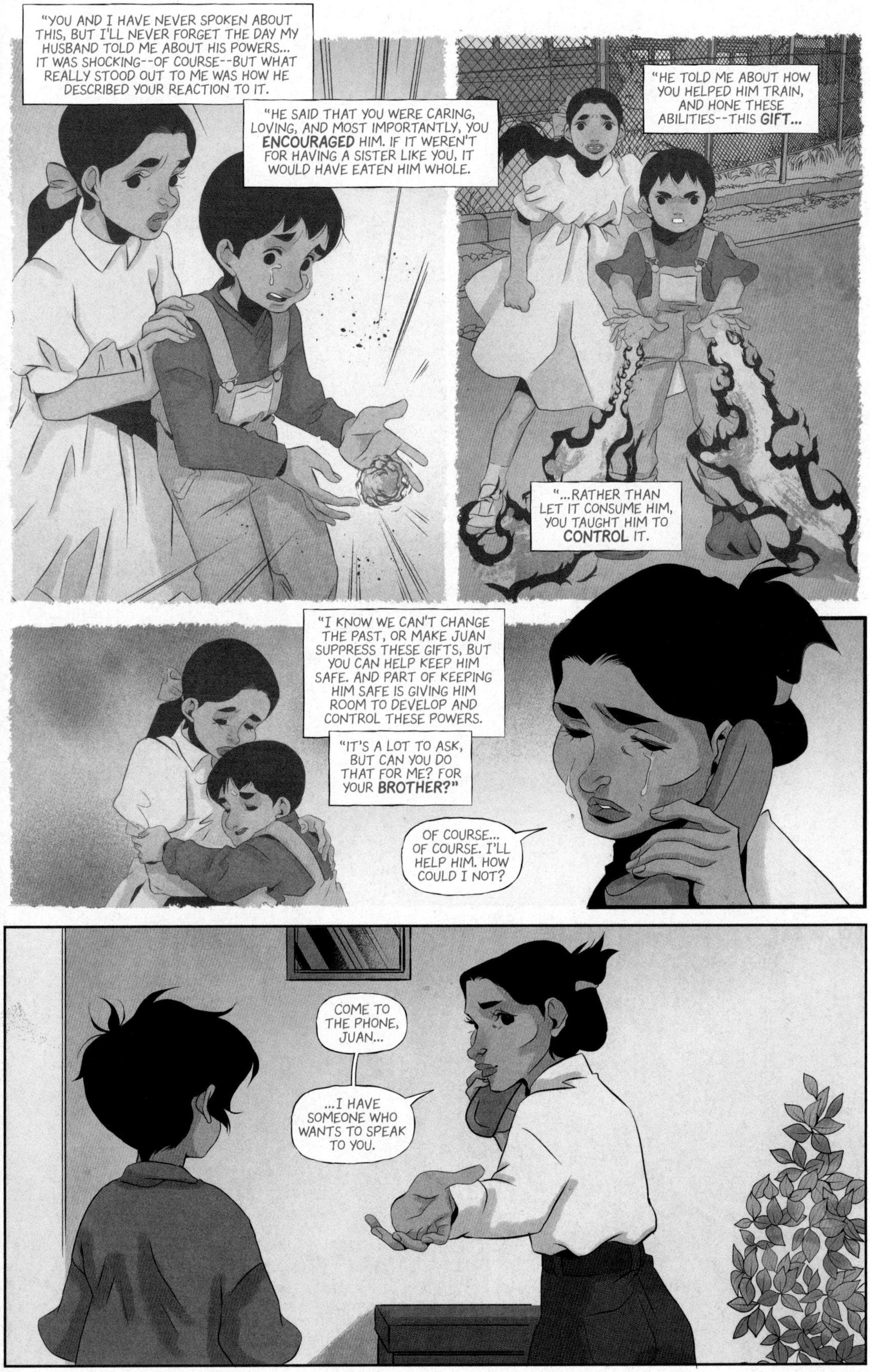
"YOU AND I HAVE NEVER SPOKEN ABOUT THIS, BUT I'LL NEVER FORGET THE DAY MY HUSBAND TOLD ME ABOUT HIS POWERS... IT WAS SHOCKING--OF COURSE--BUT WHAT REALLY STOOD OUT TO ME WAS HOW HE DESCRIBED YOUR REACTION TO IT.
"HE SAID THAT YOU WERE CARING, LOVING, AND MOST IMPORTANTLY, YOU **ENCOURAGED** HIM. IF IT WEREN'T FOR HAVING A SISTER LIKE YOU, IT WOULD HAVE EATEN HIM WHOLE.
"HE TOLD ME ABOUT HOW YOU HELPED HIM TRAIN, AND HONE THESE ABILITIES--THIS **GIFT...**
"...RATHER THAN LET IT CONSUME HIM, YOU TAUGHT HIM TO **CONTROL** IT.
"I KNOW WE CAN'T CHANGE THE PAST, OR MAKE JUAN SUPPRESS THESE GIFTS, BUT YOU CAN HELP KEEP HIM SAFE. AND PART OF KEEPING HIM SAFE IS GIVING HIM ROOM TO DEVELOP AND CONTROL THESE POWERS.
"IT'S A LOT TO ASK, BUT CAN YOU DO THAT FOR ME? FOR YOUR **BROTHER?"**
OF COURSE... OF COURSE. I'LL HELP HIM. HOW COULD I NOT?
COME TO THE PHONE, JUAN...
...I HAVE SOMEONE WHO WANTS TO SPEAK TO YOU.

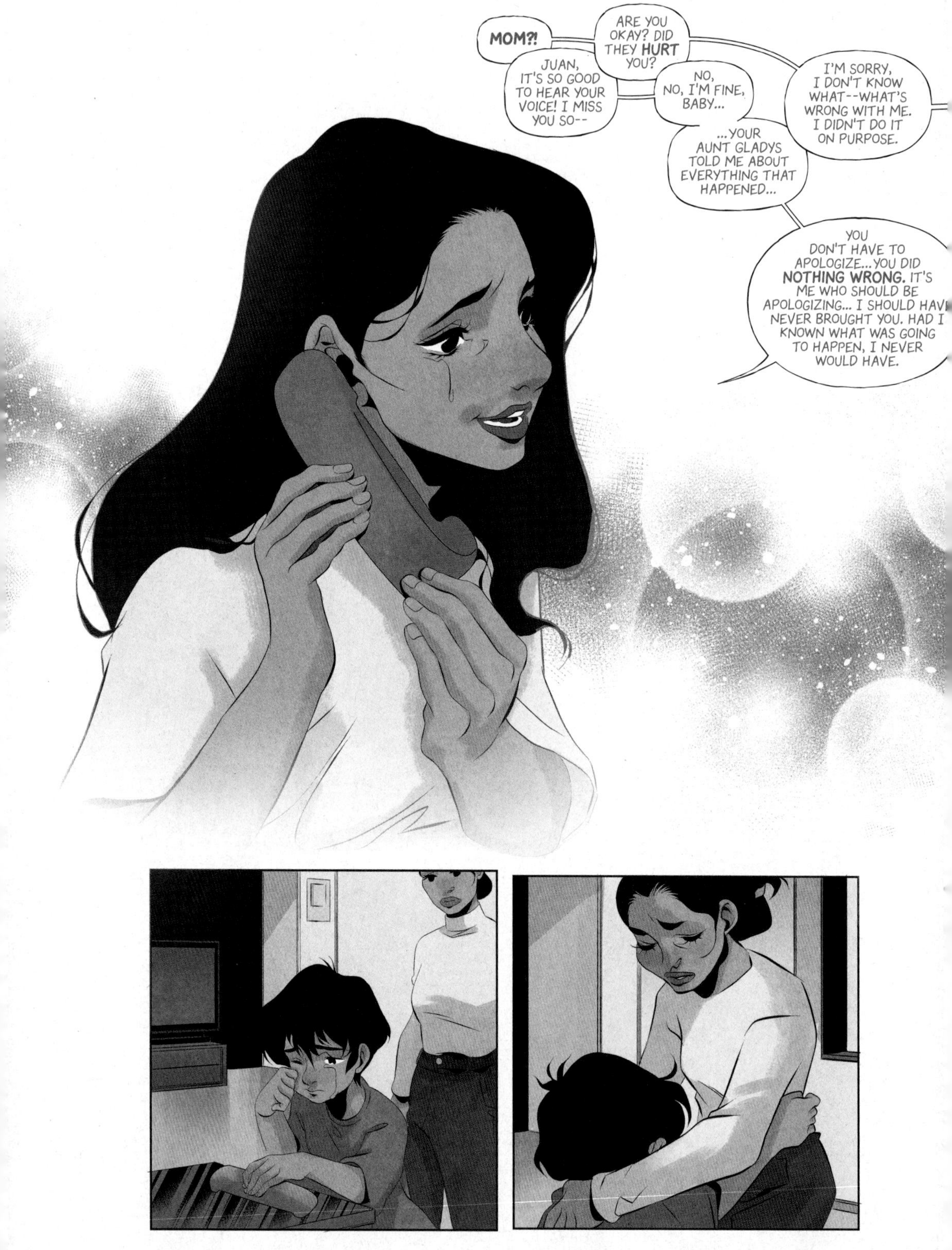
MOM?!
JUAN, IT'S SO GOOD TO HEAR YOUR VOICE! I MISS YOU SO--
ARE YOU OKAY? DID THEY **HURT** YOU?
NO, NO, I'M FINE, BABY...
...YOUR AUNT GLADYS TOLD ME ABOUT EVERYTHING THAT HAPPENED...
I'M SORRY, I DON'T KNOW WHAT--WHAT'S WRONG WITH ME. I DIDN'T DO IT ON PURPOSE.
YOU DON'T HAVE TO APOLOGIZE...YOU DID **NOTHING WRONG.** IT'S ME WHO SHOULD BE APOLOGIZING... I SHOULD HAV NEVER BROUGHT YOU. HAD I KNOWN WHAT WAS GOING TO HAPPEN, I NEVER WOULD HAVE.

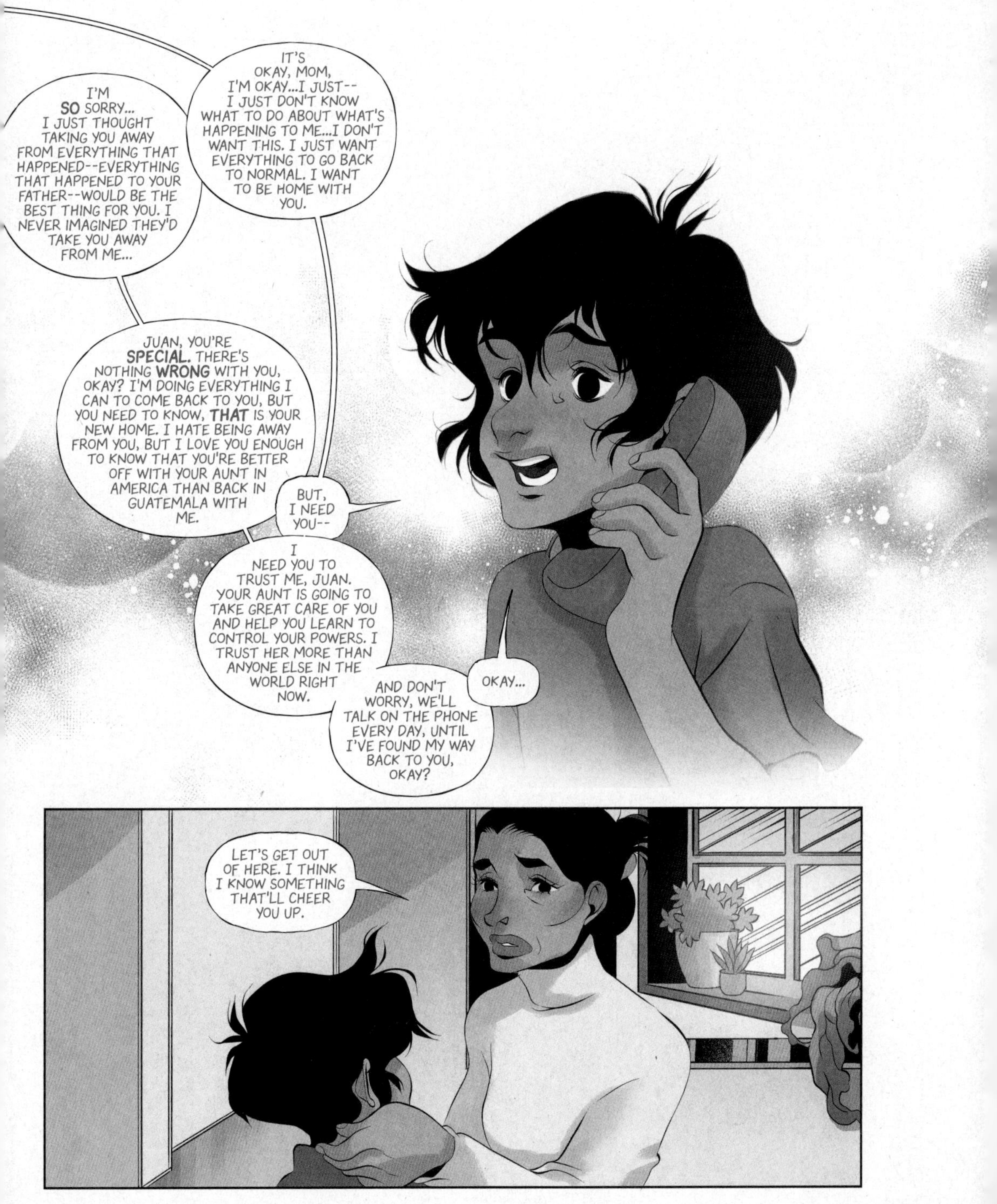
I'M SO SORRY... I JUST THOUGHT TAKING YOU AWAY FROM EVERYTHING THAT HAPPENED--EVERYTHING THAT HAPPENED TO YOUR FATHER--WOULD BE THE BEST THING FOR YOU. I NEVER IMAGINED THEY'D TAKE YOU AWAY FROM ME...
IT'S OKAY, MOM, I'M OKAY...I JUST-- I JUST DON'T KNOW WHAT TO DO ABOUT WHAT'S HAPPENING TO ME...I DON'T WANT THIS. I JUST WANT EVERYTHING TO GO BACK TO NORMAL. I WANT TO BE HOME WITH YOU.
JUAN, YOU'RE SPECIAL. THERE'S NOTHING WRONG WITH YOU, OKAY? I'M DOING EVERYTHING I CAN TO COME BACK TO YOU, BUT YOU NEED TO KNOW, THAT IS YOUR NEW HOME. I HATE BEING AWAY FROM YOU, BUT I LOVE YOU ENOUGH TO KNOW THAT YOU'RE BETTER OFF WITH YOUR AUNT IN AMERICA THAN BACK IN GUATEMALA WITH ME.
BUT, I NEED YOU--
I NEED YOU TO TRUST ME, JUAN. YOUR AUNT IS GOING TO TAKE GREAT CARE OF YOU AND HELP YOU LEARN TO CONTROL YOUR POWERS. I TRUST HER MORE THAN ANYONE ELSE IN THE WORLD RIGHT NOW.
OKAY...
AND DON'T WORRY, WE'LL TALK ON THE PHONE EVERY DAY, UNTIL I'VE FOUND MY WAY BACK TO YOU, OKAY?
LET'S GET OUT OF HERE. I THINK I KNOW SOMETHING THAT'LL CHEER YOU UP.

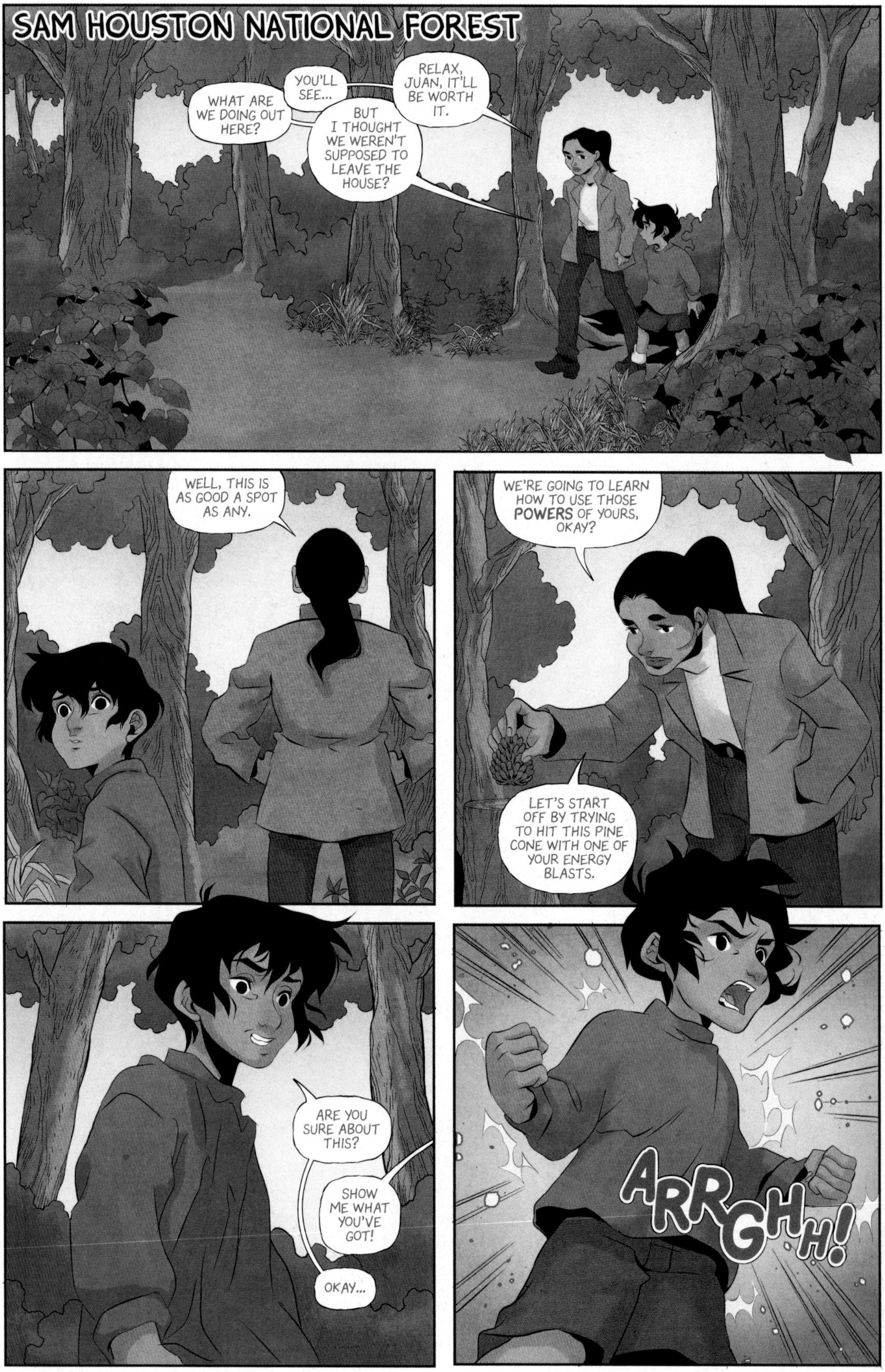
SAM HOUSTON NATIONAL FOREST
WHAT ARE WE DOING OUT HERE?
YOU'LL SEE...
RELAX, JUAN, IT'LL BE WORTH IT.
BUT I THOUGHT WE WEREN'T SUPPOSED TO LEAVE THE HOUSE?
WELL, THIS IS AS GOOD A SPOT AS ANY.
WE'RE GOING TO LEARN HOW TO USE THOSE POWERS OF YOURS, OKAY?
LET'S START OFF BY TRYING TO HIT THIS PINE CONE WITH ONE OF YOUR ENERGY BLASTS.
ARE YOU SURE ABOUT THIS?
SHOW ME WHAT YOU'VE GOT!
OKAY...
ARRGHHH!

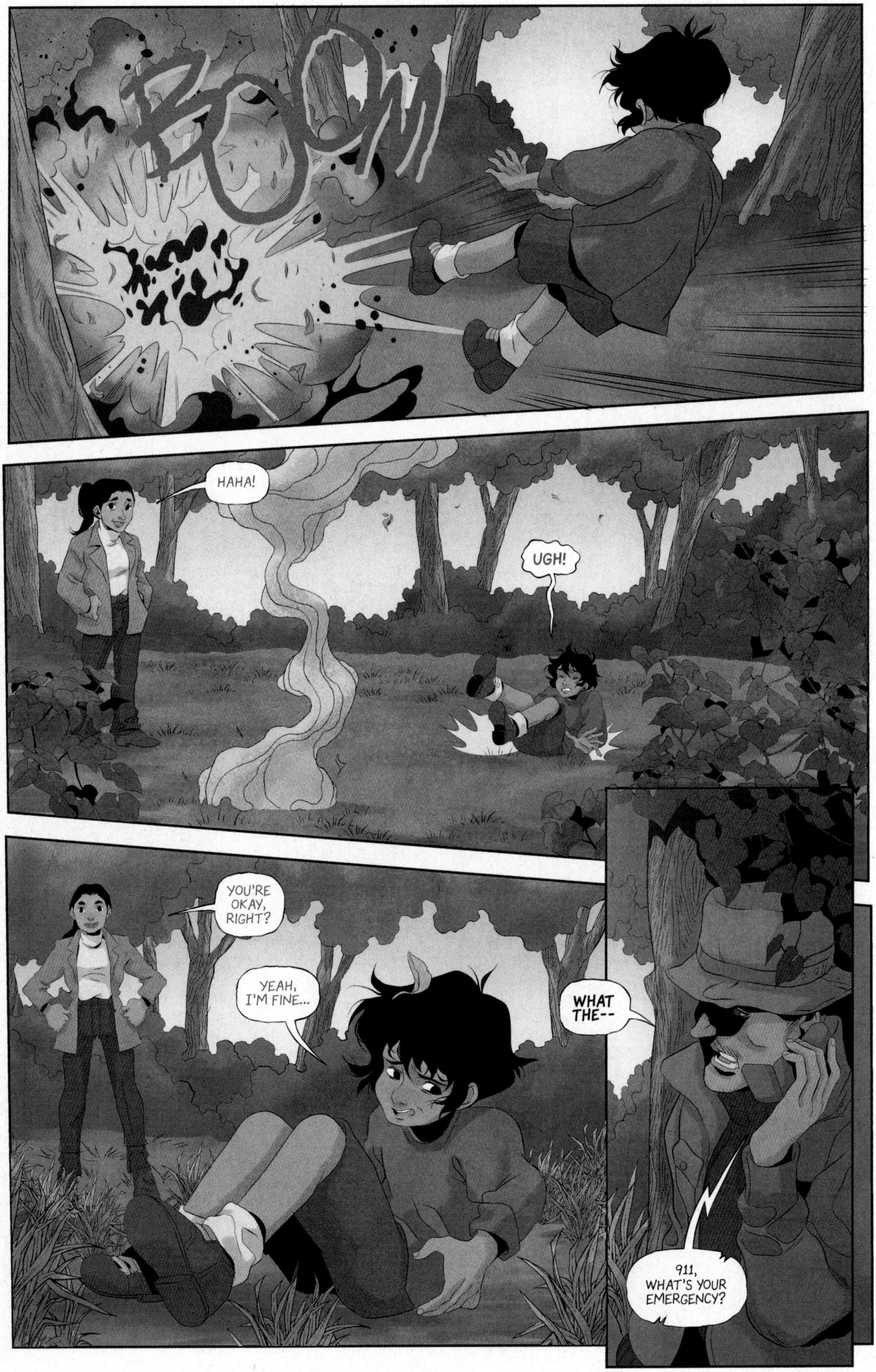
BOOM
HAHA!
UGH!
YOU'RE OKAY, RIGHT?
YEAH, I'M FINE...
WHAT THE--
911, WHAT'S YOUR EMERGENCY?

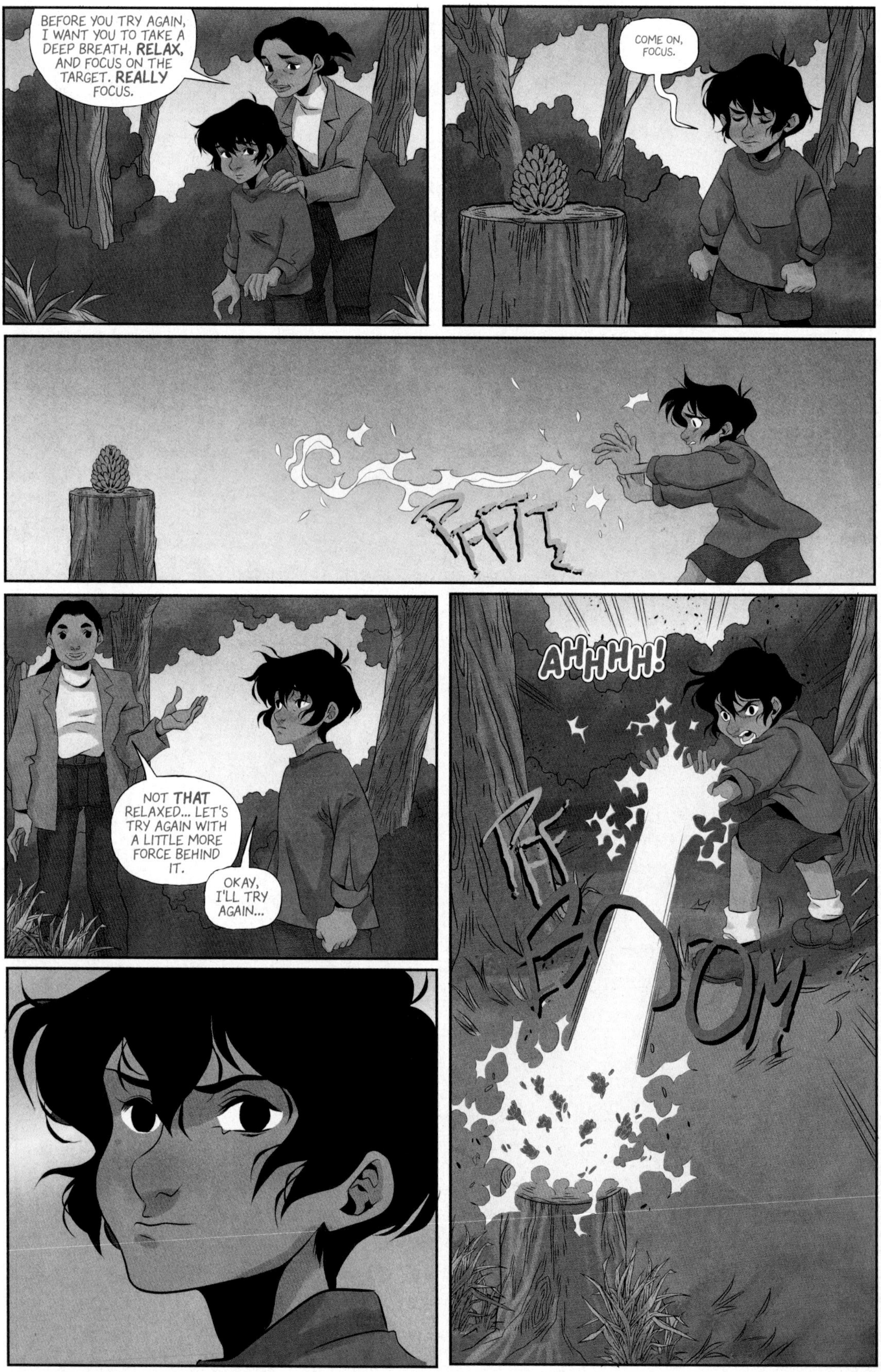
BEFORE YOU TRY AGAIN, I WANT YOU TO TAKE A DEEP BREATH, RELAX, AND FOCUS ON THE TARGET. REALLY FOCUS.
COME ON, FOCUS.
PFFTZ
NOT THAT RELAXED... LET'S TRY AGAIN WITH A LITTLE MORE FORCE BEHIND IT.
OKAY, I'LL TRY AGAIN...
AHHHH!
PHF
BOOM!

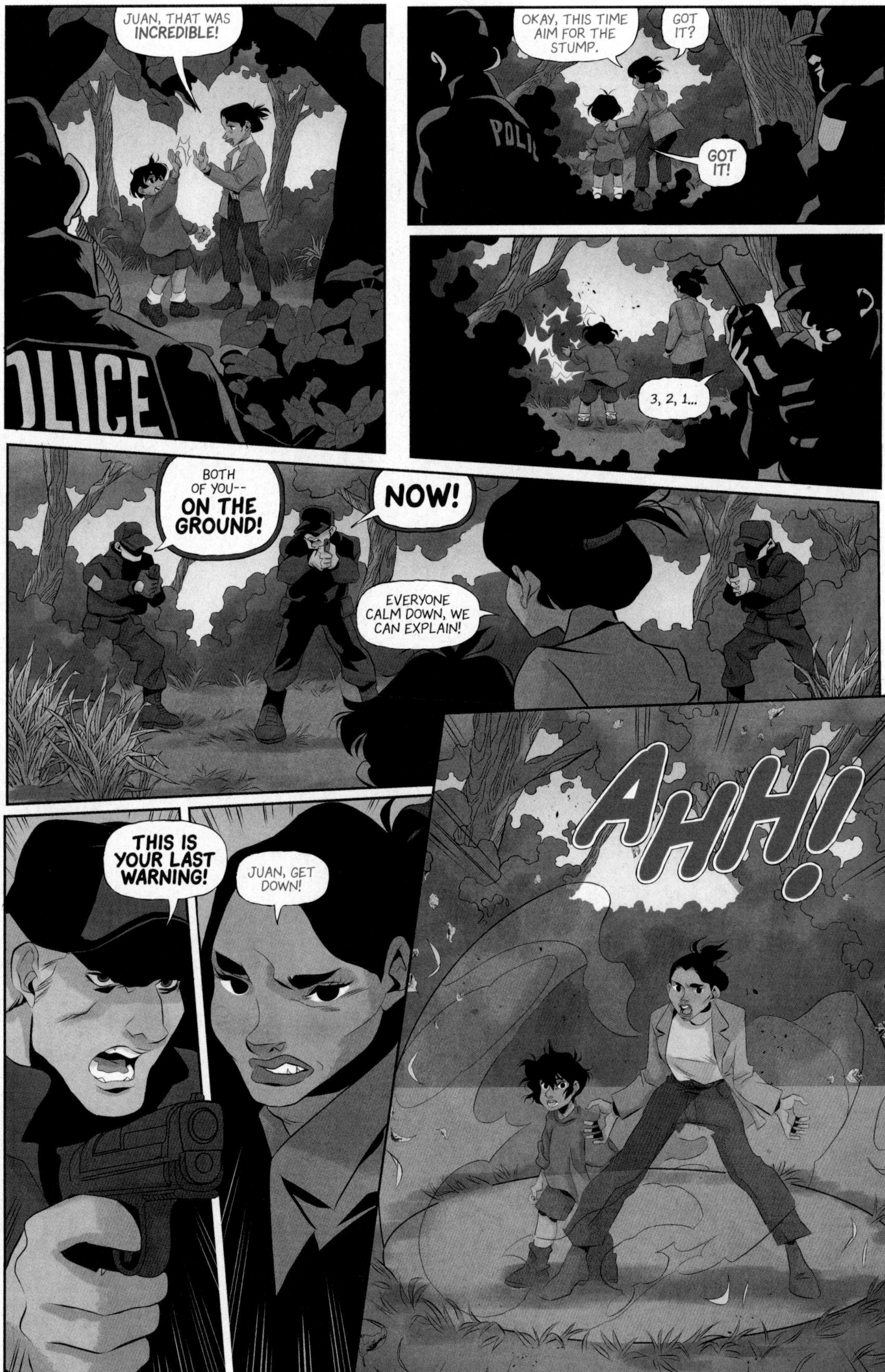

JUAN, THAT WAS INCREDIBLE!
POLICE
OKAY, THIS TIME AIM FOR THE STUMP.
GOT IT?
GOT IT!
POLICE
3, 2, 1...
BOTH OF YOU-- ON THE GROUND!
NOW!
EVERYONE CALM DOWN, WE CAN EXPLAIN!
THIS IS YOUR LAST WARNING!
JUAN, GET DOWN!
AHH!

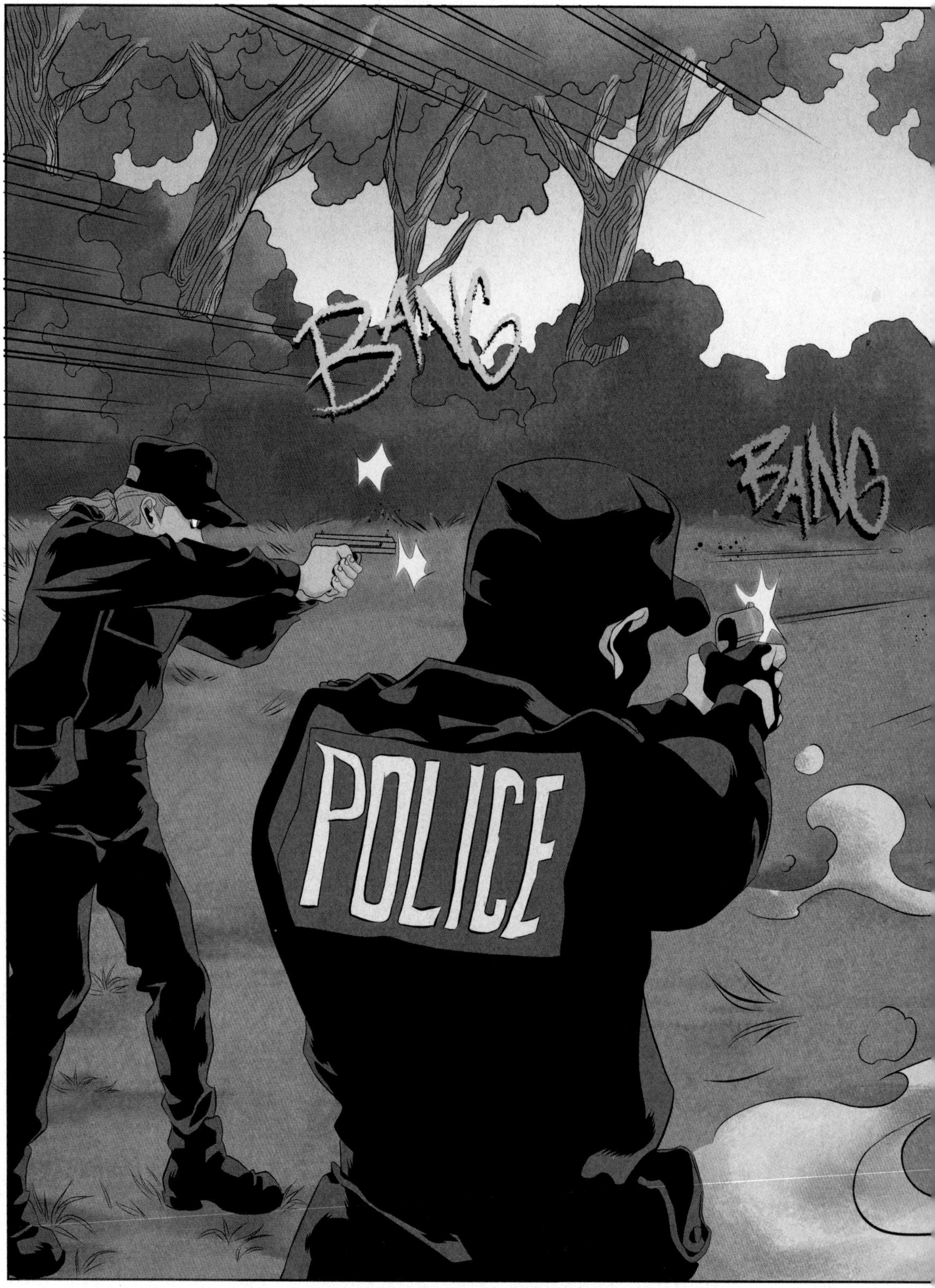
BANG
BANG
POLICE

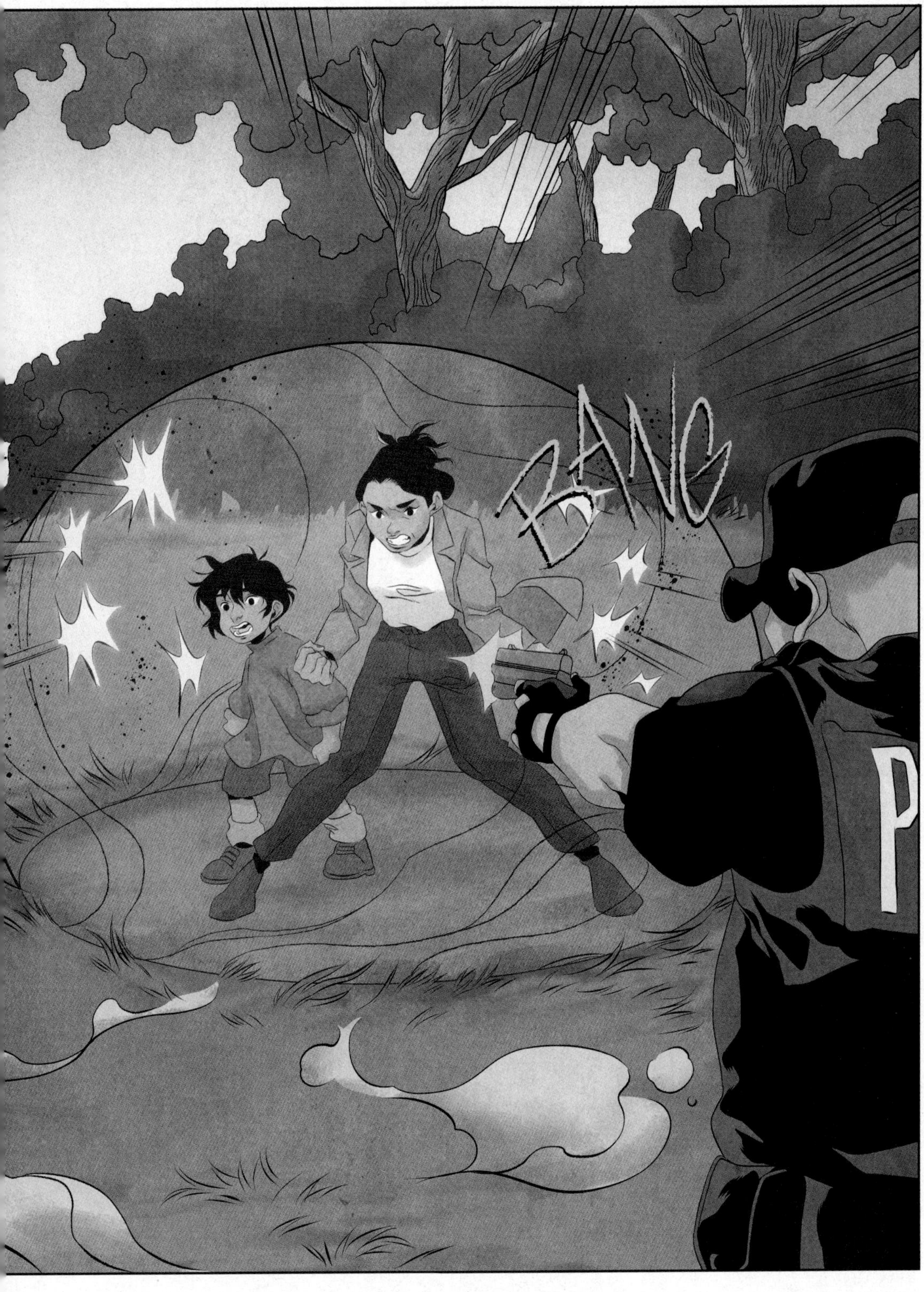
BANG
P

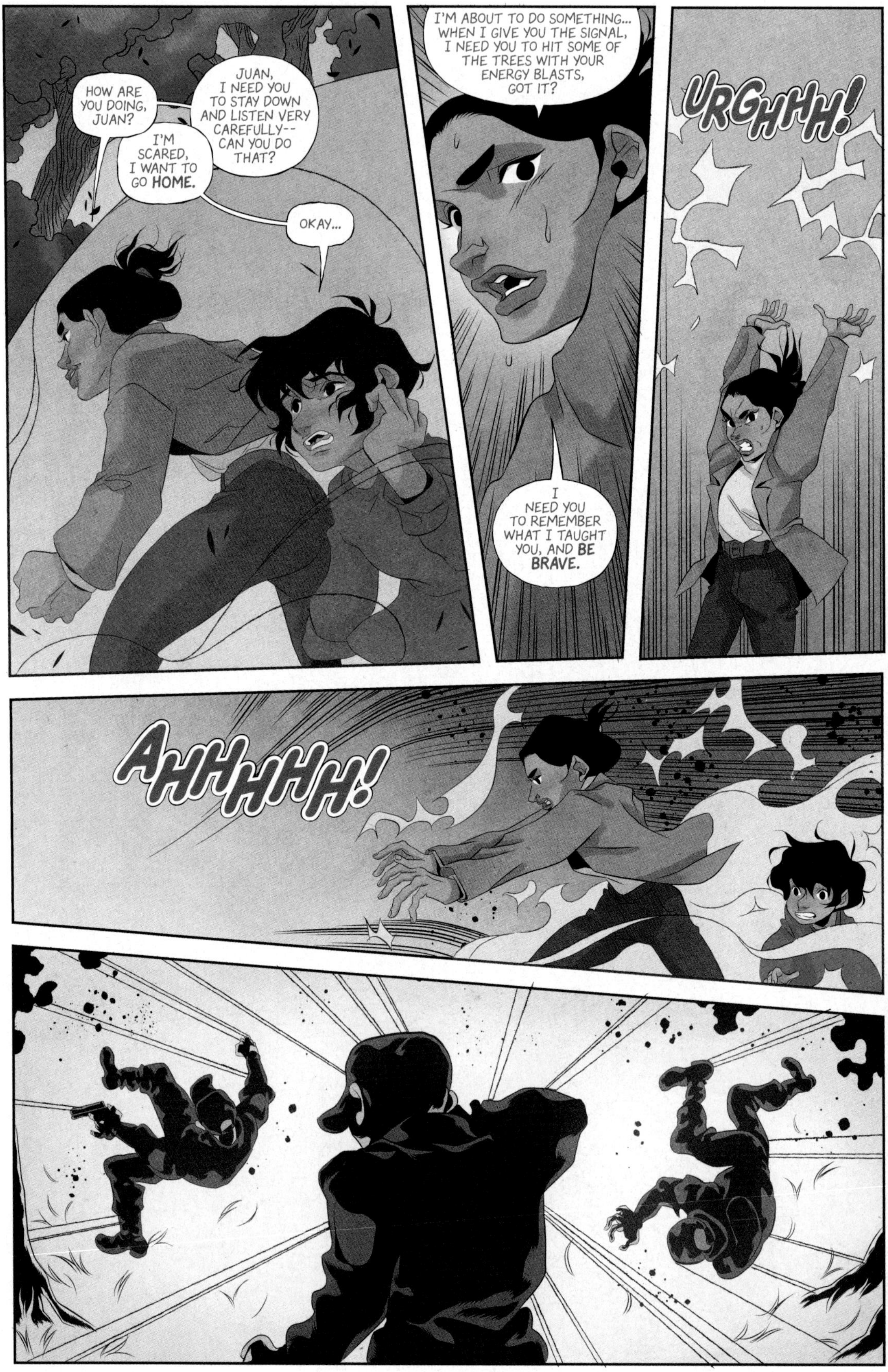
HOW ARE YOU DOING, JUAN?
I'M SCARED, I WANT TO GO HOME.
JUAN, I NEED YOU TO STAY DOWN AND LISTEN VERY CAREFULLY-- CAN YOU DO THAT?
OKAY...
I'M ABOUT TO DO SOMETHING... WHEN I GIVE YOU THE SIGNAL, I NEED YOU TO HIT SOME OF THE TREES WITH YOUR ENERGY BLASTS, GOT IT?
I NEED YOU TO REMEMBER WHAT I TAUGHT YOU, AND BE BRAVE.
URGHHH!
AHHHHHH!

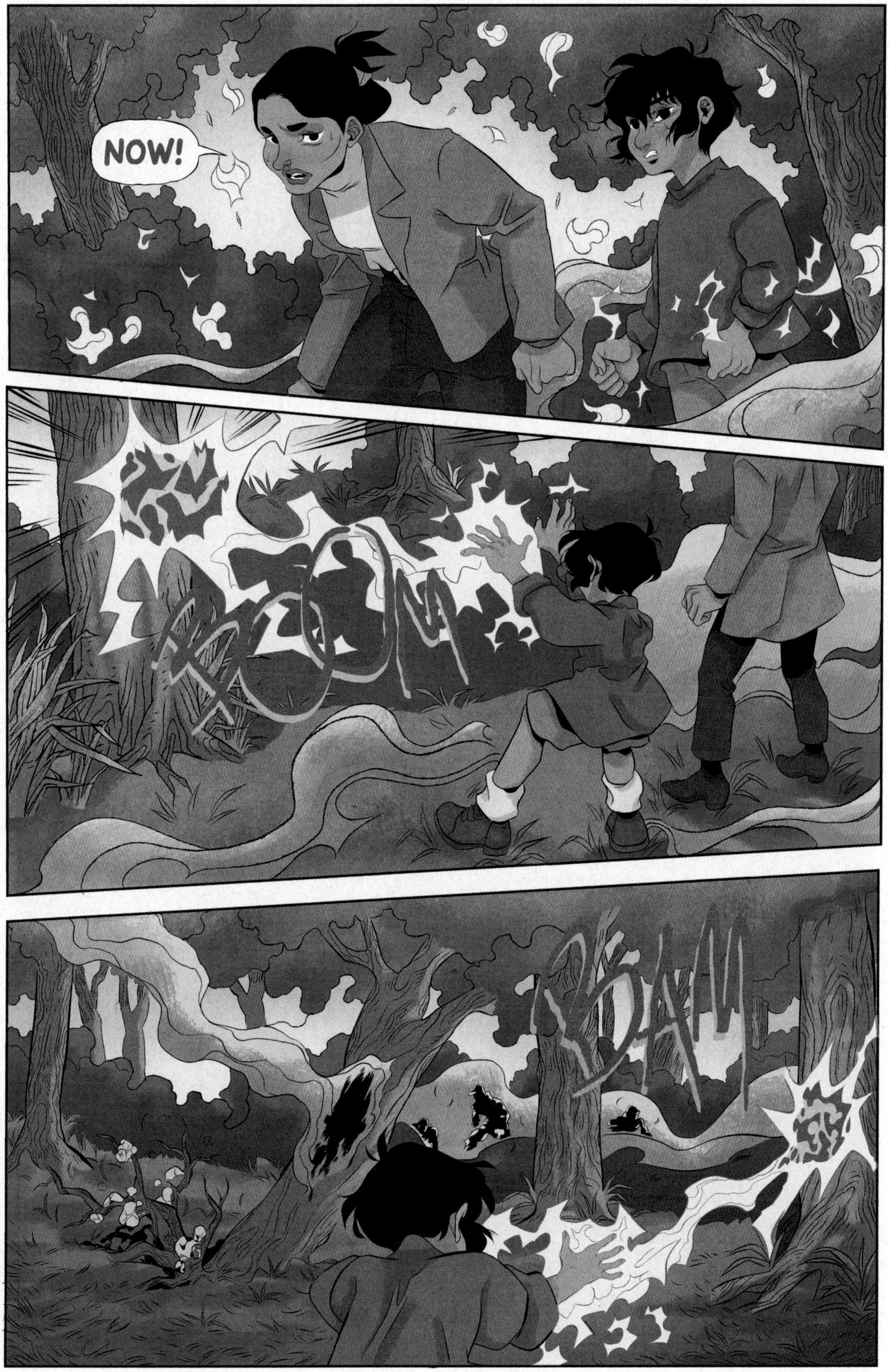
NOW!

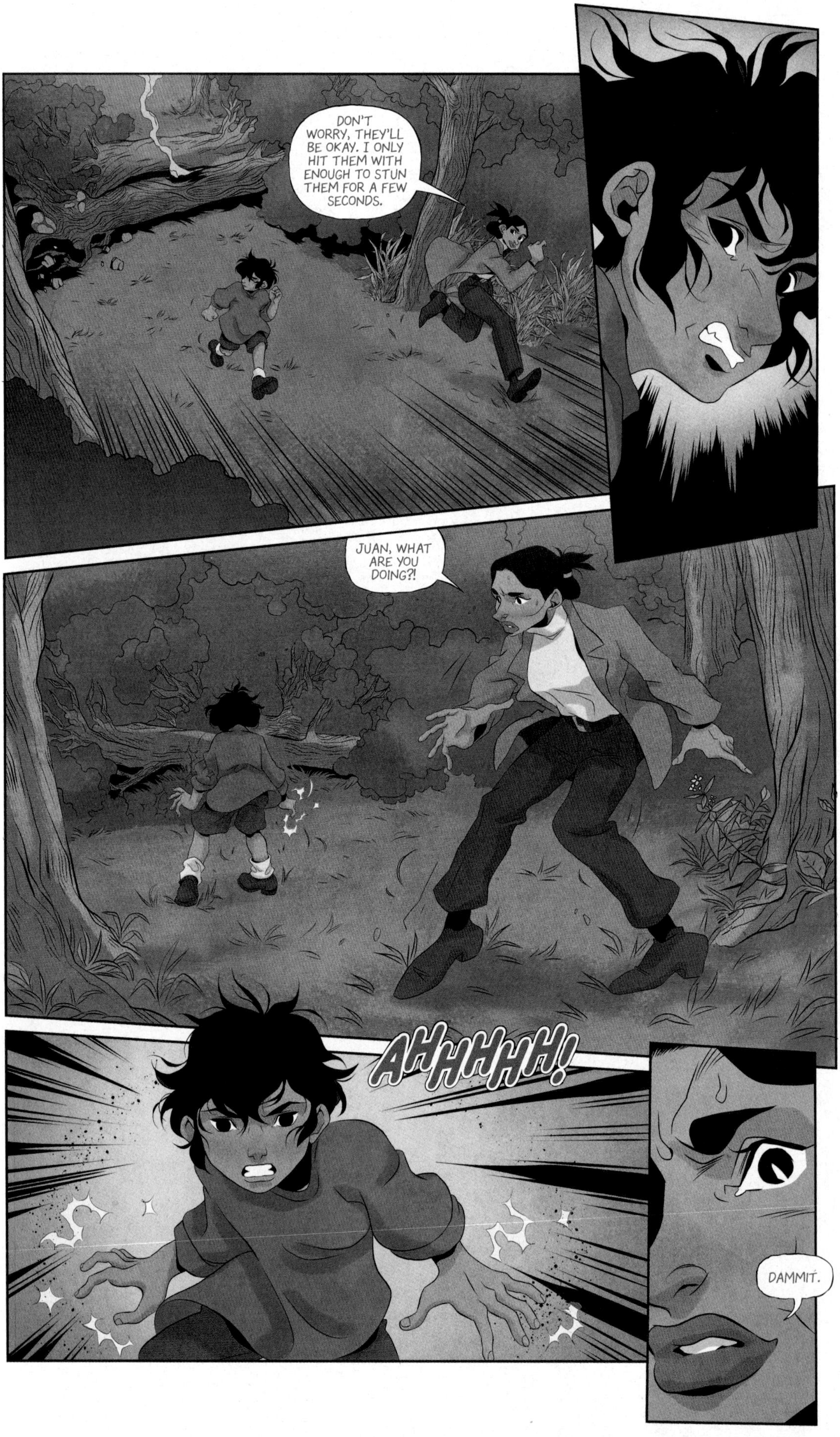
DON'T WORRY, THEY'LL BE OKAY. I ONLY HIT THEM WITH ENOUGH TO STUN THEM FOR A FEW SECONDS.
JUAN, WHAT ARE YOU DOING?!
AHHHHHH!
DAMMIT.

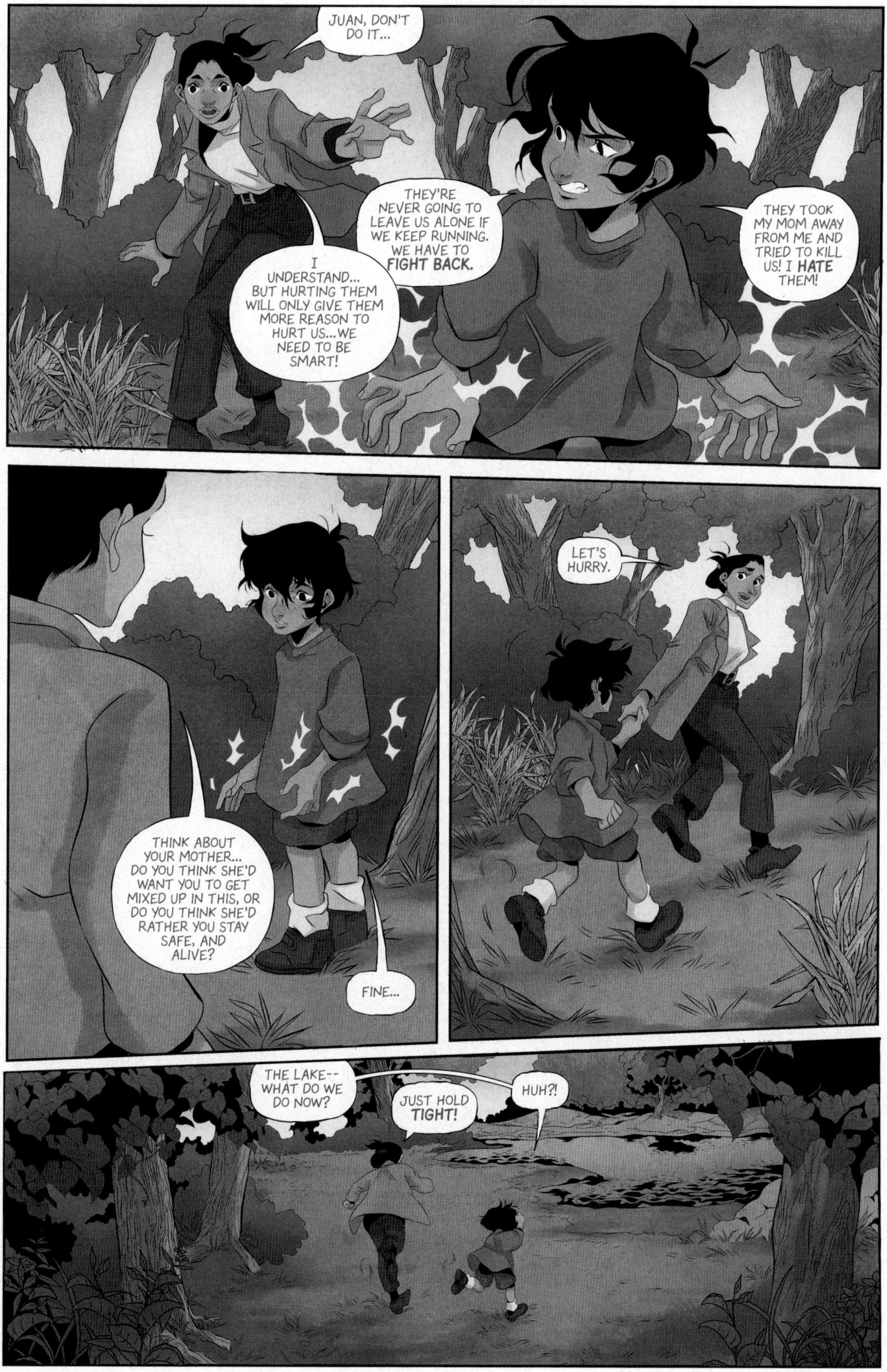
JUAN, DON'T DO IT...
THEY'RE NEVER GOING TO LEAVE US ALONE IF WE KEEP RUNNING. WE HAVE TO **FIGHT BACK.**
THEY TOOK MY MOM AWAY FROM ME AND TRIED TO KILL US! I **HATE** THEM!
I UNDERSTAND... BUT HURTING THEM WILL ONLY GIVE THEM MORE REASON TO HURT US...WE NEED TO BE SMART!
THINK ABOUT YOUR MOTHER... DO YOU THINK SHE'D WANT YOU TO GET MIXED UP IN THIS, OR DO YOU THINK SHE'D RATHER YOU STAY SAFE, AND ALIVE?
FINE...
LET'S HURRY.
THE LAKE-- WHAT DO WE DO NOW?
JUST HOLD **TIGHT!**
HUH?!

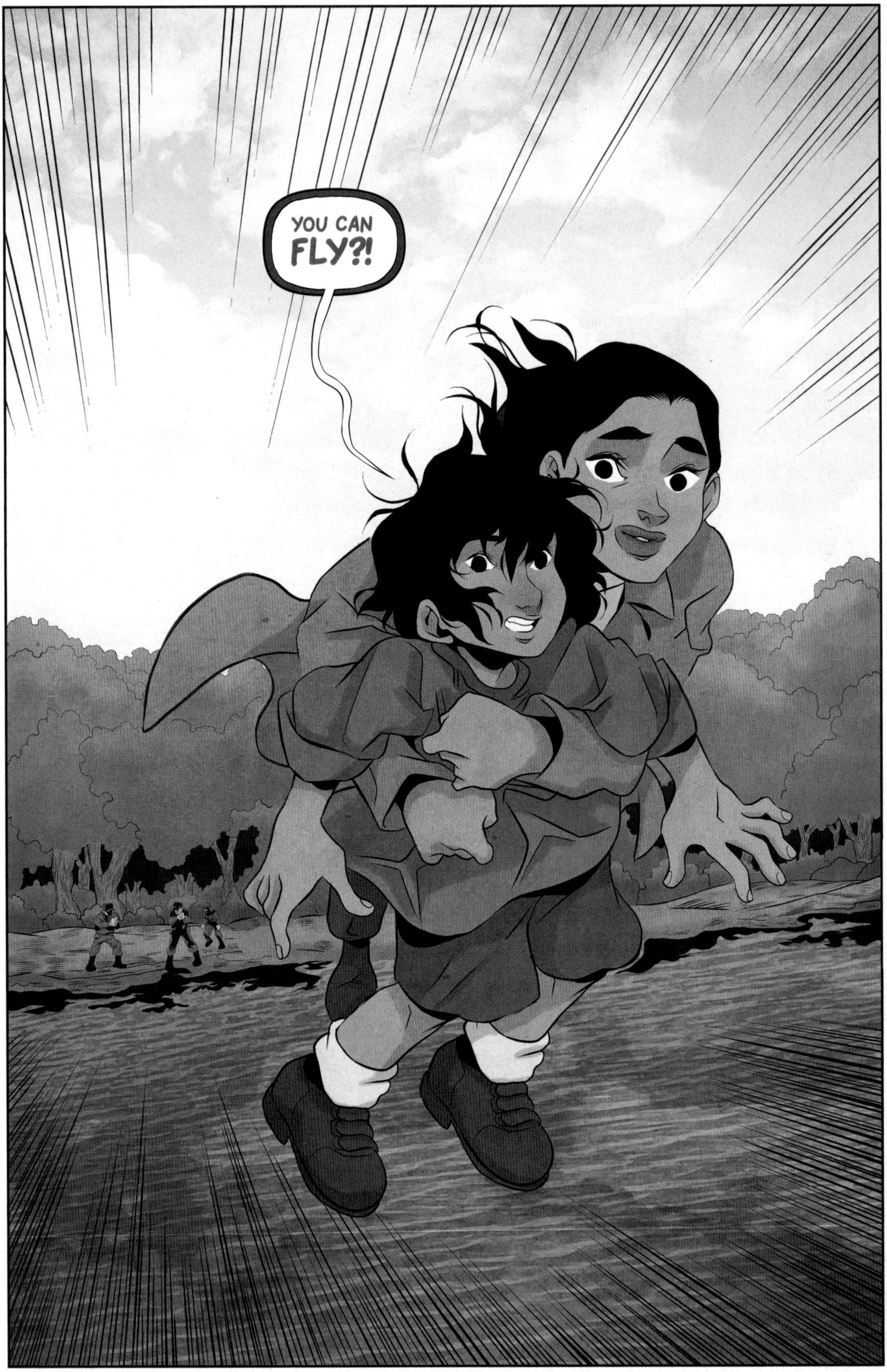
YOU CAN FLY?!

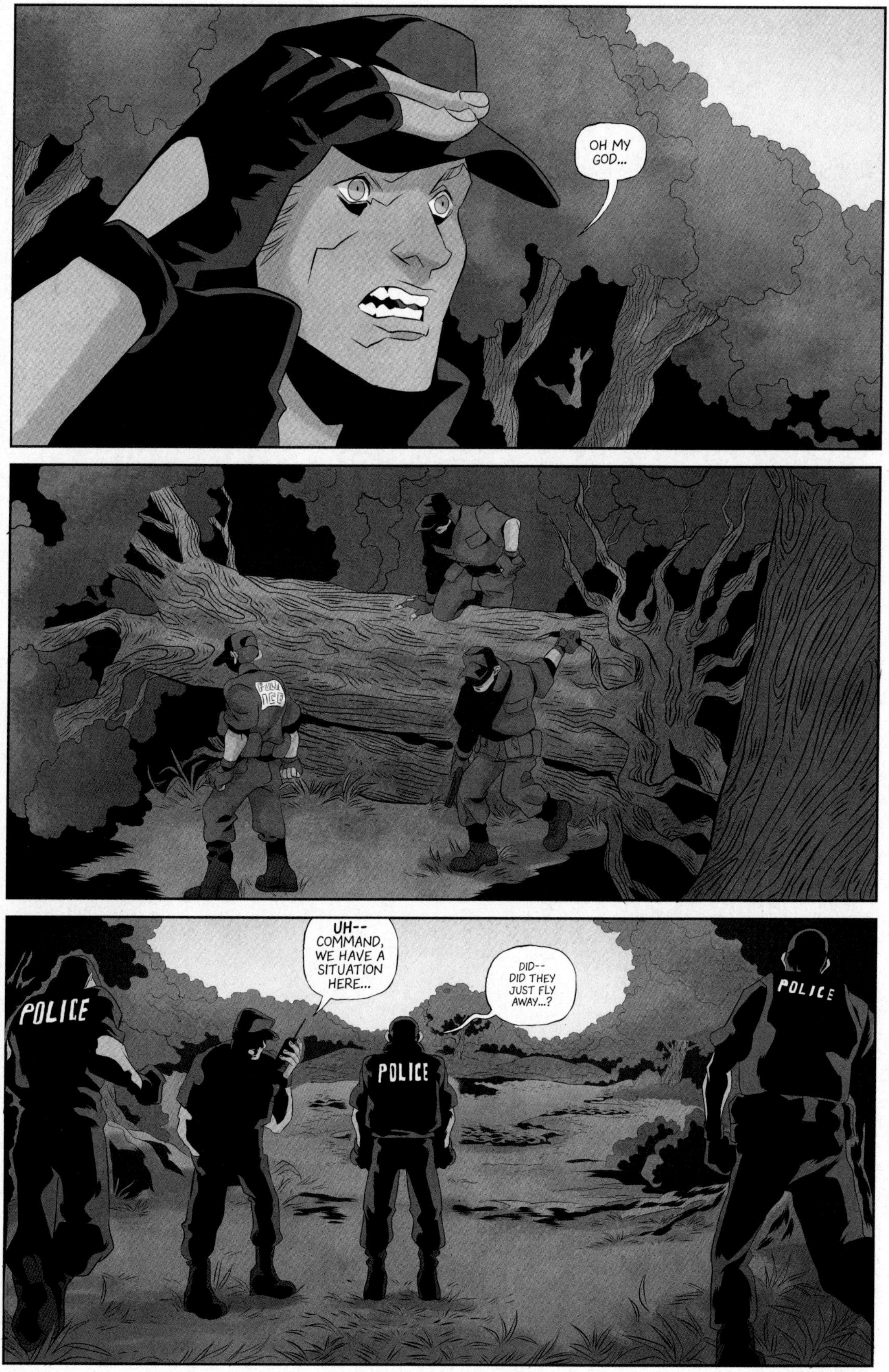
OH MY GOD...
UH-- COMMAND, WE HAVE A SITUATION HERE...
DID-- DID THEY JUST FLY AWAY...?
POLICE
POLICE
POLICE

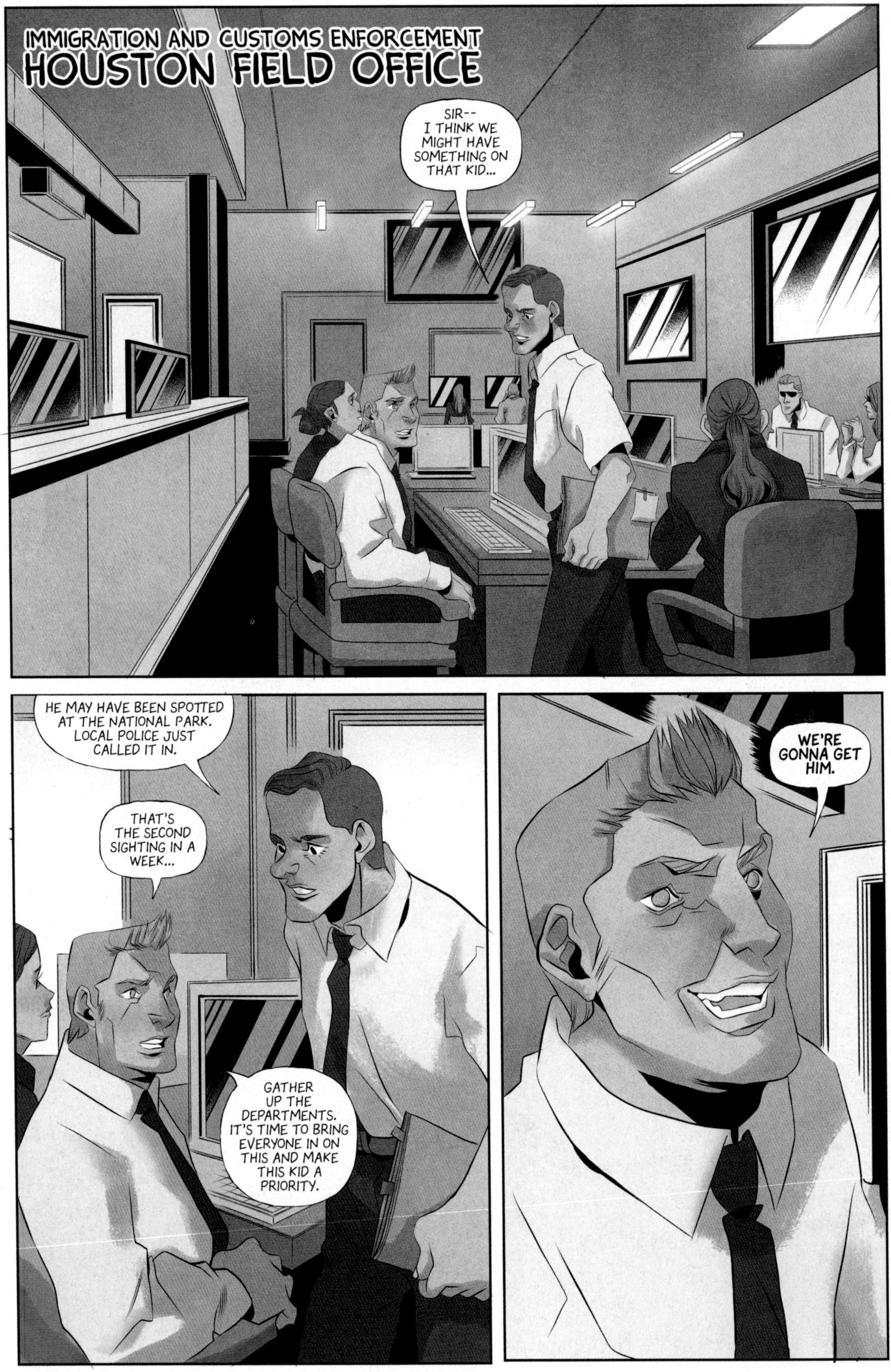
IMMIGRATION AND CUSTOMS ENFORCEMENT
HOUSTON FIELD OFFICE
SIR-- I THINK WE MIGHT HAVE SOMETHING ON THAT KID...
HE MAY HAVE BEEN SPOTTED AT THE NATIONAL PARK. LOCAL POLICE JUST CALLED IT IN.
THAT'S THE SECOND SIGHTING IN A WEEK...
GATHER UP THE DEPARTMENTS. IT'S TIME TO BRING EVERYONE IN ON THIS AND MAKE THIS KID A PRIORITY.
WE'RE GONNA GET HIM.

Chapter Four

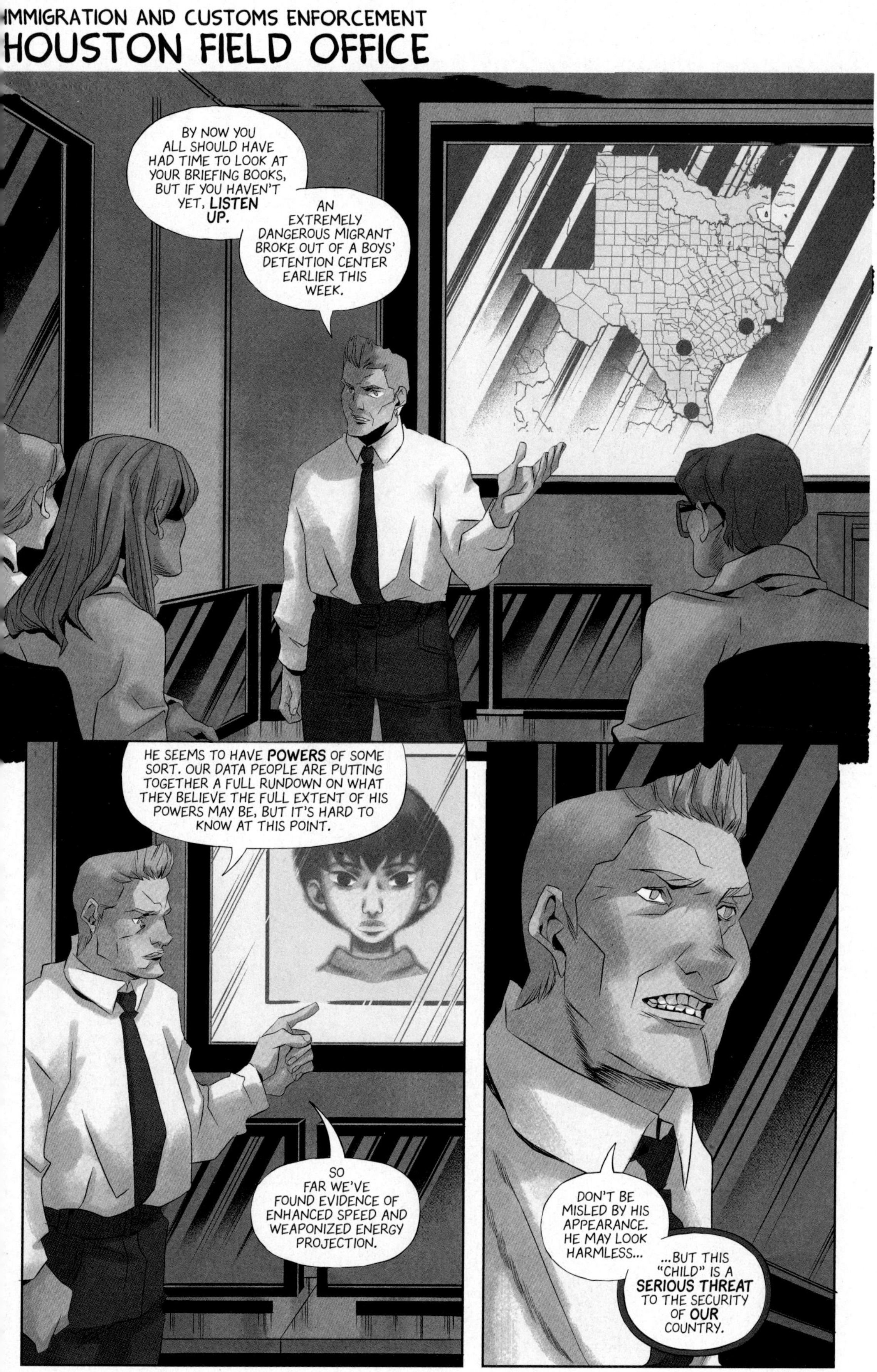
IMMIGRATION AND CUSTOMS ENFORCEMENT
HOUSTON FIELD OFFICE
BY NOW YOU ALL SHOULD HAVE HAD TIME TO LOOK AT YOUR BRIEFING BOOKS, BUT IF YOU HAVEN'T YET, LISTEN UP.
AN EXTREMELY DANGEROUS MIGRANT BROKE OUT OF A BOYS' DETENTION CENTER EARLIER THIS WEEK.
HE SEEMS TO HAVE POWERS OF SOME SORT. OUR DATA PEOPLE ARE PUTTING TOGETHER A FULL RUNDOWN ON WHAT THEY BELIEVE THE FULL EXTENT OF HIS POWERS MAY BE, BUT IT'S HARD TO KNOW AT THIS POINT.
SO FAR WE'VE FOUND EVIDENCE OF ENHANCED SPEED AND WEAPONIZED ENERGY PROJECTION.
DON'T BE MISLED BY HIS APPEARANCE. HE MAY LOOK HARMLESS...
...BUT THIS "CHILD" IS A SERIOUS THREAT TO THE SECURITY OF OUR COUNTRY.

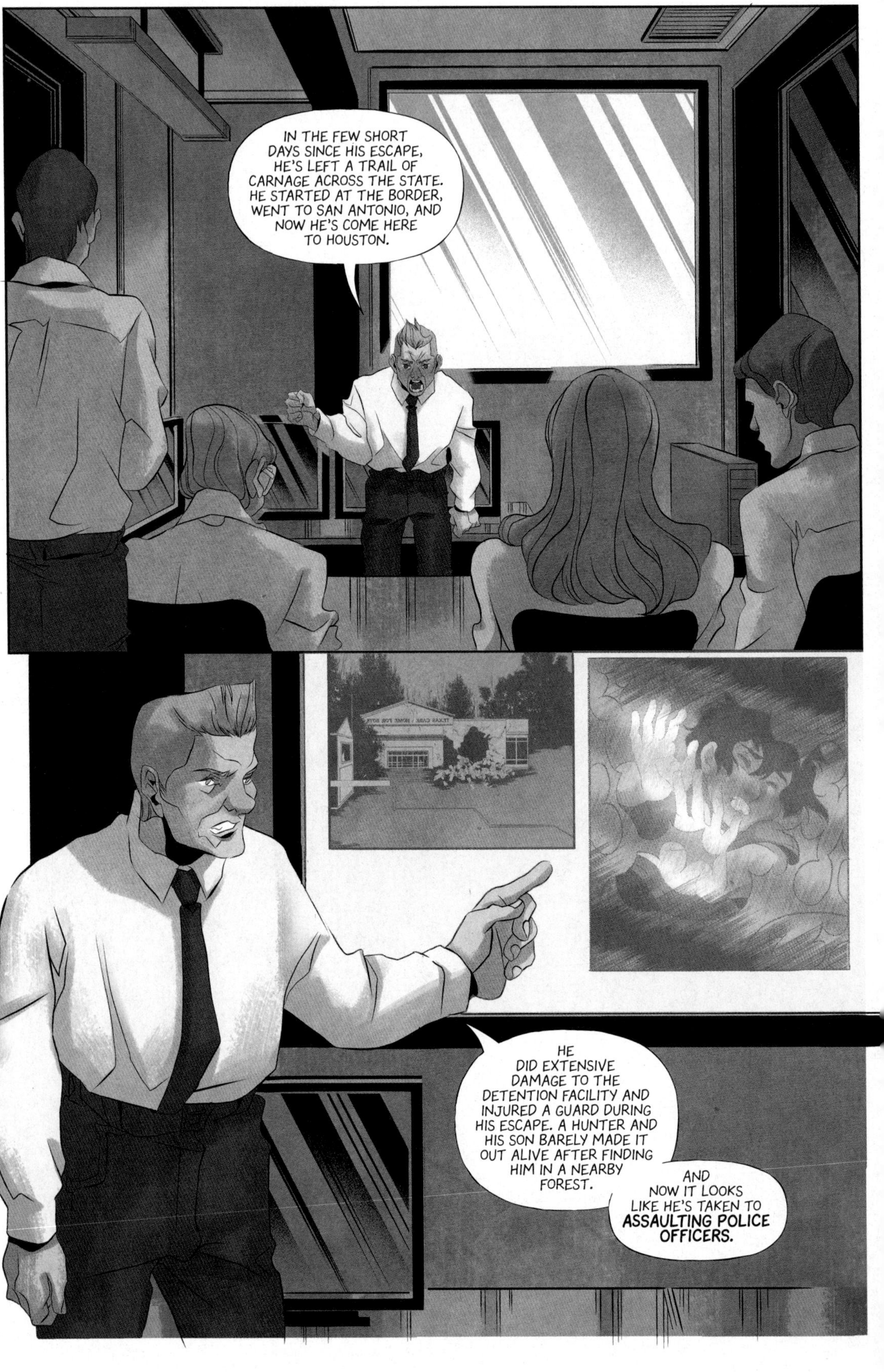
IN THE FEW SHORT DAYS SINCE HIS ESCAPE, HE'S LEFT A TRAIL OF CARNAGE ACROSS THE STATE. HE STARTED AT THE BORDER, WENT TO SAN ANTONIO, AND NOW HE'S COME HERE TO HOUSTON.
HE DID EXTENSIVE DAMAGE TO THE DETENTION FACILITY AND INJURED A GUARD DURING HIS ESCAPE. A HUNTER AND HIS SON BARELY MADE IT OUT ALIVE AFTER FINDING HIM IN A NEARBY FOREST.
AND NOW IT LOOKS LIKE HE'S TAKEN TO **ASSAULTING POLICE OFFICERS.**

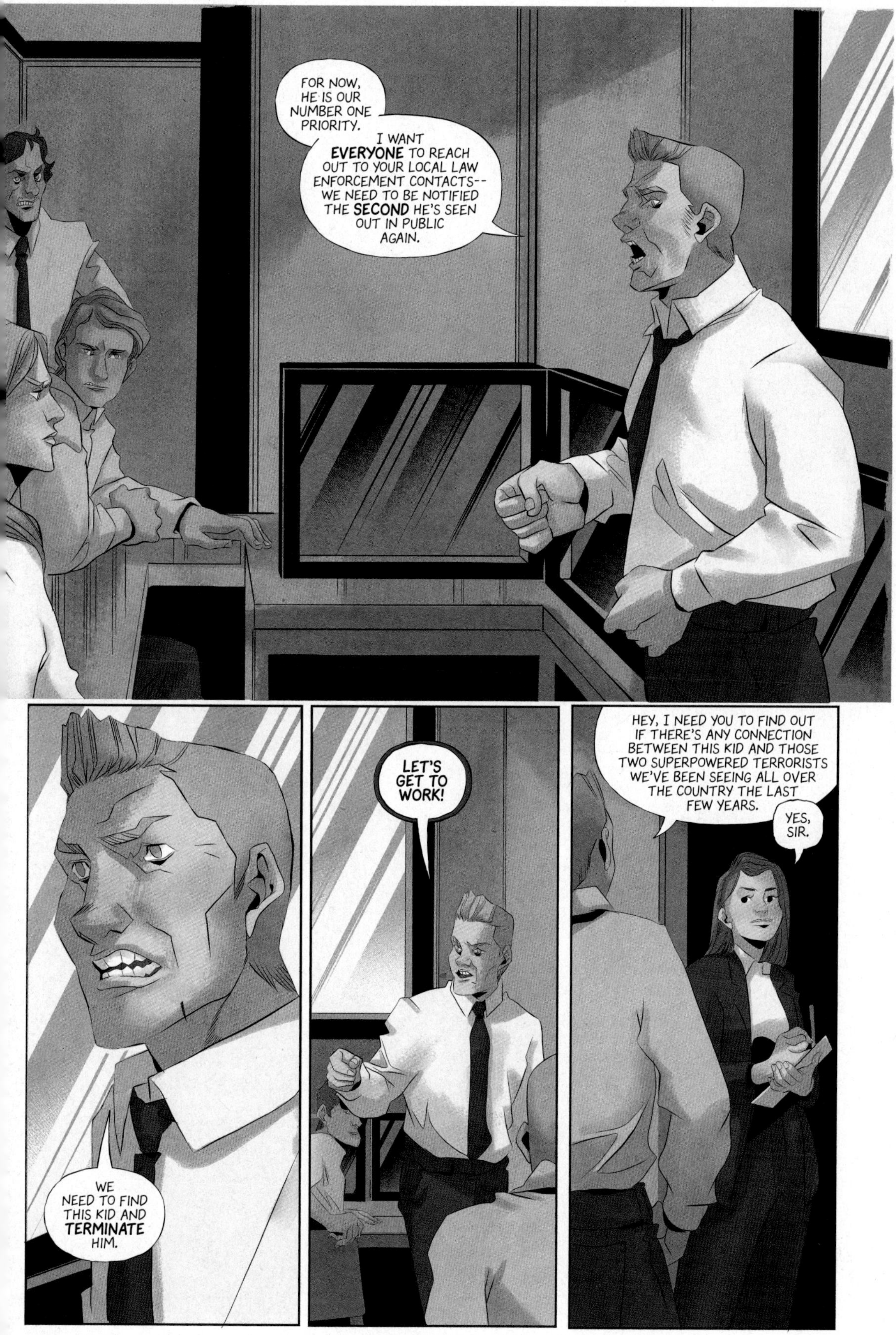
FOR NOW, HE IS OUR NUMBER ONE PRIORITY.
I WANT **EVERYONE** TO REACH OUT TO YOUR LOCAL LAW ENFORCEMENT CONTACTS-- WE NEED TO BE NOTIFIED THE **SECOND** HE'S SEEN OUT IN PUBLIC AGAIN.
WE NEED TO FIND THIS KID AND **TERMINATE** HIM.
LET'S GET TO WORK!
HEY, I NEED YOU TO FIND OUT IF THERE'S ANY CONNECTION BETWEEN THIS KID AND THOSE TWO SUPERPOWERED TERRORISTS WE'VE BEEN SEEING ALL OVER THE COUNTRY THE LAST FEW YEARS.
YES, SIR.

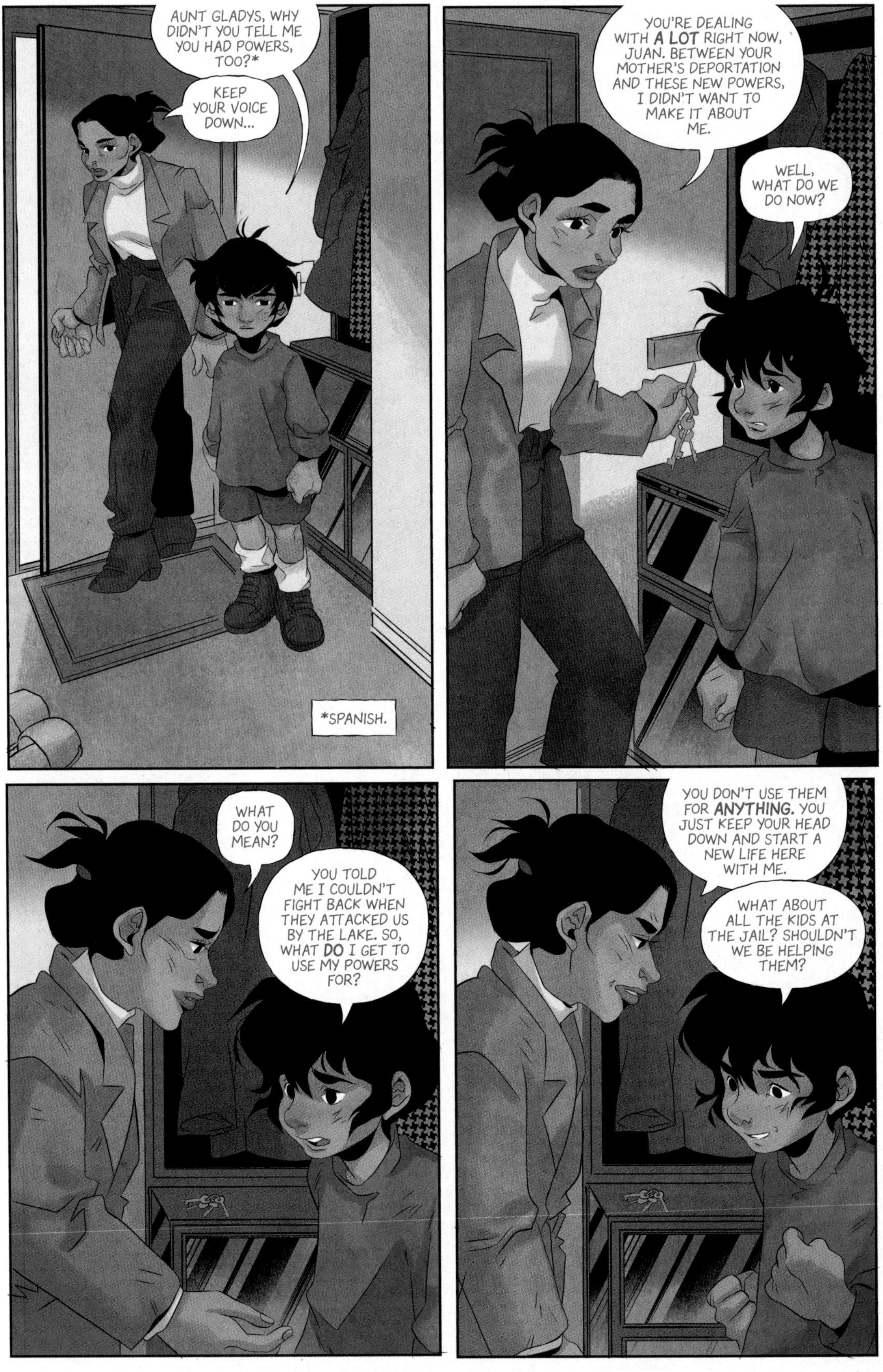
AUNT GLADYS, WHY DIDN'T YOU TELL ME YOU HAD POWERS, TOO?*
KEEP YOUR VOICE DOWN...
*SPANISH.
YOU'RE DEALING WITH A LOT RIGHT NOW, JUAN. BETWEEN YOUR MOTHER'S DEPORTATION AND THESE NEW POWERS, I DIDN'T WANT TO MAKE IT ABOUT ME.
WELL, WHAT DO WE DO NOW?
WHAT DO YOU MEAN?
YOU TOLD ME I COULDN'T FIGHT BACK WHEN THEY ATTACKED US BY THE LAKE. SO, WHAT DO I GET TO USE MY POWERS FOR?
YOU DON'T USE THEM FOR ANYTHING. YOU JUST KEEP YOUR HEAD DOWN AND START A NEW LIFE HERE WITH ME.
WHAT ABOUT ALL THE KIDS AT THE JAIL? SHOULDN'T WE BE HELPING THEM?

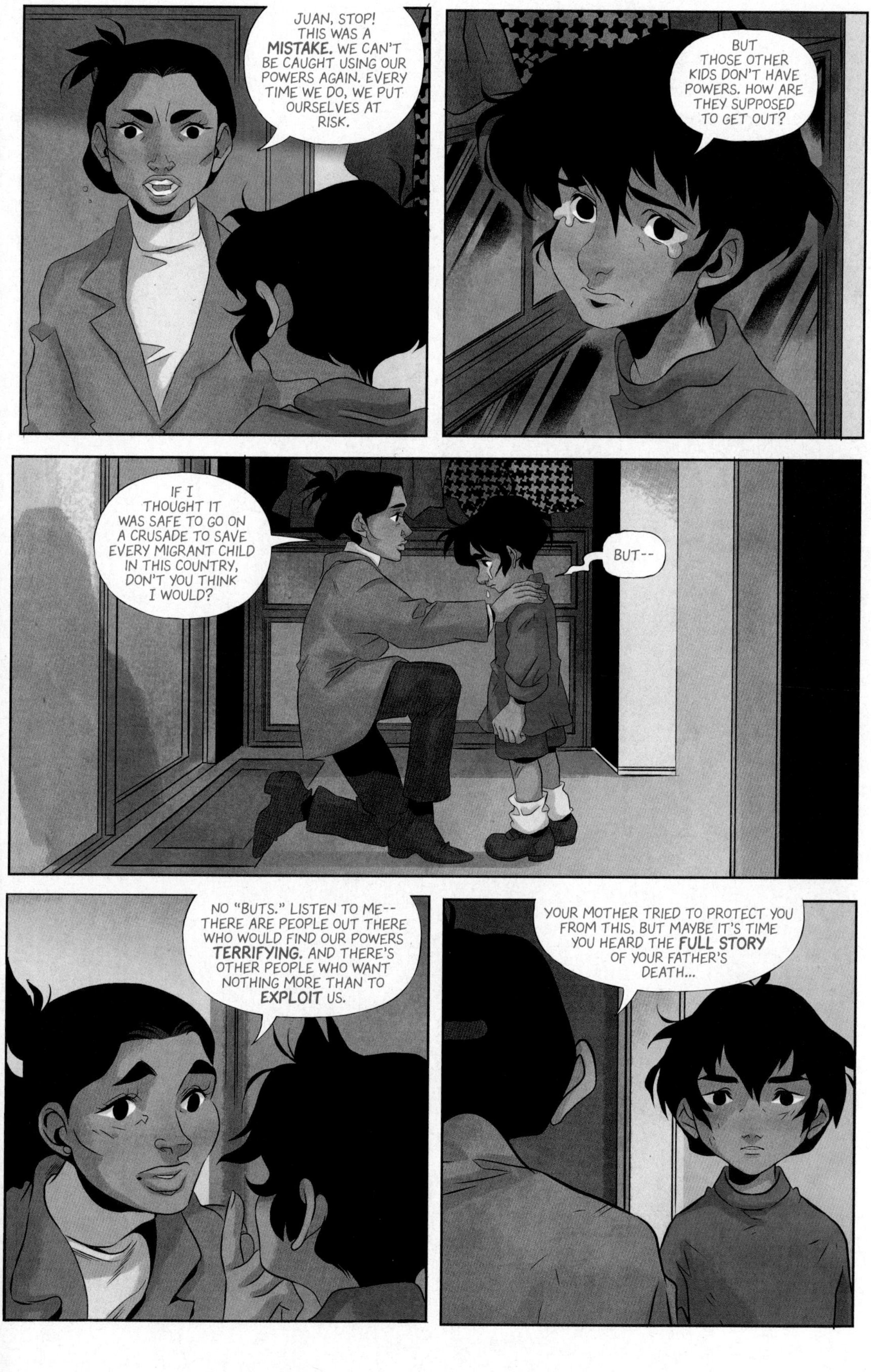
JUAN, STOP! THIS WAS A **MISTAKE.** WE CAN'T BE CAUGHT USING OUR POWERS AGAIN. EVERY TIME WE DO, WE PUT OURSELVES AT RISK.
BUT THOSE OTHER KIDS DON'T HAVE POWERS. HOW ARE THEY SUPPOSED TO GET OUT?
IF I THOUGHT IT WAS SAFE TO GO ON A CRUSADE TO SAVE EVERY MIGRANT CHILD IN THIS COUNTRY, DON'T YOU THINK I WOULD?
BUT--
NO "BUTS." LISTEN TO ME-- THERE ARE PEOPLE OUT THERE WHO WOULD FIND OUR POWERS **TERRIFYING.** AND THERE'S OTHER PEOPLE WHO WANT NOTHING MORE THAN TO **EXPLOIT** US.
YOUR MOTHER TRIED TO PROTECT YOU FROM THIS, BUT MAYBE IT'S TIME YOU HEARD THE **FULL STORY** OF YOUR FATHER'S DEATH...

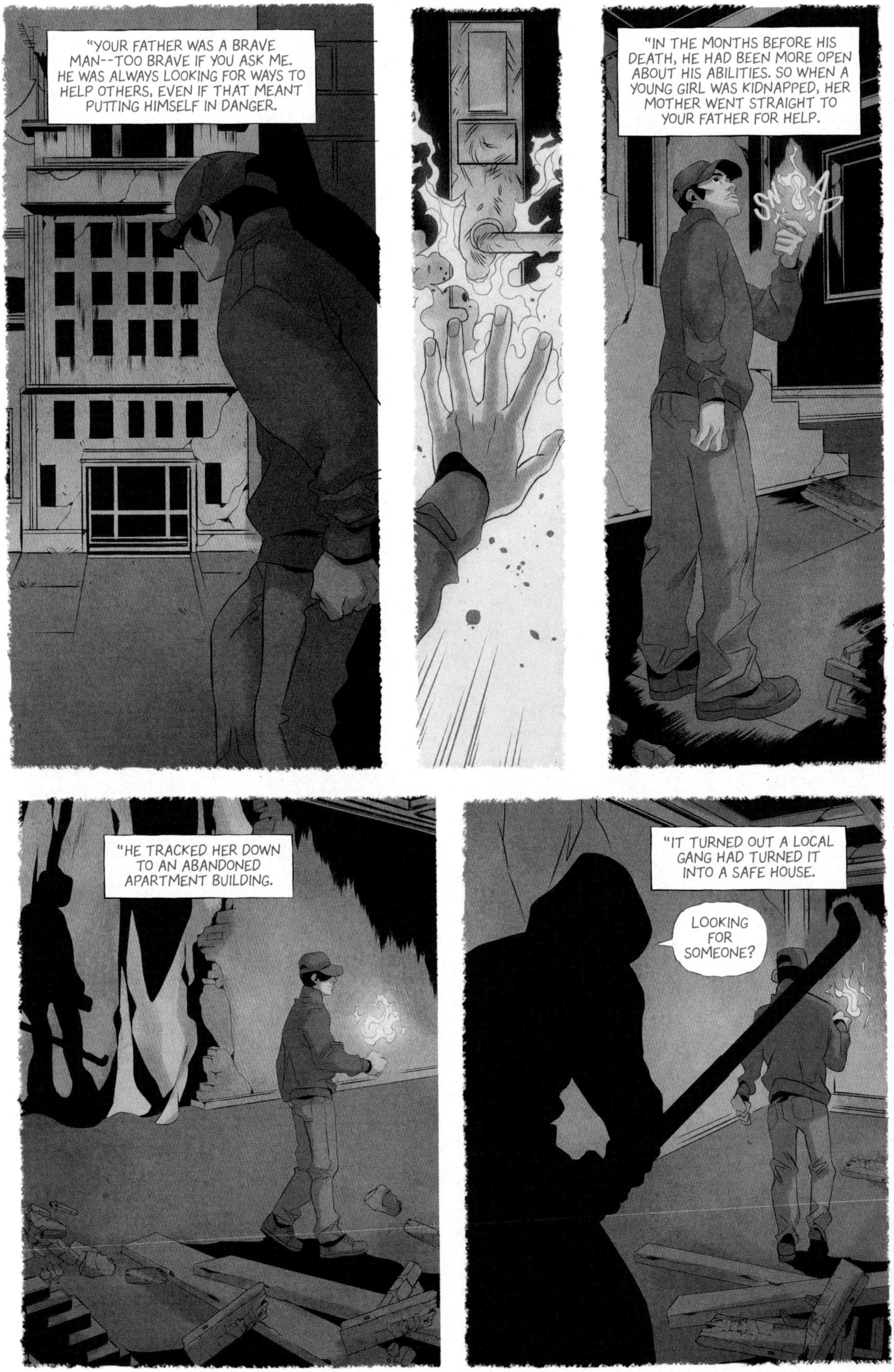
"YOUR FATHER WAS A BRAVE MAN--TOO BRAVE IF YOU ASK ME. HE WAS ALWAYS LOOKING FOR WAYS TO HELP OTHERS, EVEN IF THAT MEANT PUTTING HIMSELF IN DANGER.
"IN THE MONTHS BEFORE HIS DEATH, HE HAD BEEN MORE OPEN ABOUT HIS ABILITIES. SO WHEN A YOUNG GIRL WAS KIDNAPPED, HER MOTHER WENT STRAIGHT TO YOUR FATHER FOR HELP.
SNAP
"HE TRACKED HER DOWN TO AN ABANDONED APARTMENT BUILDING.
"IT TURNED OUT A LOCAL GANG HAD TURNED IT INTO A SAFE HOUSE.
LOOKING FOR SOMEONE?

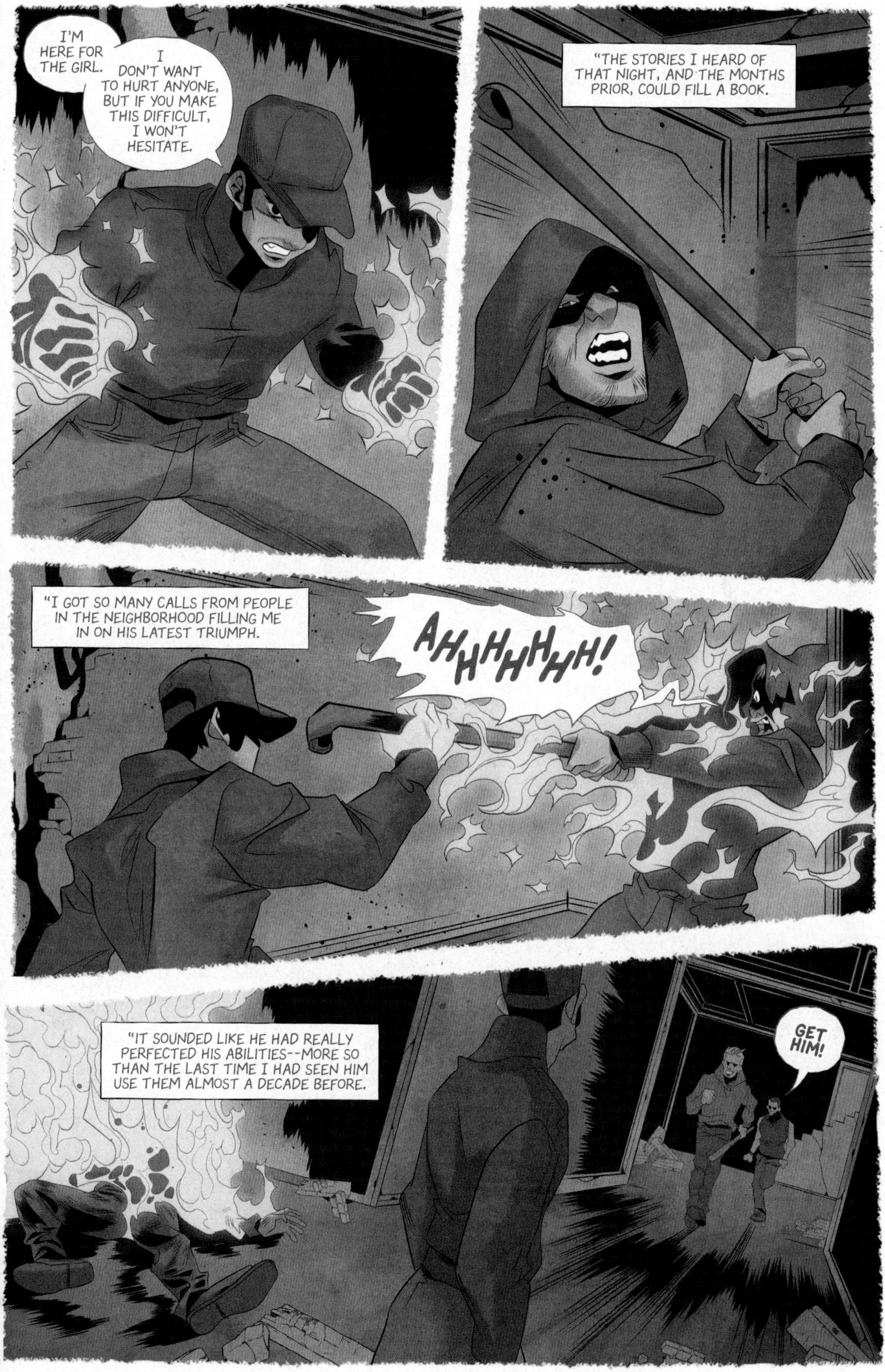
I'M HERE FOR THE GIRL.
I DON'T WANT TO HURT ANYONE, BUT IF YOU MAKE THIS DIFFICULT, I WON'T HESITATE.
"THE STORIES I HEARD OF THAT NIGHT, AND THE MONTHS PRIOR, COULD FILL A BOOK.
"I GOT SO MANY CALLS FROM PEOPLE IN THE NEIGHBORHOOD FILLING ME IN ON HIS LATEST TRIUMPH.
AHHHHHHH!
"IT SOUNDED LIKE HE HAD REALLY PERFECTED HIS ABILITIES--MORE SO THAN THE LAST TIME I HAD SEEN HIM USE THEM ALMOST A DECADE BEFORE.
GET HIM!

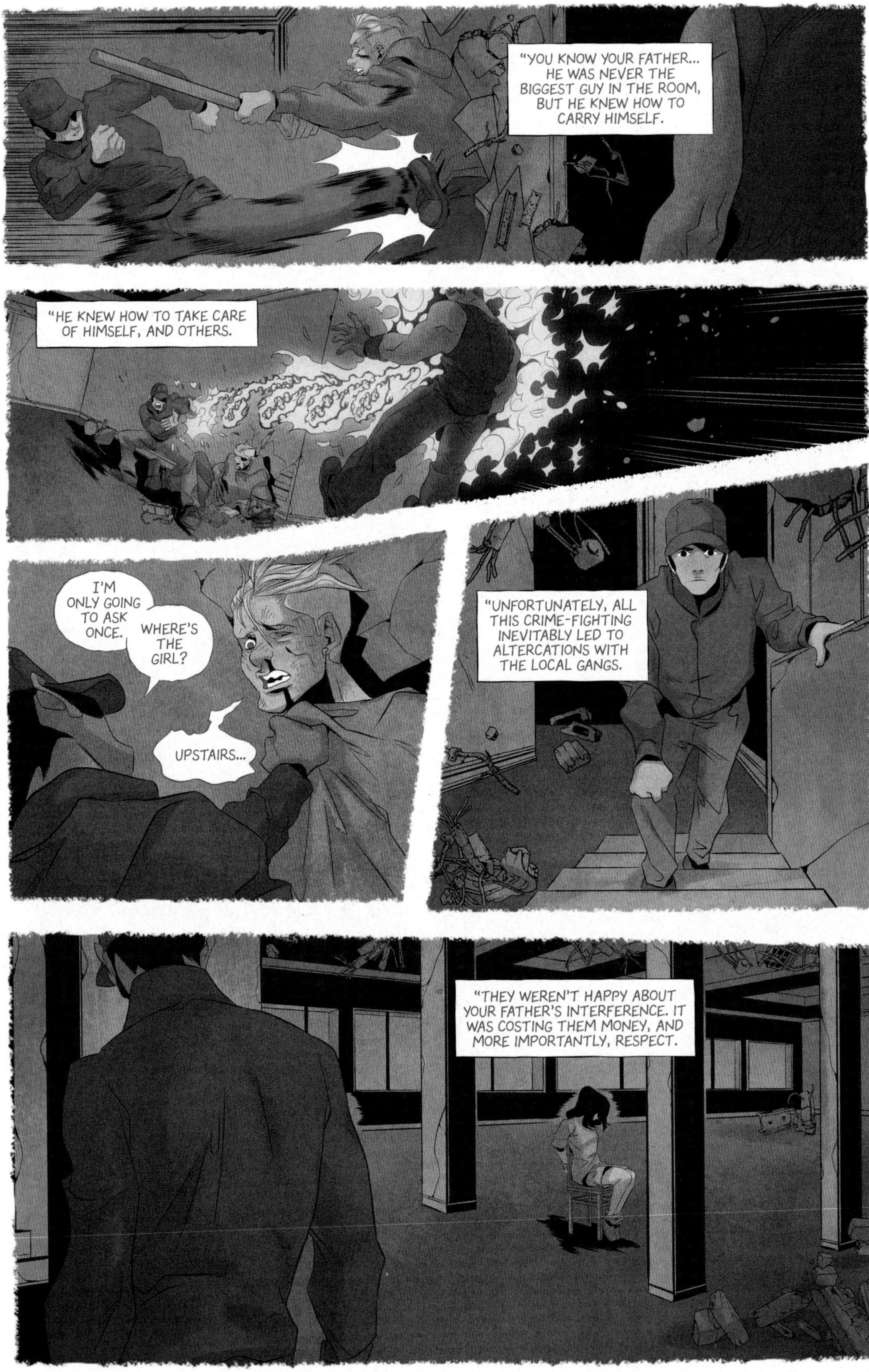
"YOU KNOW YOUR FATHER... HE WAS NEVER THE BIGGEST GUY IN THE ROOM, BUT HE KNEW HOW TO CARRY HIMSELF.
"HE KNEW HOW TO TAKE CARE OF HIMSELF, AND OTHERS.
I'M ONLY GOING TO ASK ONCE.
WHERE'S THE GIRL?
UPSTAIRS...
"UNFORTUNATELY, ALL THIS CRIME-FIGHTING INEVITABLY LED TO ALTERCATIONS WITH THE LOCAL GANGS.
"THEY WEREN'T HAPPY ABOUT YOUR FATHER'S INTERFERENCE. IT WAS COSTING THEM MONEY, AND MORE IMPORTANTLY, RESPECT.

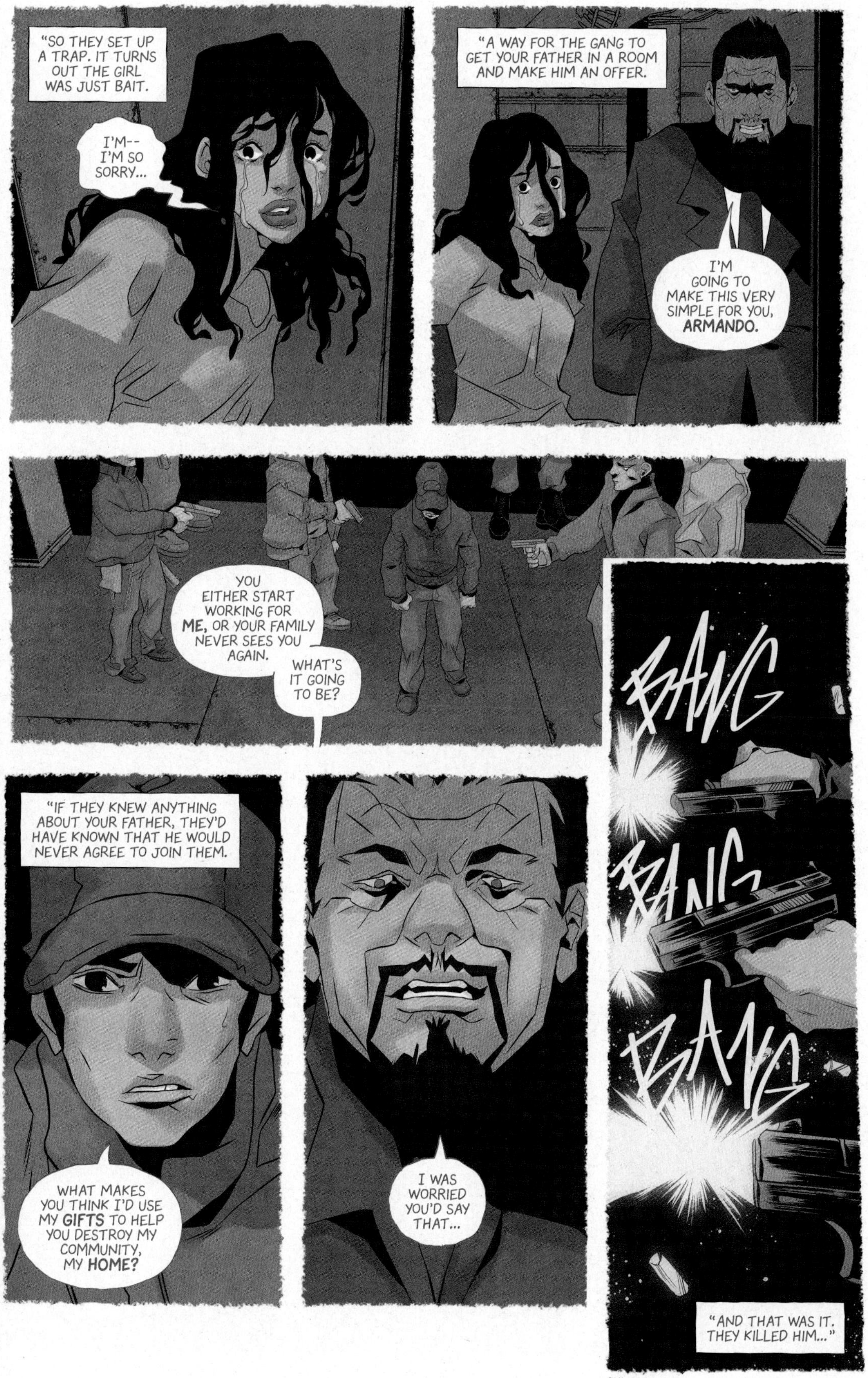
"SO THEY SET UP A TRAP. IT TURNS OUT THE GIRL WAS JUST BAIT.
I'M-- I'M SO SORRY...
"A WAY FOR THE GANG TO GET YOUR FATHER IN A ROOM AND MAKE HIM AN OFFER.
I'M GOING TO MAKE THIS VERY SIMPLE FOR YOU, **ARMANDO.**
YOU EITHER START WORKING FOR **ME,** OR YOUR FAMILY NEVER SEES YOU AGAIN.
WHAT'S IT GOING TO BE?
"IF THEY KNEW ANYTHING ABOUT YOUR FATHER, THEY'D HAVE KNOWN THAT HE WOULD NEVER AGREE TO JOIN THEM.
WHAT MAKES YOU THINK I'D USE MY **GIFTS** TO HELP YOU DESTROY MY COMMUNITY, MY **HOME?**
I WAS WORRIED YOU'D SAY THAT...
BANG
BANG
BANG
"AND THAT WAS IT. THEY KILLED HIM..."

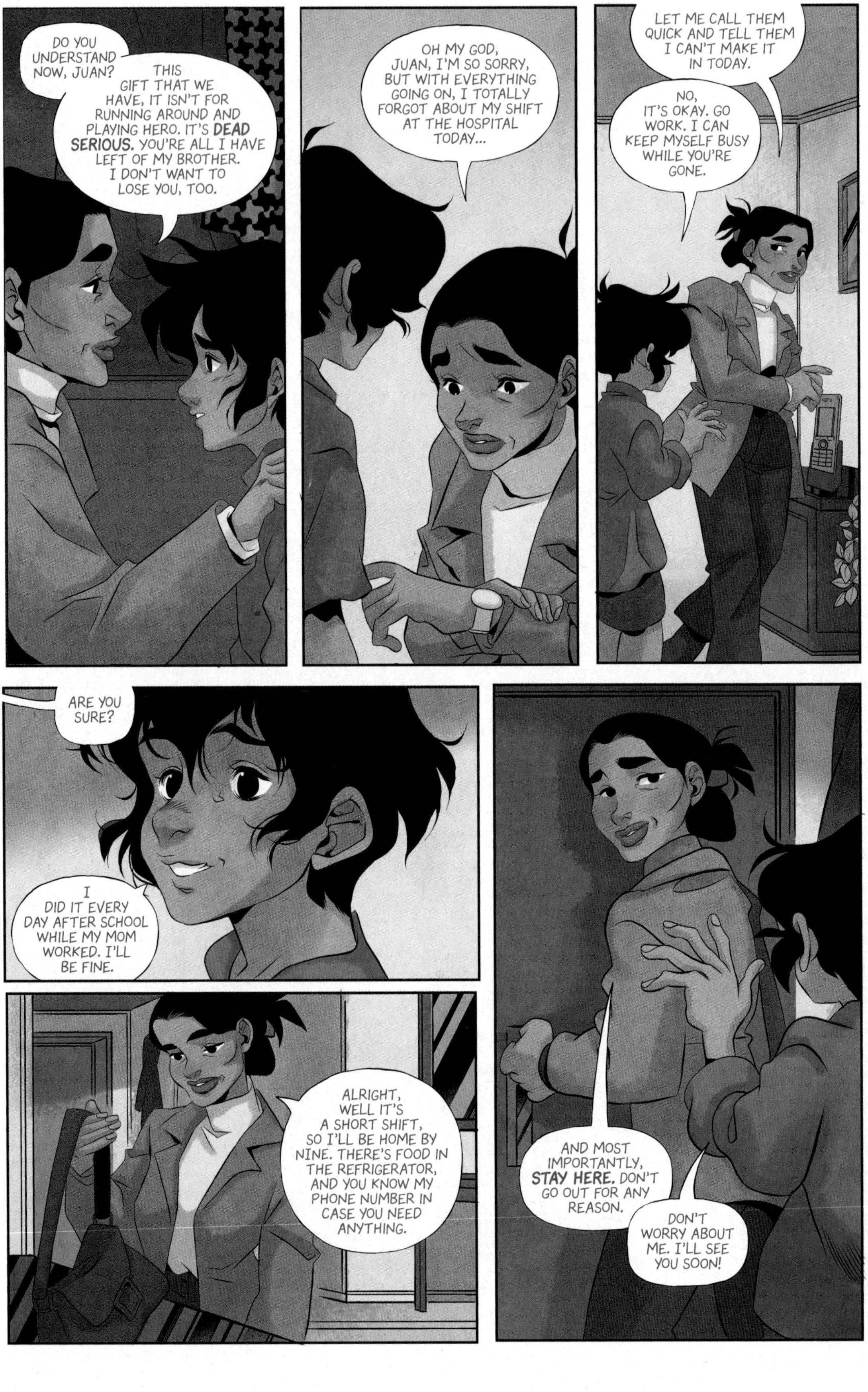
DO YOU UNDERSTAND NOW, JUAN?
THIS GIFT THAT WE HAVE, IT ISN'T FOR RUNNING AROUND AND PLAYING HERO. IT'S **DEAD SERIOUS.** YOU'RE ALL I HAVE LEFT OF MY BROTHER. I DON'T WANT TO LOSE YOU, TOO.
OH MY GOD, JUAN, I'M SO SORRY, BUT WITH EVERYTHING GOING ON, I TOTALLY FORGOT ABOUT MY SHIFT AT THE HOSPITAL TODAY...
LET ME CALL THEM QUICK AND TELL THEM I CAN'T MAKE IT IN TODAY.
NO, IT'S OKAY. GO WORK. I CAN KEEP MYSELF BUSY WHILE YOU'RE GONE.
ARE YOU SURE?
I DID IT EVERY DAY AFTER SCHOOL WHILE MY MOM WORKED. I'LL BE FINE.
ALRIGHT, WELL IT'S A SHORT SHIFT, SO I'LL BE HOME BY NINE. THERE'S FOOD IN THE REFRIGERATOR, AND YOU KNOW MY PHONE NUMBER IN CASE YOU NEED ANYTHING.
AND MOST IMPORTANTLY, **STAY HERE.** DON'T GO OUT FOR ANY REASON.
DON'T WORRY ABOUT ME. I'LL SEE YOU SOON!

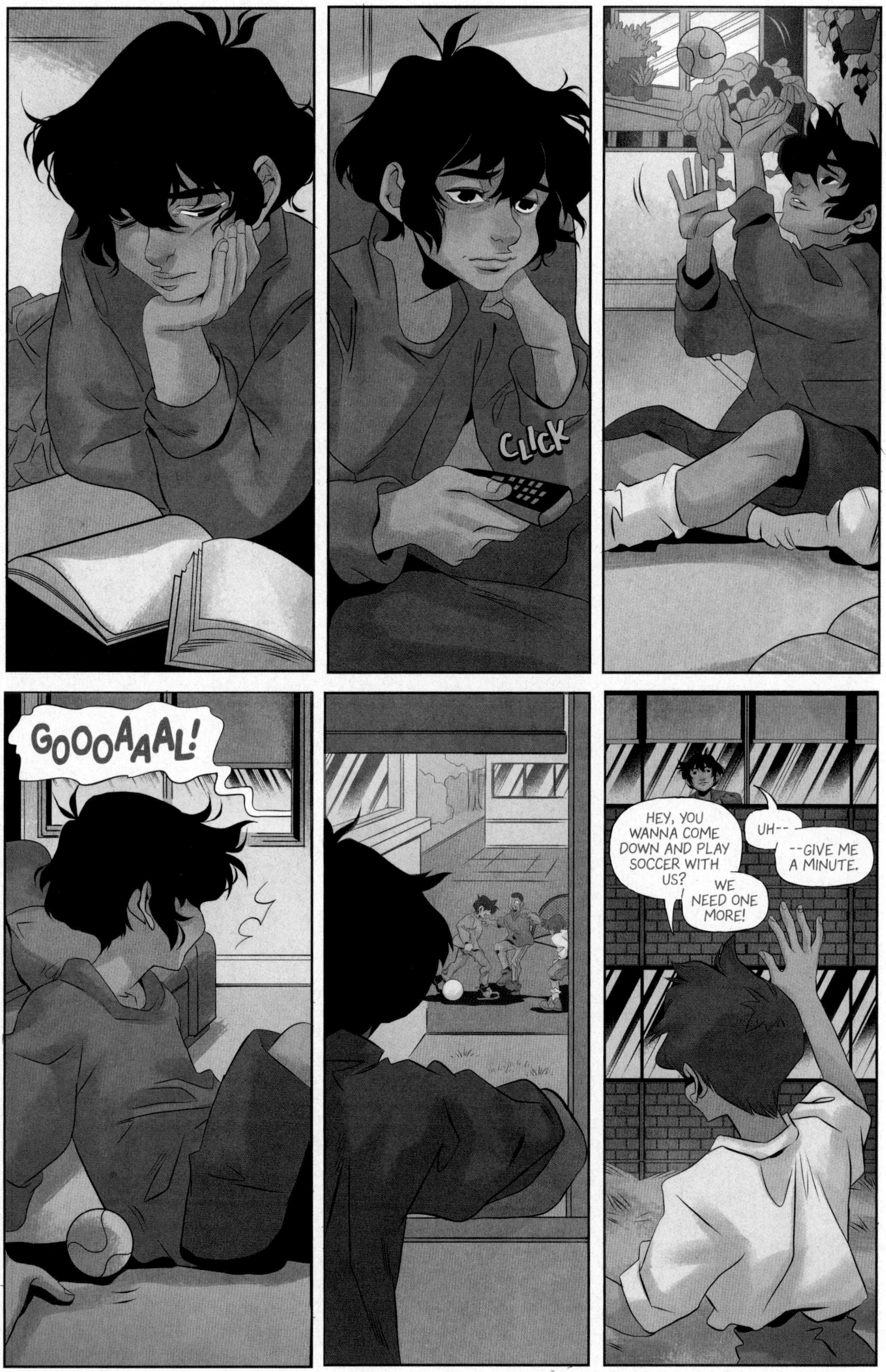
CLICK
GOOOAAAL!
HEY, YOU WANNA COME DOWN AND PLAY SOCCER WITH US?
WE NEED ONE MORE!
UH--
--GIVE ME A MINUTE.

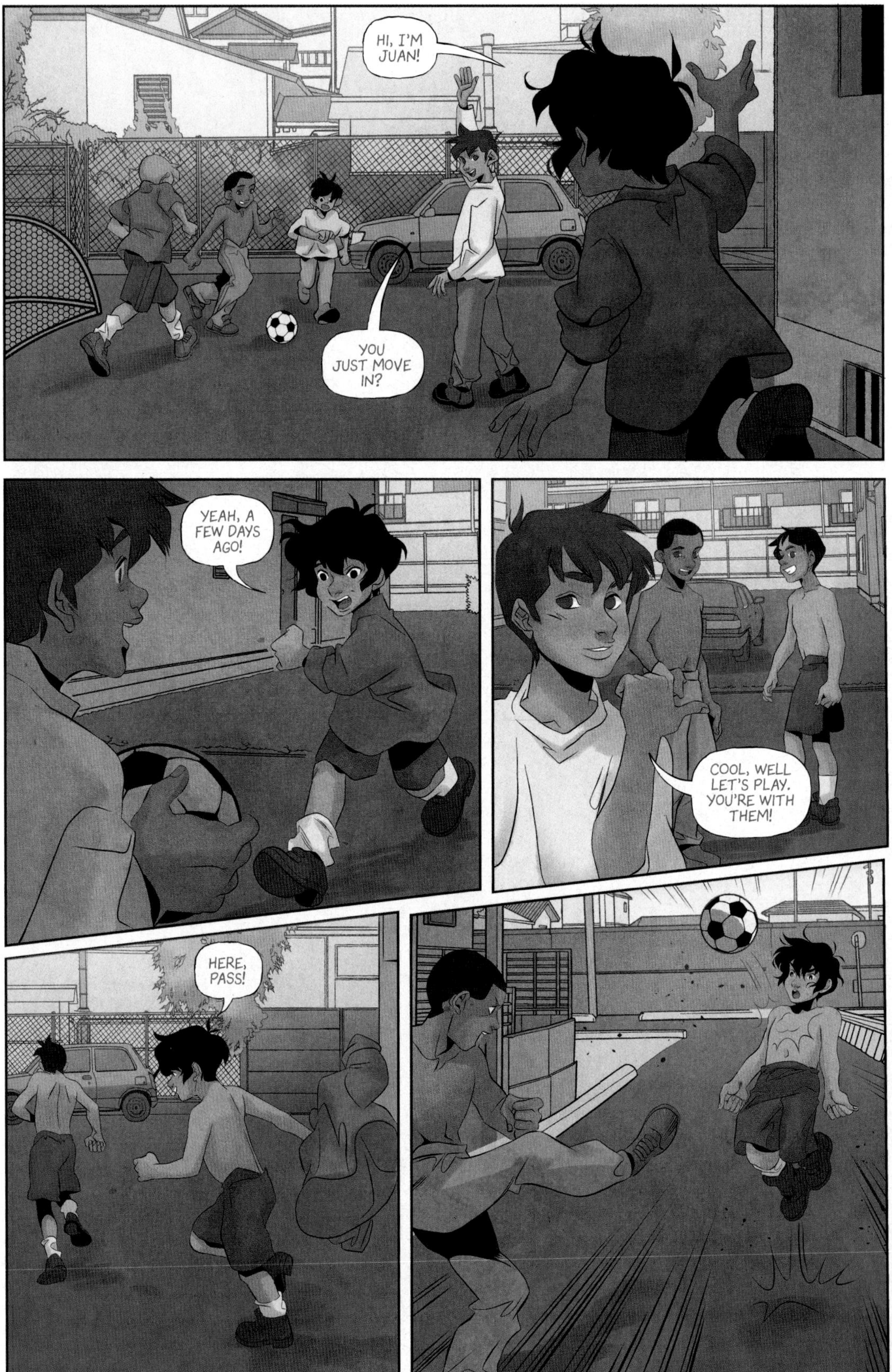
HI, I'M JUAN!
YOU JUST MOVE IN?
YEAH, A FEW DAYS AGO!
COOL, WELL LET'S PLAY. YOU'RE WITH THEM!
HERE, PASS!

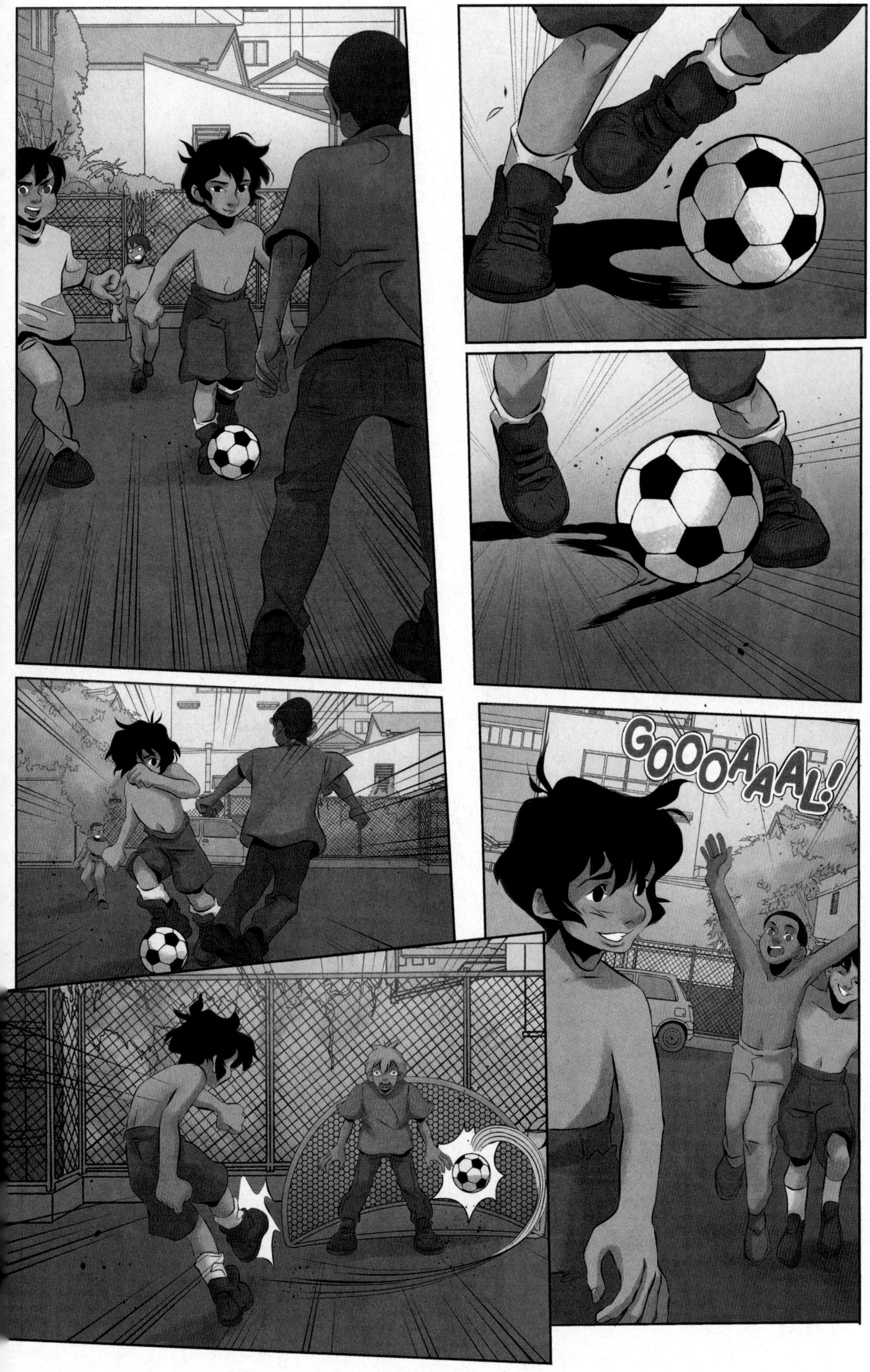
GOOOAAAL!

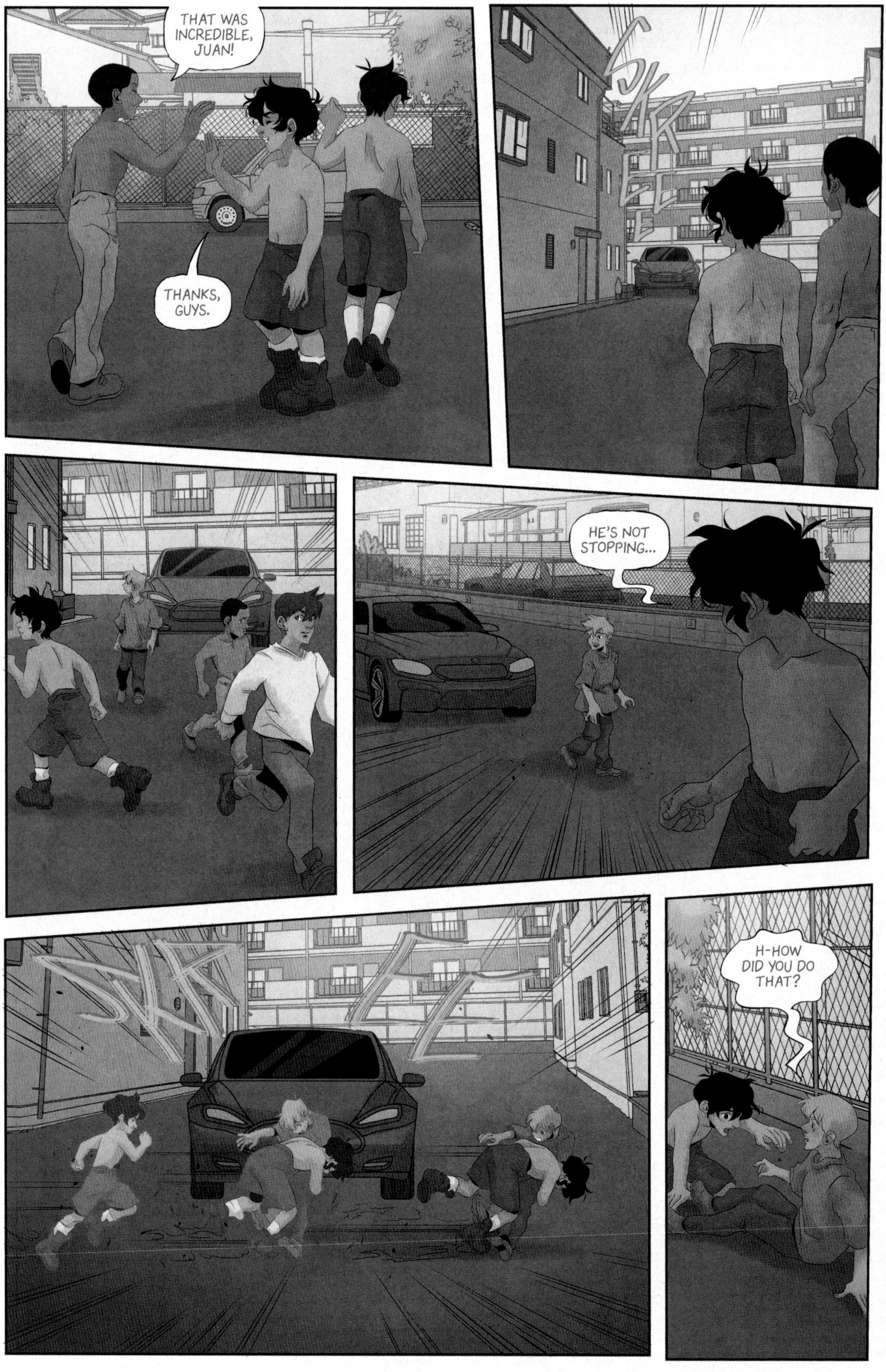
THAT WAS INCREDIBLE, JUAN!
THANKS, GUYS.
SKREE
HE'S NOT STOPPING...
SKREE
H-HOW DID YOU DO THAT?

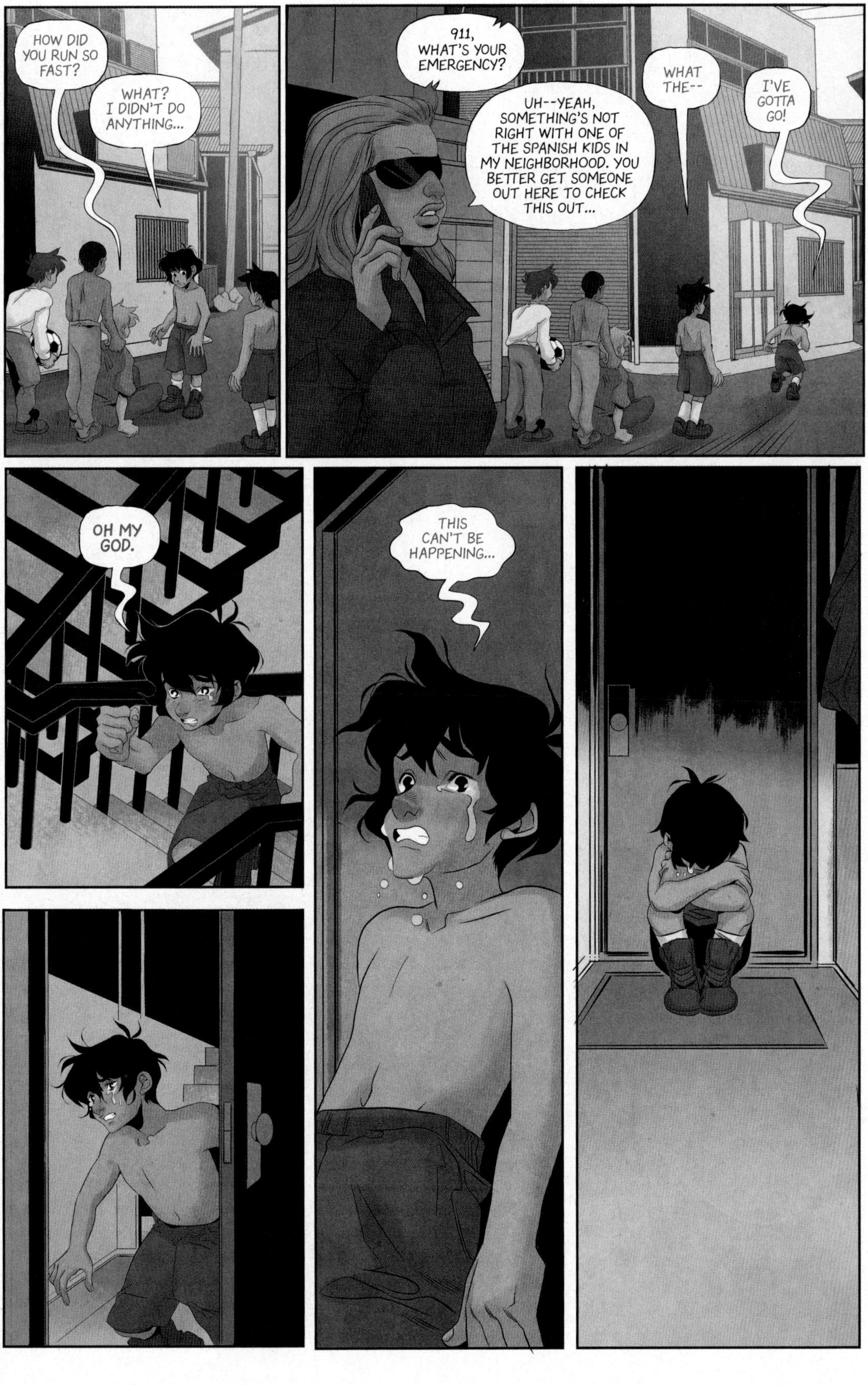
HOW DID YOU RUN SO FAST?
WHAT? I DIDN'T DO ANYTHING...
911, WHAT'S YOUR EMERGENCY?
UH--YEAH, SOMETHING'S NOT RIGHT WITH ONE OF THE SPANISH KIDS IN MY NEIGHBORHOOD. YOU BETTER GET SOMEONE OUT HERE TO CHECK THIS OUT...
WHAT THE--
I'VE GOTTA GO!
OH MY GOD.
THIS CAN'T BE HAPPENING...

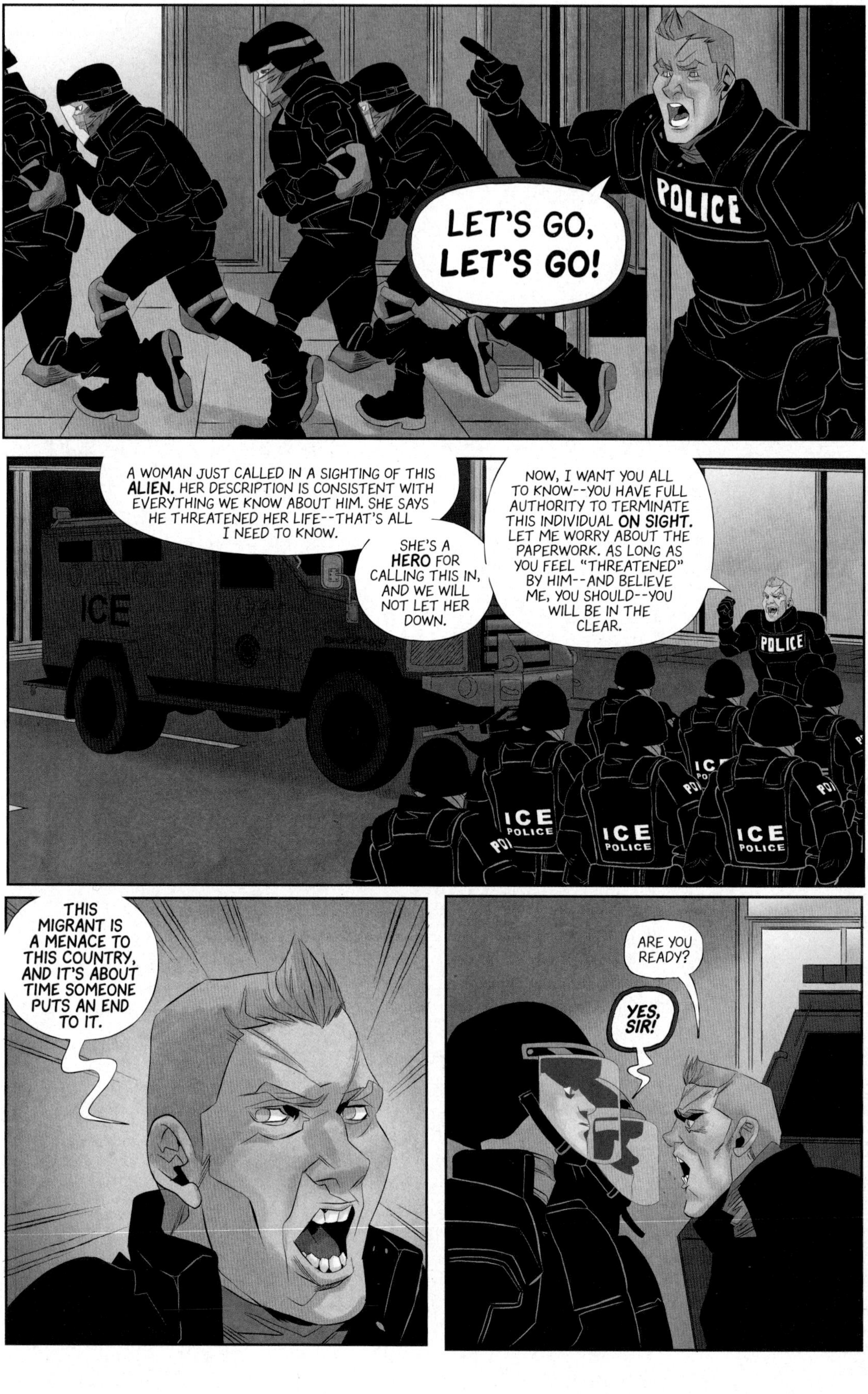
LET'S GO, LET'S GO!
A WOMAN JUST CALLED IN A SIGHTING OF THIS ALIEN. HER DESCRIPTION IS CONSISTENT WITH EVERYTHING WE KNOW ABOUT HIM. SHE SAYS HE THREATENED HER LIFE--THAT'S ALL I NEED TO KNOW.
SHE'S A HERO FOR CALLING THIS IN, AND WE WILL NOT LET HER DOWN.
NOW, I WANT YOU ALL TO KNOW--YOU HAVE FULL AUTHORITY TO TERMINATE THIS INDIVIDUAL ON SIGHT. LET ME WORRY ABOUT THE PAPERWORK. AS LONG AS YOU FEEL "THREATENED" BY HIM--AND BELIEVE ME, YOU SHOULD--YOU WILL BE IN THE CLEAR.
THIS MIGRANT IS A MENACE TO THIS COUNTRY, AND IT'S ABOUT TIME SOMEONE PUTS AN END TO IT.
ARE YOU READY?
YES, SIR!

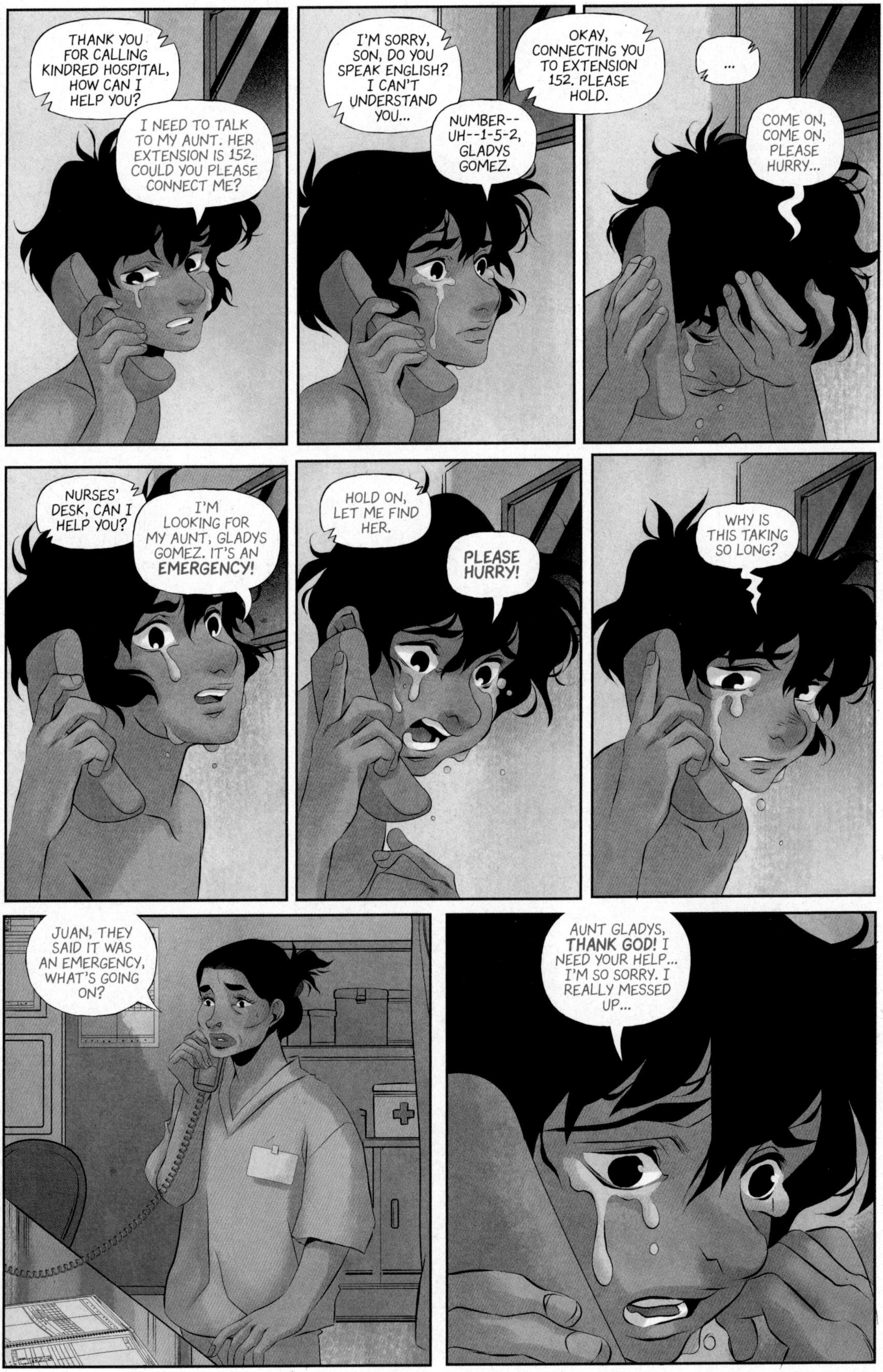
THANK YOU FOR CALLING KINDRED HOSPITAL, HOW CAN I HELP YOU?
I NEED TO TALK TO MY AUNT. HER EXTENSION IS 152. COULD YOU PLEASE CONNECT ME?
I'M SORRY, SON, DO YOU SPEAK ENGLISH? I CAN'T UNDERSTAND YOU...
NUMBER-- UH--1-5-2, GLADYS GOMEZ.
OKAY, CONNECTING YOU TO EXTENSION 152. PLEASE HOLD.
...
COME ON, COME ON, PLEASE HURRY...
NURSES' DESK, CAN I HELP YOU?
I'M LOOKING FOR MY AUNT, GLADYS GOMEZ. IT'S AN **EMERGENCY!**
HOLD ON, LET ME FIND HER.
PLEASE HURRY!
WHY IS THIS TAKING SO LONG?
JUAN, THEY SAID IT WAS AN EMERGENCY, WHAT'S GOING ON?
AUNT GLADYS, **THANK GOD!** I NEED YOUR HELP... I'M SO SORRY. I REALLY MESSED UP...

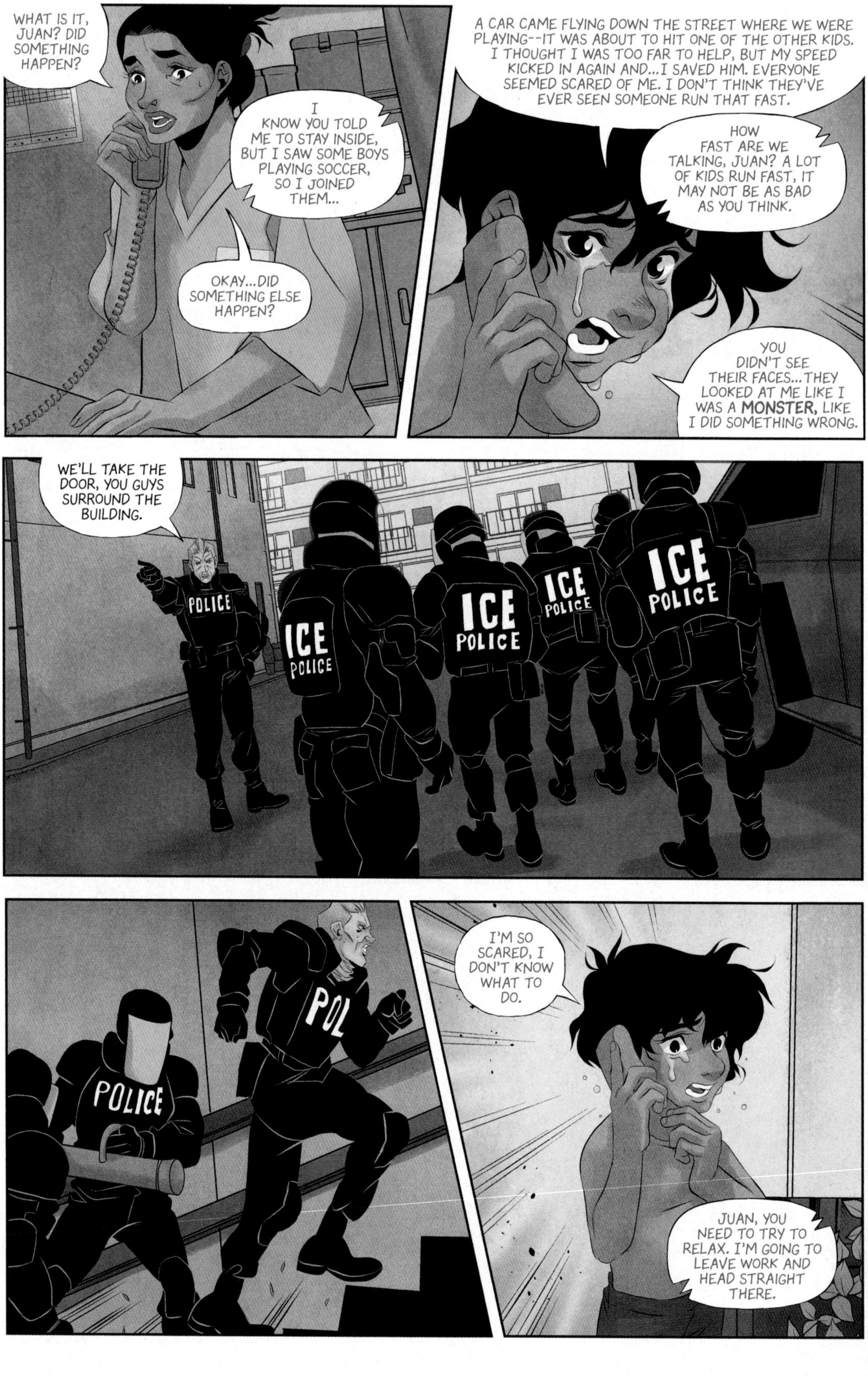

WHAT IS IT, JUAN? DID SOMETHING HAPPEN?
I KNOW YOU TOLD ME TO STAY INSIDE, BUT I SAW SOME BOYS PLAYING SOCCER, SO I JOINED THEM...
OKAY...DID SOMETHING ELSE HAPPEN?
A CAR CAME FLYING DOWN THE STREET WHERE WE WERE PLAYING--IT WAS ABOUT TO HIT ONE OF THE OTHER KIDS. I THOUGHT I WAS TOO FAR TO HELP, BUT MY SPEED KICKED IN AGAIN AND...I SAVED HIM. EVERYONE SEEMED SCARED OF ME. I DON'T THINK THEY'VE EVER SEEN SOMEONE RUN THAT FAST.
HOW FAST ARE WE TALKING, JUAN? A LOT OF KIDS RUN FAST, IT MAY NOT BE AS BAD AS YOU THINK.
YOU DIDN'T SEE THEIR FACES...THEY LOOKED AT ME LIKE I WAS A **MONSTER,** LIKE I DID SOMETHING WRONG.
WE'LL TAKE THE DOOR, YOU GUYS SURROUND THE BUILDING.
POLICE
ICE POLICE
ICE POLICE
ICE POLICE
ICE POLICE
POLICE
POL
I'M SO SCARED, I DON'T KNOW WHAT TO DO.
JUAN, YOU NEED TO TRY TO RELAX. I'M GOING TO LEAVE WORK AND HEAD STRAIGHT THERE.

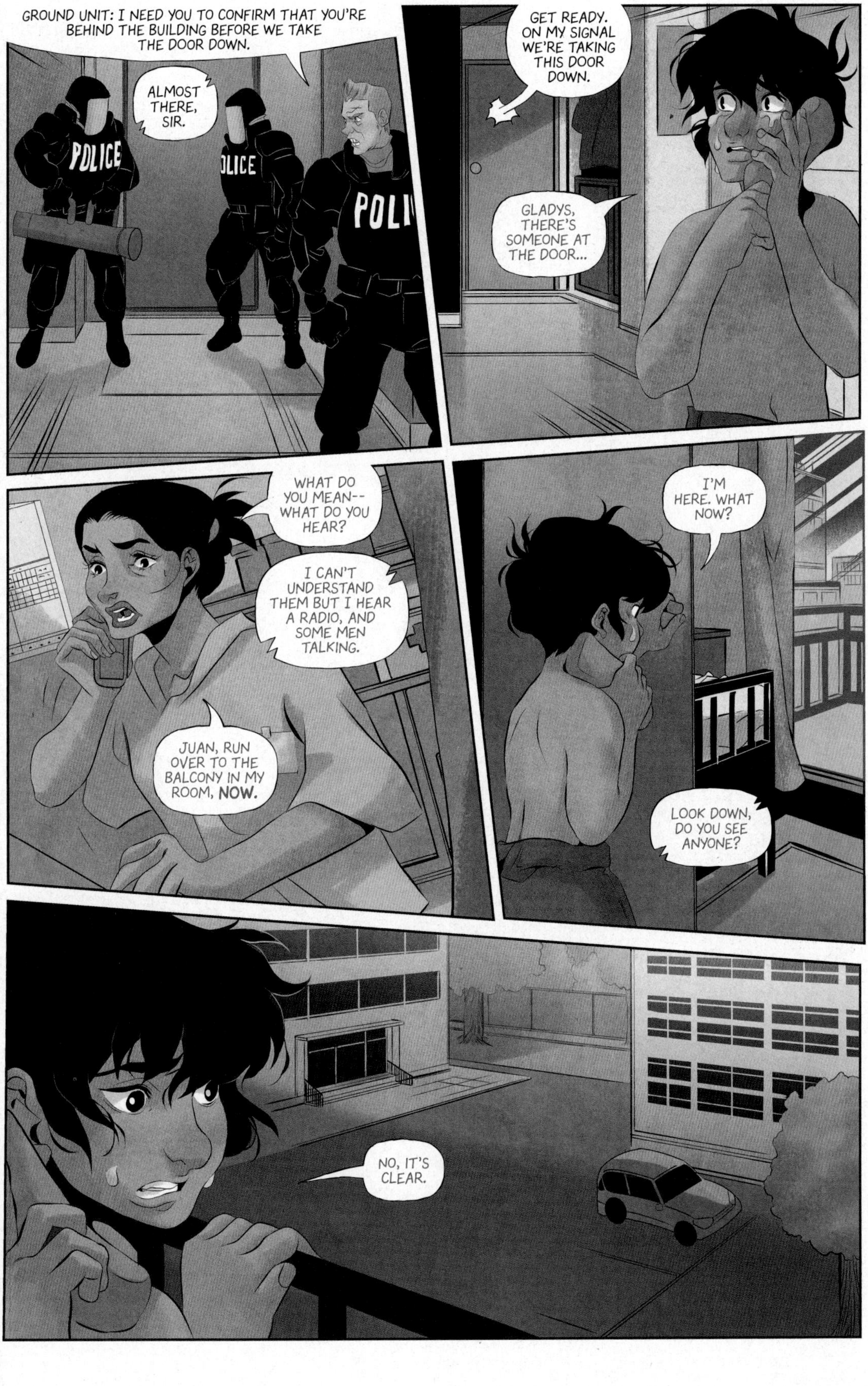
GROUND UNIT: I NEED YOU TO CONFIRM THAT YOU'RE BEHIND THE BUILDING BEFORE WE TAKE THE DOOR DOWN.
ALMOST THERE, SIR.
POLICE
POLICE
POLI
GET READY. ON MY SIGNAL WE'RE TAKING THIS DOOR DOWN.
GLADYS, THERE'S SOMEONE AT THE DOOR...
WHAT DO YOU MEAN-- WHAT DO YOU HEAR?
I CAN'T UNDERSTAND THEM BUT I HEAR A RADIO, AND SOME MEN TALKING.
JUAN, RUN OVER TO THE BALCONY IN MY ROOM, **NOW.**
I'M HERE. WHAT NOW?
LOOK DOWN, DO YOU SEE ANYONE?
NO, IT'S CLEAR.

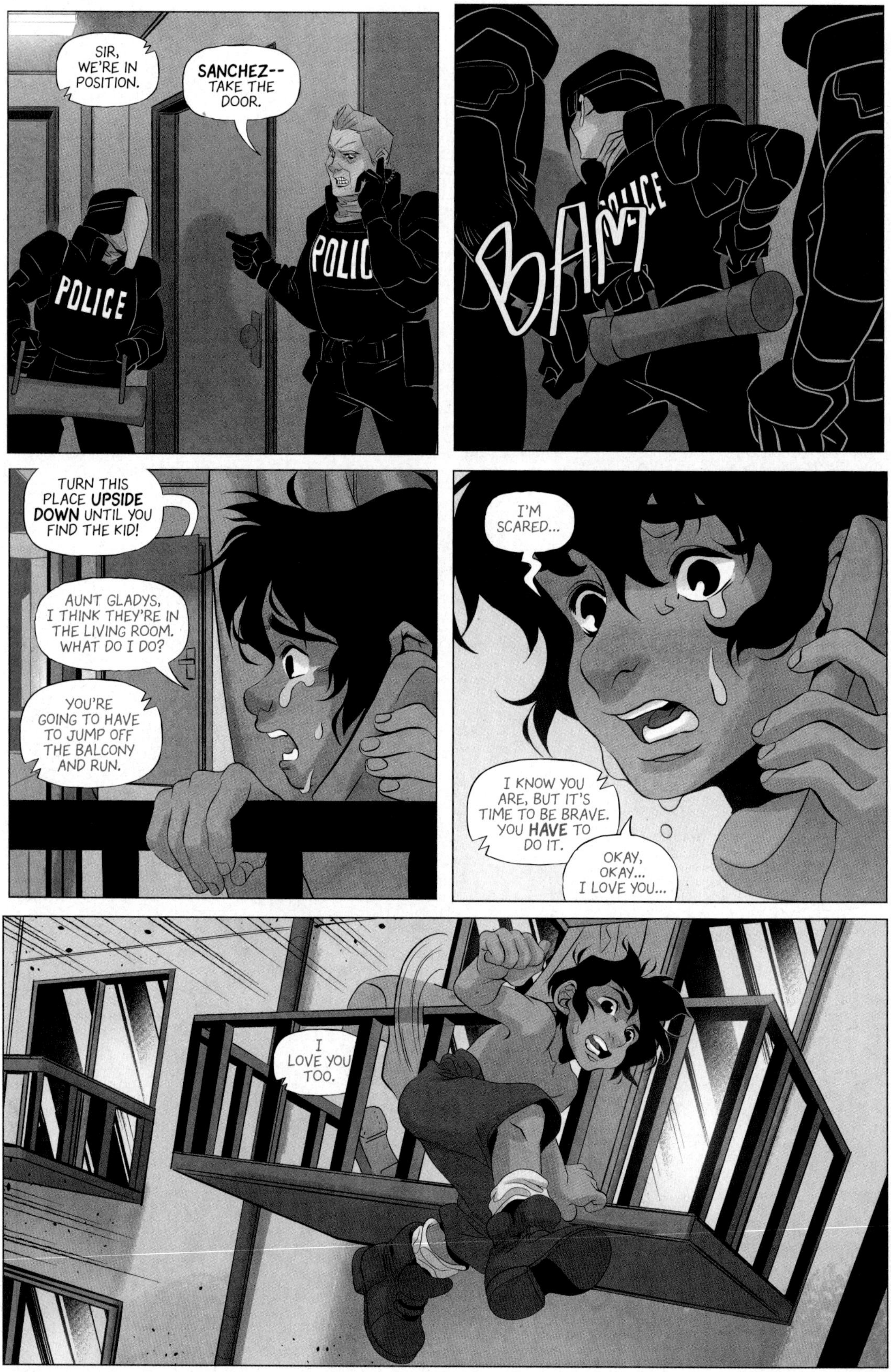
SIR, WE'RE IN POSITION.
SANCHEZ-- TAKE THE DOOR.
POLICE
POLICE
BAM
TURN THIS PLACE UPSIDE DOWN UNTIL YOU FIND THE KID!
AUNT GLADYS, I THINK THEY'RE IN THE LIVING ROOM. WHAT DO I DO?
YOU'RE GOING TO HAVE TO JUMP OFF THE BALCONY AND RUN.
I'M SCARED...
I KNOW YOU ARE, BUT IT'S TIME TO BE BRAVE. YOU HAVE TO DO IT.
OKAY, OKAY... I LOVE YOU...
I LOVE YOU TOO.

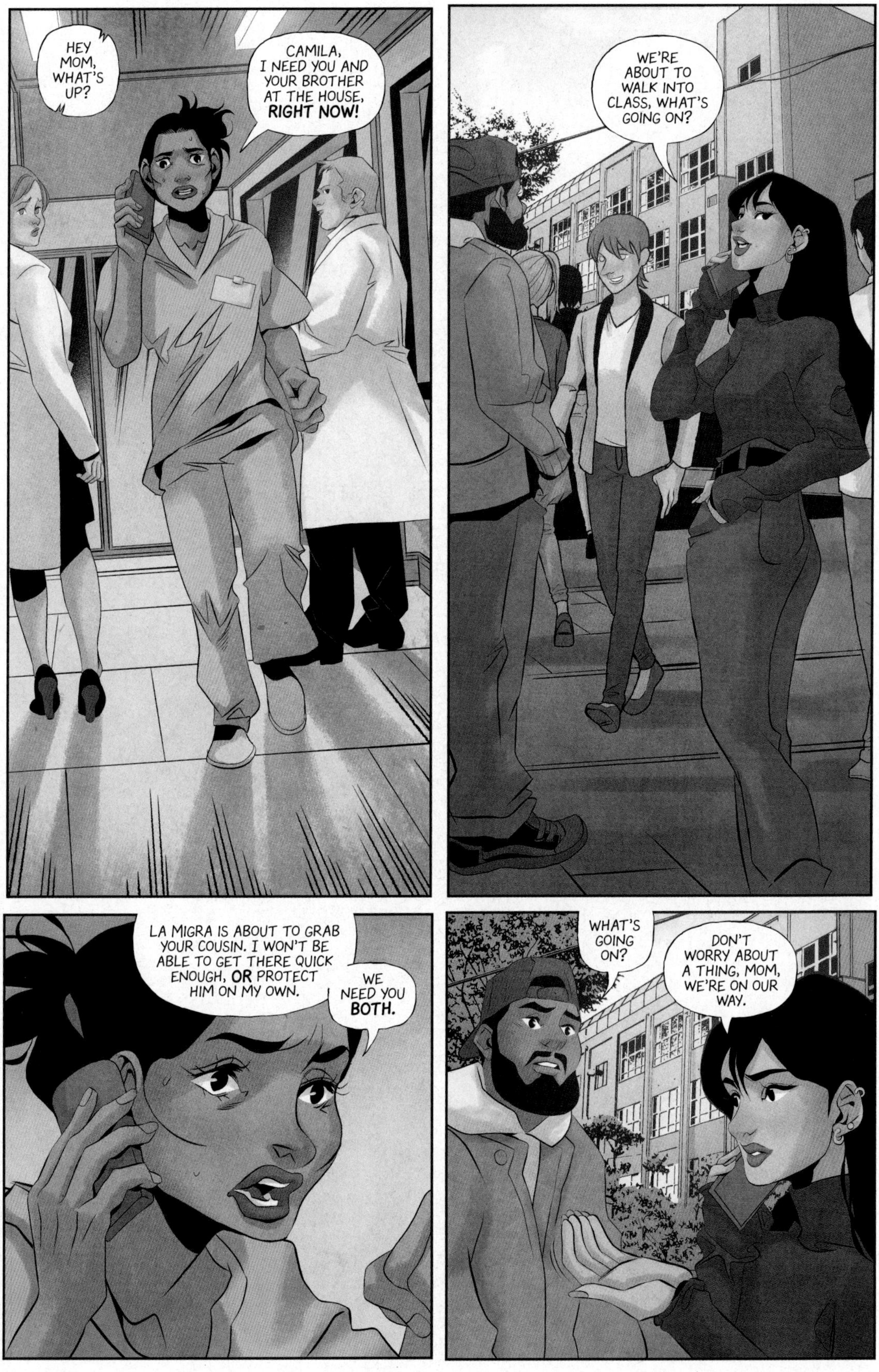
HEY MOM, WHAT'S UP?
CAMILA, I NEED YOU AND YOUR BROTHER AT THE HOUSE, **RIGHT NOW!**
WE'RE ABOUT TO WALK INTO CLASS, WHAT'S GOING ON?
LA MIGRA IS ABOUT TO GRAB YOUR COUSIN. I WON'T BE ABLE TO GET THERE QUICK ENOUGH, **OR** PROTECT HIM ON MY OWN.
WE NEED YOU **BOTH.**
WHAT'S GOING ON?
DON'T WORRY ABOUT A THING, MOM, WE'RE ON OUR WAY.

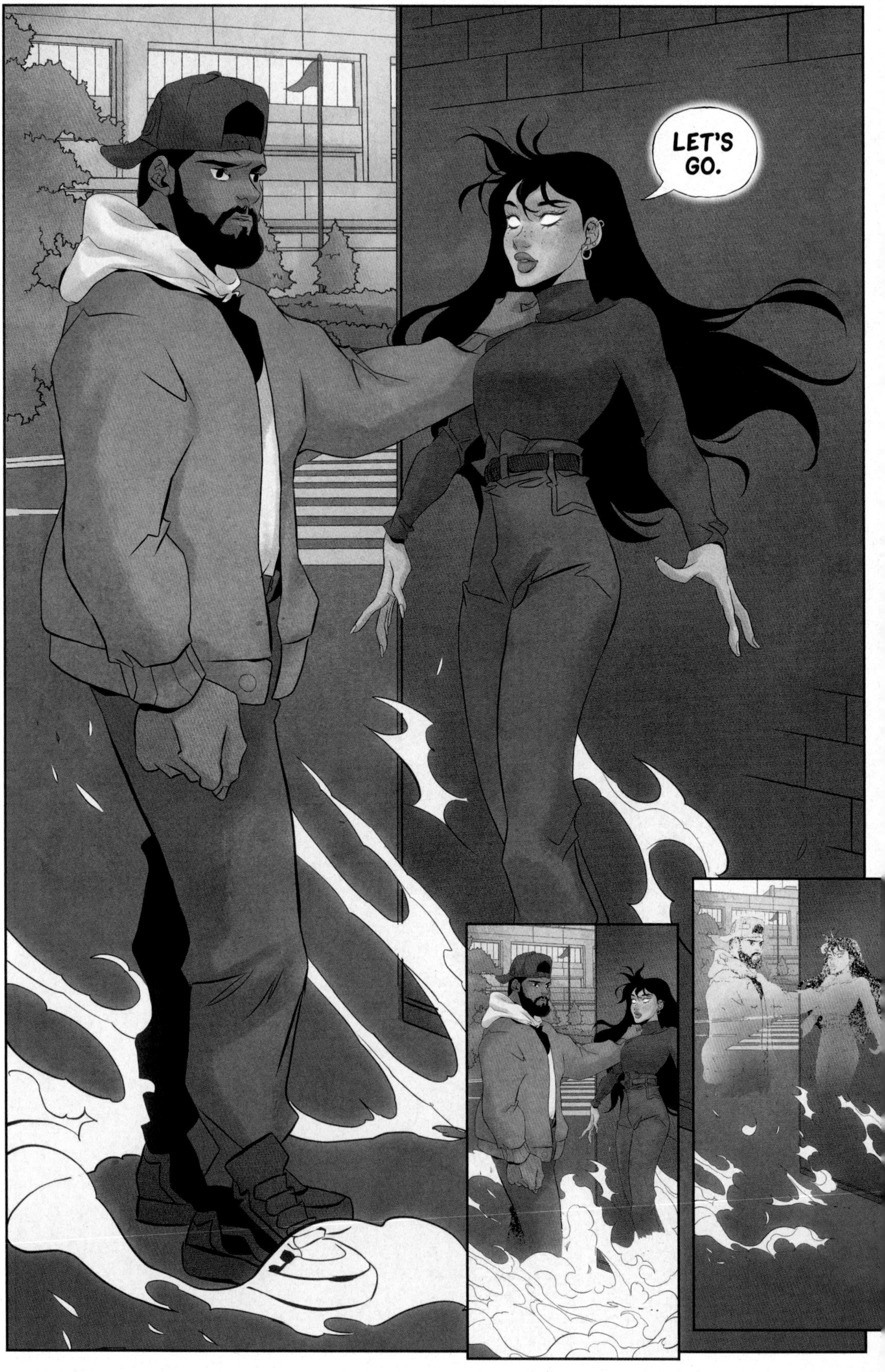
LET'S GO.

Chapter Five

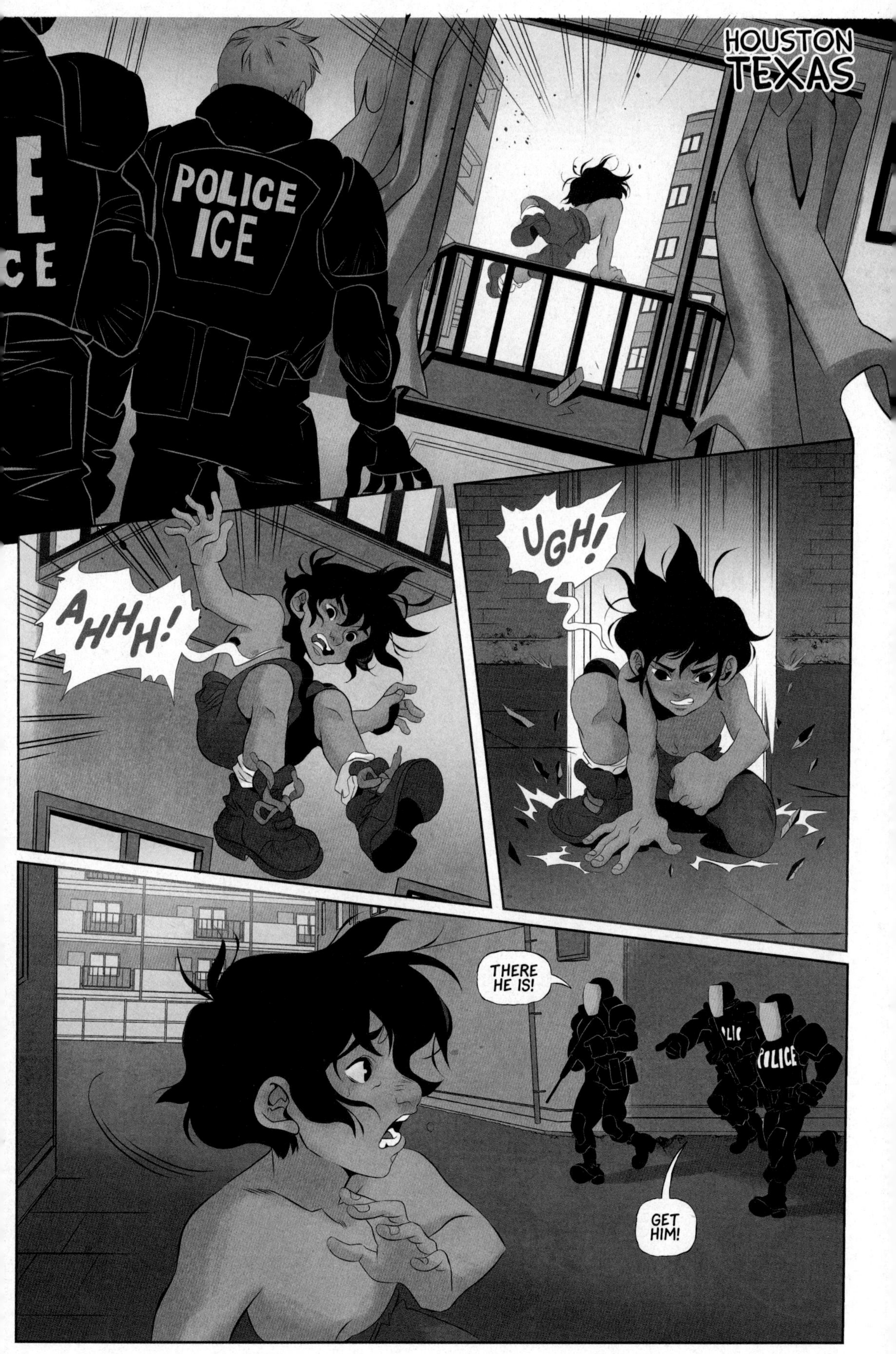
HOUSTON
TEXAS
POLICE
ICE
AHHH!
UGH!
THERE HE IS!
POLICE
GET HIM!

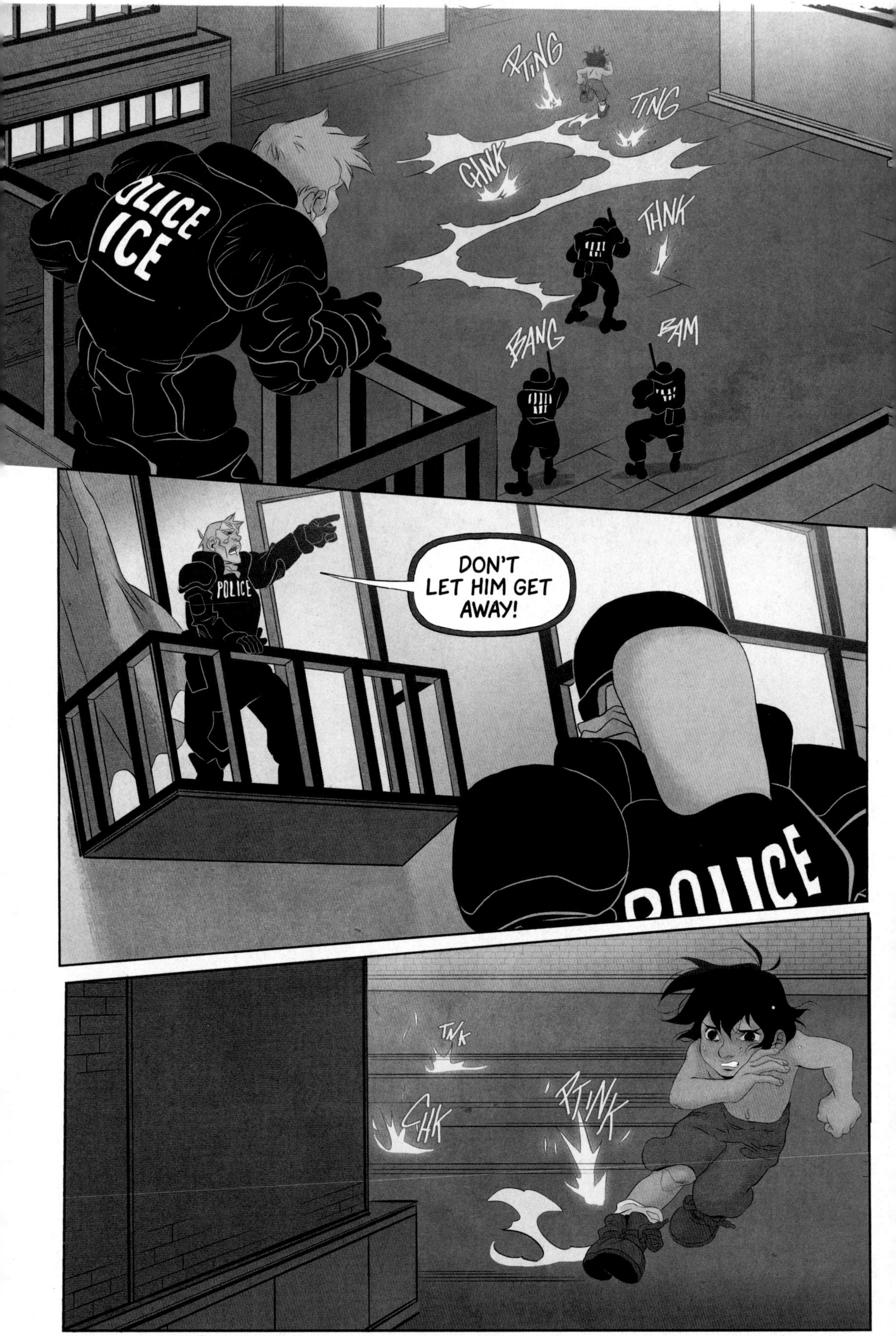
PTING
TING
CHNK
THNK
BANG
BAM
POLICE
DON'T LET HIM GET AWAY!
POLICE
TNK
CHK
PTINK

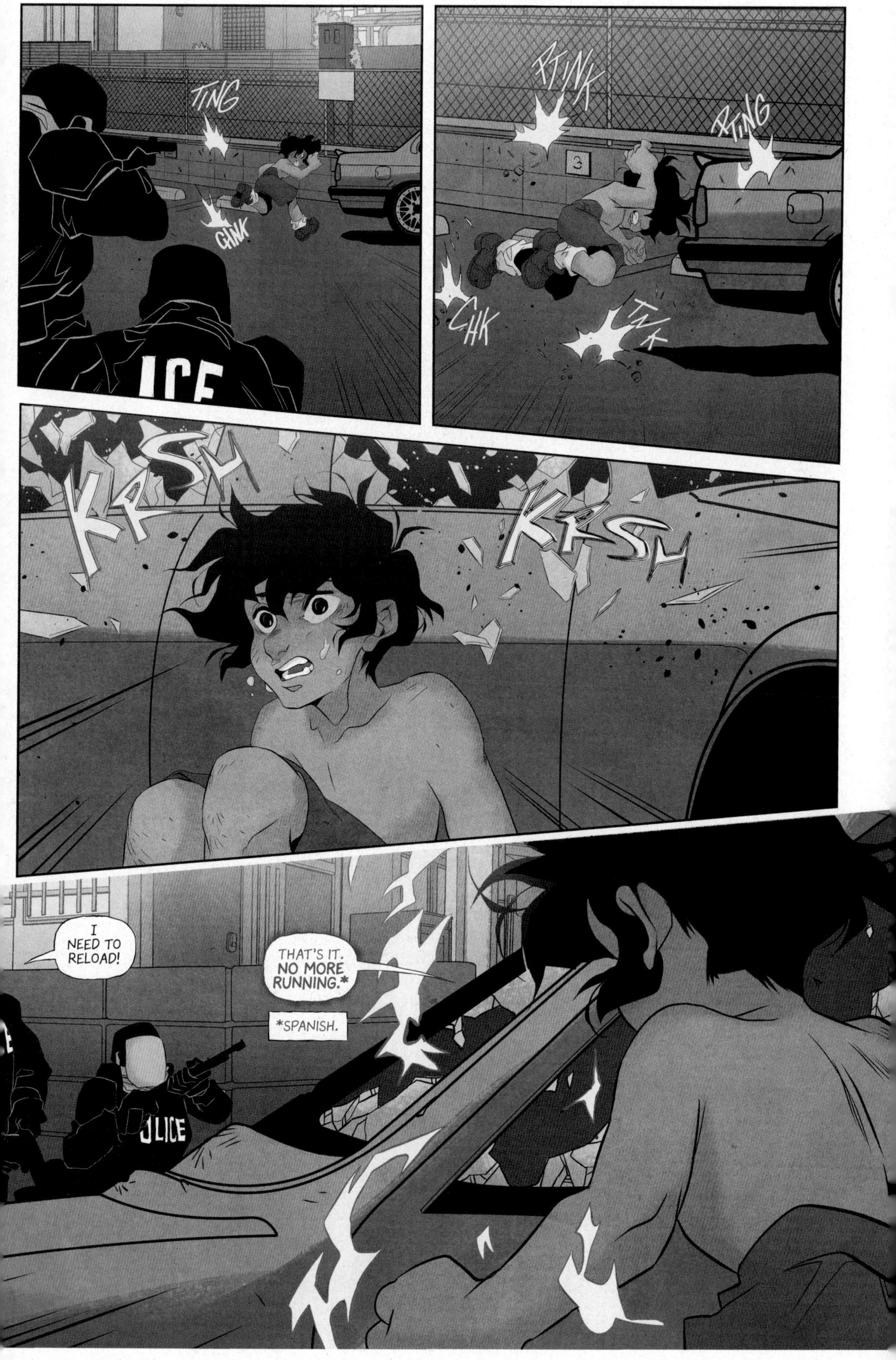
TING
CHINK
ICE
PTINK
PTING
CHK
TWK
KRSH
KRSH
I NEED TO RELOAD!
THAT'S IT. NO MORE RUNNING.*
*SPANISH.
LICE

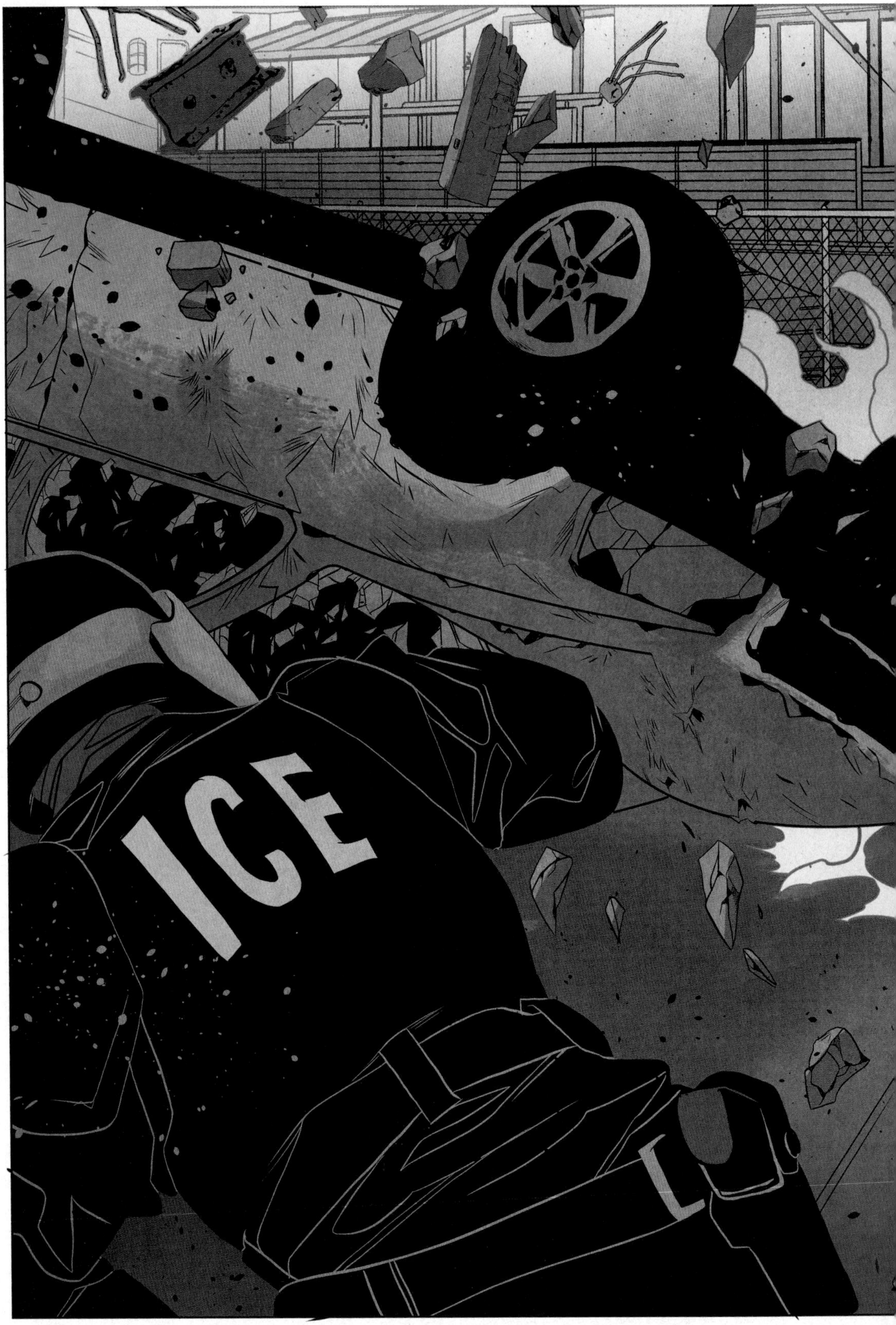
ICE

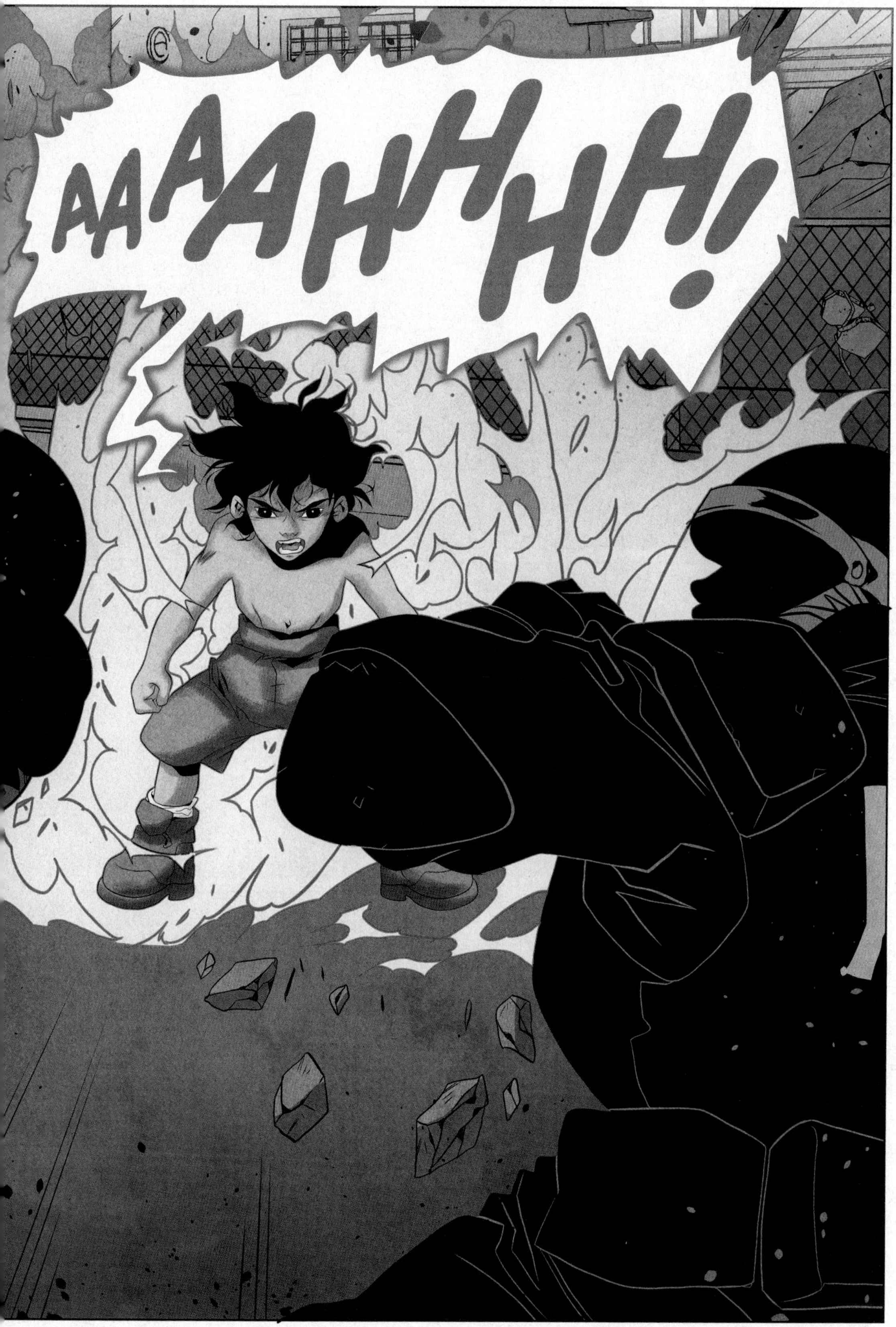
AAAAHHHH!!

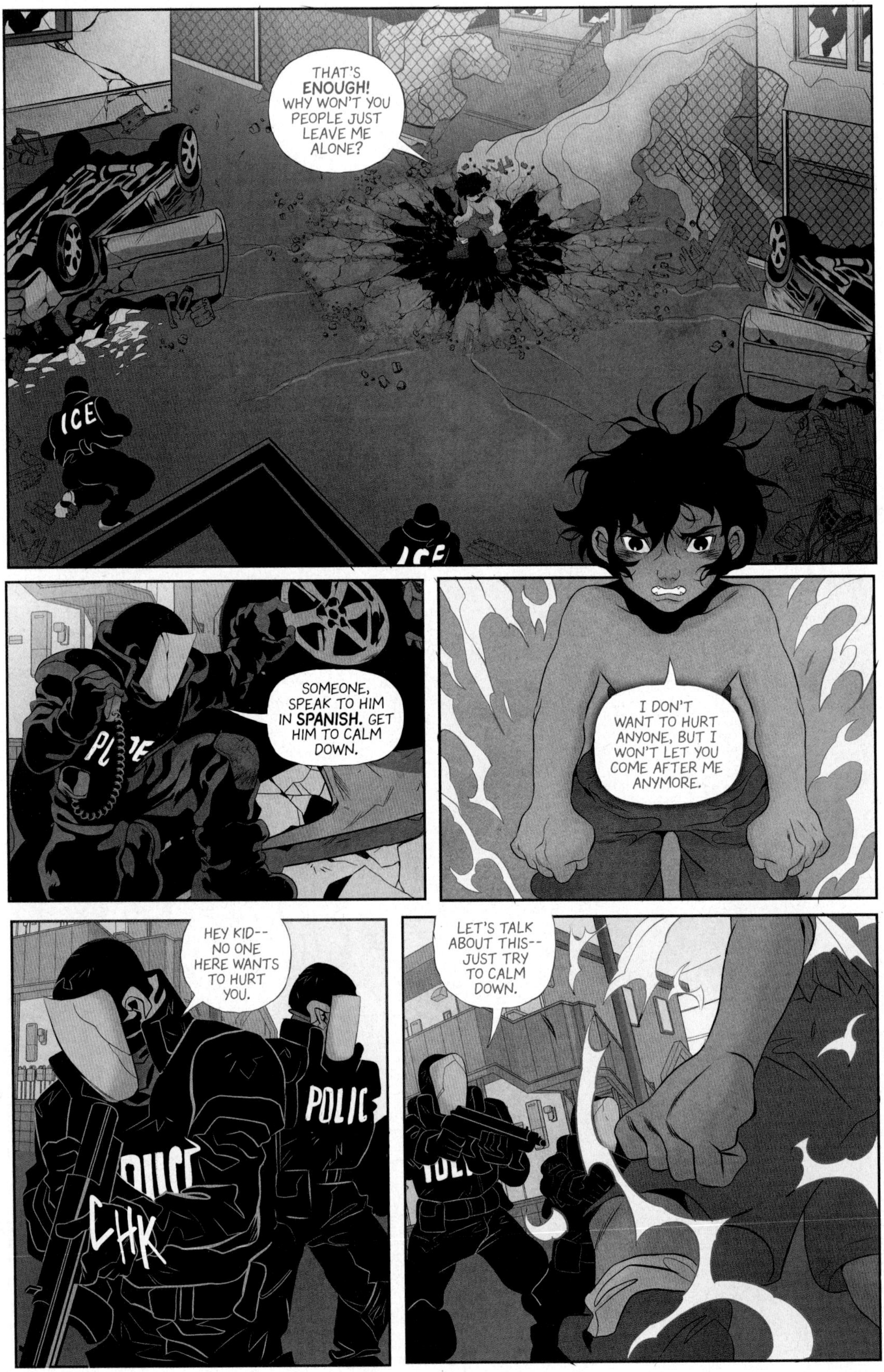
THAT'S ENOUGH! WHY WON'T YOU PEOPLE JUST LEAVE ME ALONE?
ICE
ICE
SOMEONE, SPEAK TO HIM IN SPANISH. GET HIM TO CALM DOWN.
I DON'T WANT TO HURT ANYONE, BUT I WON'T LET YOU COME AFTER ME ANYMORE.
HEY KID-- NO ONE HERE WANTS TO HURT YOU.
POLIC
CHK
LET'S TALK ABOUT THIS-- JUST TRY TO CALM DOWN.

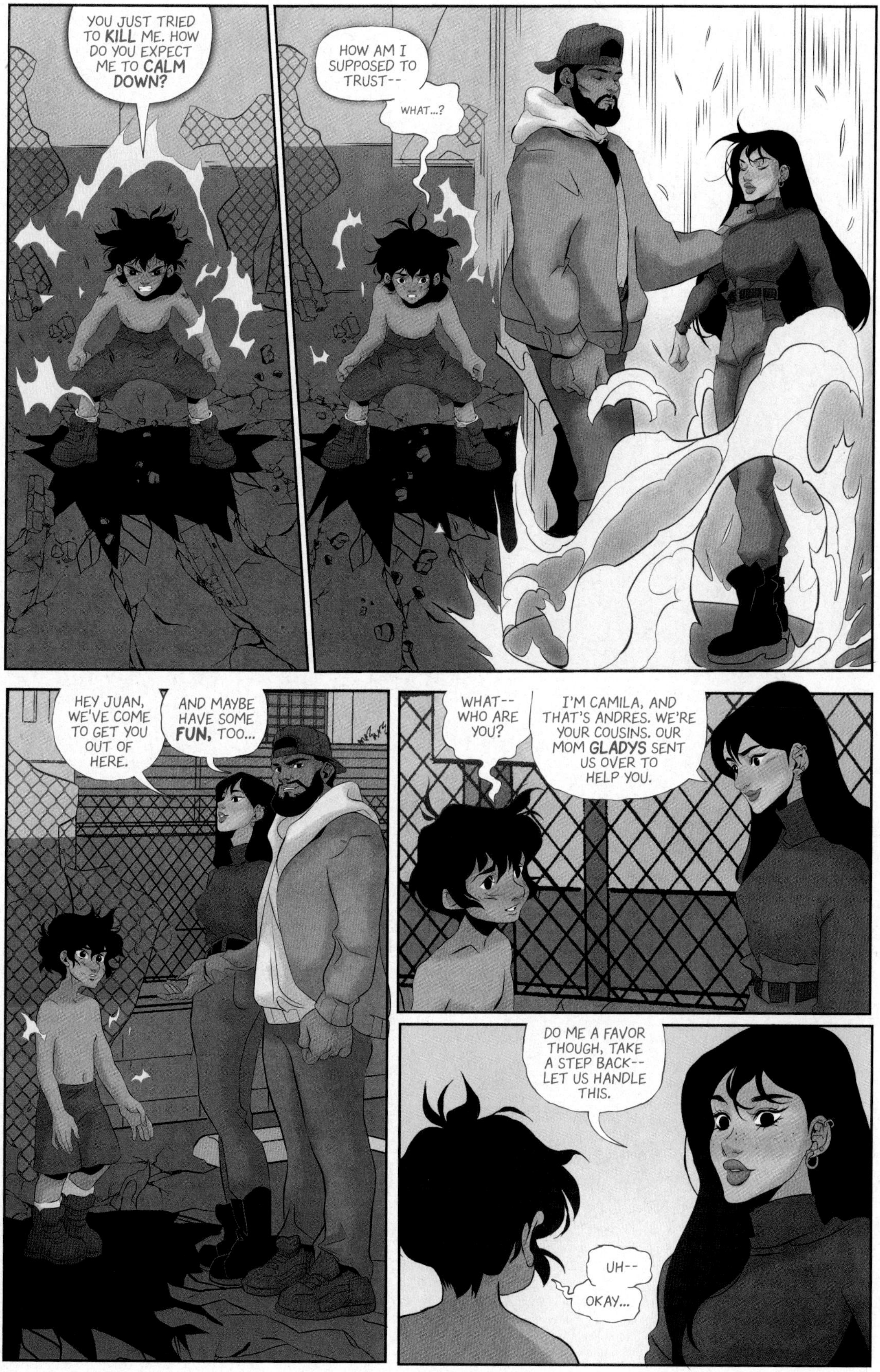
YOU JUST TRIED TO **KILL** ME. HOW DO YOU EXPECT ME TO **CALM DOWN?**
HOW AM I SUPPOSED TO TRUST--
WHAT...?
HEY JUAN, WE'VE COME TO GET YOU OUT OF HERE.
AND MAYBE HAVE SOME **FUN,** TOO...
WHAT-- WHO ARE YOU?
I'M CAMILA, AND THAT'S ANDRES. WE'RE YOUR COUSINS. OUR MOM **GLADYS** SENT US OVER TO HELP YOU.
DO ME A FAVOR THOUGH, TAKE A STEP BACK-- LET US HANDLE THIS.
UH--
OKAY...

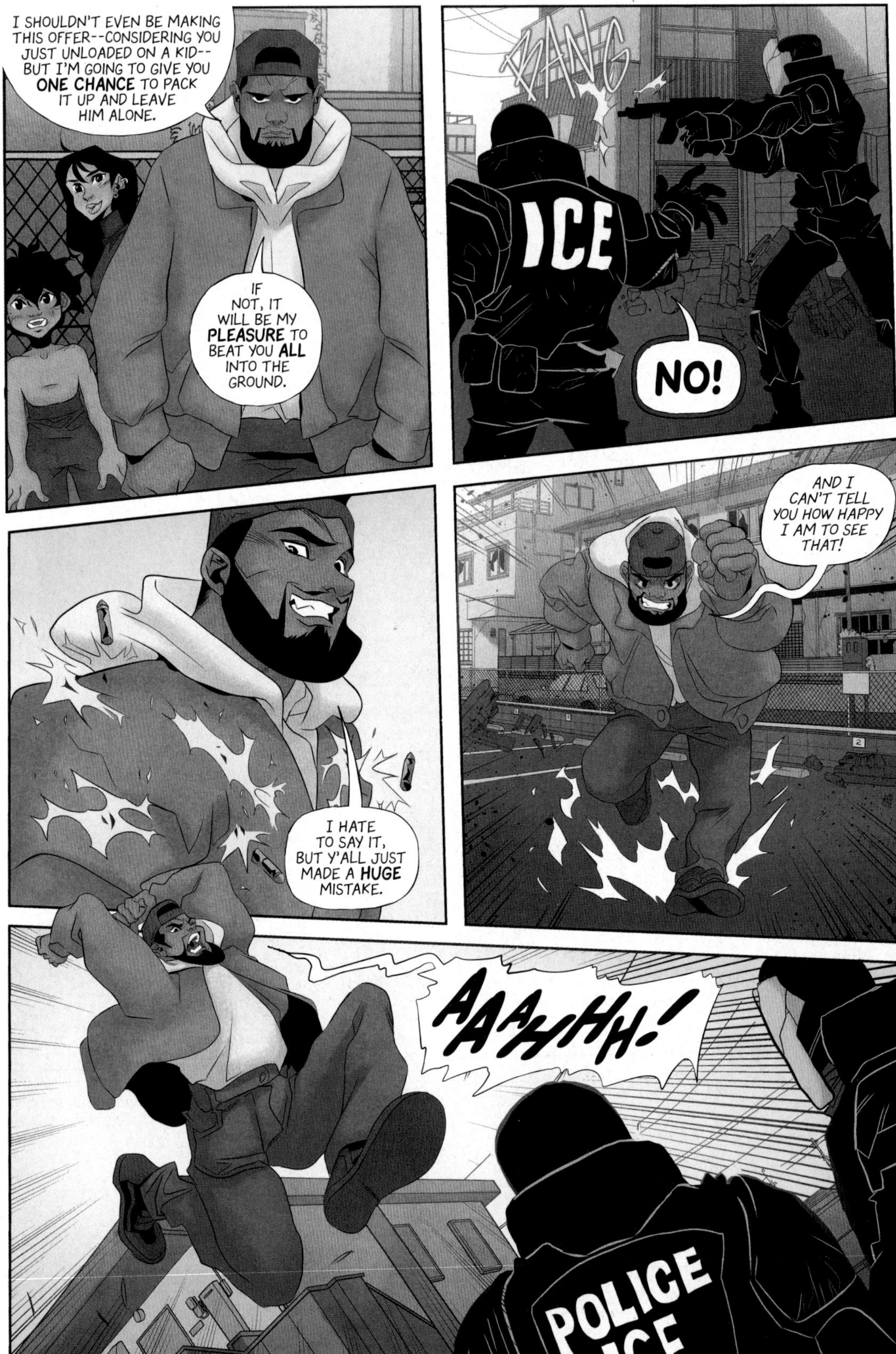

I SHOULDN'T EVEN BE MAKING THIS OFFER--CONSIDERING YOU JUST UNLOADED ON A KID--BUT I'M GOING TO GIVE YOU ONE CHANCE TO PACK IT UP AND LEAVE HIM ALONE.
IF NOT, IT WILL BE MY PLEASURE TO BEAT YOU ALL INTO THE GROUND.
BANG
ICE
NO!
I HATE TO SAY IT, BUT Y'ALL JUST MADE A HUGE MISTAKE.
AND I CAN'T TELL YOU HOW HAPPY I AM TO SEE THAT!
AAAHHH!
POLICE
ICE

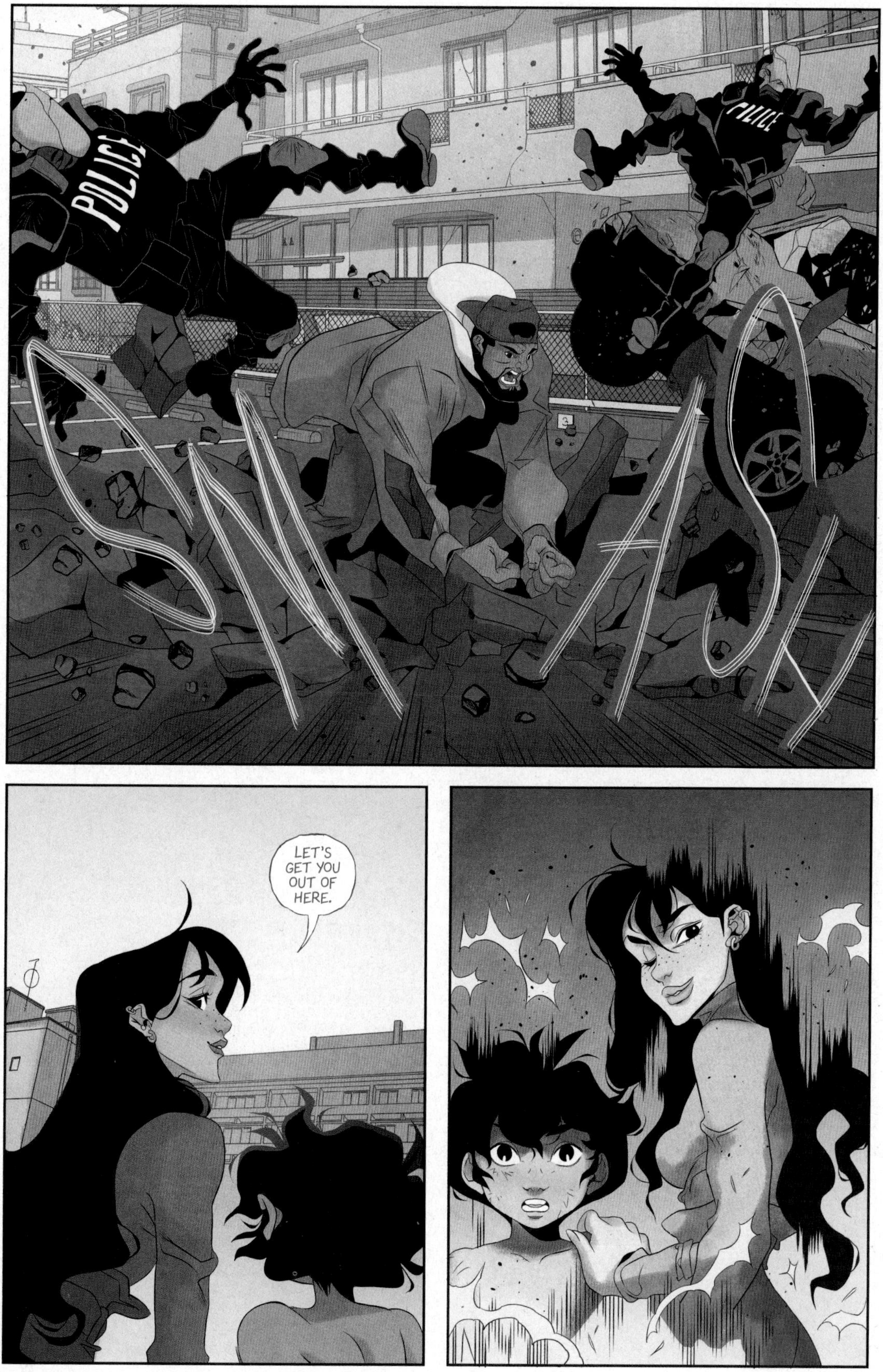
POLICE
POLICE
SMASH
LET'S GET YOU OUT OF HERE.

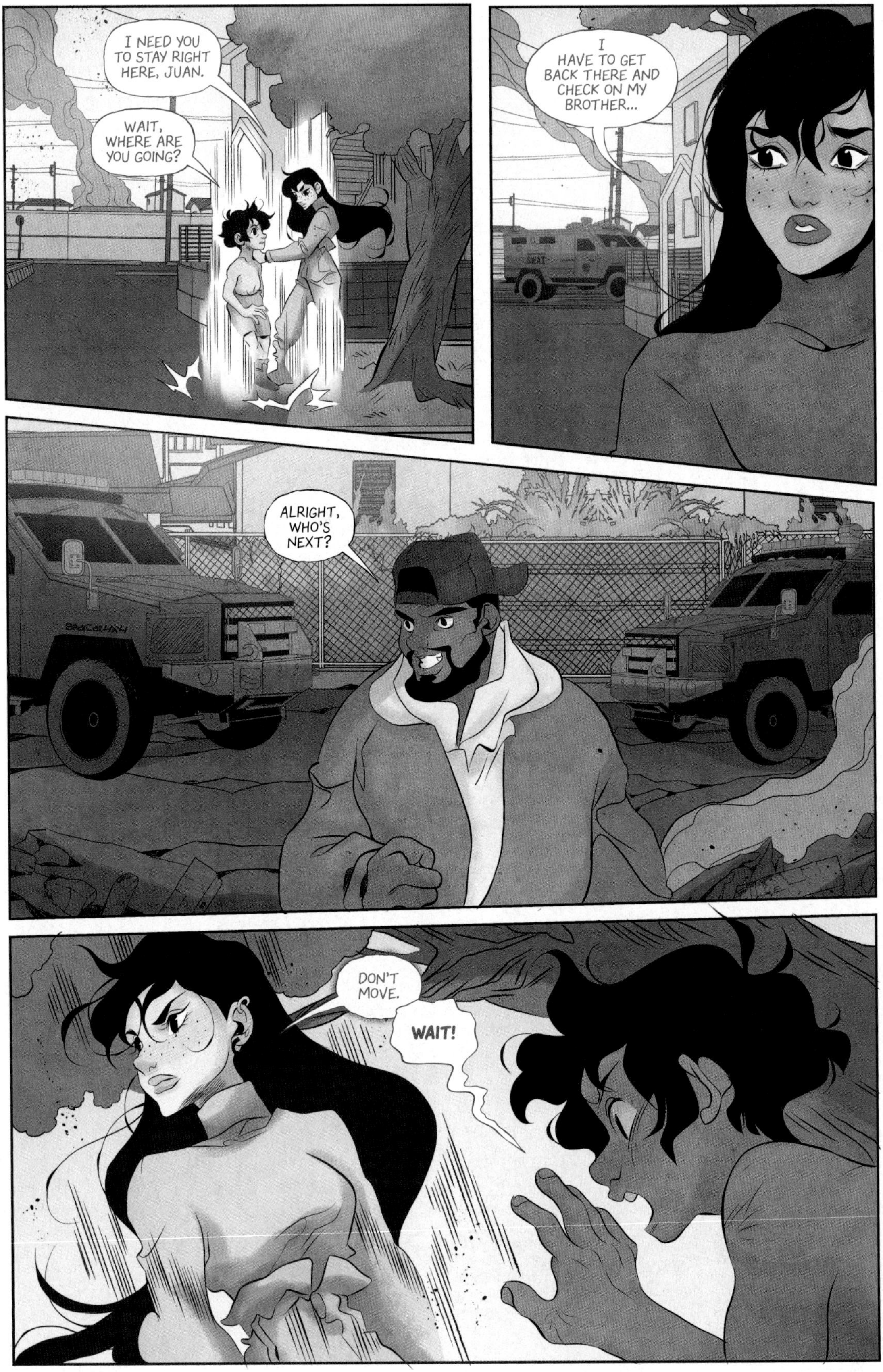
I NEED YOU TO STAY RIGHT HERE, JUAN.
WAIT, WHERE ARE YOU GOING?
I HAVE TO GET BACK THERE AND CHECK ON MY BROTHER...
SWAT
ALRIGHT, WHO'S NEXT?
BearCat 4x4
DON'T MOVE.
WAIT!

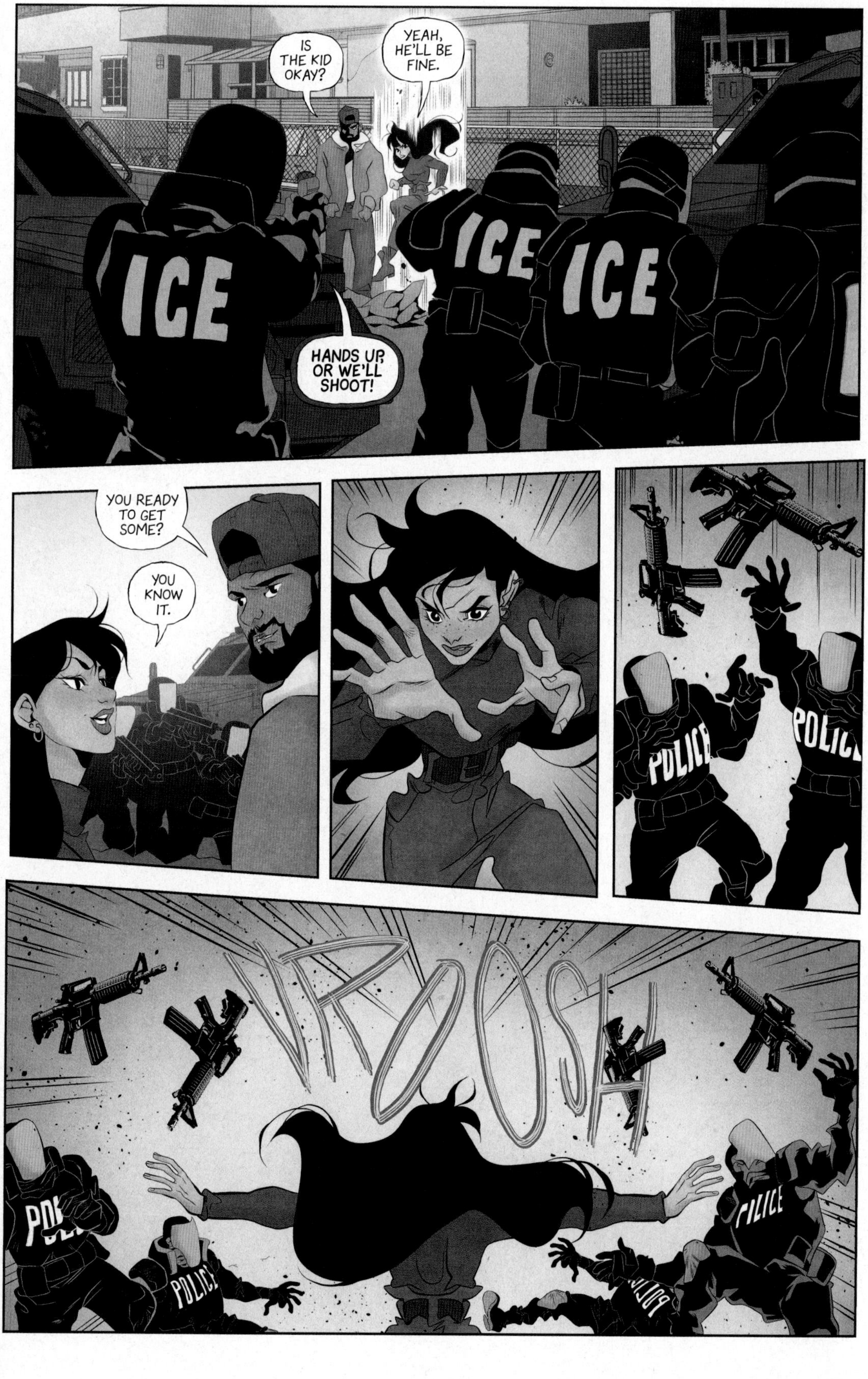
IS THE KID OKAY?
YEAH, HE'LL BE FINE.
HANDS UP, OR WE'LL SHOOT!
ICE
ICE
ICE
YOU READY TO GET SOME?
YOU KNOW IT.
POLICE
POLICE
VROOSH
POLICE
POLICE

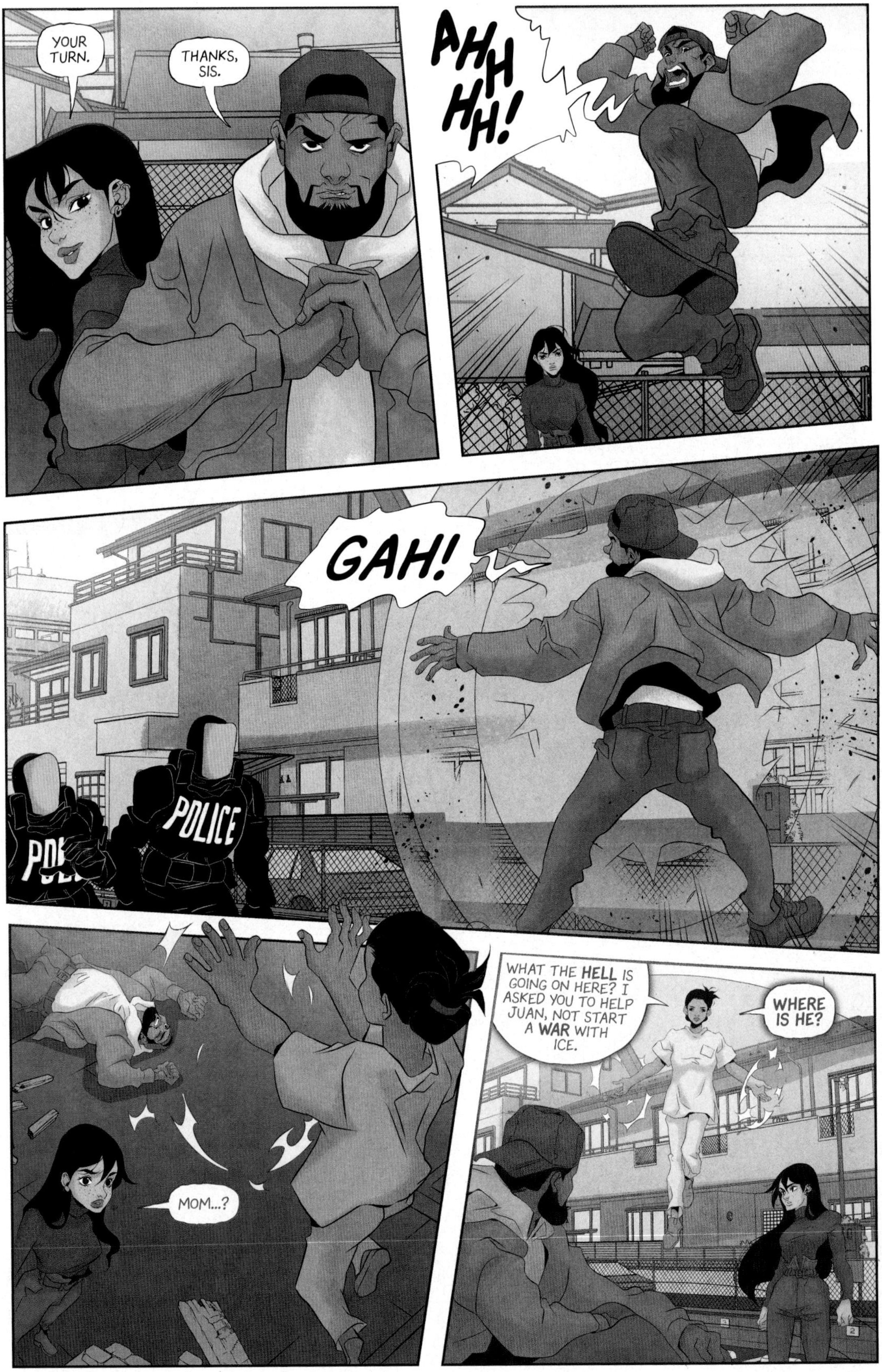
YOUR TURN.
THANKS, SIS.
AHHHH!
GAH!
POLICE
MOM...?
WHAT THE HELL IS GOING ON HERE? I ASKED YOU TO HELP JUAN, NOT START A WAR WITH ICE.
WHERE IS HE?

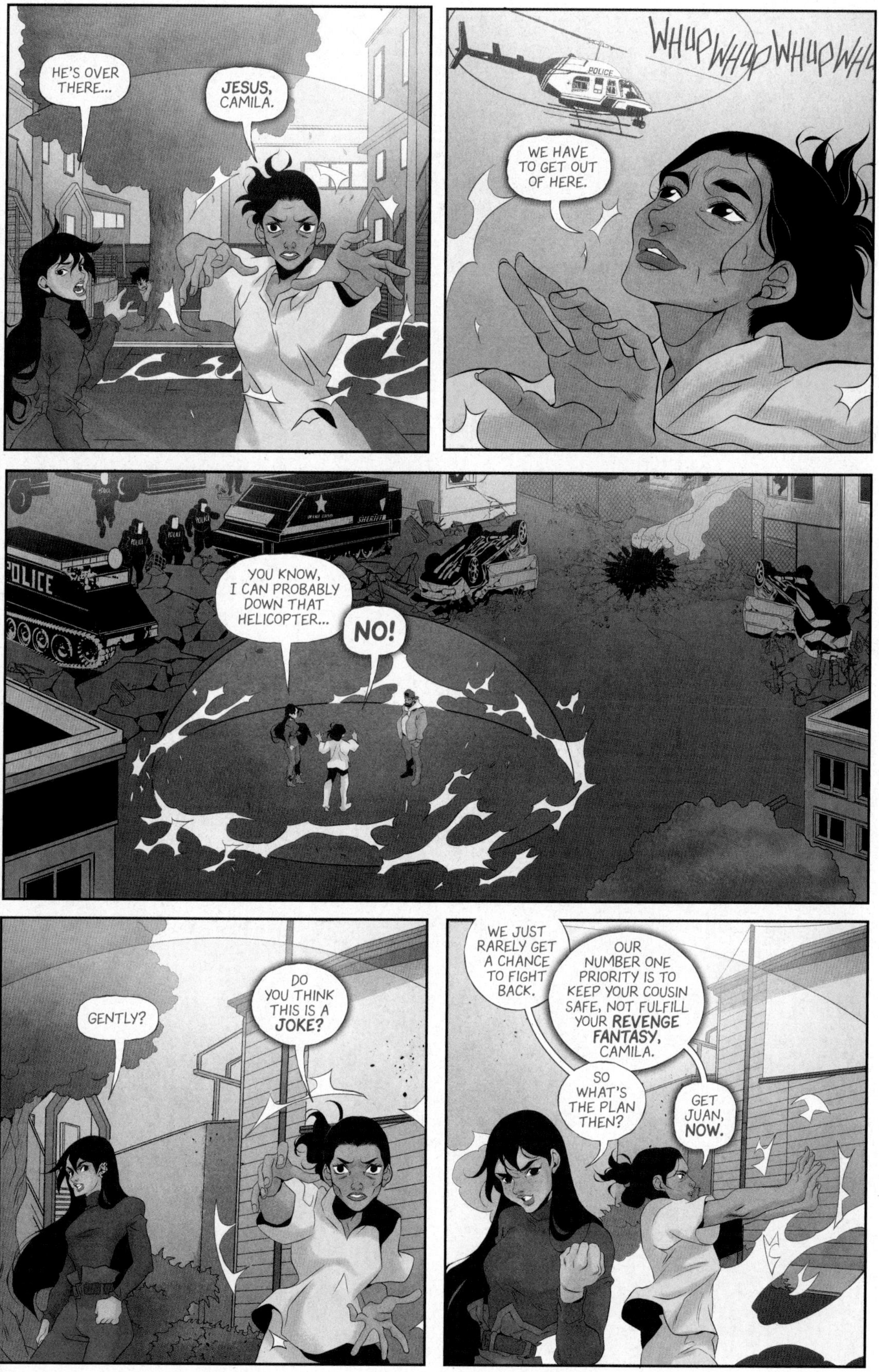
HE'S OVER THERE...
JESUS, CAMILA.
WHUPWHUPWHUPWH
POLICE
WE HAVE TO GET OUT OF HERE.
POLICE
SHERIFF
YOU KNOW, I CAN PROBABLY DOWN THAT HELICOPTER...
NO!
GENTLY?
DO YOU THINK THIS IS A JOKE?
WE JUST RARELY GET A CHANCE TO FIGHT BACK.
OUR NUMBER ONE PRIORITY IS TO KEEP YOUR COUSIN SAFE, NOT FULFILL YOUR REVENGE FANTASY, CAMILA.
SO WHAT'S THE PLAN THEN?
GET JUAN, NOW.

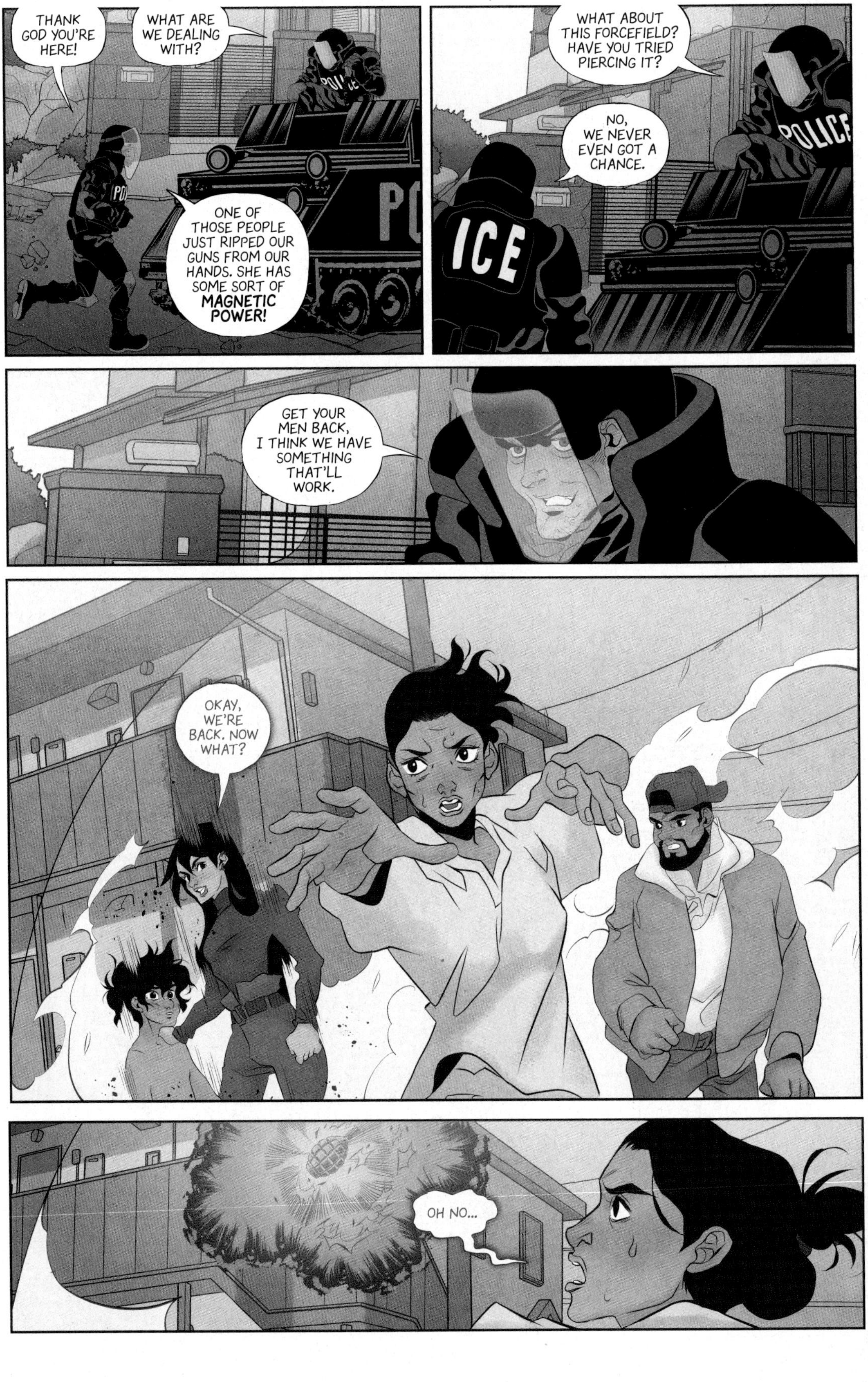
THANK GOD YOU'RE HERE!
WHAT ARE WE DEALING WITH?
ONE OF THOSE PEOPLE JUST RIPPED OUR GUNS FROM OUR HANDS. SHE HAS SOME SORT OF MAGNETIC POWER!
WHAT ABOUT THIS FORCEFIELD? HAVE YOU TRIED PIERCING IT?
NO, WE NEVER EVEN GOT A CHANCE.
GET YOUR MEN BACK, I THINK WE HAVE SOMETHING THAT'LL WORK.
OKAY, WE'RE BACK. NOW WHAT?
OH NO...

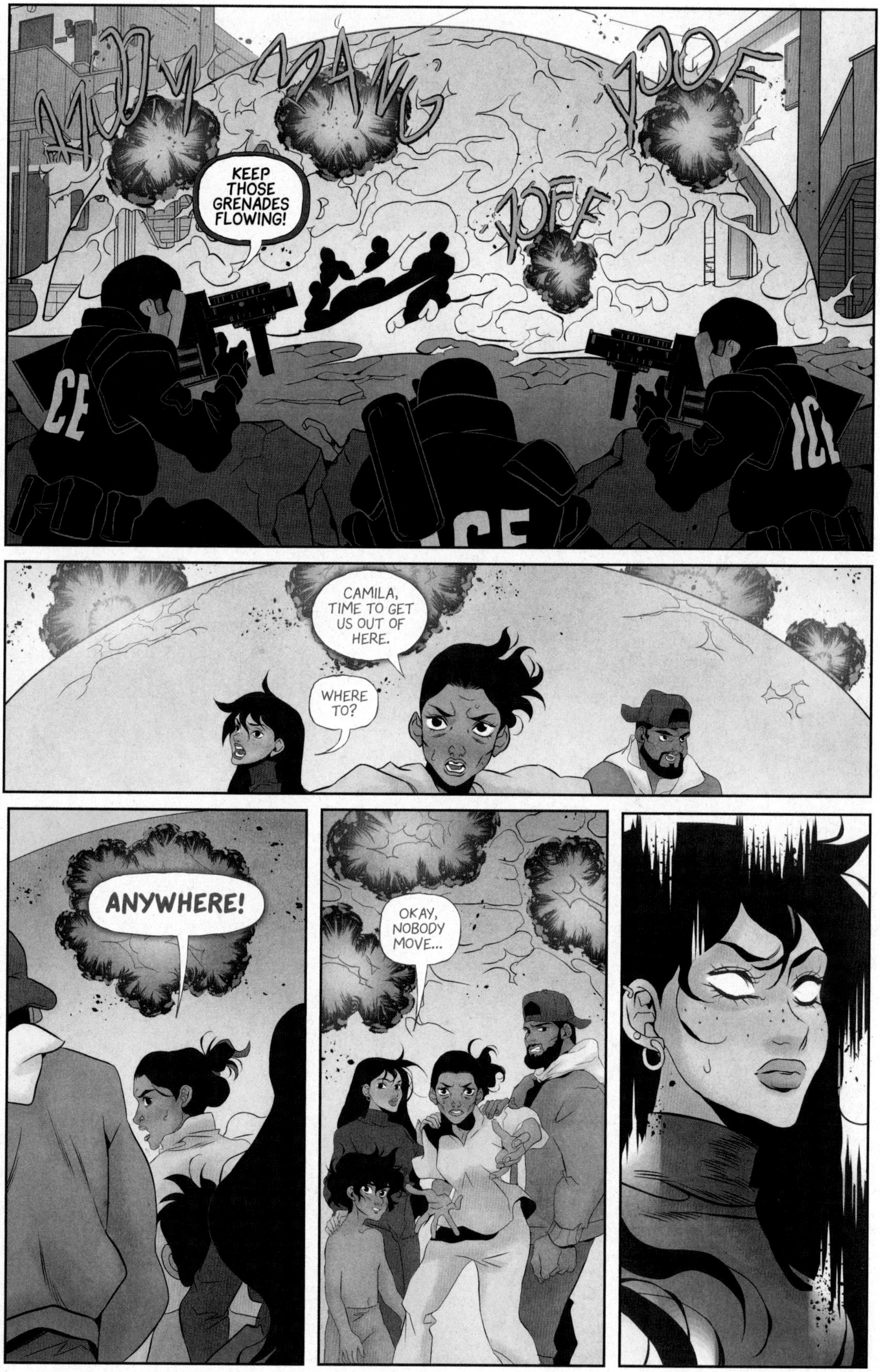
KEEP THOSE GRENADES FLOWING!
CAMILA, TIME TO GET US OUT OF HERE.
WHERE TO?
ANYWHERE!
OKAY, NOBODY MOVE...

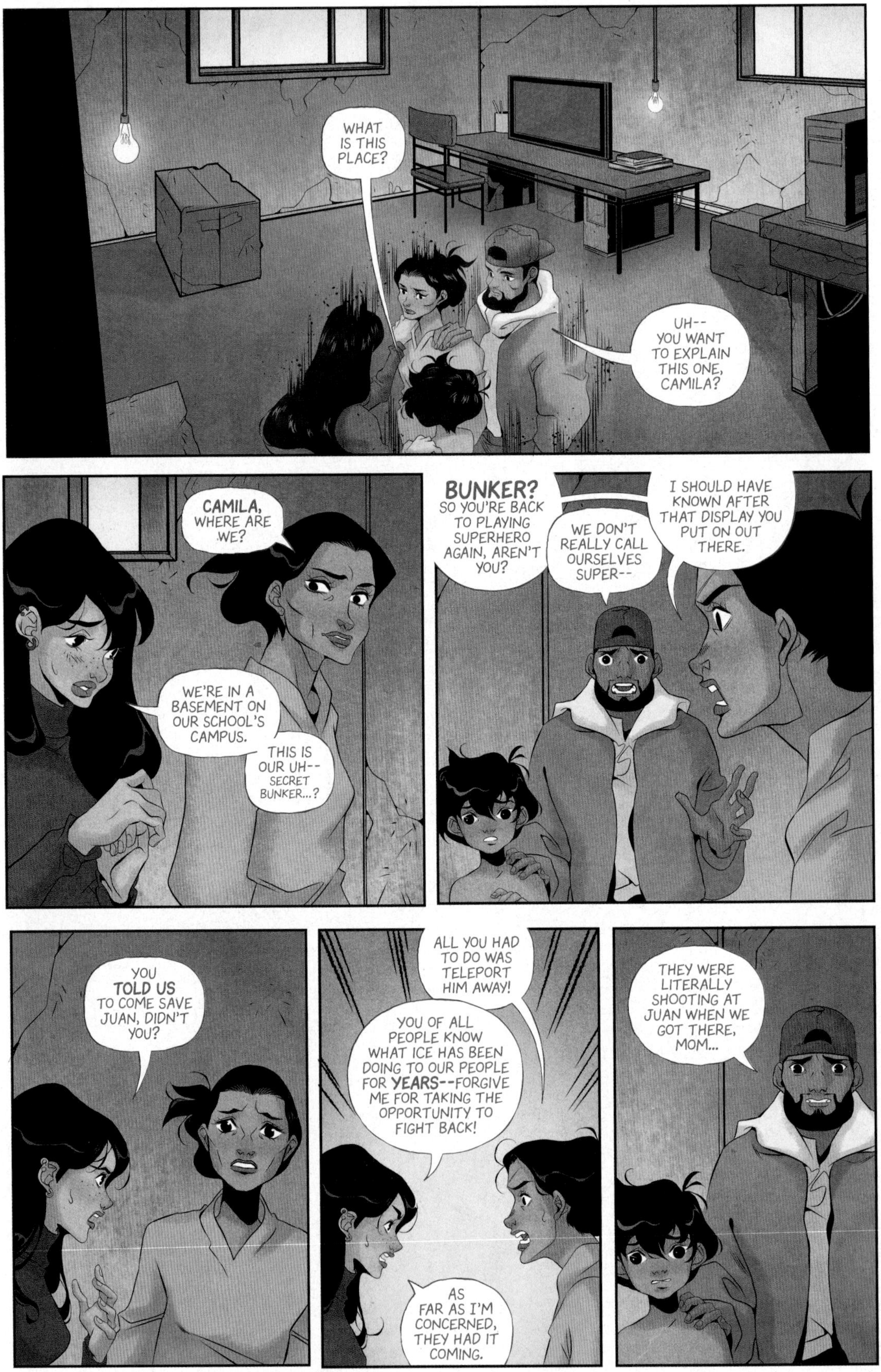
WHAT IS THIS PLACE?
UH-- YOU WANT TO EXPLAIN THIS ONE, CAMILA?
CAMILA, WHERE ARE WE?
WE'RE IN A BASEMENT ON OUR SCHOOL'S CAMPUS.
THIS IS OUR UH-- SECRET BUNKER...?
BUNKER? SO YOU'RE BACK TO PLAYING SUPERHERO AGAIN, AREN'T YOU?
WE DON'T REALLY CALL OURSELVES SUPER--
I SHOULD HAVE KNOWN AFTER THAT DISPLAY YOU PUT ON OUT THERE.
YOU TOLD US TO COME SAVE JUAN, DIDN'T YOU?
ALL YOU HAD TO DO WAS TELEPORT HIM AWAY!
YOU OF ALL PEOPLE KNOW WHAT ICE HAS BEEN DOING TO OUR PEOPLE FOR YEARS--FORGIVE ME FOR TAKING THE OPPORTUNITY TO FIGHT BACK!
AS FAR AS I'M CONCERNED, THEY HAD IT COMING.
THEY WERE LITERALLY SHOOTING AT JUAN WHEN WE GOT THERE, MOM...

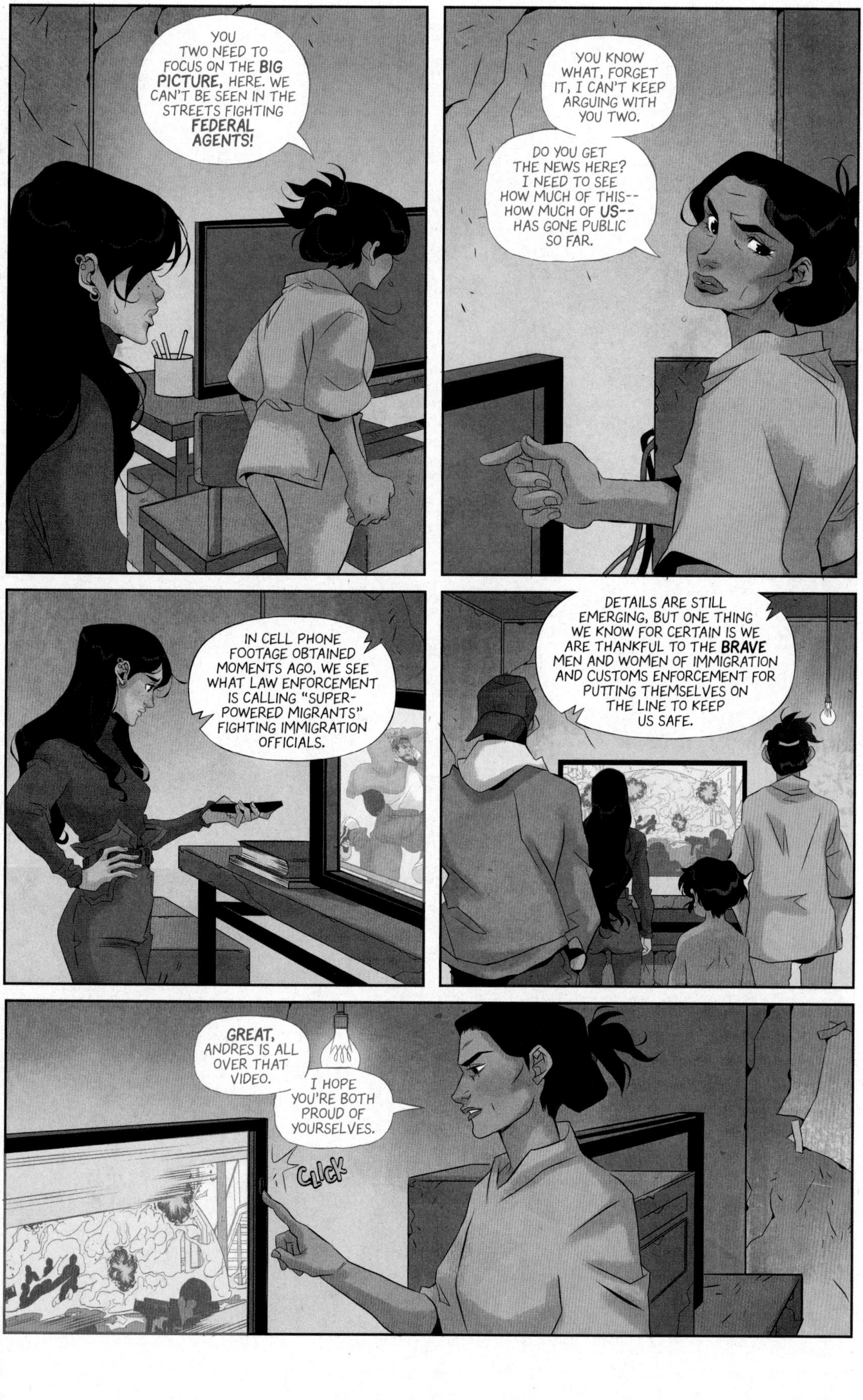
YOU TWO NEED TO FOCUS ON THE BIG PICTURE, HERE. WE CAN'T BE SEEN IN THE STREETS FIGHTING FEDERAL AGENTS!
YOU KNOW WHAT, FORGET IT, I CAN'T KEEP ARGUING WITH YOU TWO.
DO YOU GET THE NEWS HERE? I NEED TO SEE HOW MUCH OF THIS-- HOW MUCH OF US-- HAS GONE PUBLIC SO FAR.
IN CELL PHONE FOOTAGE OBTAINED MOMENTS AGO, WE SEE WHAT LAW ENFORCEMENT IS CALLING "SUPER-POWERED MIGRANTS" FIGHTING IMMIGRATION OFFICIALS.
DETAILS ARE STILL EMERGING, BUT ONE THING WE KNOW FOR CERTAIN IS WE ARE THANKFUL TO THE BRAVE MEN AND WOMEN OF IMMIGRATION AND CUSTOMS ENFORCEMENT FOR PUTTING THEMSELVES ON THE LINE TO KEEP US SAFE.
GREAT, ANDRES IS ALL OVER THAT VIDEO.
I HOPE YOU'RE BOTH PROUD OF YOURSELVES.
CLICK

ONE WEEK LATER

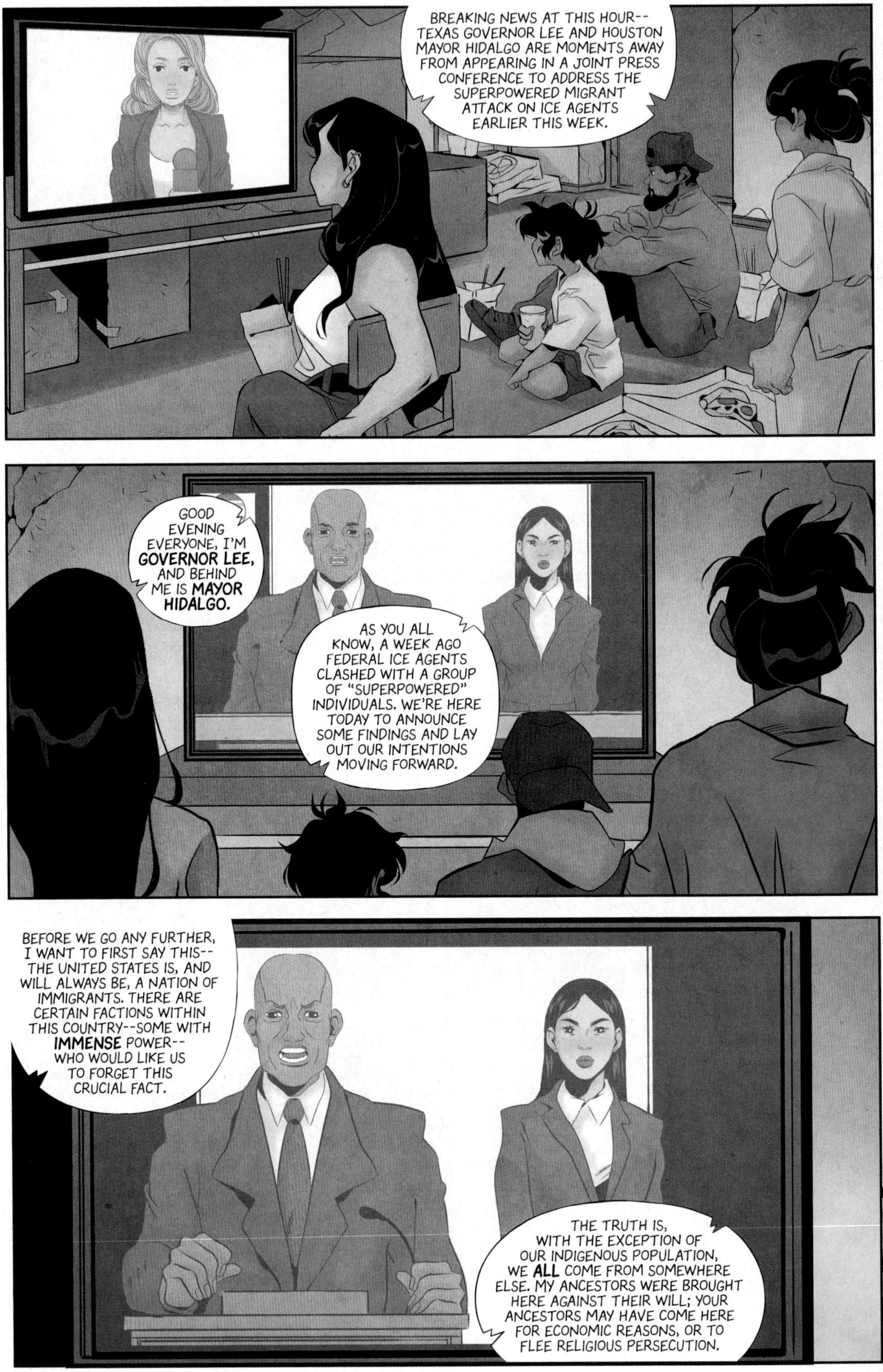
BREAKING NEWS AT THIS HOUR--TEXAS GOVERNOR LEE AND HOUSTON MAYOR HIDALGO ARE MOMENTS AWAY FROM APPEARING IN A JOINT PRESS CONFERENCE TO ADDRESS THE SUPERPOWERED MIGRANT ATTACK ON ICE AGENTS EARLIER THIS WEEK.
GOOD EVENING EVERYONE, I'M **GOVERNOR LEE,** AND BEHIND ME IS **MAYOR HIDALGO.**
AS YOU ALL KNOW, A WEEK AGO FEDERAL ICE AGENTS CLASHED WITH A GROUP OF "SUPERPOWERED" INDIVIDUALS. WE'RE HERE TODAY TO ANNOUNCE SOME FINDINGS AND LAY OUT OUR INTENTIONS MOVING FORWARD.
BEFORE WE GO ANY FURTHER, I WANT TO FIRST SAY THIS--THE UNITED STATES IS, AND WILL ALWAYS BE, A NATION OF IMMIGRANTS. THERE ARE CERTAIN FACTIONS WITHIN THIS COUNTRY--SOME WITH **IMMENSE** POWER--WHO WOULD LIKE US TO FORGET THIS CRUCIAL FACT.
THE TRUTH IS, WITH THE EXCEPTION OF OUR INDIGENOUS POPULATION, WE **ALL** COME FROM SOMEWHERE ELSE. MY ANCESTORS WERE BROUGHT HERE AGAINST THEIR WILL; YOUR ANCESTORS MAY HAVE COME HERE FOR ECONOMIC REASONS, OR TO FLEE RELIGIOUS PERSECUTION.

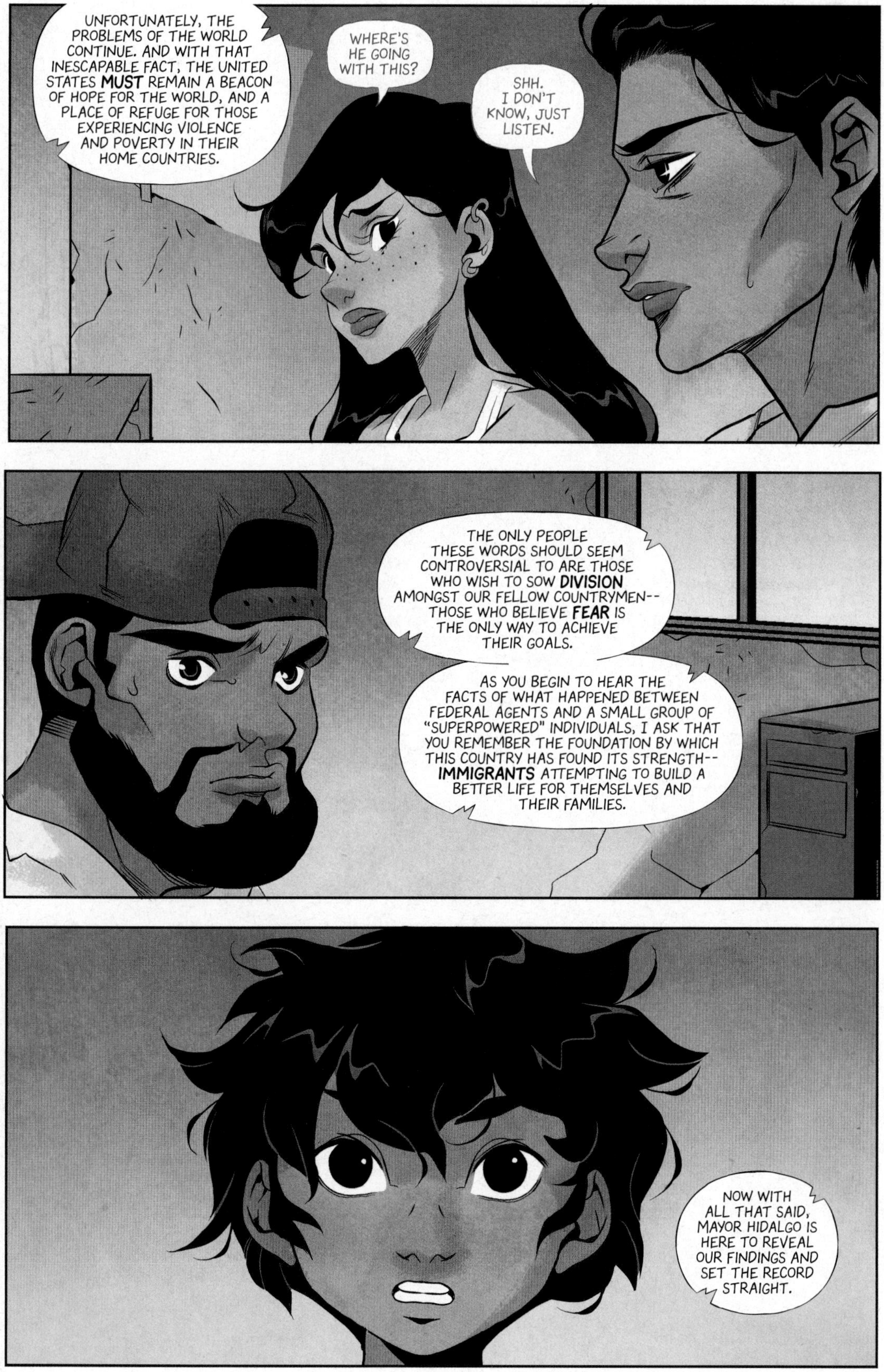
UNFORTUNATELY, THE PROBLEMS OF THE WORLD CONTINUE. AND WITH THAT INESCAPABLE FACT, THE UNITED STATES MUST REMAIN A BEACON OF HOPE FOR THE WORLD, AND A PLACE OF REFUGE FOR THOSE EXPERIENCING VIOLENCE AND POVERTY IN THEIR HOME COUNTRIES.
WHERE'S HE GOING WITH THIS?
SHH. I DON'T KNOW, JUST LISTEN.
THE ONLY PEOPLE THESE WORDS SHOULD SEEM CONTROVERSIAL TO ARE THOSE WHO WISH TO SOW DIVISION AMONGST OUR FELLOW COUNTRYMEN-- THOSE WHO BELIEVE FEAR IS THE ONLY WAY TO ACHIEVE THEIR GOALS.
AS YOU BEGIN TO HEAR THE FACTS OF WHAT HAPPENED BETWEEN FEDERAL AGENTS AND A SMALL GROUP OF "SUPERPOWERED" INDIVIDUALS, I ASK THAT YOU REMEMBER THE FOUNDATION BY WHICH THIS COUNTRY HAS FOUND ITS STRENGTH-- IMMIGRANTS ATTEMPTING TO BUILD A BETTER LIFE FOR THEMSELVES AND THEIR FAMILIES.
NOW WITH ALL THAT SAID, MAYOR HIDALGO IS HERE TO REVEAL OUR FINDINGS AND SET THE RECORD STRAIGHT.

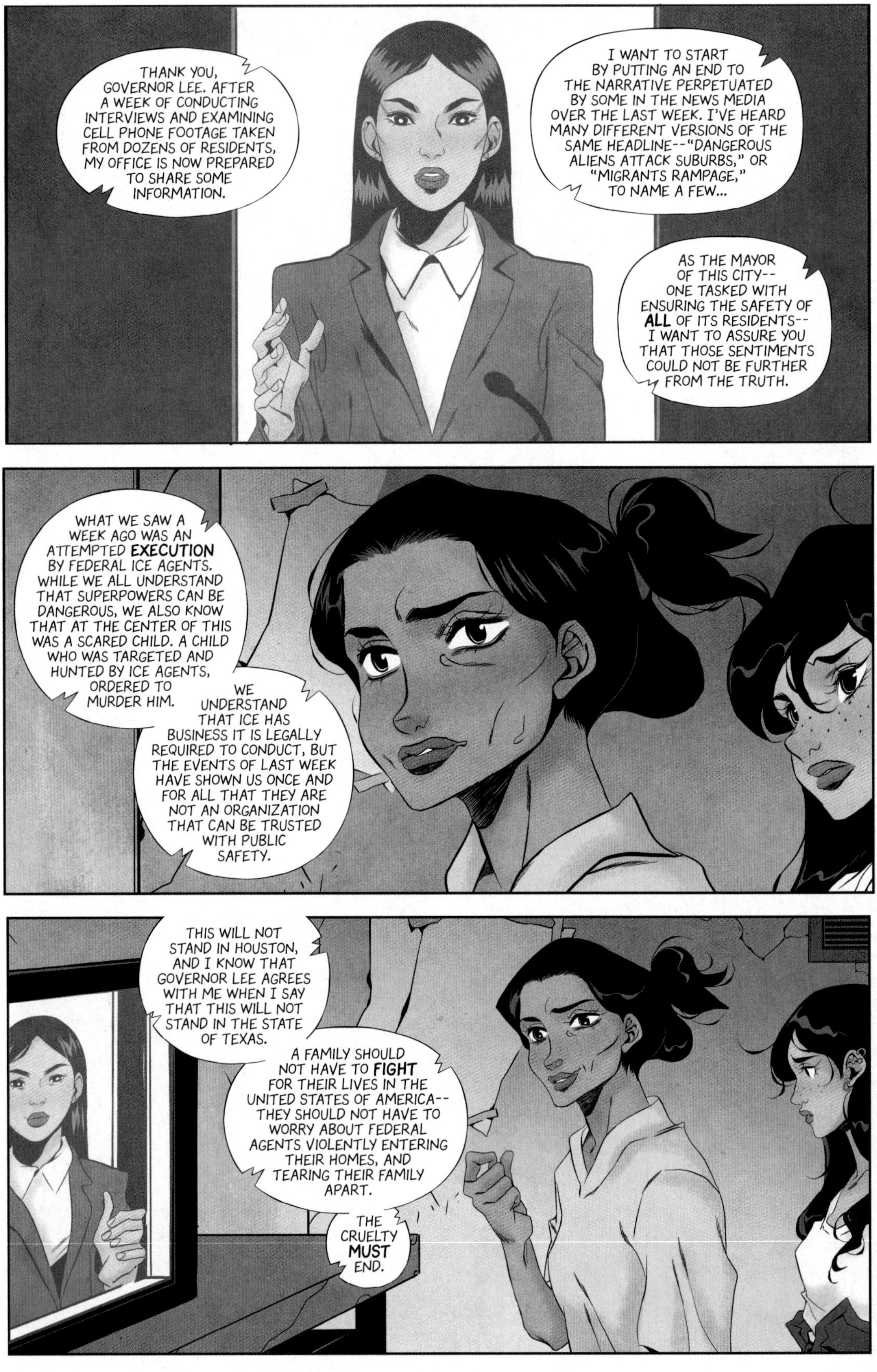
THANK YOU, GOVERNOR LEE. AFTER A WEEK OF CONDUCTING INTERVIEWS AND EXAMINING CELL PHONE FOOTAGE TAKEN FROM DOZENS OF RESIDENTS, MY OFFICE IS NOW PREPARED TO SHARE SOME INFORMATION.
I WANT TO START BY PUTTING AN END TO THE NARRATIVE PERPETUATED BY SOME IN THE NEWS MEDIA OVER THE LAST WEEK. I'VE HEARD MANY DIFFERENT VERSIONS OF THE SAME HEADLINE--"DANGEROUS ALIENS ATTACK SUBURBS," OR "MIGRANTS RAMPAGE," TO NAME A FEW...
AS THE MAYOR OF THIS CITY-- ONE TASKED WITH ENSURING THE SAFETY OF **ALL** OF ITS RESIDENTS-- I WANT TO ASSURE YOU THAT THOSE SENTIMENTS COULD NOT BE FURTHER FROM THE TRUTH.
WHAT WE SAW A WEEK AGO WAS AN ATTEMPTED **EXECUTION** BY FEDERAL ICE AGENTS. WHILE WE ALL UNDERSTAND THAT SUPERPOWERS CAN BE DANGEROUS, WE ALSO KNOW THAT AT THE CENTER OF THIS WAS A SCARED CHILD. A CHILD WHO WAS TARGETED AND HUNTED BY ICE AGENTS, ORDERED TO MURDER HIM.
WE UNDERSTAND THAT ICE HAS BUSINESS IT IS LEGALLY REQUIRED TO CONDUCT, BUT THE EVENTS OF LAST WEEK HAVE SHOWN US ONCE AND FOR ALL THAT THEY ARE NOT AN ORGANIZATION THAT CAN BE TRUSTED WITH PUBLIC SAFETY.
THIS WILL NOT STAND IN HOUSTON, AND I KNOW THAT GOVERNOR LEE AGREES WITH ME WHEN I SAY THAT THIS WILL NOT STAND IN THE STATE OF TEXAS.
A FAMILY SHOULD NOT HAVE TO **FIGHT** FOR THEIR LIVES IN THE UNITED STATES OF AMERICA-- THEY SHOULD NOT HAVE TO WORRY ABOUT FEDERAL AGENTS VIOLENTLY ENTERING THEIR HOMES, AND TEARING THEIR FAMILY APART.
THE CRUELTY **MUST** END.

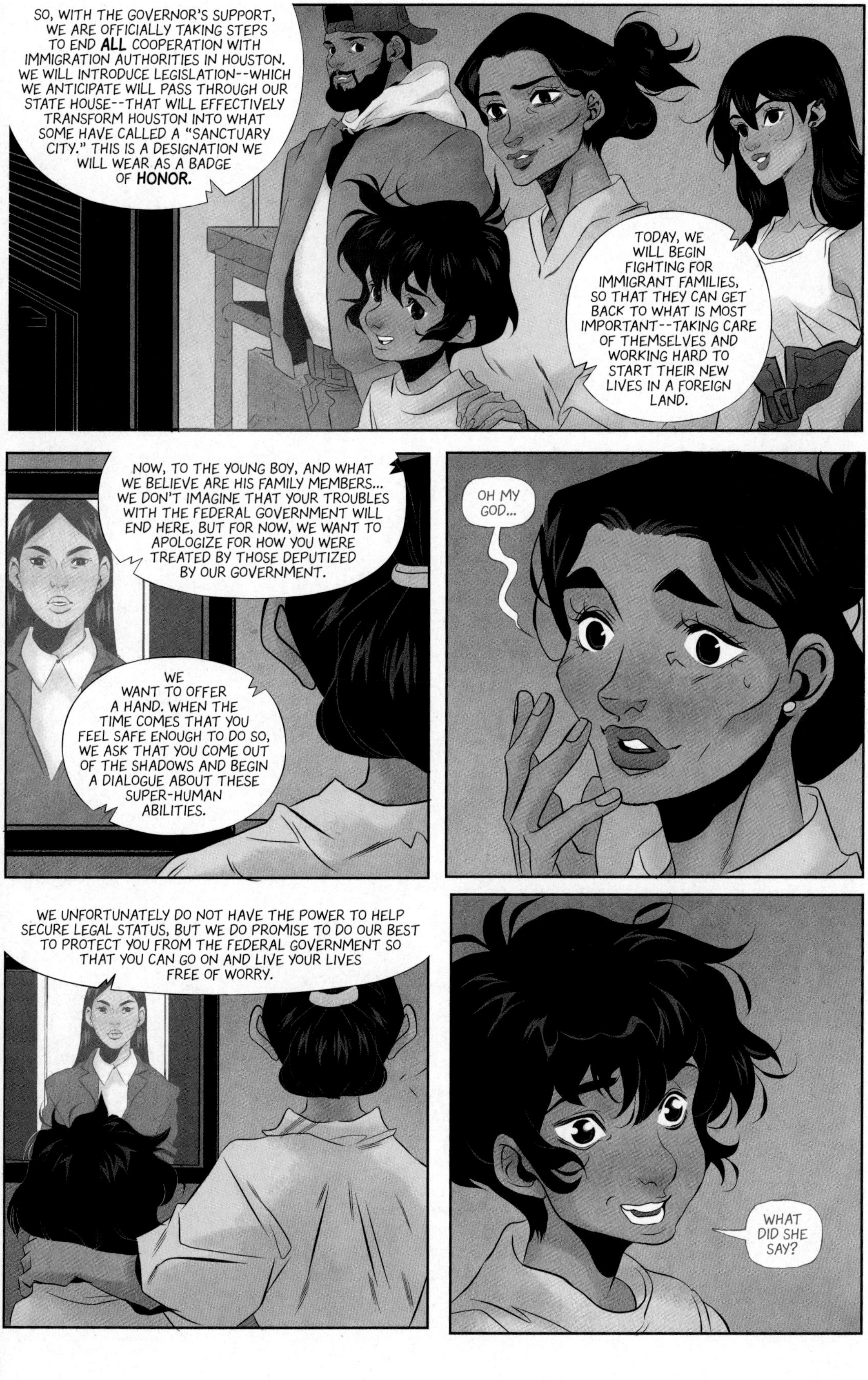
SO, WITH THE GOVERNOR'S SUPPORT, WE ARE OFFICIALLY TAKING STEPS TO END ALL COOPERATION WITH IMMIGRATION AUTHORITIES IN HOUSTON. WE WILL INTRODUCE LEGISLATION--WHICH WE ANTICIPATE WILL PASS THROUGH OUR STATE HOUSE--THAT WILL EFFECTIVELY TRANSFORM HOUSTON INTO WHAT SOME HAVE CALLED A "SANCTUARY CITY." THIS IS A DESIGNATION WE WILL WEAR AS A BADGE OF HONOR.
TODAY, WE WILL BEGIN FIGHTING FOR IMMIGRANT FAMILIES, SO THAT THEY CAN GET BACK TO WHAT IS MOST IMPORTANT--TAKING CARE OF THEMSELVES AND WORKING HARD TO START THEIR NEW LIVES IN A FOREIGN LAND.
NOW, TO THE YOUNG BOY, AND WHAT WE BELIEVE ARE HIS FAMILY MEMBERS... WE DON'T IMAGINE THAT YOUR TROUBLES WITH THE FEDERAL GOVERNMENT WILL END HERE, BUT FOR NOW, WE WANT TO APOLOGIZE FOR HOW YOU WERE TREATED BY THOSE DEPUTIZED BY OUR GOVERNMENT.
WE WANT TO OFFER A HAND. WHEN THE TIME COMES THAT YOU FEEL SAFE ENOUGH TO DO SO, WE ASK THAT YOU COME OUT OF THE SHADOWS AND BEGIN A DIALOGUE ABOUT THESE SUPER-HUMAN ABILITIES.
OH MY GOD...
WE UNFORTUNATELY DO NOT HAVE THE POWER TO HELP SECURE LEGAL STATUS, BUT WE DO PROMISE TO DO OUR BEST TO PROTECT YOU FROM THE FEDERAL GOVERNMENT SO THAT YOU CAN GO ON AND LIVE YOUR LIVES FREE OF WORRY.
WHAT DID SHE SAY?

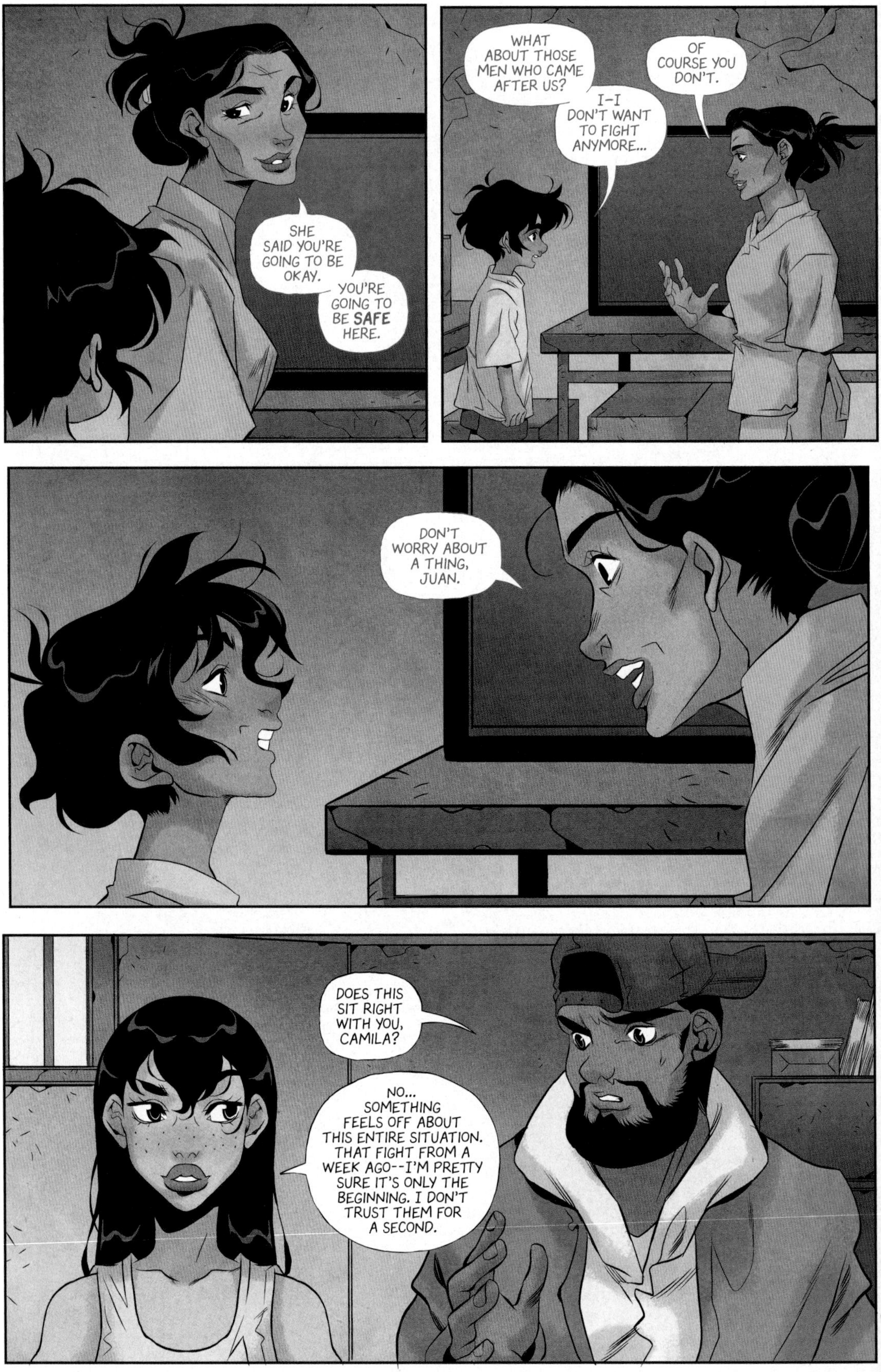
SHE SAID YOU'RE GOING TO BE OKAY.
YOU'RE GOING TO BE **SAFE** HERE.
WHAT ABOUT THOSE MEN WHO CAME AFTER US?
I-I DON'T WANT TO FIGHT ANYMORE...
OF COURSE YOU DON'T.
DON'T WORRY ABOUT A THING, JUAN.
DOES THIS SIT RIGHT WITH YOU, CAMILA?
NO... SOMETHING FEELS OFF ABOUT THIS ENTIRE SITUATION. THAT FIGHT FROM A WEEK AGO--I'M PRETTY SURE IT'S ONLY THE BEGINNING. I DON'T TRUST THEM FOR A SECOND.

One month later

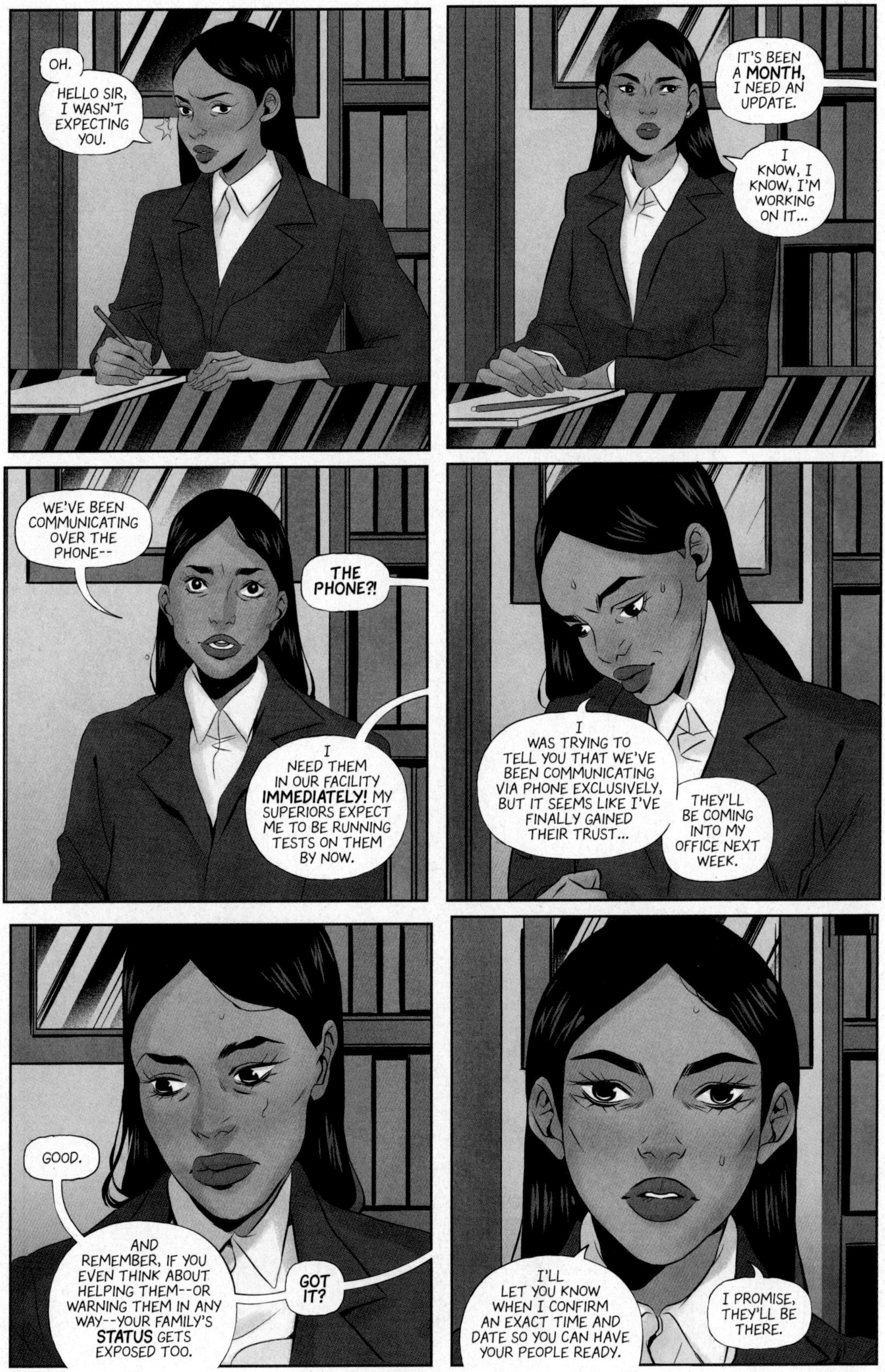
OH.
HELLO SIR, I WASN'T EXPECTING YOU.
IT'S BEEN A **MONTH,** I NEED AN UPDATE.
I KNOW, I KNOW, I'M WORKING ON IT...
WE'VE BEEN COMMUNICATING OVER THE PHONE--
THE PHONE?!
I NEED THEM IN OUR FACILITY **IMMEDIATELY!** MY SUPERIORS EXPECT ME TO BE RUNNING TESTS ON THEM BY NOW.
I WAS TRYING TO TELL YOU THAT WE'VE BEEN COMMUNICATING VIA PHONE EXCLUSIVELY, BUT IT SEEMS LIKE I'VE FINALLY GAINED THEIR TRUST...
THEY'LL BE COMING INTO MY OFFICE NEXT WEEK.
GOOD.
AND REMEMBER, IF YOU EVEN THINK ABOUT HELPING THEM--OR WARNING THEM IN ANY WAY--YOUR FAMILY'S **STATUS** GETS EXPOSED TOO.
GOT IT?
I'LL LET YOU KNOW WHEN I CONFIRM AN EXACT TIME AND DATE SO YOU CAN HAVE YOUR PEOPLE READY.
I PROMISE, THEY'LL BE THERE.

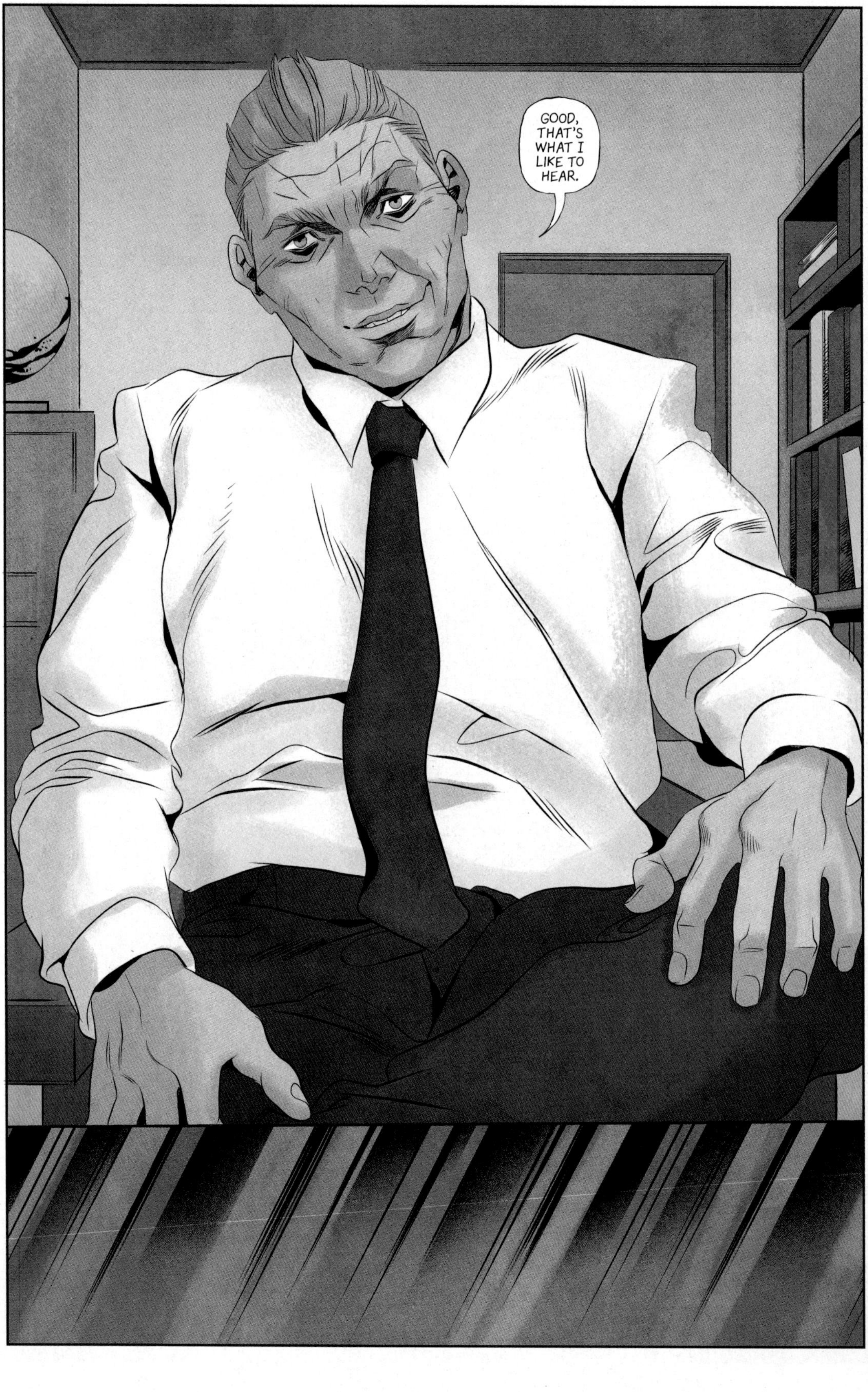
GOOD, THAT'S WHAT I LIKE TO HEAR.

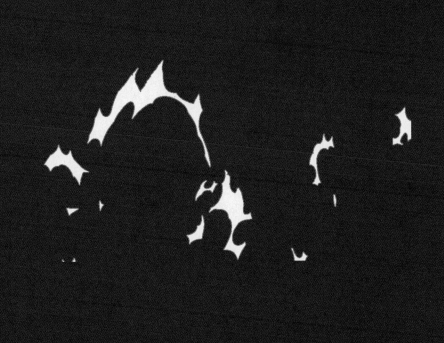

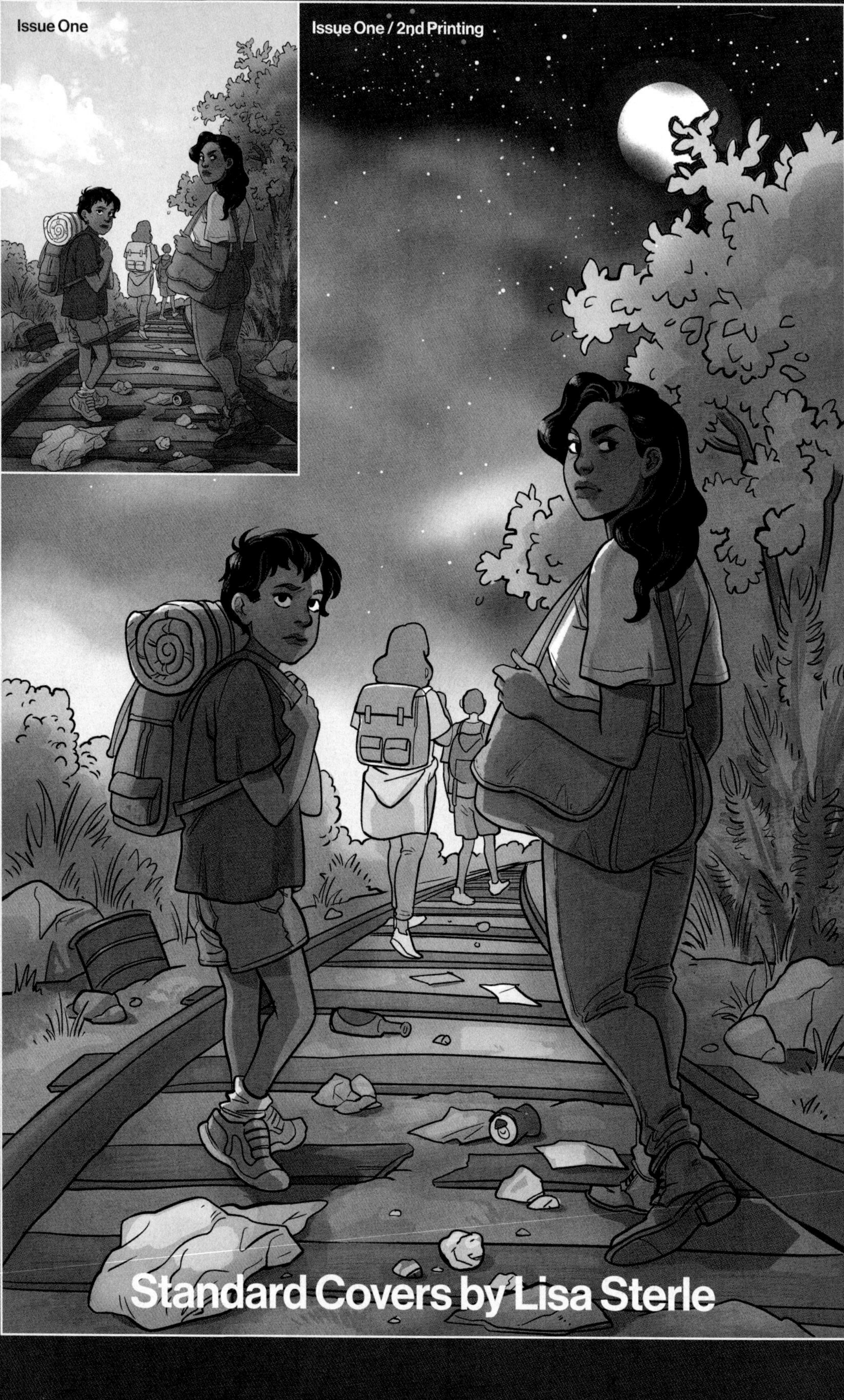

Issue One

Issue One / 2nd Printing

Standard Covers by Lisa Sterle

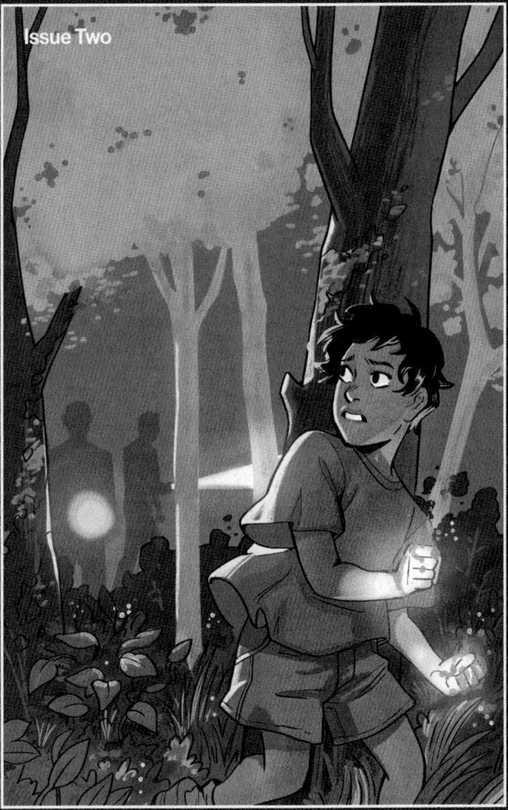
Issue Two

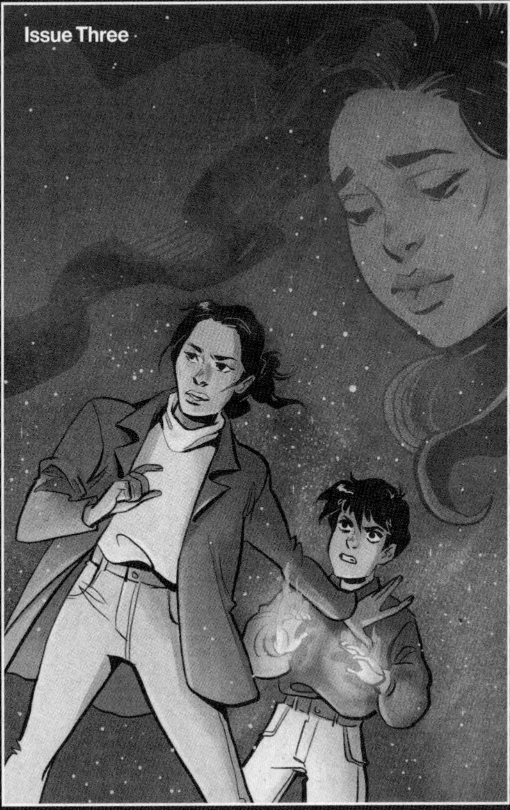
Issue Three

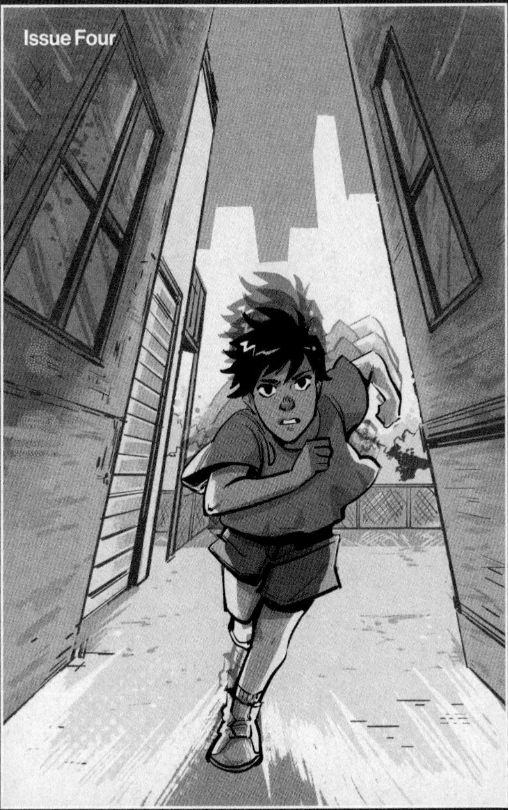
Issue Four

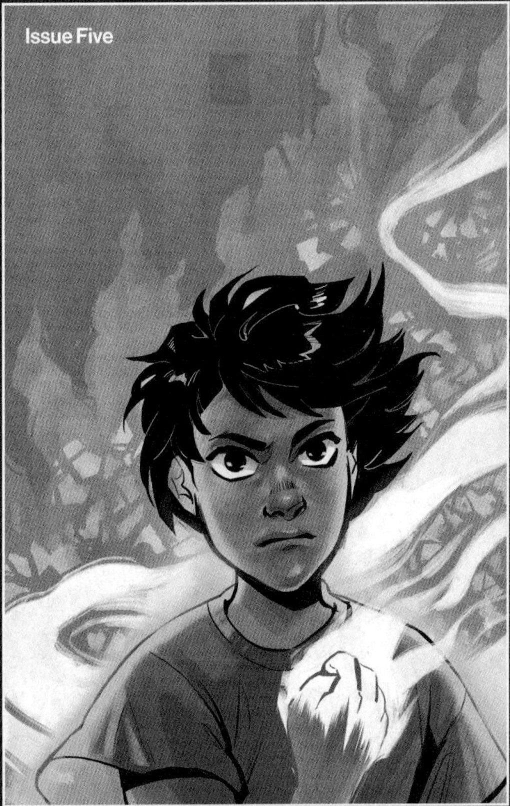
Issue Five

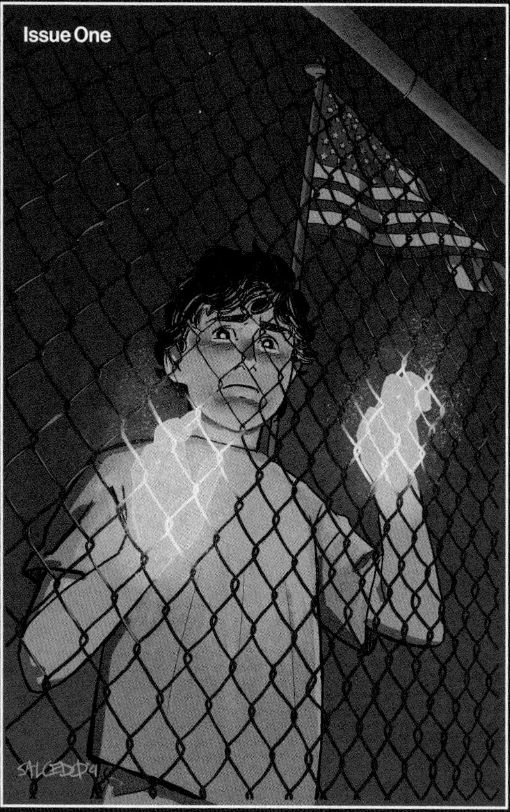
Issue One

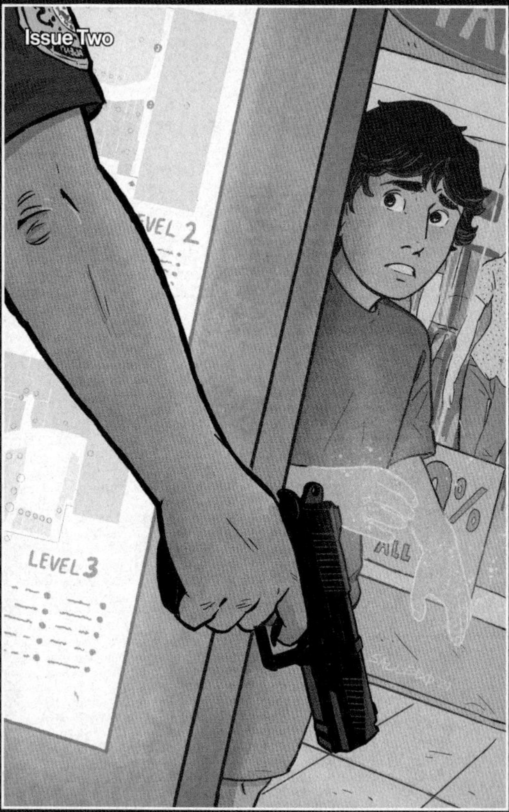
LEVEL 3
Issue Two

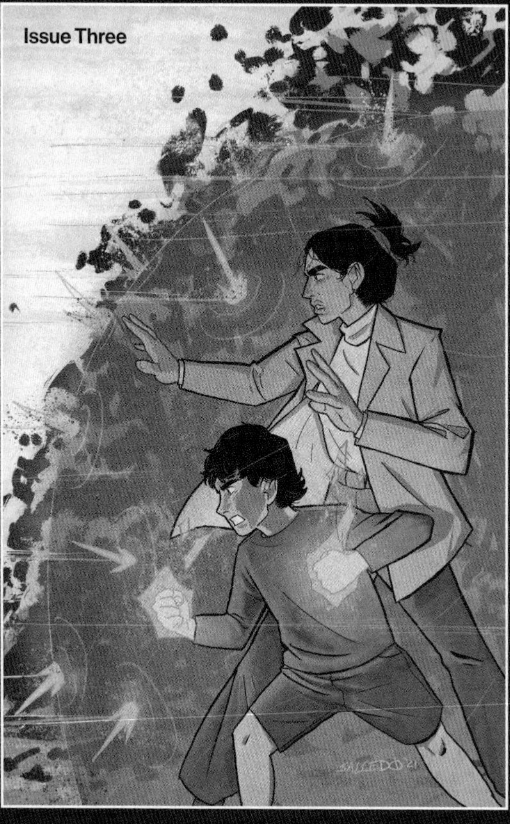
Issue Three

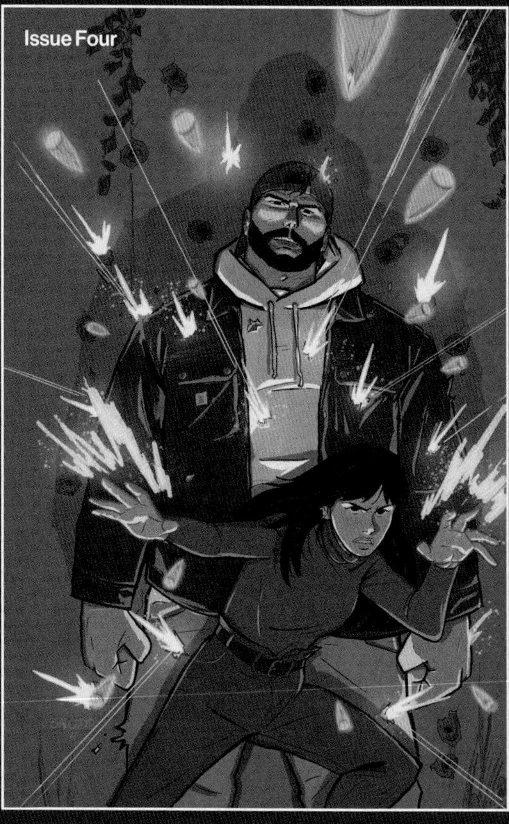
Issue Four

Issue Five

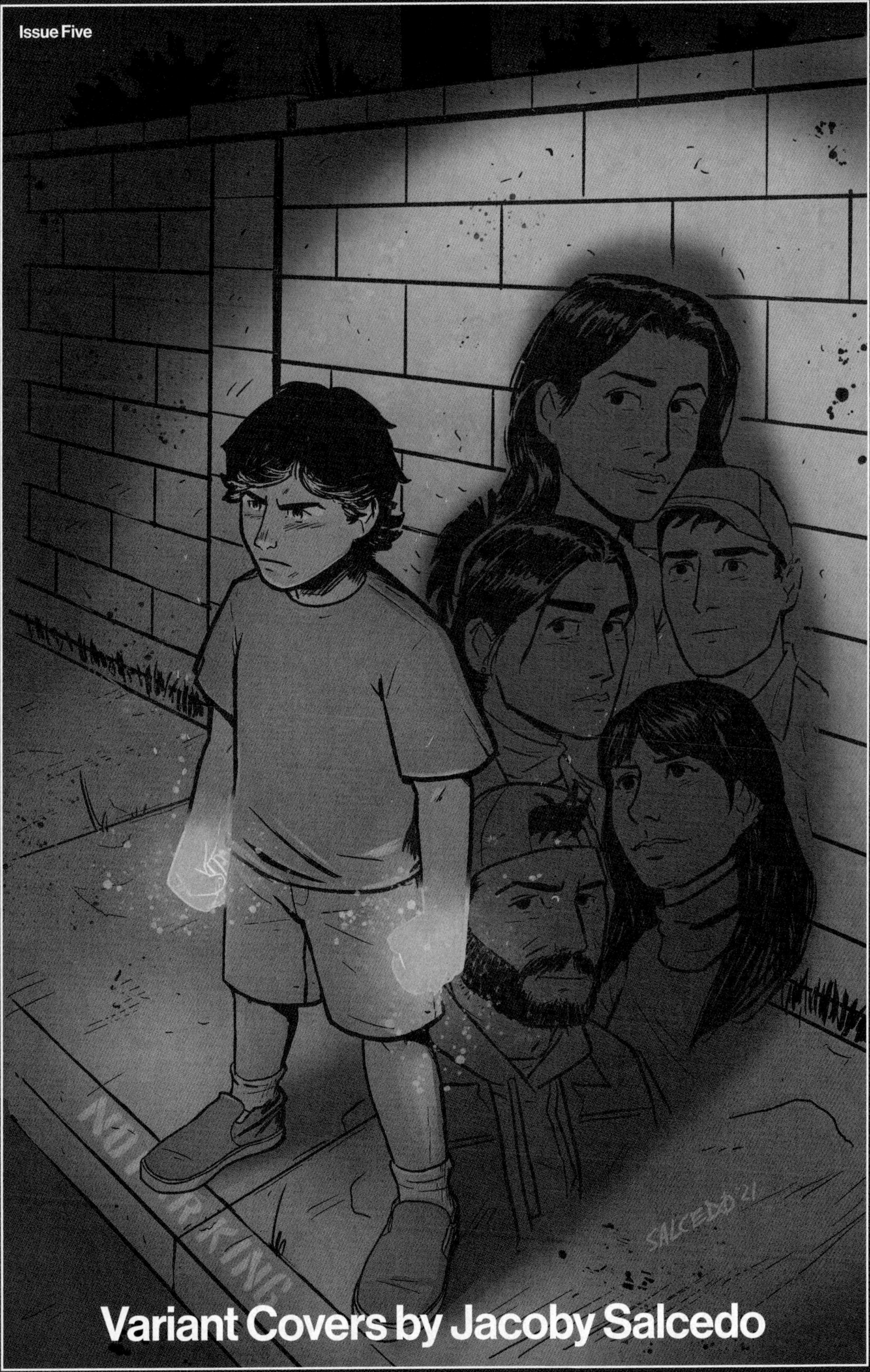
SALCEDO '21

Variant Covers by Jacoby Salcedo

Teaching
HOME

A Re-Imagining Migration
Educator's Guide

Contributors:

Abeer Shinnawi
Amber Cook
Jodi Grosser
Robin Hawley-Brillante

Contents

Re-Imagining Migration

Acknowledgments

Re-Imagining Migration would like to thank Julio Anta for his kind attention, his wonderful book, and his contributions to this guide. We would also like to thank our director, Adam Strom for introducing us to *Home* by reaching out to Julio via social media to make this ed guide a reality, and, of course, his editorial insights. In addition, we would like to thank our co-founder Carola Suárez-Orozco for her groundbreaking research which serves as a quiet background to all of this work. Veronica Boix-Mansilla also deserves credit for her leadership developing our framework and learning arc. Special thanks to the educators Amber Cook, Jodi Grosser and Robin Hawley-Brillante, who helped construct all of the activities and questions for this guide. Without them, this work would not be possible.

Part One

Before Teaching Home

1.1
Introduction

Home is the story of a young boy who is torn away from his mother while seeking asylum at the US border just as something begins to change in him. He doesn't know it yet, but it's the onset of super-human abilities that will change his life forever. Julio Anta is joined by artist Anna Wieszczyk, color artist Bryan Valenza, letterer Hassan Otsmane-Elhaou, and cover artist Lisa Sterle.

According to the *Washington Post*, "The Trump administration separated at least 5,500 children from their parents along the border between July 2017 and June 2018 in an attempt to deter migration." On February 2, 2021, President Biden issued an executive order that created a task force to reunite the remaining families. Imagine the anguish these children are experiencing given the grueling experience they encountered fleeing their own country. It is that experience that is at the heart of Julio Anta's *Home*. Imagine the guilt, fear and anger parents must feel when their children are taken away from them. The plethora of emotions rage within because they believe they failed their children again. *Home* illustrates the experiences of both parent and child but also adds a layer of heroism to the main character that gives the reader another perspective on what it means to have superpowers.

In the spring of 2021, NPR[1] reported that the number of asylum-seeking migrants, including unaccompanied minors, crossing the southwest border into the U.S. is soaring, leaving the Biden administration scrambling to find appropriate care and housing for thousands of children. Experts explain that the recent increase of migrants has been on the rise since April 2020 due to ongoing violence, natural disasters, food insecurity, and poverty in Guatemala, El Salvador, and Honduras. Not all of them apply for or are granted asylum.

---

[1]   https://n.pr/3mrTja8

1.2
Home and the Re-Imagining Migration Learning Arc

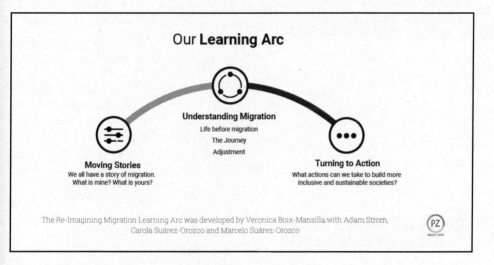

Our **Learning Arc**

Understanding Migration
Life before migration
The Journey
Adjustment

Moving Stories
We all have a story of migration.
What is mine? What is yours?

Turning to Action
What actions can we take to build more
inclusive and sustainable societies?

The Re-Imagining Migration Learning Arc was developed by Veronica Boix-Mansilla with Adam Strom, Carola Suárez-Orozco and Marcelo Suárez-Orozco

Home powerfully explores several key themes from the Re-Imagining Migration Learning Arc. As a graphic depiction of a family migration story, *Home* provides an opening to discuss the questions at the heart of the Moving Stories section of the learning arc including:

▶ We all have a story of migration—what is my story? What is yours?

▶ In what ways do stories of migration help us understand who we are?

▶ What can we learn from the many visible and invisible stories of migration around us?

▶ How can we approach the sharing of stories of migration with understanding and compassion?

The book's focus on Juan and his mother's journey to the US speaks powerfully to the journey section of the learning arc. Their story, if introduced and discussed with context and care, can help readers better understand and empathize with those who, like Juan, have risked their lives to cross the border. To discuss these experiences, consider adapting the following guiding questions.

1.3
The Journey

What do people experience as they move from one place to another?

▶ In what ways are people's migration journeys similar and different from one another?

▶ How much control do migrants have over their journey and what are the choices and dilemmas they face during their journey?

▶ What do these journeys reveal about human nature?

How do borders impact people's lives?

▶ What is the purpose of borders?

▶ How do the visible and invisible borders that people encounter shape their lives?

▶ How can borders work in an ethical way?

How do individuals and societies navigate ambiguous status?

▶ What are the rights of people with ambiguous status (people who are not clearly recognized by the State)?

▶ How do individuals and societies manage ambiguous status?

▶ What are our responsibilities toward people on the move with ambiguous status?

As we think about both the books we read and the way we teach them, we often find ourselves reflecting on a fundamental observation articulated by Dr. Rudine Sims Bishop. Dr. Sims Bishop explained "Books are sometimes windows, offering views of worlds that may be real or imagined, familiar or strange. These windows are also sliding glass doors, and readers have only to walk through in imagination to become part of whatever world has been created or recreated by the author. When lighting conditions are just right, however, a window can also be a mirror. Literature transforms human experience and reflects it to us, and in that reflection, we can see our own lives and experiences as part of a larger human experience. Reading, then, becomes a means of self-affirmation, and readers often seek their mirrors in books."

With her words in mind, we should recognize that *Home* will impact different readers differently. For some, the book will introduce them to a world that may be unfamiliar or only known through media, myth, or stereotype. For others, the book might serve as a mirror in the way that many readers of graphic novels and comics identify with the superhero abilities that arise during times of adversity, just as Juan discovered his during his tumultuous journey. Our challenge as educators is to provide opportunities to recognize experiences that we bring from *Home* and enhance them with a deep engagement with the story, then reflect on them with our peers whose perspectives and personal experiences might be different than our own.

Finally, as teachers and readers, we need to remember that Juan's story is one of migration and family sacrifice. There are others, and it would be a mistake to let a single story represent all migration experiences. Indeed, migration has been an integral part of our experience since humans first walked the earth; while it has ebbed and flowed over time, it is ubiquitous. Across history, the skepticism, fear, and intolerance associated with differences have developed into deeply ingrained class and culture hierarchies leading to conflict, intolerance, and violence. In a world with more and more people on the move, educating young people to learn to live with, work with, and respect our differences is essential for the survival of democracy. This is not an option—it is imperative.

1.4
Dispositions We Seek to Develop in Students

By Veronica Boix- Mansilla

Re-imagining Migration's educational framework identifies five core dispositions that we deem essential to navigate a world of increasing mobility, diversity, and complexity. One way to think about the dispositions is as the overarching learning goals of the curriculum preparing young people for a world on the move. They are introduced below, highlighting cognitive as well as social, emotional, and ethical dimensions of learning and development.

Five Core Dispositions

The capacity, sensitivity, and inclination to...

1
Understand Perspectives: Others and One's Own

Understand and value oneself. Recognizing one's own emotions, thoughts, values, cultural lenses, and worldviews—and the multiple influences on them. Acknowledging one's strengths and capacity to contribute to our environments, as well as our proclivity to hold stereotypes or blind spots. Recognizing that others may have views of the world and of ourselves that are different from our own.

Empathize with others, honoring their dignity and seeking to understand their experiences and perspective. An embodied disposition to share in the experiences and emotions of another person. A disposition to seek to understand their values and worldviews, multiple cultural affiliations, and influences. A disposition to care about who another person is (a peer, a literary character), minimizing "othering" and recognizing other people's human dignity.

Recognize, value, and bridge complex emotions, identities, intersections, and influences. Appreciate the dynamism of cultures and perspectives. A disposition to recognize that there is always more than one perspective, that individuals may participate in multiple cultures, and that cultures influence one another. An openness and disposition to appreciate intersections, mixture, and hybridity in people and cultures.

2
Inquire About Migration with Care and Nuance

The capacity, sensitivity, and inclination to...

Exhibit care and curiosity about our shared and divergent human experience of migration. Feel connected and belonging to a larger human story, viewing migration as a shared human experience—past, present, and future. Pose relevant and informed questions, exhibiting curiosity and the desire to learn.

Investigate and recognize patterns across time, place, and identities reasoning with diverse sources of evidence. Gather, weigh, and reason with evidence to make sense of migration-related issues or situations, seeking out quality sources and media and interpreting them carefully and critically. Consider, for instance, evidence on causes for and impacts of migration on individuals, communities, and nations, combining disciplinary lenses to make sense of a world on the move. Consider patterns across time, space, and identities.

Form informed and ethical personal positions. Examine matters with compassion, managing complex ideas, contexts, and emotions to draw informed conclusions about issues related to migration.

3
Communicate and Build Relationships Across Difference

The capacity, sensitivity, and inclination to...

Listen empathically and mindfully. Listen openly, empathically and mindfully to the many languages people use to communicate (verbal, visual, body languages). Appreciate communicative styles as expressions of identity, culture, and communities of belonging, and recognize that people's humanity, cultural assets and complex thinking capacities are often vaster than what emerging linguistic competences can show, or how non-dominant forms of expression are often interpreted.

Express with purpose, audience, and context in mind. Use multiple languages to communicate (feelings, values, ideas, stories), express oneself (one's identity, culture, belonging) in ways that keep purpose, audience, and context in mind. Appreciate and engage in cultural and linguistic straddling, code-switching, and combining languages to improve communication, and build bonding and bridging relationships within and across groups.

Appreciate and reflect on respectful and inclusive dialogue across race, nationality, gender, religion, and ethnicity. Appreciate respectful dialogue building on the desire to understand and be understood. Recognize, critically, that language can serve as a gatekeeper or a gateway for inclusion and for understanding other people's lives, cultures, and the world. Recognize and reflect on communication and relational challenges recognizing the source of difficulties (e.g., language of exclusion, differences in communicative norms), and seeking inclusive solutions.

The capacity, sensitivity, and inclination to...

Recognize power and inequities in various forms. Recognize racial, class, religious, ethnic, and gender inequities and power disparities regarding self and known and distant others—in daily experiences as well as across past and present, local, and global cases of migration. Uphold values of human dignity and diversity that are foundational to inclusive societies, social belonging, and moral development.

Understand one's own position vis-à-vis power and inequities. Understand one's own position vis-à-vis inequities navigating the ideas, feelings, and relationships associated with responding to inequities from specific positions and contexts (e.g., compassion, respect, and admiration vis-à-vis persons who experience marginalization, as well as pride in one's own family story of migration, freedom, and courage to share one's language, values, and roots).

Envisioning inclusive and sustainable societies. Imagine possible equitable and just futures, enriched by the inclusion of marginalized voices in dialogue and relationships that embody the values of human dignity and diversity central to our democratic life.

4
Recognize Power & Inequities in Human Experience and Migration

The capacity, sensitivity, and inclination to...

Recognize our circles of belonging, care, and influence. Develop a sense of belonging to a learning environment, a community, and a society and an inclination to participate regarding issues or situations involving human migration. Be sensitive toward opportunities to act constructively in groups, contexts, and relationships, and a desire and inclination to make a difference.

Employ understanding, voice, and action to foster equitable and inclusive societies. Seek to understand experiences and systems associated with human migration and how earlier change makers have attempted to make a difference. Use the capacity to express one's perspective, experiences, and story to change minds. Use civic engagement tools (political action, community projects, digital campaigns) to take informed and compassionate action.

Reflect and revise our actions. Reflect on actions and strategies (learn from the stories of the past, examining prior attempts, voicing perspectives, engaging others, planning, and executing). Assess and adjust them to foster well-being among immigrant and host communities; foster equitable and inclusive societies strengthening civic life and democratic institutions.

5
Take Action to Foster Inclusive and Sustainable Societies

1.5
Author's Note from Julio Anta: Reflections on Migrants' Stories

In the Spring of 2018, news of family separation at the border began trickling in. Like many Americans, I was devastated by what I was seeing. But as the son of a Cuban refugee, and the grandson of undocumented immigrants from Colombia, this news hit me particularly hard. Seeing images of children in cages, listening to interviews with parents who had no idea when, or even if they'd ever see their children again...it broke me.

Not only did I see my Cuban father—whose parents brought him over as a five-year-old nearly 60 years ago—in the eyes of these children at the border, but as a new father myself, I saw my own three-year-old son.

So, after months of obsessively researching the issue, I began developing the idea for *Home*. I wanted to expose my readers to the cruelty immigrants–particularly Latin American asylum seekers–are subjected to by our government, and, in the process, hopefully influence these readers to think differently. That's how *Home*, the comic book, was born.

What Should Educators Know Before Teaching *Home*?

1.6

For more information on how family separation impacts youth, here are two resources written by Carola Suarez-Orozco:

The Science is clear: Separating Families has Long-term Damaging Psychological and Health Consequences for Children, Families, and Communities[3]

I Felt Like My Heart Was Staying Behind: Psychological Implications of Family Separations & Reunifications for Immigrant Youth[4]

What should educators know before teaching *Home*, and how should that knowledge shape their approach to teaching the novel? One can find an answer after watching a conversation with Re-Imagining Migration's program leads, Abeer Shinnawi and Carola Suárez-Orozco, about family separation and the impact of the trauma on children and their families: What should educators know, do, and understand before teaching *Home*?[2]

---

2   https://bit.ly/3l9U1tq

---

3   https://bit.ly/2Yi743q
4   https://bit.ly/3uDEAgd

CAROLA SUÁREZ-OROZCO *is the chair of Re-imagining Migration's board of directors. She is also a Distinguished Professor of Education and Human Development at the University of Massachusetts, Boston and the co-founder of Re-imagining Migration. Her books include* Children of Immigration *(Harvard University Press),* Learning a New Land *(Harvard University Press), as well as* Transitions: The Development of the Children of Immigrants *(NYU Press). She has been awarded an American Psychological Association (APA) Presidential Citation for her contributions to the understanding of the cultural psychology of immigration, has served as chair of the APA Presidential Task Force on Immigration, and is a member of the National Academy of Education. Her latest book is* Immigrant-Origin Students in Community College: Navigating Risk and Reward in Higher Education.

Reading Graphic Novels

1.7

> "...When you look at a photo or realistic drawing of a face, you see it as the face of another.
> But when you enter the world of the cartoon, you see yourself."
>
> —Scott McCloud, author of *Understanding Comics*

Here are some resources to help you build a foundation for teaching *Home* or any other graphic novel.

According to *Literacy Today: Reading Graphic Novels*[5], the popularity of graphic novels have taken on a new form of learning in schools across the nation. Educators are finding that teaching graphic novels allows students to learn using various modalities while being entertained. Although graphic novels are not new, knowing how to teach them is vital to creating a better understanding and appreciation for the genre within a curriculum. According to *Literacy Today,* graphic novels lend themselves to being used:

Graphic Novels/Comics and Terms and Concepts[6] (Read-Write-Think): brief vocabulary concepts about graphic novels.

Comic vocabulary definitions and examples[7] (Read-Write-Think): text containers provide examples of how to read comic panels using the different designs used in graphic novels and comics.

Comic Book Grammar and Tradition:[8] website that explains the aesthetic nature of comic book lettering.

To launch a genre study • As mentor texts for author's craft • As writing prompts • To introduce complex themes and issues • As a prompt for expository writing • For engaging students in critical literacy
To encourage authentic discussions in literature circles or inquiry groups

---

5   https://bit.ly/3uHmWIn

---

6   https://bit.ly/3a5cbG6
7   https://bit.ly/2Yt1gE1
8   https://bit.ly/3Aa0mt1

Part Two

Teaching *Home*

2.1
Pre-Reading Activities

Identities in Context:[9]

All of us develop our identities within a social and cultural context. To a certain extent, that context influences the opportunities we have in life and our ability to express ourselves as we wish. Psychologist Uri Bronfenbrenner tried to capture the influence of the environment on people's identities in what he called the Ecological Theory of Identity. In it, he tried to identify the various forces that shape the way we develop our sense of self.

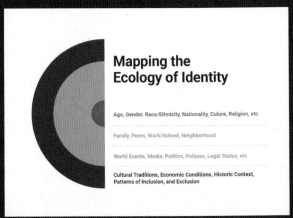

Mapping the Ecology of Identity

Age, Gender, Race/Ethnicity, Nationality, Culure, Religion, etc

Family, Peers, Work/School, Neighborhood

World Events, Media, Politics, Policies, Legal Status, etc

Cultural Traditions, Economic Conditions, Historic Context, Patterns of Inclusion, and Exclusion

Identifying the way each layer of the ecological model relates to our identity is particularly helpful for exploring the ways that newcomers develop their identities in a new land because they, or their family members, have recently transitioned from one social and cultural context to another. Therefore, the relationship between their identities and their environment has changed. Helping to isolate those changes can help to clarify the way people navigate their lives in a new land.

Before beginning a discussion of the book, create an ecological identity map for yourself. Throughout the guide, we encourage students to create a similar map for the characters they encounter in the book.

---

9   https://bit.ly/3A4ImjG

Moving Stories:

All of us have migration stories, whether in this generation or in the past, across internal borders of within, by choice, by force, or something in between. Before turning to the novel, you might encourage students to share their own moving stories using ideas from our learning guide. The core of the activity is having students interview each other, with proper contracting and guidance, using a set of questions that were developed by a group of learning scholars including educators, sociologists, and psychologists. Follow this link[10] to the learning guide for ideas on how to structure the activity.

Exploring The Theme Of A Moral Compass:

Home is a graphic novel that allows the opportunity for students and educators to develop conversations around the concept of using a *moral compass*. A moral compass is a reference to a person's ability to judge what is right and wrong and act accordingly. Prior to reading the book, use the following questions as a guide:

▶ Look at each character through a moral compass—how do they project being morally just?

▶ How can we bring awareness of the treatment of migrants and their families at the border?

▶ How can we, as a society, help to bring about change?

▶ How is being complicit considered to be morally corrupt? Examine the role of White supremacy culture in the novel and the complicit behavior of the characters of color.

1.
Ask students to answer the following question and complete the activity:

What do(es) _____ mean to you? Pick one:

Power • Justice • Migration • Identity • Responsibility • Borders

Draw a comic to illustrate how it shows up in the United States in different contexts -- in your community, in your school, in your family, in your friends, in your pop culture, in social media.

2.
Rate each statement from
1: Strongly Agree to 10: Strongly Disagree:

People with power are obligated to use it for good, no matter their age.

When people are in danger, they have a human right to leave the dangerous place and seek freedom elsewhere.

When someone is new to our community, we should welcome them warmly and include them in activities.

Pick one statement and compose a written, audio, or video journal entry. Consider examples from your own life and media you have consumed. Revisit your entry throughout your reading of the comic book series and consider how it confirms, refutes, and/or enriches your understanding of the issues.

10   https://bit.ly/3BaixQw

Part Three

Reading *Home*

Note: *Home* is a series of books but uses the power of images and words. You may choose the book as a read-aloud, assign each book to smaller clusters of students for them to read together, or ask students to read the book on their own. Regardless of how students encounter the text, we believe that it is vital that you make time to explore the text in a reflective conversation. To be clear, when we say text, we are referring to both the words and the illustrations.

3.1 Teaching Suggestion Pre-Read:

Too often readers skip through the illustrations in books, focusing on the words to carry the narrative. In a graphic novel, the words and images work together to tell the story. That is true of *Home*. One way to ensure that readers engage with the illustrations is to ask them to read each book one time without looking at the text. After completing the book, individually or in groups, use the see-feel-think-wonder[11] thinking routine from Project Zero to structure the reflection.

With students' observations, feelings, thoughts, and wonders noted, read each book a second time, this time including the words and revisit the thinking routine. What would students add? How did the words influence their responses to the story? Are there wonders that were answered? Did new wonders surface?

---

11   https://bit.ly/3uJ5ZgO

3.2 What Do We Know and What Don't We Know?

After recording student wonderings, consider what we know and what we don't know about Juan's story.

Individually or in groups ask students to record what they know about Juan's story on a piece of paper or computer document: in one column note what we know and, in another column, add what we don't know. Consider using the following guiding questions to structure this exercise:

- What was Juan's life like before he migrated?
- Why did he migrate?
- How much choice did he have in the decision to migrate?
- What did he experience as he migrated? How did this impact the relationship with his mother?
- How much control did he have over his journey and what are the choices and dilemmas he faces along the way? How were the dilemmas different for his mother?
- What physical and psychological borders did he have to cross along the way?
- What are the conditions like for him in the US?
- Is Juan's migration story typical? Does it represent the experiences of most immigrants? If so, how? If not, what is unique about his experience?
- Consider what you learn about migration from media and public officials. How is this story like what you see and hear coming from politicians and in the media? How is it different? How does the author use quotes from politicians to emphasize the narrative of migrants coming to this country?
- What did you learn about migration from this book that you didn't know before?

After considering the questions, look at what you said you knew. Now note what you don't know. How might you find the answers?

3.3 What's Below the Surface of Juan's Story?

Use the iceberg diagram exercise to reveal what is under the surface of the story told in *Home*. While the book focuses on his journey, what are the other themes and issues that are raised by his story?

Migration Story
What's below the surface?
Life before migration
Culture, language, relationships
Reasons people leave their homes
Choice, pressures, environment
Experiences during migration journeys
Journey, borders
Ambiguous status
Laws, asylum/refugees, mixed family documentation
Conditions in the new land
Social discourse (current/historical), opportunities, adjustment
Local stories of migration and global patterns
Perspective, unique/universal
Re-Imagining Migration

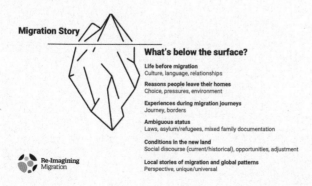

Part Four

4.1
Connecting, Extending, and Challenging Our Knowledge and Understanding

---

▶ How does the story in *Home* connect to what you already know about immigration?

▶ How does it extend your knowledge of immigration?

▶ How might it challenge what you already know about immigration?

Using Project Zero Thinking Routines

Following are a series of thinking routines[12], almost all of which come from Project Zero at the Harvard Graduate School of Education.[13] Senior Project Zero Principal Investigator Veronica Boix Mansilla explains that thinking routines are "thinking structures or malleable micro-teaching tools carefully designed to be used in a wide range of learning spaces. Meant to be used frequently, across content, over time, and as an integral part of a learning environment, these routines are essential contributors to creating a classroom culture where learners are engaged thoughtfully, and their thoughts and voices take center stage."

---

12   https://bit.ly/3FioRYz
13   https://pz.harvard.edu

4.2
Text to Text, Text to Self, Text to World

- How is the story in *Home* like another text that you have read, seen, or listened to?

- How does the story in *Home* connect with your story or experiences? How might it be different?

- How is the story in *Home* similar to something else you know about or have learned about from the world at large?

4.3
Same, Different, Gain

Take the ideas in the last thinking routine deeper by exploring one connection you made to another text or event.

- How are they similar?

- How are they different?

- What do we gain by comparing them? And what might we lose in the comparison?

4.4
Three Whys

Consider the significance of the story in *Home*.

- Why does it matter to you?

- Why does it matter to your community?

- Why does it matter to the world?

Part Five

Reading
Home

5.1
Chapter One: Who Has the Power?

In this chapter, the reader is introduced to Juan and his mother, Mercedes, after they cross the border into Texas. This provides an opportunity to focus on perspective-taking, as we consider the ways in which people are impacted by the decisions they make, but also how they can become accomplices to policies that affect the lives of others

▶ Who has the power in this issue?

▶ Who does not have power?

▶ What do individuals/groups do with the power?

▶ Who benefits from the power?

Reflection Questions

1. How does it impact you as a reader to know that the series is grounded in actual, real-world experiences of Guatemalan immigrants—both children and adults?

2. What are the factors pushing the characters away from their homes and pulling them to migrate elsewhere—social, political, and/or environmental? What connections and patterns can you identify from your own stories of migration?

3. What values are reflected in each character's actions? In your community, what are the values that you see expressed?

4. What makes an action morally justifiable? Whose actions in this chapter are morally just? Why?

5. Who has power? Who doesn't have power? What do individuals and groups do with power? Who benefits? Track shifts and how power dynamics change over time. How do power dynamics work in your community?

6. Determine which political and social systems are at work here. Think about what Juan and his mother experienced from government employees when they arrived at the border. How do the impacts of the political and social systems show up in ways that are either obvious or hidden? What patterns do you see? How do they echo in your own community?

7. How does the illustrator make the characters' emotions visible? How can we help others visualize our emotions, and others' emotions, to build empathy through both words and images?

8. Words matter. How does the use of the words *scourge*, and *criminals* help shape a particular image of immigrants coming into the United States?

9. Examine the image of "The Icebox." What message does the illustrator portray using the color scheme? Compare the illustration with images in the media of detention centers holding children at the border.

10. What was the "zero tolerance" rule under the Trump administration? Do some research on "zero tolerance." Using your information, think about how that affected mi/immigrants living with ambiguous status in the United States.

11. After reading the chapter, what do you know about how long the journey was from Guatemala to the United States border? What type of planning do you think is necessary for the journey? Besides physical materials, what else would one need to prepare to take the journey?

12. Juan was placed in solitary confinement for having extra food. Do you think he should be punished for having extra food? Do you think the punishment was just? Discuss.

13. Juan realizes he has superpowers while in solitary confinement, but by accident. Describe Juan's superpowers. How does this change his role in the story? How do you think this will affect the story?

5.2 Chapter Two: Survival and the Single Story

After Juan escapes from the detention center, he seeks to find his relatives so he can be reunited with his mother. The struggle continues as Juan tries to avoid being caught by ICE and other members of the community.

Guiding Questions

▶ How do we navigate our own strengths and weaknesses during times of struggle?

▶ How does Juan's family history dictate his fate?

▶ How does fear ignite mob mentality?

Reflection Questions

1. What do we give up or sacrifice when we make choices about our survival? How do we weigh the needs of individuals with the needs of the group?

2. What skills or knowledge does Juan bring to the situation? How does he use them?

3. What types of media messages do we receive about mi/immigrants coming into the United States? How do you know what is real, what is fake, and what is not a fair representation of the story? For a deeper explanation, research best practices in news literacy[14].

4. How has the media shaped our understanding of mi/immigration patterns in the United States? How do you know what is real from fake news?

5. How do the guards describe Juan before he escaped?

6. There are flashbacks that take the reader back to before Juan and his mother left Guatemala. How do the flashbacks help us understand why they left their homes? How does their experience help us understand why people seek asylum?

7. When Juan is united with his aunt Gladys, what family truth does he discover? How does this truth help him make more sense of his own reality?

8. What happens to Mercedes, Juan's mother? Dissect the images that show her fate and how that influences public perception of immigrants and migrants coming to the United States.

9. How does Juan adapt quickly to tense situations as he navigates his survival after escaping from the detention center?

---

14   https://bit.ly/3FioX2n

Chapter Three: A Family's Secret

Juan now must learn to live not only with the deportation of his mother, but also the new family secrets his aunt reveals to him. Juan learns to own his power, maneuver without his mother, and adapt to a new family dynamic.

Guiding Questions:

▶ What responsibility does one have when provided with a particular power?

▶ Why do family relationships matter so much to Juan?

▶ Why is it hard sometimes to do the right thing? What can be the consequences of doing the right thing?

Reflection Questions

1. What theme or message is the author crafting about Latine characters by depicting them with superpowers? How might this message apply to other marginalized peoples?

2. What are the repercussions when people act upon incomplete rumors, stereotypes, or misinformation or incomplete information?

3. What are your working definitions for the following words:

   • Asylum   • Asylum seeker   • Undocumented immigrant   • Refugee

   Consider what, who, or where do you think of when you hear these words?

4. The first few pages of this chapter have minimal words and only images. Create your own dialogue to convey the emotions portrayed in the panels.

5. Why do you think Juan's father had to control his powers? How would certain powers consume a person?

6. Describe the relationship between Juan and his mother, Mercedes. How does their relationship help with their constant struggles?

7. Aunt Gladys takes Juan to Sam Houston National Forest. Why does she take Juan to that forest? Does the trip help Juan? What does Juan discover about his aunt while in the forest?

8. Extension: Research the history and legacy of Sam Houston. Consider how what you have learned influences your understanding of the setting.

9. How does Juan learn to use his powers responsibly? Do you agree with his decision after the conversation he has with his aunt? What does Juan discover about Aunt Gladys as they try to escape from the police?

5.4

Chapter Four: With Great Power Comes Great Responsibility

Juan learns about the tragic death of his father while learning the importance of how to control his "gift." He learns the hard way that doing what is right using his powers can lead to grave consequences.

Guiding Questions:

▶ Are there times when a person's understanding of their civic duty can endanger others?

▶ Whose point of view and perspective is being represented in this chapter? Whose is left out?

▶ Who might be the person(s) who lose, are affected negatively, or are left out and how?

Reflection Questions

1. In a few sentences, interpret the author's perspective on immigration and asylum issues from what you have read thus far. Now compare the author's perspective with yours. How did the text/chapter/issue align with your existing beliefs? How did it differ? How has the story impacted your perspective?

2. How do you explain why different people might interpret a text or an event differently? As a reader, what factors influence your interpretation of a text? Who gets to decide what the truth is? What is the difference between a legitimate perspective and twisting the truth? How can an author guard against misinterpretation of their work? How can people guard against misinterpretation of their words or actions?

3. How can exposure to differences of opinions and practicing active listening encourage new understanding and develop empathy?

4. Consider the discussion between Juan and his aunt Gladys about what their roles should be and how they should use their powers. How might the ideas in this conversation connect to you as an individual, to your community, and to the larger world?

5. What is the role of the superhero? How is it like being a social activist? How might it be different? What are productive ways to recognize and interrupt injustice?

6. What words are used by ICE officers to describe Juan? How similar are the custom agent's words when describing other national threats? What words would you use to describe Juan? Compare and contrast them with those of the ICE officers. How do you explain the differences?

7.   How does Juan rationalize using his superpowers to help other students in the detention center?

8.   Do you believe Juan's father, Armando, made the right decision about when and how to use his powers?

9.   The woman who called 911 to report Juan was called a "national hero." Why do you think people called her that? Do you agree with that characterization? Why or why not?

10.   Why do you think the woman might have considered it her civic duty to report Juan? How would you define your civic duty in that situation? Are their times in which a civic duty and an ethical responsibility might conflict?

11.   Who are Luis and Camila? How do they respond to Juan needing help?

Chapter Five: Who is Safe in a Sanctuary?

5.5

After being pursued by ICE agents, Juan is confronted by his cousins, who use their superpowers to save him from being detained. Aunt Gladys does not approve, but Juan and his cousins are now in a dilemma on how to remain in hiding from ICE agents who are after them for "waging a war" against them.

Guiding Questions:

▶ What are the values, policies, institutions, and actors that make up the immigration system in the US? What role does ICE play in that system?

▶ How do people in the system interact with each other and with the parts of the system?

▶ What are elements of the system that block change?

Reflection Questions

1.   How do Luis and Camila save Juan? How does Juan react?

2.   Do you believe that Luis and Camila did the right thing? Explain.

3.   Why is Aunt Gladys upset with her children?

4.   Consider familiar media images and public perceptions of Latinos in the US. How does the depiction of Juan as a superhero challenge that perception? How do media images shape the way people act? Why might some people find the idea of a Latino superhero particularly important?

5.   What does the ending of the series suggest about the nature of power

and alliances among groups of people? How can we interrupt this kind of corruption?

6.   What is a sanctuary city? Research the purposes of sanctuary cities and why some people protest them.

7.   To learn more about how students can become involved in civic action, introduce the Quinceaneras at the Capitol Protest[15] in Texas where 15 young women took a stand in support of sanctuary cities.

8.   What are some ways that the US immigration system shapes the experiences of newcomers, and the way people respond to them? What messages are sent by different parts of the system about immigrants, asylum seekers, and refugees? What can people do to create more safe, welcoming, and inclusive communities? What changes in our immigration system might be necessary? How do you anticipate how people might respond to those changes? What might people be able to do to build allies and support?

---

15   https://bit.ly/3019TX7

After the Text: Taking Action

How can we take action toward more inclusive and sustainable societies?

The Re-Imagining Migration Learning Arc culminates by encouraging students to reflect on their roles in creating communities of inclusivity and shared belonging. We offer the following guiding questions to begin that process:

▶ What issues related to migration do we care about and why?

▶ What can we learn from individuals and groups who have addressed migration in the past?

▶ How might we use our voices and spheres of influence to create and sustain inclusive and welcoming communities?

Thinking about where to begin taking action on an issue as large as migration can be intimidating. Help students break the experience of migration down. Earlier in the guide we suggested using an iceberg diagram to make the different experiences, themes, and issues underneath Juan's migration story visible. Now is a good time to return to that chart. Ask students if there are things they would like to add.

As a class, spend some time with the chart and ask students to identify an issue that speaks to them and how it relates to life before migration, issues related to their journey, or life in the United States.

To guide that process, you might share the Mapping Opportunities for Action graphic below:

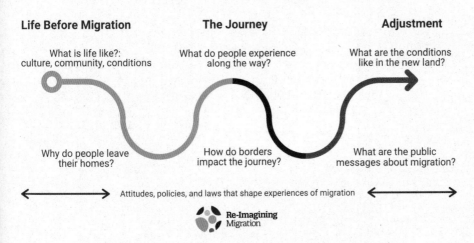

Human Migration: Mapping Opportunities for Action

Life Before Migration

What is life like?: culture, community, conditions

Why do people leave their homes?

The Journey

What do people experience along the way?

How do borders impact the journey?

Adjustment

What are the conditions like in the new land?

What are the public messages about migration?

← → Attitudes, policies, and laws that shape experiences of migration ← →

Re-Imagining Migration

Once students have identified an area of interest. You might share this story[16] of a creative civic action led by 15 teenage immigrant young women in Texas as a model.

If you would prefer to move straight to having students design their own civic action projects, consider using these Project Zero thinking routines to structure their planning.

1. Start with People, Systems, and Wedges[17] to identify the elements within the system they are seeking to change.

2. Help students think consider their spheres of influence with Circles of Action.[18]

3. Moving from big goals to tactics can be hard. The What Else Can I Do? And Why?[19] thinking-routine can be helpful when students seek to identify concrete tactics and actions they can take.

4. Before moving to action, encourage students to reflect on their plans with Compass Points.[20]

16   https://bit.ly/3019TX7
17   https://bit.ly/3Da3HtP
18   https://bit.ly/3AbnZRK
19   https://bit.ly/3Bgj9Ek
20   https://bit.ly/3a8HrUK

Creator Bios

Julio Anta is a writer based in New York City. Raised in Miami, in a Cuban and Colombian family, Julio strives to tell narratively rich stories about diverse and empowered Latinx characters for Adult, Young Adult, and Middle Grade readers. Forthcoming work includes *Frontera*, a YA graphic novel from HarperAlley, and *Si Se Puede*, a non-fiction graphic novel from Ten Speed Press.

Anna Wieszczyk is a comic book artist from Poland. She is the artist behind *Lucid* and *Interesting Drug* published by Boom! Studios, *Godkiller* and *Ocuppy Comics* published by Black Mask, as well as various anthologies. Anna is actively involved in the budding Polish zine scene. Her aspiration is to find her voice as feminist and activist and have it heard.

Bryan Valenza is a comic book colorist, and the founder of coloring studio Beyond Colorlab based in Jakarta, Indonesia. He currently occupies his time coloring various projects, including *Skies of Fire*, *InSexts*, *Golgotha* and *Mighty Morphin Power Rangers*.

Hassan Otsmane-Elhaou is a British/ Algerian letterer, who has worked on comics like TIME BEFORE TIME, WHAT'S THE FURTHEST PLACE FROM HERE?, and *Red Sonja*. He's also the editor of the Eisner-winning *PanelxPanel* magazine and voice behind *Strip Panel Naked*.